The Sea Glass Gift

The parish,

In all things:
breathe, love, ~~And~~ create!

Julie RayMarti

The parish,

In all things.

breathe, love, And create.

Julie Bartel

The
Sea
Glass
Gift

Julie Rogers-Martin

ARCHWAY
PUBLISHING

This is a work of fiction. All of the characters, names, incidents, organizations, and dialogue in this novel are either the products of the author's imagination or are used fictitiously.

Archway Publishing books may be ordered through booksellers or by contacting:

Archway Publishing
1663 Liberty Drive
Bloomington, IN 47403
www.archwaypublishing.com
1 (888) 242-5904

Because of the dynamic nature of the Internet, any web addresses or links contained in this book may have changed since publication and may no longer be valid. The views expressed in this work are solely those of the author and do not necessarily reflect the views of the publisher, and the publisher hereby disclaims any responsibility for them.

Any people depicted in stock imagery provided by Thinkstock are models, and such images are being used for illustrative purposes only. Certain stock imagery © Thinkstock.

Scriptures taken from the Holy Bible, New International Version®, NIV®. Copyright © 1973, 1978, 1984, 2011 by Biblica, Inc.™ Used by permission of Zondervan. All rights reserved worldwide. www.zondervan.com The "NIV" and "New International Version" are trademarks registered in the United States Patent and Trademark Office by Biblica, Inc.™

ISBN: 978-1-4808-5439-0 (sc)
ISBN: 978-1-4808-5437-6 (hc)
ISBN: 978-1-4808-5438-3 (e)

Library of Congress Control Number: 2017918290

Print information available on the last page.

Archway Publishing rev. date: 8/14/2018

For Brian-Your life changed mine forever...
moving me toward health, wholeness and hope.

Everyone has the same question, whether they ask it or not. How could you? How could you give away your own child, your own flesh and blood? However tactfully they say it, what they are really asking is: what kind of a monster are you?

That question brings it all back, like a shard of glass piercing wounds so deep I have to navigate out of a house of mirrors to answer it. I've encountered a lifetime of shards, some of my own making, and some strewn my way from the paths of others. I'm tired of determining which is which. The scars are there just the same. I think other people, in their questions, are looking for validation. They too have made a ravaging choice for their own reasons, hoping that someday, someone will absolve them. Somehow it will turn out right. I understand the desire for confession. So for those who really want to know, here's my story, real and uncensored.

Chapter 1
Shard

Silica is the primary ingredient in glass. In nature, silica
is most commonly found in sand and quartz. When
lightning strikes sand, quartz can turn into glass.

As usual, I found myself in a flurry when leaving for the holidays. At least, I didn't have to prepare anything for Thanksgiving this year. I'd packed myself and my spunky dog, Sunday, watered the plants, cleared my desk, and was checking emails when it glared from the green screen.

"I'm looking to speak to Jenna Khoury. Would you happen to have a personal email address? -Jeffrey Brisures"

The message clutched my throat, triggering an airless gasp. Blood plummeted to my feet. Could it be?

"I am Jenna," I hammered back.

Minutes later I received another.

"Well then, hopefully, the name sounds familiar-Jeffrey Brisures. I think I might be your son. I've wanted to reach you for quite some time now. Hope you don't mind my making contact, much less contact through email."

A moan escaped. I saw him clearly now, the shard that shredded my soul into tiny pieces. The bond, though invisible, was a thread stretching miles of anonymity. I never allowed myself to hope this moment would happen. If I had let my longing rise to the surface, I'd have never been able to live with myself. If I could ever learn to trust my emotions, I would say the feeling was pure, unadulterated joy. Someone that was once a part of me, whom I talked to, read to, sang to, prayed for, and cried endless tears over, found me. Once I was lost, now I am found. But the pain, the real pain, was in the remembering.

Chapter 2
The Gift of Music

Glass is somewhere on the threshold of materiality, an element on the borderline between the visible and invisible. It is a fascinating material, known chiefly for its transparency, luster, and lightness.[1]

People walk through their lives with reflections of others guiding their perceptions. By some, we are blinded, but others offer a luster, a gleam of an image we can't help but gravitate toward. Musicians have that influence on me. I've never felt as connected to life as when enveloped in music. Singing expands my soul. Whether in the shower or to the radio, it transports me to places I never fathomed existed in real time and space. Somewhere in the blend of tones, a bond is formed connecting souls that feel each other's depths, and share in the reverie and desolation. This is the shorthand of passion.

My infatuation with music began at the age of six when I was begged into duets with my father.

"Sing us another, Eddie," his friends shouted at parties, "with your daughter this time."

Fascinated by the graceful dance of his fingers on the guitar, I was never more than a few feet away. We always started with "Scarlet Ribbons." His velvety tenor voice drew them in, a father watching his child in prayer. On the chorus, I chimed in with the melody, and he the cascading harmony.

My parent's friends hooted and hollered, demanding another. So we sang our showstopper: "Sunrise, Sunset" from *Fiddler on the Roof*. You could hear a pin drop as we sang. Even the children, running around like wildcats, quietly inched up. This time, I sang the harmony.

The lyrics told of a young girl growing up to be a bride, standing side by side, under the canopy, with her lover. He sang from a father's perspective, clenching the heart of every parent in the room. The time would come when they would have to say goodbye to their children at the altar of marriage.

A reverent pause lingered after the song, hovering like a magic spell and then came their animated applause. I bowed, hugged my dad, and walked off. Truly we shared the most special bond in the world-the gift of music.

We'd spend many hours at our home in New Orleans with his guitar, playing new songs and old, until that heartrending night when I was twelve years old. My parents sat my eight-year-old sister, Jordan, and me down in the living room, and they told us they were getting a divorce. Dad was moving out.

What child was surprised by divorce when her parents wrangled and roared every night? The icy chill pierced the security within. We knew it was coming, but that didn't make it any easier. I flung myself on the ground, cried, and begged him not to go, but he left nonetheless. The blow of abandonment was overpowering. It knocked the wind right out of me, and I felt that I'd never be able to catch a full breath again.

All I could see was what was left behind-his bare closet, and the stripped garage. All I could hear was the empty sound of my heart beating wildly when I'd sit on the orange lounger where we used to have our nightly music sessions. The gut realization that he was not coming back bore a hole in me so deep that I identified with the hollowness of his guitar, its insides carved out and exposed for all to see. So I lay horizontally on our orange chair and pretended that's what I was, held in his arms, being strummed while he hummed.

After Dad left, I couldn't find myself anywhere I went. Emptiness lurked around every corner. In school, the chalkboards were filled with undecipherable hieroglyphics, and friends were full of laughter I couldn't fathom. Classes I used to love like Language Arts and Social Studies were endless agony.

"Jenna, are you paying attention? Jenna?"

"Uh, huh," I responded as the cloud cleared.

"And your answer...?

"Uh...I'm not sure."

"C'mon, Jenna. What is going on? You know this."

"Uh, huh."

"See me after class, please."

The teachers queried, but the words, convoluted and tangled, were a jumble when I tried to let them out. How could you explain a caving world? Each day another room collapsed. My friends knew about the divorce, but since no one had experienced one, they didn't know what to say. They started avoiding me like they did the neighborhood boys who tortured animals.

Tears flowed freely between Mom, Jordan, and me. If one of us started, we all cried, as if we could see the drops welling inside each other. I tried my hardest to bite my lip and hold them back so as not to cause Mom any more pain. Any hint of "Dad" was painful, so in my conversations I used "him" if there was no other way around it. Before long, "Dad" just fell out of my vocabulary.

I placed words together so vigilantly that soon it became easier not to talk. So I retreated to my room for a few months and wrote poetry. The paper and pen absorbed my stark words with understanding. With them, I could say whatever I wanted, and no one would get hurt.

The more I wrote, the more I desired the solitude. It was the only thing I hungered for in weeks. Mom pleaded with me to come out of my bedroom, but I couldn't face the world without him, or our music. She left me alone, at first. Then I'd hear her approach my door, and knock. I'd take a deep breath and muster up enough energy to look composed when she popped her head through the crack, but I couldn't say anything. I just nodded or shook my head to whatever she said. No, I wasn't coming down for dinner. Yes, I was ready for the bus. No, I did not finish my chores. No, I was not hungry.

Church provided a haven for me. Although Mom didn't feel welcomed anymore because of the divorce, I pleaded to go to the tiny church in our neighborhood. It helped to replace the emptiness I felt since Dad left. So, when I saw the poster outside the sanctuary: *Youth Choir Members needed,* my heart pounded.

The other junior high girls and I demurely whispered when Roy, the handsome young director, walked into the choir room.

"Wow, he's cute, " a girl beside me said with a huge, dreamy sigh.

Someone had written on the chalkboard a quote, and I was pondering its meaning before he began.

Music is the mediator between the spiritual and the sensual life. ~Beethoven

"Everything you ever need to know about vocal music can be found in one piece by Handel called 'Passacaglia,'" Roy announced in a resounding voice. "Handel loved music, but his father, intent on him becoming a lawyer, forbid him to study it. Have your parents ever forbidden you to study something? Well, when George Frideric was a teenager he visited a relative who worked in the church. Scouting around, George started playing the church organ. Hearing him, Duke Adolf was so impressed that he begged him to stay and take lessons from the organist at the Lutheran church. With the duke's influence, Handel persuaded his father. Before long he so exceeded his teacher's skills that even as a teenager he replaced his teacher as organist."

"Wow, a teenager!" We shook our heads and grinned.

"You'll get to know this piece very well because, to me, it epitomizes music. 'Passacaglia' is a type of composition with variations on a bass theme done in three-fourths time. Now, I know you're saying, 'What does all that mean?' but by the end of the day, you will know what it means, because I believe it has all the elements of a brilliant piece of music-a strong bass line, point, counterpoint, as well as cadence and phrasing that will knock you out of your seats!"

From slumped postures, we straightened up with attention. As Roy turned on the stereo, we scooted our metal chairs up closer, being sure to keep them in a straight line.

"Listen first for the tone or feeling of the piece. I didn't tell you what 'Passacaglia' means because I want you to discover it on your own from what you hear."

I felt like an adult for the first time in my life, listening for the intricacies of classical music. I cocked my ears closer to the speakers. The purity of the first notes struck a chord deep within me, almost bringing tears. The passion was deep and daunting, but then it became playful and fun, like a dance. My head bounced with the beat. It was as if they were in a race with each other, the harp and violin. He stopped the recording and we almost fell out of our seats wanting more.

"So, what was the feeling in that section?" he asked.

"Somber," "serious," "with a little hope," others imparted.

"Great. You are on it. What activity does it sound like?"

"Like they're on a walk," Lewis, the pastor's son said. "The notes are kind of doing a walk down there."

"Then it gets playful," I added. "It almost makes you want to dance."

"Did you hear that, everyone?" Roy jumped up on a chair with excitement. "Jenna, you're very insightful. 'Passacaglia' means street dance, or street waltz."

Then, climbing down, he turned the music back on and begged for our interpretation. The more we inferred, the more animated Roy became.

Our bounces and wide-eyed nods seemed to be saying, "This choir thing is going to be fun!"

On again, off again, Roy paused the music at various points for discussion and applauded our analysis. You are a brilliant choir. You've got it. You've experienced what Passacaglia actually means-street dance. It's a playful form of music. Isn't it?"

We all nodded.

"Passacaglias are bass-led. When you learn to hear the bass in music, it's as if at once the birds and trees start singing to you even though you've been outside all day. Those who can only hear the melody, miss out on the richness, the depth, and the soul of the music.

"Distinguishing the bass line gives you the anchor. Listen again. Which line is picking up tempo, the bass or melody?"

"The bass!" we screamed.

"Exactly. The bass is the rhythm of the piece. If there are drums, the bass line follows them. If there are no drums, the bass serves as the pulse of the piece. You guys are amazing. Now, let's see what you know."

Roy fired question after question. We shouted the correct answer for every query.

"Look how much you already know. For a piece of candy, who can hum part of the bass line of our exquisite Passacaglia?"

I raised my hand and sang its sweet sultry song.

"Bravo," he said, clapping his hands. Then he "airmailed" me a piece of my favorite candy, Bit-o-Honey. How did he know?

When we finally opened our music, we were exhilarated.

"Look there's the time signature and that must be the bass line," I observed.

As we sang our piece, he asked questions about feeling, tempo, and pitch. We answered like scholars. Learning a lifetime of music in that one-hour lesson, we were all hooked. We quickly spread the word about the cool new director who had waltzed into town. The girls giggled and whispered every time he came near. Our choir grew from eight to twenty in three weeks. We never looked at music in the same way again; never heard it without listening for the bass line.

Chapter 3
Fused Quartz

Fused quartz is the purest and strongest of all the glasses. Its stability and transparency afford its use as semi-conductors, optic fibers, and lenses. But most glassworkers prefer to work with glasses that will fuse at lower temperatures so they add minerals for color and stability. [2]

No one realizes (until its absence) the stability and strength a family offers. The gravity of life pulls us ever downward if the forces of love and nurture don't balance us out. Without them, we could end up as shattered shards on the floor. Layers and layers of life's lessons reflect to and through us by our family connections. Even with the changing dynamics, ours was no different.

Greeting my sister Jordan and me every Saturday morning with a list of chores, Mom waved the flimsy paper in the air urging us to choose our poison. I complained incessantly, but Mom didn't hear because her hips were swaying to the Latin beats of Carlos Santana blasting on the stereo. Each week, we chose our instruments for dusting, sweeping, and washing every particle of dirt from our house. I don't think I'd ever seen Mom dance before "he" moved out.

Singing and dancing as we cleaned, I found our work a rhythm, a time marker in the endless sprawl of the week. We used brushes to mimic mics, empty trash cans as bongos, and mops as dance partners. When the last stray item was twirled into place, we'd pile into the car for errands and extracurricular activities.

Grocery shopping was a contest. Mom would give each of us a part of the list and proclaim that whoever got to the checkout line first with all her items was the winner. The prize was a piece of candy, or chips from the coveted checkout aisle. Jordan always shared her prize with me, but I couldn't bring myself to reciprocate. With the occasional chip purchase, I might part with one or two, but no way was I sharing my peanut butter cups with anyone.

Jordan and I were catapulted into my mother's jam-packed world. Up at dawn cooking omelets (because I couldn't stomach sweet things for breakfast) Mom was a pre-school teacher by morning, and an office clerk until 7PM. When I turned thirteen, I was charged with being the babysitter for Jordan. I was less than thrilled with the arrangement, because aside from watching my bratty sister, I was expected to have dinner on the table when Mom walked in from work, so we could eat as a family.

Gone were my joyous days of watching *Star Trek*'s Captain Kirk foil every galactic foe. Unless I timed it well and had dinner ready and warming in the oven, my *Star Trek* hour was spent fending off the evils of hunger in our family with the simple hamburger and hot dog meal. Eventually, I began to venture into real meals, complete with vegetables and an occasional dessert. When my days were a disaster at school, I looked forward to Mom and Jordan praising my cooking adventures.

My inquisitive mind started to see the kitchen as a science lesson. I was mesmerized by the physical changes in food such as asparagus glowing a bright green after just seconds in the water. My science teacher, Ms. Dufresne, was energized by my questions, and helped me research the cause-the tiny air cells of the asparagus pop and change to bright green when it interacts with the surface of boiling water. When I overheard the grocer advise a woman to place an apple inside a brown bag with the avocado to ripen it faster, I couldn't wait for Ms. Dufresne's class so I could find out why. Her eyes gleamed to match her smile when she explained the powers of ethylene emanating from the apple's skin.

So, somewhere between learning to use acids such as vinegar and lemon juice to make everything from buttermilk to pickles, I began seeing the grocery list as my ticket to exploration. After our store contests, Mom would nudge me back to the pre-packaged dinner section to get new ideas for the week while she and Jordan endured the checkout lines.

Family life as I knew it had fallen apart all around me, but in the kitchen, I could do my part to hold it together. On delectable nights, after eggplant Parmesan, or fried shrimp po-boys, the three of us would sit for hours reminiscing, even acting out the scenes of the day for each other. And although we were missing our integral fourth, we were reworking the mosaic of our lives in his absence. I began to see cooking as the grout that held us together. Since I was able to choose the tiles, arranging varied colors and textures on the plate became my art.

Unfortunately, ten-year-old Jordan was not an art connoisseur.

"I hate turkey. I'm not eating it," Jordan complained as she dissected the turkey from the tetrazzini.

"I hate turkey too, but it was on sale so we have to eat it."

"It has too much white meat, and it's dry."

"You have to eat it. It's dinner."

"You can't make me," she snooted, bottom lip furrowed down like a bulldog.

Jordan snubbed my cooking when Mom had late meetings. I took her obstinacy personally, so personally, that on occasion I would even pinch Jordan's nose and force her to open her mouth so I could shove bites of the shunned dinner down her throat. I learned early on that forced feeding is not healthy for relationships.

Although our time with Mom was limited, we managed a good amount of laughter. Mother subtly demanded it. If we ever uttered the words, "I'm bored," her response was immediate: "Boredom is a lack of creativity. And nothing cures boredom more than good hard work!" She would grin from ear to ear as she handed us scouring powder and a sponge.

But most of our days were full of fun. If ever there was a party or an outing that was excruciatingly dull, Mom had plenty to say about it.

"Ladies, you create your own happiness, so make a party wherever you go."

Whatever was necessary to breathe the fresh air of life into something, Mom was there to the rescue. She created her own party even in the midst of raising two young girls. And she imparted an energy and vibrancy in us that could not be squelched without visions of scouring powder and a sponge.

Mom's vivaciousness was contagious. Although Jordan and I were in a constant battle for her attention, our days were filled with the spontaneity of pillow fights and raucous dance parties. Somewhere along the way each evening we ended up on Mom's bed with a tray of snacks of either popcorn or cut up lemons with salt. My mouth waters just thinking about it.

Chapter 4
The Music Room

Though fused quartz glass contains only silicon and
oxygen, industrially produced glass contains impurities,
which can cloud, discolor, or create instability. [3]

With the Fall Musical Fest fast approaching, our church choir director, Roy, scheduled extra rehearsals. Everyone loved to come because he was so animated. When we blended our harmonies well, he would stand up on a chair and sigh.

"Oh me, oh my. That was amazing," he declared as he pounded his heart with his hand. "It gets me right here." Or if things weren't going so well, he'd lie on the ground and say, "You're killing me, altos. You're dragging the tempo, and it's killing me."

At the end of each practice he'd drill us in Italian musical terms, and candies would soar through the air. One never knew what to expect with Roy.

Since I was one of the leads in the musical, he phoned to arrange a pool party/practice for soloists at his house on Saturday.

"I'll have to switch around my piano lesson," I noted, "but I'm sure that will be okay."

"I didn't know you took piano," Roy told me. " How long have you been playing?"

"About three years."

"That explains why you're far above the rest in reading music and pitch. You might be our next George Frideric Handel."

"I doubt that. But I do like to play."

"What are you working on now?"

"'*Moonlight Sonata*', but I have a long way to go before I get that one down."

"That is a tough piece. The notes aren't that difficult, but Beethoven demands a depth of passion. It's as if he is getting beyond music itself. His ideas break new ground."

"I know what you mean. I think for Beethoven, the music is just a path toward something else, almost like a religious journey."

"Wait 'til you get to his later pieces," Roy replied. "They're so complex that you can find more logical and interesting patterns each time you study it. I hope you'll play for me soon."

"Sure thing," I said calmly, though my heart raced at the thought.

My mom had to catch up on a few things at the office that day, so she was relieved when I told her that Roy volunteered to pick me up and bring me home from the rehearsal. She rolled the new bathing suit she had bought me in a towel and laid it by the door on her way out so I wouldn't forget it.

"Do you have your suit?" he asked as I got into his tiny sports car. "We'll be swimming in the pool at our apartment complex. I'll have you back by four."

Roy and I sauntered out to his pool. His bronze body glistened with sweat. Summer was a sauna in New Orleans, so we jumped into the calm clear water to cool off. The sun played swivel sticks with the reflections on the bottom. Splashing and playing chase, we waited for the other choir members to arrive. After swimming for a while, we got out and wrapped the big beach towels around us like a cigars.

"When are the other kids coming?" I asked.

"They'll be here soon," he said. "I had you come early because you have the most solos. We'll get back in the pool when they get here. Just grab a snack, and meet me in the music room."

I grabbed some chips and a Coke and went to the back room and sat next to him on the piano bench.

"Let me hear you play." I found "Moonlight Sonata" positioned on the piano and I began to play. At first, I strained. I was used to my teacher's posture but Roy had a different pose, which seemed to melt the more I played. It wasn't my best rendition but the passion came through my fingers the more I played. When I finished, he tilted his head, took a breath and offered only one word: "Intriguing." He said it drawn out, like each syllable was a mountain to be climbed. I didn't know how to read his tone, but he moved quickly to our fall musical score, so I didn't have to think about what he meant.

The intro he played for my solo sounded familiar, but did not have the fullness like during youth choir. In choir practice, I always prided myself in being able to produce the first note (in perfect pitch) when he would pause at the intro and point to me. But at his house, I struggled to find my cues. Either he was leaving out notes, or I was distracted, but the piece was definitely not coming together.

After a few fumbled attempts, he inquired, "Are you cold in that wet suit?"

"No, not really. I just can't find the notes I'm supposed to come in on. And the rhythm is different from what we have practiced."

"Maybe you just need to loosen up a bit," he said with a wink. And with that he reached over and started rubbing my shoulders.

His firm kneading relaxed me. I was a little tight after all. His fingers were strong and deliberate. They massaged up my neck and near my ears. But then they slipped to my breasts. I squirmed and moved to push his hands away. But before I knew it, he had pulled the strings to my bathing suit top and it crumpled onto the piano bench. I looked at him with horror and disbelief, and scrambled to cover myself with the towel I was sitting on, but within seconds he had me off the piano bench and pinned to the ground. His hands grasped mine and moved them over his body. He squeezed my hands around his hard flesh and lay on top of me. I gasped and tried to wriggle away.

"Stop! Get off of me." Off went my bottoms. "We are supposed to be having a rehearsal."

"*This* is a private party," he replied with a sickening grin.

"Stop, you're hurting me," I screamed as loud as I could.

"You know you love this. You've wanted this for a while. I can tell by how you look at me. We have a special connection."

His words were like a branding iron etching my skin. I most certainly did not want this! He positioned himself on top of me again. Thrashing and scratching, I bit his neck, which made him angry. He got rougher, and meaner. His scratchy hands were all over me, and his grunts were getting louder.

In between gags and tears, I screamed, "Please, help me!" I closed my eyes so I wouldn't see his face.

Then, there was a pain that sliced through my body from top to bottom. I couldn't believe the piercing scream that came from deep inside me. It reminded me of the helpless animal scream I heard in a science class film that week about hyenas ripping at flesh. The hyenas got more ravenous as the blood gushed and the screams turned to whimpers. Something felt like spiders crawling on my arms and legs, feathery and creepy. It was the last thing I remember as clouds filled my head.

There was a knock at the door. He froze like a statue. More pounding. "I know you're in there, open up."

He quivered uncontrollably for a few seconds, then looked at me with an expression of absolute disgust, like I was filled with hundreds of maggots. He bounced up, threw me across the room, found a towel, and ran to the door. I raced to the bathroom and locked the door behind me. I gagged, which teased the food I had just eaten, almost up through my throat. I heard tense conversation from the door, but my ears were filled with the sounds of his grunts and my screams from the floor of the music room.

My stomach retched again and this time and I threw up all over the sink. Splashing water on my face, I looked around for a towel and found a tiny one that read, "He who sings, prays twice." I hung my head in shame. I felt the life drain out of me and fall to the floor. Seeing my shorts and tank top there from before, I fumbled to cover up my naked body. Were there any outward signs of the tattered heart within? How could he do this? Trample the connection we shared: Beethoven, piano, music, and God! Looking in the mirror, I noticed the tears streaming down my face and the horror that stretched from eye to eye. Could this really be happening to me?

Running to the phone in the kitchen, I called my mother. It rang and rang but she was not at her desk. I tried the main office number, to no avail. Where was Roy?

Before I knew it, he was there beside me. Blood surged through my veins, and a strong throb pulsed in my head. I was dizzy again, but I pretended to talk to my mom saying she needed to come get me. He snatched the phone from my ear and growled, "We're done here. I'm bringing her home." I stared in disbelief, but he wouldn't look at me. Breathlessly, I ran toward the front door. He yanked my arm and wrestled me out the back. With his eyes to the ground and a soft voice he said, "Get in the car, I'm taking you home."

Is he for real? Will I end up in a ditch somewhere along the way? I froze, but he pushed me full force into the front seat of his car. My head hit the steering wheel with a thud, and I began to cry. He got in from the other side and started the car with a jerk. I cried and cried the entire time he drove, not knowing whether to leap from the speeding car, or trust that he truly was taking me home to safety. I would've jumped but the ditches seemed deeper and the traffic speed faster than usual. My heart raced and I whimpered like the hyena-chased animal until the neighborhood sno-ball stand came into view. Roy made jerks and sounds that were hard to analyze. Then he said in a twitchy whisper, "Please pray for me. I am a sick man." It felt like spiders crawled all over me, but I used every bit of energy I had to fling myself out the door and run through the neighbor's yard toward home.

That is the tape that continually runs in my brain, haunting and confusing me down to the very core of my being. "You know you wanted it. I can tell by the way you look at me. Please pray for me. I am a sick man."

Roy resigned the next day with no explanation. The kids and parents were horrified that such a talented young director would leave with no notice just before the fall musical. I didn't have it in me to let anyone know I was involved. It carried too much shame. "You know you wanted it. I can tell by the way you look at me. Please pray for me. I am a sick man."

The physical pain was excruciating, especially since I confided in no one. But his words were a cancer that grew and took hold of my life. And they have tortured my soul every day since. They've clouded my decisions and made me second-guess every motive I've ever had. They've made me distrust even the feelings that run through my veins. I hate him most for that.

Chapter 5
Glass Transition Temperature

Glass is formed by heating materials to an elevated temperature above which melting occurs. Each material has a different melting point so there is no one glass transition temperature. It is just that at this temperature, the atoms are in a fixed position and the material is considered to be a glass.[4]

There was a burning inside me I couldn't name. Its heat gathered and stung as it moved through my body like lava in a volcano. Sometimes it began in my stomach, other times in my back, but eventually it went to my head. I tried everything to shake it: sleep more, move more. But it just got stronger and stronger until one day I opened my eyes to find people standing over me asking me what happened. What did I remember before I blacked out? This happened time after time.

The blackouts had me perplexed. First there was burning, then dizziness, then a creeping spider sensation through my brain into my veins and back again, like a cloud working its way through my body and head. Then I came to. I didn't ever remember going down. There was no rhyme or reason to the blackouts. They only happened a few times, but that was enough for my mom to say I needed to see a doctor. She took me to the main hospital and clinic in New Orleans. After my doctor ran tests and couldn't find anything, he suggested that she take me to a psychologist.

The waiting room was good for my imagination as I concocted diagnoses for each person in a chair. The woman with the bandana was a single mother suffering from a fatal bout of cancer, depressed because of her inability to find homes for her four children. The teenage boy across from me was addicted to acid and was losing his grasp of reality. He didn't even know whether the woman sitting near him was his mother, or the evil social worker sent to make sure he went to therapy. I was annoyed when they called my name and I had to be the one diagnosed.

After the initial lines-what happens in here is confidential-your parents will never know anything that you say, so you are safe in these walls-he started his interrogation.

Are your parents still together?
No, they're divorced.
With whom do you live?
My mother and sister. I see Dad every other weekend.
How do you get along with your sister?
She is an annoying little brat that I have to watch endlessly.
How do you get along with your parents?
Mom is so busy with her two jobs that luckily she stays out of my life. We stay with Dad at his new apartment every other weekend.
What do you do for fun?
Sing and cook.
What are your favorite subjects in school?
Writing and music.
Why is he asking such lame questions?
Do you have a lot of friends?
A few.
How are your relationships with boys?
UGH! (I growled under my breath.)
Is there a problem there?
Yeah, they are all disgusting pigs and only want one thing.
What is that?
You're a man-you know. Sex.
And have you had sex before?

———— «◉» ————

Jenna?
Grunts, screams, and cries filled my head. This is where the rubber meets the road, Jenna. You know what you need to do. Mom doesn't have a lot of money to drag this out...so...
It's a long story.
We have time. Why don't you sit back and tell me?
It was horrible. I screamed, I bit, I kicked, I cried. He was a monster...I trusted him.
Who?

My church's youth choir director. We all loved him. He made us feel talented and creative. He said I had a special talent and we a special connection.

What happened?

I told him the worst parts of the story.

The film in my head keeps playing, and it won't go away. I keep remembering what he said and it won't go away.

What did he say?

That I wanted it, that he could tell by the way I looked at him, that I wanted it for quite some time.

If you kicked and screamed and bit, then you didn't want it.

I know, but...the other choirgirls and I used to talk about how cute he was-how we wish he wasn't married so he could date us. I wasn't thinking about sex though, but maybe kissing.

Even if you were thinking about it before, if you told him to stop, you did not want it.

But what if he heard us whispering about him and saying how cute he was?

Stop it. Stop it right there. You are a child. He forced you. He is wrong. He is a sick man.

I know. He said that too. He said he was a sick man, and that I should pray for him.

When did he tell you that?

After it was all over and he was driving me home.

Did you tell anyone?

No. He resigned the next day.

So you have been keeping this inside all this time?

Yes.

The drops started leaking out of my eyes.

Why?

Because, he may have been right. The other girls and I were talking about how cute he is. What if he overheard us? I can't get all of this out of my head. It's like a horror movie that keeps playing in my head no matter how many times I try to turn it off.

More drops leaked, enough to form puddles on my arm. As I wiped them off, I noticed the Kleenex on the table in front of me. But I didn't want them dried away; I wanted to feel the tears on my skin. I felt lighter as they leaked. They had been bottled up for so long.

It may take some time, but we can work on getting those thoughts and images out of your head. Why didn't you tell your mother?

She has her own issues: the divorce, dad missing child support payments because his business went under. She's working two jobs just to keep us afloat. She can't handle any more than what I've already put her through.

More tears. I sucked in all the mucous, sounding like a croaking bull frog.

That's why I'm here. Now I'm having blackouts. I come to and can't remember where I am or how I got there. I told Mom I needed help with my problems. It's all mixed up in my head. It's cloudy with cobwebs, and sometimes I can't tell if I dreaming or awake.

How often are the blackouts?

Every week or two.

What brings them on?

I don't know. That's what's confusing.

You have no idea?

No idea.

What are your biggest fears?

Being abandoned, like when Dad left. Lately, though my fears is death. I guess it's because I came pretty close to it with Roy.

How often do you think about death?

A lot. I write lots of poems about it.

Have you ever had thoughts of suicide?

Yes, and no.

What do you mean by that?

Yes, I wonder who would care. I wonder who would come to my funeral. I wonder how long they would even talk about me before I was forgotten.

What kept you from it?

I never planned how, or when. I don't like blood, so thinking about it is better than the real deal. Pills don't always kill you, and you could end up even worse than dead: a vegetable somewhere in a nursing home.

What was it about your life that made you want to end it all?

His words and his grunts. I can't bear to hear those in my head every day for the rest of my life.

Have those noises in your head gotten any better?

No, they are getting stronger.

When do they get stronger?

Usually, when I get around boys.

Which boy makes those voices stronger?

Any of them. All of them. Once they start acting like sniffing dogs and try to touch me or get in my pants, then I hear those sounds, and it makes me sick. I gag and sometimes I even throw up when his voices get inside my head.

Pools of tears now.

Boys think I'm a freak. I think I am a freak. All the other girls love boys. They love kissing, holding, and touching boys. Will I ever be normal?

You are normal.

I am not normal.

You are hurting, and confused. You've had a very traumatic thing happen to you, and you kept it inside for a very long time. It's normal to react the way you do to similar situations.

Will I ever stop hearing those sounds?

That's what we are going to work on.

When?

Next week.

Can't we start now?

Yes, you can start now.

How?

Well, you like to write, correct?

I love to write.

Write it out. Write everything you just told me, and then some. Write your feelings about everything, about this visit, about him, about not being able to tell anyone. Do you have a journal?

Yes, where do I begin?

Start with a letter. It can be to your mother, or to him.

I don't think I can ever tell my mother these things.

You don't have to share it with anyone. You are writing these things for *you*. You want to subdue these sounds in your head, right?

A river of tears was streaming down my chest.

Yes, God, yes.

Then give them a place to speak, a place to be heard. If you get anywhere near thinking about death, you give me a call immediately. Here is my card, with my emergency number. Do you understand?

Yes.

Now, let's go make an appointment for next week, and we can get this sick man out of your head and where he belongs.

I couldn't wait to write when I got home.

Dear Roy,

I hate you! Hate is not even a harsh enough word to describe my feelings about you. My skin crawls when I think of you. It's like boils ready to erupt and ooze slimy puss when I think of where and how you touched me. I hate every part of my body because of you, especially my insides.

I trusted you. You stole from me. I trusted when you said I was talented; we were talented. I trusted when you took us to new heights of musical performance. I trusted the special connection we had. I thought that you cared about me and had my safety in your hands. But all you cared about was getting off, feeling my flesh, and taking something precious from me.

You took my soul. It was not good enough that you violated and hurt me, but then you twisted it around like it was my fault. It was not my fault. You are a perverted, sick man, and I will never pray for you except for you to die. I hope you rot on top of someone else so the whole world will know kind of man you are. But then I wouldn't want that pain for anyone else. I only want it for you.

What was your wife thinking when she married you? What was the church thinking when they hired you? What was my mom thinking when she let me go to your house? Did anyone ever have a hint of suspicion that you are the wretched human being that you are?

Do you even know what damage you've done to me? I can't even be around boys without gagging or throwing up. Any time they touch me it's like the boils erupt. I can't trust

any man. Even my own father, and he is a good man, a won-
derful man. I keep wondering if he is doing that to little girls
on the side like you did to me.

At church I have to think of God, and how he forgives.
And I don't want him to forgive you. I want you to rot in hell
and beyond. I want you to have to watch your wife, your chil-
dren, your loved ones, each raped in front of you. But then
again, you are such a sick man that you might enjoy that!

When I think of you, my insides burn inside my body; I
have so much rage. I hate that you asked me to forgive and
pray for you. You know you are sick.

Why couldn't you have let me forgive you on my own? Why
did you have to ask for it? Now I don't want to. I'll never want
to, because of what you said. You twisted everything around.
You know I didn't want it. You have scratches, bruises, and
bites to prove it. Why would you say something like that? Do
you know what it's like to have your thoughts and feelings
twisted and turned on themselves from the inside out?

I can't trust anything anymore, nothing. Not even my
own feelings.

I hate you. I hate you. I hate you. And that hate spills
over on to me. I will never forgive you. Ever. You hear that,
God? Never.

-Jenna

Chapter 6
The Melt

Glassblowing involves several furnaces, the first of which
contains a crucible of melted glass. A long metal blowpipe
is used to gather "the melt" from the furnace. [5]

Ms. Melancon, our high school choir teacher, announced we would be traveling to Italy for the International Choral Competition. I flicked my thumb with my index finger for the hundredth time that day, irritating the tiny flap of skin that hung next to my thumbnail. Although I winced, I couldn't stop the rubbing.

"We'll land in Rome and stay there for four days."

As Jacquie, my choir mate, got excited, her words became quickened as if in a race.

"Can you believe we'll get to see the origin of western civilization? Galileo, Caesar, the Sistine Chapel, the Coliseum, and the martyrs. We'll be there where it began." Her lips were thin and crimson, and when she spoke, they moved as if in a dance, with the top trying to catch up to the bottom. I tried to concentrate on her words, but those lips.

Stop it. Leave your hangnail alone.

She continued, "Then, we spend four days in Florence with all the masters, Botticelli, DaVinci, Michelangelo, and Bernini." Each name brought forth images from the slideshow our art history teacher had shown us to prepare for the trip.

Who is Bernini? I had to go straight to the school library to look it up before the bell rang. Knowledgeable about art, music, and life, Jacquie was the favored student of teachers and students alike. And she was so intense. Every word was packed with power, and she wore her emotions on her sleeve. I pulled on that nasty hangnail again. I shook out of my trance.

"I'm crazy for Venice. Water everywhere-and we get to ride in the gondolas. It'll be like New Orleans after a hurricane," I said remembering when Camille hit and how we canoed for hours through our once car-filled streets.

"Except in Venice, everything won't look as though a bomb went off. Their water world will still be intact and exquisite," Jacquie added.

"And colorful, and enchanted."

"My mother has never been out of the country, so she can't believe we get this opportunity to sing for the pope on Easter Sunday if we win!"

I felt my forehead wrinkle as I replied; "I wish I were Catholic so I could get how incredible it is to sing for the pope. I know it's a big deal, but I'm not ripping apart at the seams about it, like the rest of you."

The advanced choir at our all girl public high school had already won the National Competition in New York City, and now we were entering the International High School Choral Competition in Italy. We were singing our way through the numerous Catholic churches and eateries in New Orleans, raising support for our trip. We were ecstatic!

Jacquie was a junior. She was one year older than I was, but because we took the same hour-long school bus trip each day to and from school, she was nice to me. Her long dark hair flowed as ribbons in the wind from the bus window. "I've written a song," she confided. "I stayed up all night one night and it just kind of came to me. It's weird how it happened."

"I'd love to hear it. Can you play it for me at lunch?" My voice cracked with excitement. She was known for how her fingers moved effortlessly on the guitar and her soothing crystal clear voice. Now she was trying her hand at songwriting. "They've rearranged my schedule so I have an upperclass-man's lunch to prepare for the trip. Thank God I don't have PE anymore this semester," I quipped, relieved that my klutziness would no longer be on daily display for my classmates.

"Sure thing," she added. "Just meet me in the music library at lunch. Thanks, Jenna. I could use the practice." I exited the bus feeling like I was in on the biggest and best secret of the world! I closed the door of the music library behind me and sat near her. Her song was like diamonds: rich, deep, and transparent. It started my finger rubbing and pulling again.

"Let celestial quiet still your soul, the beat of heart you feel as one, in the rhythm, find your peace and dreams, and the battle raging will be won."

Her lyrics were more enticing with each verse, speaking of a power that can overcome all. I desperately needed peace and to believe that the war in my head would one day cease. She sang it like a poet on a hill. And as she did, my heart stopped, like it forgot its purpose was to pump and pound oxygen through my veins. Dazzled, I sat back. My eyes tried to regain focus. As I tried to catch my breath, snuffles escaped. I couldn't find words to describe how the fingers of her song reached out and captured my life: my fears, my pain, never fitting in, never finding peace, or another soul that could understand the combat within. Drops poured from my eyes.

The silence that connected us those brief moments evoked the most stirring feeling I'd ever felt in my life. As the words failed, the music lingered like the fragrance of magnolias after a rain. Our eyes were fixed on each other, our nods a covenant fused in space, afraid of ruining the precious bond with any movement. We sat there in the music library, crying quietly until the bell blared, breaking the synergy. Fumbling, we collected our book bags. As she ran out of the room, I noticed the guitar pick she had just used laying behind on her seat. As I rubbed it between my fingers, I felt the warmth, the energy, the connection we had just shared. How could such a small piece of plastic bring so much passion? I tucked it away in a very special place in my wallet and ran to class.

⸺ ((◍)) ⸺

> *How strange a vehicle a gondola is, coming down unchanged*
> *from times of old romance, and so characteristically black, the*
> *way no other thing is black except a coffin-a vehicle evoking*
> *lawless adventures in the splashing stillness of the night.* [6]

Touring Italy was magical, like darning a Disney fairy tale to the pages of history. Each city-Rome, Milan, Florence, and Venice-had its own story to tell, with its own accent, nuance, and fragrance that lingered far after the happily ever after. Vatican City was a bustling business district. Quite the spectacle, thirty girls in handmade red dresses, we had a trail of followers believing we were supporters of the Communist red party in the approaching elections.

St. Peter's Basilica was the epitome of what humanity could form from stone, wood, and pure perseverance. Splendidly crafted in marble from ceiling to floor, it exuded awe. Bernini's pulpit, carved out of the largest piece of bronze in the world, towered a hundred feet above the altar. It was designed to serve as a visual link between Michelangelo's dome above, and the congregation at floor level below.

Light filtered in through the dome, dancing with the images on the colorful mosaic tiles. My knees became weak at the sight of such splendor. I was glad that my principal, Ms. Ventura, guided me to a nearby bench. We were able to sit for a while and study the architecture instead of being paraded through like the rest of the chorus.

"I've never seen anything so, so...so..." My head bobbled trying to find a word.

"I know," she whispered. "Ralph Waldo Emerson claims it to be 'an ornament of the earth...the sublime of the beautiful.'"

"I'm sorry I had to stop. My knees wobbled, and I started to feel faint."

"I'm glad you did. It gives us a good excuse to sit here for a minute." And we did, in silent awe. After a time we joined the other girls.

The next part of the tour was to the coliseum. Elephant leg pillars bore the marks of the thousands who were martyred there. *How could they have hated the Christians so much as to cut them open and send them into the ring with lions that devoured them alive? What kind of people would do that?* I couldn't help but compare them to Nazi Germany. Be careful whom you demonize so as to not become one yourself.

Venice was a water wonderland. Our tour guide gave us the story of how it was built. "Running away from the evil Attila and his Huns, the neighboring villagers of Padua and Torcello fled to the archipelagos (tiny islands), and hence Venice was born. Since they had the best artisans, philosophers, doctors, musicians, architects, writers, and astronomers in the world at that time, they constructed elaborate canals and waterways between the marshes and islands. "Venezia" became the chief carrier between the east and the west, bringing the wines of the Greek Isles, the goods of Christian Constantinople, and the silks, carpets, and spices from the Orient. The mosaics that fill the town are rich in Arabic color, pattern, and influence."

That intense Venetian passion and eye for color created a palette of vivid buildings, reflected as the gleaming water swirled around the ever-passing gondolas. It was as if the water bred beautiful art and music like those crystal rocks you put in liquid that grew into colorful stalagmites before our eyes.

We continued our tour of Venice at St. Mark's Basilica. Our guide continued, "This basilica was built to hold the relics of St. Mark. They were stolen from Alexandria by two Venetian merchants in 828 and taken to Venice.

The mosaic on the wall shows how the sailors covered the relics with a layer of pork while smuggling it out of Alexandria. Since Muslims are not allowed to touch pork, they would not search or confiscate them."

Sitting outside on the square of Piazza San Marco, we ate Panini sandwiches while a full orchestra serenaded us under the stars. Though we couldn't speak each other's languages, the musicians were communicating our past and present: Chopin, Beethoven, and even our own Gershwin. Did they know that playing "Rhapsody in Blue" would forever weave our American girl hearts to the rich tapestry of Venice? The world was so much grander than I had ever imagined.

Our excursion to the nearby island of Murano to tour the glassblowing factory was mesmerizing. The glassblowers twirled fingers of fire gathered from a furnace and then shaped them into marvelous pieces of art while giving brief explanations on the physics of glass. "When water freezes, we call it ice. When sand freezes, we call it glass." Each time a blower reached into the furnace to add to the glowing orb, my innards collected energy as well. Connecting science and art, passion, and power, the glass swelled with the breath of its creator. Seeing in living color how we, like that delicate glass, were laced together with inspiration, revelation, and complexity, caused my insides to broaden like a bubble on a wand.

I walked through the studio studying each item, amazed at how those colorful pieces could originate from the simple elements of sand and fire. The exhibition of shapes, colors, weights, textures, and light was better than any museum we had seen thus far. My heart raced the entire time I was there. It only settled down, found solace again in its skin, when on the sunset water taxi ride back to our hotel, we saw the gondolas and begged our chaperones to let us ride them that night. Each boat could hold two or three, so Jacquie and I paired for the ride.

Black with gold carvings, the gondola appeared like a canoe shaped treasure chest. Red paper lanterns were strung across a line running from the front of the boat to the back. The gondolier greeted Jacquie and me. Then he took his oar, guiding the long craft through the canals with ease, and when necessary, the help of a long black pole.

Under bridges, we looked up to see hundreds staring and waving. And soon, you could hear the inevitable refrain, "Can we ride one too?" The gondolier's voice was rich and sweet as he sang arias from operas as well as popular tunes. When Jacquie and I sang along to *"Volare" and "Que Sera?"* our marine serenades received applause from the many bridges above.

The moon kissed the water at an angle forming a long moon path, guiding us to a world beyond. And once again we shared that silent space where souls collide. Sitting together on that bench, we held hands, hugged, and pinched ourselves to ensure it was all really happening.

And then, when we were far down a quiet ravine, following our own moon river, in the stillness of the gleaming water, skimming like a water bug through the canal, I reached over and kissed her. She didn't look surprised, or offended. As I leaned in, her luscious lips, framing the toothy grin, kissed me back with the lingering touch of one wanting the moment encased in time.

We stayed there for what seemed like an eternity locked in love and longing. But not in the ordinary sexual way, in a way that connected souls not just to each other, but to the myriads of other souls in time, who long to be joined to something greater, something real and timeless, something lawless and adventurous in the splashing stillness of the night.

Chapter 7
Adding Color

Many ingredients can be added to common glass to change its properties. Adding substances such as cobalt for blue, gold for red, manganese for purple, and iron for green creates color.

The Rimini International Choral Competition was a fanfare of choruses from around the globe competing for a gold medal and a chance to sing for the pope on Easter Sunday. The youth chorus component allowed fifty of the most talented choirs to sing prepared pieces, sight read, and then work with another conductor. The criteria by which we were judged were: intonation, fidelity to the score, sound quality, program choice, and overall artistic impression. The competition was intense as only national champions could qualify. We had earned the U.S. title that fall in New York City.

In the first round we sang the pieces we had rehearsed for months. The intricacies of Norman Della Joio's "O Jubilant Song" and Bach's "Dona Nobis Pacem" wooed the judges. Adamant about intonation, Ms. Melancon coached us to sing with a smile rather than an O-mouth, as most directors instruct. She believed that singing on the vowel with the smile shaped mouth kept us tone and pitch perfect.

Even though our senior accompanist, Traci, was sick with the flu, she never missed a beat. Our performance was seamless, with all the necessary dynamics and passion that proved we truly understood the sacred score. When we finished, there was a reverent stillness before the claps of acclamation.

Then came the challenge. Each choir had to perform while sight-reading a piece of music it had never seen before. Ms. Melancon pumped us by reminding that we sight-read every day as part of our advanced chorus class. We were extremely good at it, much better than with any choir she had ever worked. But before we went on, another senior girl got sick. (What was up with the senior girls-too much wine?)

The sickly one, Paula, was the lead first soprano, and I was her support. Jacquie was the lead second soprano, and she was looking a little peaked too. When they handed us the music, we were all relieved. It was straight-forward and much easier than the pieces we were used to. Ms. Melancon tapped her music stand, and we looked up, a fine tuned music machine trained to stop dead in our tracks at her words or taps. She spread her hands across her face, giving us the signal to smile and get in vocal position. We always smiled and looked like we were having fun. Usually we were.

Traci started the intro. The first page was rocky with a few flats and weird harmonies, but we kept focused, and before long it was as if we were on a sailboat race, anticipating the wind before it came. Ms. Melancon over-exaggerated the crescendos, and our dynamics were powerful. Before long, people in the audience were looking up from their programs to see the American girls in red dresses perform. First whispers, then hushes, then clapping and yelling filled the music hall. Even the judges looked dazzled as they tallied our scores.

In the last round, we had to work with another conductor. This was what scared us the most. We were totally devoted to Ms. Melancon, the magic of the Lakeside High School Chorus. We were convinced no one could bring the music out of us like she could.

She gave us encouragement the night before. "Look at how easy this piece is. The director may change the tempo, or the dynamics, but this is a piece of cake. Mostly the judges want to make sure that I have trained you to follow the conductor's lead. If he wants the altos to dominate a section, do it. Just watch closely, and you will be fine. Show 'em what you know. Let us shine!"

"How do you think we are doing so far?" I asked.

"Are you kidding, we are already a winner because we've made it to the finals," she replied.

"But are we first, second or third so far?" I continued.

"So far I think we're first. Our sight-reading was incredible."

She was right. Most people had not made it this far in the competition. They were already headed home, and we had a chance at Easter, only two days away. As we ambled to the risers, Paula, the lead 1st soprano, stumbled and fell. She was dizzy, so they brought her some water, but either the nerves or the flu, got her again. She apologized and whispered to me as she left the stage, "You've got to pull us through. You can do it." With that she ran off gagging.

Was Roy around? Perhaps he had that effect on her too. *Stop it. Concentrate. You can do this. No, I can't. I love the challenge of performing. No, you don't, not since Roy.*

At that instant, Jacquie looked at me with those lips that I longed to kiss each night. Then she smiled, gave me a thumbs up, and I felt my feet sprout wings that could lift me through the roof.

"You can do it," she mouthed.

The male director used a baton, and he tapped on the music stand. It was a different sound than we were used to but our concentration was summoned. The first notes were much more staccato than we rehearsed but we flowed through the piece, until the chorus. He was drawing out the sopranos. I was struck with fear, as the notes were too high for me to lead. I could support them, but to be the lead-no way.

More and more he drew from the sopranos. My heart hammered, and my throat strained as we neared the descant. Then, the music had the same chord progressions as in the song *"Volare"*, and I was back on the gondola, serenading my love for all who could hear. I sang that descant like an angel, hitting the notes with such nuance, such intensity, such a straight tone that it lingered through the rest of the piece. We were breathless by the end, but we received a standing ovation.

Our scores came back almost perfect. We were the winners of the International High School Choral Competition, and we were headed to the Vatican! The notes of the descant could not approach the musical high we were on that night. We ate in the hotel so as to have a good night sleep before our Vatican debut the next day. Wine was flowing freely as we toasted and celebrated our success. (In Italy, if our parents gave written permission, we were allowed to drink wine with dinner.)

After lights out, the two senior girls we were rooming with snuck out, which left Jacquie and me alone. "Look what I have." Jacquie pulled out an opened bottle of wine.

"Where did you get that?"

"Necessity is the mother of invention."

"Why do you need it? Didn't you have enough at dinner?"

"Oh loosen up, it'll be fun."

"We aren't supposed to drink except at dinner."

"When did you start being Mother Theresa?"

While enjoying the Italian radio, we drained most of the bottle. We made up harmonies to songs we didn't even know, and we laughed with the heartiness of thick chested men. "I was really nervous today, you know. I didn't think I could do it. Thanks for giving me the thumbs up."

"I knew you could do it. You are better than Paula anyway. You're just not a senior, that's why you're not the lead."

"I never could've done it without that encouragement. I was about to lose it."

"You gave me the same encouragement with my song. I'll never forget that day when you cried. I felt as though I reached out and took your heart in my hand."

"That's because you did. I've never felt that way before. I've never felt that I fit in, anywhere. I've never felt that anyone could understand the things I've been through, but you sang how I feel." I gulped, "And...you gave me hope."

"That's what you did for me when you cried. It was the ultimate connection. It's what all artists clamor for when they create something. You put your heart and soul on the line, or the page, beating with all its might, all defenseless and open, just for someone to feel what you feel, even for a second."

"I know," I said, as I inched toward her on the bed.

"You feel way deep down too; I can tell. You feel in a place where most people don't want to go, or don't even know exists. I can see it in your eyes." She snuggled in closer and continued, "When I look in your eyes, I'm not scared when I'm down in the depths, because I know I'm not alone." Her words were a savory dish after a desert journey.

"You know what got me through the competition?" I offered.

"What?"

"Remembering the gondola ride. When the song started to sound like 'Volare', I remembered..."

"The kiss?" Her eyebrows rose with the same smile as her lips.

"Yes, the kiss."

"Why haven't we talked about it?" she inquired.

"I don't know. What is there to say?"

"That it was the best thing that ever happened to me, and I didn't want it to ever end," she said taking my hand to her chest.

"I know."

"You don't want to talk about it, do you?"

"No." I didn't want to talk about it. I wanted to do it, over and over again. With that, we were locked in an embrace as tight as if we were dangling over the ravenous lions at the coliseum, and our death grip was the only thing keeping us alive. Impassioned kisses, caresses, exploring each other's bodies and accepting the pleasure the other had to give was ours all night. It was fresh and new. The exquisite feel of satin and fire simultaneously crept into the crevices of our curiosity.

When it was over we both cried.

"Why are we crying?" I asked.

"You know this is wrong, right?" My heart sunk to the lobby four floors below.

"But, why? I love you. I've loved you since the bus, when you spoke of the artists and their passion. And since I heard your song."

"You know why it's wrong. We are here in Rome, near the Vatican, where we will sing for the pope tomorrow. How can you say it's not wrong?"

"I'm...not Catholic," I stammered. "I love you." *What a sorry attempt for an excuse. I am beginning to sound like Roy.*

"And I love you, too. But that doesn't make it right."

"I've never felt this connection with anyone before. Ever!"

"But that still doesn't make it right. The Bible is pretty clear on homosexuality."

"It doesn't feel clear to me. It feels like I love you and I'm ok with that. Besides, nothing works with me and boys. I'm only normal when I'm with you."

"Me too, but that doesn't make it right."

"How do you know for sure?"

"We were both crying, weren't we?"

Jacquie and I fell into an awkward silence as we dragged ourselves out of bed the next morning. Filing into the same line for the same continental breakfast as we had every other day on the trip, our moves were mechanical, and the small talk was excruciating. It was hard to fathom that it was Easter. Where was the Easter basket, and the Macy's parade on TV? New Orleanians expect parades on all the major holidays: Mardi Gras, St. Patrick's Day, Independence Day, St. Joseph's Altar, and Christmas. It couldn't be Easter without the fanfare of trumpets, banners, bands, and horses. Could it? I tried to resolve myself to the notion that a Vatican celebration was all about piety and ritual. "How many other choirs get to sing? What parts of the mass are they singing?" were the questions at meals.

Because of the throngs expected for Easter, we had to arrive at the Vatican at dawn. Even then, the lines of people drew a maze around the city. Each person grasped his ticket like it was pure gold. Our bus, ushered on to a special lane (since we were singing at the service) meandered through the maze.

The mass was held outside with a huge white canopy framing the marble mosaic altar. Pots of blooming flowers formed a pink and purple corridor all around the Vatican stairs. The choir sang "Alleluia" as the processional hailed the giant golden cross and paraded it from St. Peter's basilica to the outdoor altar.

Bishops and priests marched and nodded to the waving crowds. When the pope came out, the cheering escalated. Banners waved, and I turned to Jacquie, "It's a pope parade, but it's a far cry from Mardi Gras."

She rolled her eyes and tersely replied, "That is *exactly* the point!" How in the world did I forget that Mardi Gras was the opposite of Easter? Mardi Gras, or Fat Tuesday, is the last gorge, or bacchanalia, before Ash Wednesday. Ash Wednesday marks the beginning of the Lenten season when all good Catholics abstain from things, such as alcohol, sweets or meat on Fridays. If a restaurant didn't serve fish, it may as well close on Fridays in Lent. Nary a soul would enter its doors.

Pope Paul took about ten minutes to proceed to the altar, but the pageantry of each step matched royalty walking on air. Although there were no horses, floats, or ladies in fancy hats, the pomp and circumstance of the cross, the incense, and the Bible processing gave new meaning to the word parade. Even with all the commotion, most people's eyes were fixed intently on the golden cross, as it had finally been freed from its Lenten black drape.

After the pope blessed and kissed the Bible, our choir rose up to sing. That's when we could finally see him closely. We couldn't take our eyes off Pope Paul. *Did he ever get used to all those eyes boring holes in his skin?*

We sang Bach's "Dona Nobis Pacem" in Latin. Our long rehearsals fused our harmonies, and our confidence was amplified through the streets of Rome, sending chills through my spine. All those months practicing and it didn't make sense, but there, *Lord, grant us peace*, came alive with the acoustics, the majesty, the splendor and the turmoil of the night before.

Even though Ms. Malencon had cut us off, our voices echoed through the crowds. Moving back to their places, most girls shivered with exhilaration. Pope Paul walked to the podium, nodded his head toward us, smiled, and said, "Proprio come gli angeli." It took a moment to translate, but we heard whispers around the crowd saying, "Just like angels." The pope said we sounded just like angels!

Our entire choir was crying at the experience, except for me. *Why wasn't*

I crying? While everyone else was overflowing with joy, the piercing question stabbed again: *What is wrong with me? Why can't I feel what others feel?*

He took out the Bible and spoke with the charisma of fire. I didn't understand Latin, but I listened like Ms. Melancon taught us to listen to opera, every pore attuned to the nuance and passion that transcended language. When his voice became intense I knew he was talking about sin. When Pope Paul looked up in love to the cross, I knew he was talking about a relationship with Jesus and the power of God to forgive anything, even those who caused his death on a cross.

I listened for his pacing and fell in love with the language. I didn't understand any of it, but I believed it all, every single Latin lilted word of it. And I felt its power over me, shaping and calming me. Everything I ever learned in Sunday school about forgiveness, love, mercy, power, and peace, I felt it. *Lord, grant us peace.*

All the grunts, groans, and twisted taunts of Roy...peace.

All the anger at my dad for leaving us...peace.

Help me, Lord; forgive my father even though he abandoned me.

And all the tumbles of the night before, the intense joy, the connection, and the sadness at the revelation, came pouring out like the wine for communion...peace.

All the anger at God for asking me to forgive...replaced with peace.

Now I needed his forgiveness, more than ever. Because I had sinned like never before. Hadn't I? *Lord, grant us peace.*

Chapter 8
Marvers

The most powerful tool in the studio is the marver: a
flat, smooth, metal or steel surface, which is ideal for
adding color while shaping and cooling the glass.

Have a seat, Jenna.
(He pointed to the couch. Needing a hug, I moved to the overstuffed
chair and let its arms envelope me.)
Sure, you can take the chair.
(He chuckled.)
You like to change things around, I see.
Yep. The last time I took the couch.
(I smiled, thinking of all the things we've discussed in our sessions.)
**So, I'd like to explore the blackouts again today. Can you give
me some information on where you were when they happen**?
But I want to talk about why his grunts are back, big and strong,
all the time.
(His pen started writing.)
So that means they were gone for a while?
Well almost. Not gone completely, but much quieter.
How did that happen?
(My heart leapt just thinking about the whole trip to Italy, the
abrupt ending, still seeing her every day in class. My skin tingled.)
I went to Italy and fell in love, and they got kind of drowned out for
a bit. We were practicing or performing round the clock.
I see. That was with your school choir, right?
Yes.
The Lakeside High School Choir, right?
(I nodded.)
So where in Italy did you fall in love?

Actually, I fell in love before we left. We just bonded in Italy. (I adjusted myself on the chair. It was not as comfortable as I imagined.)
Bonded? Does that mean you had sex?
Good Catholics would call it sex. But we didn't go that far. It was not with a boy though.
I see. Did you gag, or throw up or anything like that?
No, it was perfect. I didn't want to stop.
Then why are the voices back?
You tell me. Probably, because we broke it off.
Why?
Because it's wrong.
Who says it's wrong?
She does, and the church. We were in the Vatican, for God's sake, singing for the pope on Easter Sunday.
Do you believe it's wrong?
No. Yes...I don't know.
So, when did the voices come back?
When I had to sit in my bed and think about how screwed up I am, and how I will never fit in anywhere. About how wonderful the trip was and how perfectly we fit together and how the uh...whatever you call it...was the only time I ever felt like you're supposed to feel in that situation...getting close to someone, I mean. How is it that the only time I felt right, it was wrong?
If he's writing that much in his notes, I'll bet there will be psychiatric journals written about me in the future.
Am I a lesbian?
What do you think?
I think I'm really screwed up.
What about bi-sexual, could you be bi-sexual?
Yeah, that'd be great if I could ever get to the part where guys don't make me throw up.
Are there any guys that you like?
I go to an all girls' school. It's kind of hard to meet boys. And the boys in my neighborhood know I'm kind of fragile in that area. So, we're just friends.
Are there any kinds of clubs or activities that could foster your creativity and also help you feel more comfortable around guys?

(I remembered they had announced tryouts at McDonald High, our brother school for the Parish Players Theater. They were casting *Wizard of Oz* next week.)

There's the drama club/theater group for the combined high schools. I saw their performance of *Bye Bye Birdie* last year, and I remember thinking that might be fun. Do you think I should sign up for that?

Why is my heart pumping so fast?

That sounds good. And why don't we also look at what attracted you to...what is her name?

Jacquie.

Very well then, tell me about Jacquie.

I told it all. Like a romantic novel, I played it out with steamy page-turners. As I relived with words, I imagined the Parish Players acting it out, with flowing curtains and candles on the windows, a symphony playing "Nessum Dorma" outside, and soft sighs and moans coming from within, although I didn't think anyone would ever come to a performance of a lesbian love story.

I left that session with a few assertions in the bass line of my life: He wasn't appalled at the possibility of me being a lesbian. Jacquie's deep passion for life and especially the arts are what drew me in. Her song that sang of my soul was the chain that connected me to the outside world. But more than anything, I learned that sex was going to be a very bittersweet thing for me, no matter how you sliced it!

———— ((•)) ————

The theater was bustling in every direction. Its blood-tinted curtains had an immense stretch of velvet so smooth and silky that it took all of my resolve not to run and bury myself amidst them. When I heard the tinny announcement from the stage manager's bullhorn, I knew we were off to see the Wizard!

"All cast report to the stage for a word from our director."

Mr. Dunn was a plump middle-aged man with gray hair and stylish glasses. When he took the stage, there was no doubt that he was in charge.

"Our first performance of *Wizard of Oz* will be the middle of November. That means we have three months to get this show on the road, literally.

First, we'll perform for the public elementary schools here on the East Bank. And then we'll pack up and perform it for the elementary schools on the West Bank.

"We'll begin auditions for the various roles starting with Dorothy. Write your name under the ones you're auditioning for. The pages in your script that you'll read from are at the top of the sign in sheet. Don't come on stage unless you are prepared!"

Since this was our first show, my classmate, Ada, and I were a little hesitant to try out for any major roles. "What are you auditioning for?" she asked.

"I'm not about to try out for Dorothy, but I could definitely see myself as one of the witches," I snickered. Everyone scrambled to the sign in sheets.

"I don't sing well enough for Glenda. Maybe I could be the wicked witch of the west."

"I could see that," I replied.

"I'll get you for that later when you want a ride home."

"You know I'm only kidding."

"I know. Good luck."

"It's 'break a leg,' here, remember."

"You're right. Break a leg."

"Break a leg to you too."

Being sophomores, we didn't get any of the major roles, but we were happy with the chorus tidbits: the munchkin lollipop guild, and citizens of Oz. What a way to begin in musical theater! *Wizard of Oz* summoned both good and bad witches, munchkins, and fiends to high drama.

The drama club members paraded their new personas and costumes each day to school. Whether we wore purple boas, top hats, or checkered pants, fitting into the mainstream was no option, because we had our own stream, and eccentric was its name. We followed no current or direction patterned by anyone else. Drawing from three high schools in the parish, we were rich with blacks, Hispanics, Jews, gentiles, gays, straights, and everything in between.

Each day we headed to the auditorium directly after class to rehearse, and we didn't come into the fresh air until around 9:00 p.m. If money jingled in anyone's pockets, we headed to Pizza Hut or Krystal for a quick bite. With the cast, you never knew who would stand on the tables and sing a song from *Oz*, recite a Shakespearean sonnet, or even better, dance the Charleston to the Muzak on the speakers.

We were always breaking out in song or dance regardless of location or invitation. And we could change direction at the drop of a hat. Most of the time, people loved our exuberance and applauded us, but other times we were met with wrinkled brows and frowns. Once we got it out of our system, we could be tame for a few hours...almost.

Our director, Mr. Dunn, started us on the path of character association. He studied our every move, and had us analyze each other's, to see what it said about our temperament. When we could get inside the brain of our character, noting what each would have in his purse or pocket, what type of drink she would order at the bar, what item he would rescue first in his house, then we got to block our own scenes. Oh, the contagion of creativity; it clamored for more.

There was never a dull moment: never a time together when we were bored or indifferent. As if on a quest to find our stages and selves, we shaped each other, back and forth: flitting from one new experience to the other, trying on lifestyles, and personas like costumes from a chest.

I felt like the Tin Man, always wanting to feel something real, from my own organs and tissues, not a reaction imposed on me by the evil Roy. And so I searched for my heart, on the stage, on the risers, in church, at the disco, with my new friends in the gay bars...anywhere and everywhere I would journey to feel real again, like those splendid nights in Italy.

Chapter 9
Fracture

There are hundreds of ways to apply color to pieces. Although color is one of the most fascinating elements of glass, it is also a stumbling block, as it can lead to fracture. [7]

They started and ended pretty much the same, like spiders. I felt this soft and feathery thing creeping up my arm. In a fog, I saw it, but I didn't want to believe it was there. I wanted to pretend it was a butterfly kiss, the soft petal kind with eyelashes, but then I came eye to eye with all those legs, their brown and hairy reality, and my silent scream jolted me into panic. Fade to black. Foggy feathers and spotted spider legs crawled up my arms, until I shook them to awaken. Was I sleeping? I couldn't have been, because I was in the middle of a conversation with someone.

You're going to have to give me something to work with, Jenna.
I know, but I really don't remember why I blacked out. She had something in her hand.
Where were you?
At school.
Where at school?
In her room. It was a....
(It began to take shape)
it was a...microscope.
Who's she?
My science teacher, Ms. Holmes. It was a microscope. She said she had something to show me, and because I was her best student, with keen insight and a special ability to see patterns in things, she wanted me to tell her what I thought.
And...

And she rubbed my shoulders as I looked and said, "I'm so excited for you to see this. What do you think?"

And...

That's it.

That's it?

That's it. The spiders came in. Then they went out again, and I came to with her asking me if I was okay. I guess I had fallen or something, because I was in another chair, and she looked really worried.

Tell me about the other blackouts.

They're random. One time, I got in a really crowded elevator, and it felt like people were all over me. It was also hot and muggy in there. It could've been that.

Yes, it could've been. Any more?

The last one happened at church. I don't remember what we were talking about. We were in a meeting, actually leaving a meeting, and I just collapsed. This is the strangest one because church is where I usually go to help my head to *stop* spinning.

Hmm...That's interesting. What about the church makes your head stop spinning?

I guess it's because I know God will be there.

You see him?

No.

This man really does think I'm crazy!

But I can feel him. My Sunday school teachers are so cool. One is a New Orleans Saints football player, and the others are a married couple, and they just had a new baby. They bring the class over to their house, and we play games and have really deep discussions.

Like what?

Like what makes God cry. Like how the angels jump up and down with joy whenever someone finally gets how much God loves him. I think that's cool, to be able to make the angels dance with joy. And God smile.

That is a pretty cool image.

That's what I try to concentrate on when I hear Roy's grunts and groans in my ears. On the good days it works.

What happens on the bad days?

I can't get out of it. The film starts playing in my brain and his sounds take over, second by second, and I start questioning what kind of a person would've let that happen to her? What kind of a church hires perverts? Why all men are dogs? Why I'm a freak? What kind of a God lets horrible things like this happen? Why am I so crazy? Why shouldn't I just end it all? Should I continue? I have thousands more where those came from.

So how do you get out of the bad days?
Some days, I don't. I just have to ride with them, and the next day is usually better. Other days, I concentrate on good things, and I get to a good place faster.

What kinds of good things do you concentrate on?
Peace, joy, hope, beauty, love, and God.

You talk about God and the church a lot. Do you feel safe at the church, since it was the choir director who raped you?
It's the main place I feel safe.

What makes you feel unsafe?
Anything and everything when I get out of my element. I feel well... confused, like there is darkness and danger around every corner. I start thinking about Jacquie, about Roy, about guys and why I don't like them, about why they have one-track minds. Like the other day I was playing pool with my friend Scott. He's fun, and I really like his mother. She hangs out and talks to us. But I found him just staring at my boobs, just staring at them. I didn't get nauseated or anything. So I guess that's progress. I just got angry. I felt like hitting him. Actually, I did, with the pool stick, and it shook him out of his trance. He acted pretty weird after that. Why do boys have to do that? Go and ruin everything with sex. What is their problem? Do normal girls think about sex as much as boys do?

Why don't you ask your girlfriends what they think?
I only have one friend I could ask about that, and I'm not sure I really want to know. Then I'd have to admit how crazy I am.

What if you find out that you're just like all the other girls?
I think I'd like that.

Then why don't you ask her? What's her name?
Ada...Maybe I will.

You know, Jenna; it's natural for boys to find you attractive. It's how they are wired. You are a beautiful young woman.
(I looked at the clock and squirmed at the time.)

I need to go early today. My mom is waiting with my sister because we have to take her to the orthodontist.

(I ran to the door, and he followed me.)

Come on back. We don't have to go down that road. Let's finish this session. Tell me about Ada.

Uh...no. I really have to go. Mom said she'd be waiting in the car. I'm actually late, and I have to take the elevator....

It's all right Jenna. It's natural for...

(That's the last thing I heard).

He reached out and brushed my shoulder when he spoke. His hand felt like spiders, brown, hairy, creepy, crawling spiders.

Chapter 10
Solitary Confinement

People are like stained-glass windows. They sparkle and shine when the sun is out, but when the darkness sets in, their true beauty is revealed only if there is a light from within.[8]

I didn't really like or trust the therapist, but I did like how he got me to talk about everything. I felt lighter than air when I left his office, except for the last time. I felt sick for days. I locked myself in my room and wrote poetry, and refused to go see a psychologist ever again.

Mom tried another one, but I made excuses each time the appointment rolled around. I had a speech tournament. We had a dress rehearsal. I had a research paper to write. Each time I cancelled an appointment, I felt a door slam: locking me into a solitary confinement of the soul. For as rotten as the therapist was, he chiseled away to the core and the deep down stuff was starting to come up, such as: Why was I having blackouts? *Is it because of men touching me? If boys touch me, I gag and want to throw up, and if men touch me I black out. But what about the science teacher; she was a woman. And I really liked and trusted her. Is it about trust? Am I going to be this screwed up for life?*

The therapist had said in one of our many sessions, "We go through life, showing only a portion of who we are to each other. We keep a part of our heart hidden and tucked away. So when others tell us or show us they love us, we can't believe it because our inner voices are saying, "If you only knew the real me, the part hidden behind this wall, you wouldn't love me.'

"Intimacy, is finding someone you can trust, someone you can pull off the bricks and show that un-walled heart to. Then, when he or she shares love with you, you can really feel it, and know it is true because that person knows all of you."

I craved that sentiment and knew it was out there, somewhere. The only hope I had that it could ever happen to me was holding Jacquie's guitar pick in my hands. It brought a mixture of pleasure and pain that I didn't know how to process. I was tired of keeping my heart behind walls. But all I could feel was row after row of slamming doors.

———— ((◦)) ————

I went through the same routine each day: brushing my teeth, deciding which of twenty shirts I was going to wear, choosing oatmeal or eggs for breakfast. Should I make a meatloaf sandwich from the leftovers last night or eat the yuck at the school cafeteria? Had I known when I woke up that day that it would change my life forever, I might have dressed a little better, took notes, or something. How could one know?

My car was in the shop, so I had to take the city bus to my high school across town. I felt so mature, and my sense of accomplishment was so heightened, that I wanted to do it again. But it meant I had to ride a bus back home that afternoon. How did I forget that part of the equation?

I was standing on the street waiting for the bus, when she appeared, dark skinned, with long braided hair, holding a baby. The young woman exited the bus, struggling to manage her child and the bag of groceries. As she stepped off the bus, the bag ripped and a bottle of juice, a half-gallon of milk, some bread, and cheese fell at my feet. She winced. Behind me, the people in line started to get irritated at the holdup. So I stooped down to help her, but the bag was ripped to shreds. We loaded some items into her diaper bag, but the milk and juice wouldn't fit and she had no hands to carry them with baby in tow.

"Don't worry. I'll carry them for you," I said, captivated by the baby's slender smile.

"Oh, no, you don't have to do that," she replied unnerved. "You can just have them. Actually, I need the milk for Ebony, so if we can just rearrange my bag and put the milk in, you can have everything else."

"No, really, it's fine. I don't mind carrying them home for you, or at least until we can find another bag," I couldn't believe what was coming out of my mouth.

"There's no other store around here; that's why I take the bus."

I didn't back down. "It's okay. I have time. I was just on my way home."

"Okay. It's a bit of a walk, but that…would be…helpful," she said cautiously.

We moved aside, and the bus loaded while people stood in disbelief at the scene before them. I never minded walking in New Orleans because of the rare architectural gems to be found: beautiful columns, triumphant arches, whimsical embellishments, cascading steps, and bay windows. Her building was not a gem, but a giant dilapidated house with window shutters hanging at odd angles and moldy paint peeling from every side.

We walked in the dark hallway, up two flights of creaky stairs in the pitch black, and I couldn't believe she would attempt this on her own, much less with a baby. When we finally reached the top, a ray of light pierced the darkness, peeking from underneath her door. It was only enough to illuminate the last few dangerously high steps. "Aw, crap," she mumbled. "I forgot to get the key out of my purse while I could see. Can you hold the baby?"

I fumbled to put the milk and juice down so I could reach for the baby. She felt so good in my arms. The young woman groped around in her purse for a while, found the keys and opened the door to the tiny apartment. I wasn't ready for what I saw.

A mattress, a bare mattress on the floor in front of a TV, looked like it served as both bed and couch. A baby crib stood to the right of the makeshift bed, and next to it was the kitchen, or rather, the closet with refrigerator and stove. A small table with two chairs stood over to the side.

"How would you have managed the stairs by yourself in the dark?" I asked as she took the baby from me. The lights flickered on and off.

"Oh, you get used to it. We keep telling the landlord about the broken light fixtures, but it's been months. I would've left the bag on the first floor and brought the baby up. Then I would go back and get the groceries, if they were still there, of course. It takes a lot of luck to survive in this neighborhood. Especially at the end of the month before my boss cuts checks." She laid the baby in the crib and went to the refrigerator for a bottle. "Would you like something to drink?" She looked uncomfortable when she opened the fridge door because the only thing inside was one lonely bottle.

"No, thanks," I said. "I really have to get back." She gave the baby the bottle and fell exhausted in the chair. As she began unpacking the items from her bag, she introduced herself.

"I'm Carrie, and that's Ebony."

"I'm Jenna," I said, thinking Ebony was a great name for a baby with such beautiful dark shiny skin. We chatted for a moment about the baby until the Ebony shrieked with a wail that could curdle milk, "Aaaaayak!" My eyes strained in disbelief. A rat, a giant hairy beady-eyed rat was inching toward the empty bottle that was lying in her crib. Even as Ebony cried, the rat stood firm. It was not until Carrie flung herself like a crazed woman and banged the crib with her palms that it finally scurried away through the giant hole in the wall behind the TV leaving the bottle behind.

Carrie screamed, grabbed Ebony, and held her close. But now it was the mother who was hysterical.

"These rats! I can't believe I have to fight off the rats so my baby can eat in peace!" She cried as she rocked her child into silence. "This is not how it's supposed to be!"

As she sobbed, Ebony's innocent eyes looked up and melted me. *So this is what it's like on the other side of the tracks.*

I felt a rage well up inside me, curdling the flesh on my skin like acid. Those innocent eyes just kept looking at me. I reached for Ebony, which allowed Carrie to run to the restroom, dry her eyes and compose herself a bit.

While she was gone, there was a gnawing inside me that I couldn't explain. It was like the rat scratching and biting until it chewed its way through to my heart. That instant I knew that this would be one of those moments in life I would never, ever, forget no matter how hard I tried.

As Carrie returned from the bathroom, she thanked me profusely, and added, "You really better be on your way. It's starting to get dark. Thanks for everything. Sorry about the rat."

I left in silence because for the first time in my life I had absolutely nothing to say.

Chapter 11
Non-Crystallized

What is glass? Virtually any material is capable of glass formation. The only requirement is that the material be cooled from the liquid rapidly enough that crystal structures are given insufficient time to develop. [9]

The theater provided creativity, companionship, and collaborative wackiness. Together every waking moment, we played guitars on the levees, sipped cider through cinnamon straws, made costumes, painted sets, and called lines.

But were we friends? If friends were whom you told that you were in love with a girl you had sex with over a year ago, then, no. If friends were with whom you discussed your suspicion that one of the female teachers was making passes at you, then no. If friends were those whom you told that your shrink put his filthy paws on you and said, "You have to understand that men are going to be attracted to you, because you are a very beautiful young woman," then, no, we were not friends.

I'm not sure why I kept everything inside, why I built the walls so high. People shared with me their problems-divorce, drug addictions, or abortions. I just never did. I couldn't figure out how. When the conversation came to the juncture where I could share a tidbit that explained how I understood pain all too well, I became rigid, and tense: the metal doors slamming so tightly I could almost hear their successive bangs. Perhaps it ran too deep, and if I laid part of my heart on the table, the other parts would escape and hurricane out of control.

People tried to reach out to me; I just couldn't reach back. How could I let anyone know the deep longings within? So I drank and smoked, wandered and sought, and continued in my solitary confinement of the soul. I went through the typical high school years surrounded by people who didn't really know me at all. Sure we went to proms, danced at discos, boiled crabs at the levees, even got in trouble together for traipsing around in the French Quarter way past curfew.

I didn't have to worry about theater people judging me, because they were out there, wild and crazy with reckless abandon, just as I was. Were we connecting, or were we parallel play acting together, trying on roles from the script of life and tossing them into the fire after each scene?

Many from the theater crowd were gay or bisexual. But after watching and hanging out with them, I was not sure I fit in with them either. Sex was not casual to me, no matter how you undressed it. It was a combination of piercing knives and nausea at the same time.

I did talk to my friend Ada about sex. Actually I didn't have to ask. She spilled it all, about the night she and Kevin spent together. I'd been watching their relationship develop pretty rapidly. Shy, except when he brought out his guitar, Kevin came to life with song. We all loved to hear him sing. I even thought I was attracted to him for a while because the songs he wrote reminded me of Jacquie.

But one day, at the lakefront, I leaned against a tree, and he came up and put his arms, like a cage, on each side of my shoulders. It took every drop of my power not to kick him where it hurts, but I knew he meant nothing by it. He was just starting up a conversation. I moved his arm, ducked out, and ran away. He stood there looking at me with squinted eyes and a dumbfounded look. I never had feelings for him ever again. I was glad he and Ada were hitting it off, though. He was a good guy, and she really liked him.

"Kevin was supposed to be watching his little sister, but she got invited to spend the night out. When he found out we could be alone the whole night, he came and got me," she said, beaming.

"Where were his parents?" I asked.

"They were driving back from a wedding in Atlanta and wouldn't be home until 2 a.m. I had to be home at midnight so we had the house to ourselves for 7 hours."

My stomach began to churn for her. "And you went?"

"Of course I went," she added. "We've been going out for six months. I love being alone with him."

"You do?" my voiced stammered.

"We've been trying to figure out how to *do it* for about a month now. He comes up with a plan. Then I come up with a plan. But it never seems to work out. His car is too small, and I didn't want my first time to be in a car. I wanted the whole romantic deal, candles and all," she said dreamily.

"You mean you *did it*?" I gulped and gagged simultaneously.

"Oh my God, yes," she bragged.

"Oh...wow." I tried to act excited for her. "How was it?"

"It was perfect! A little awkward at first until we figured out what we were doing, but he is so amazing, so gentle and tender."

"Did it hurt?" I couldn't wait to ask.

"A little at first, but oh my God it was worth it in the end."

"You liked it?" I couldn't believe my ears.

"Liked it? I loved it! I can't wait to do it again. So...my parents are going away next week. May I say I'm spending the night at your house? We'll sneak back to my house, and then I'll come to your house during the day."

"I'm sure that'll be fine," I said, feeling like a part of a conspiracy against parents. It was exhilarating.

"Thanks a million. I can't stop thinking about it; I'm so excited. I'm going to make dinner first, so can you help me plan the menu?" Taking out a notebook and pencil, Ada said, "Can you teach me to make something before Friday?"

"Spaghetti and meatballs is easy, how about that?" I would've preferred fettuccine Alfredo, but with her burn-the-toast cooking skills, we'd better stick to the basics.

"That is perfect. It will take my mind off seeing him naked. It's all I can think about since our first time. I can't even study for my exams I'm so ready to do it again." Her last words were the revelation I was afraid of: I was a sick human being. The big metal doors slammed shut on my soul. Solitary. Again.

Chapter 12
Chemical Composition

There are two factors that affect the durability of glass: stress and chemical environment. Stress is caused when glass cools unevenly. Each time a substance is added for color, it brings with it a new temperature and chemical composition. This affects the strength and durability of the piece, if not properly managed.

College was fresh. You could recreate yourself over and over again. I was determined to recreate myself as normal, as in sorority sisters, boyfriends, football games, and fraternity parties. I was going to get it right this time.

Walking into my dorm room on move-in day, my mom and I surmised a hurricane had come through. An old pizza box with a half-eaten pizza, clothes, dirty underwear, magazines, and books were strewn around the room. I walked backward out of the room to check the room number. *Surely there is some mistake!*

I carefully threw the dirty clothes that were on my twin bed to the floor, making a huge pile. My mom and I glanced at each other and sighed. At that instant, a broad, shorthaired, boyish looking girl popped into the room. "Oops," she said. "I was hoping to clean this up before you got here." She moved her pile of dirty clothes and threw them into her already stuffed closet. "I'm Dawn. I got here yesterday and haven't really cleaned up yet, but I will... now." She reached her hand out for a shake.

"Hi, I'm Jenna," I said half-heartedly extending my hand. *How dirty were those clothes?*

"You need help with your things?" she asked, looking around the room. "On second thought, why don't I clean all this up while you bring everything in?"

"That sounds great," I replied, wedging my suitcase into the little square she had cleared off. "Let's go and get everything else, Mom. There's a lot of room in the closet."

Things were somewhat better when we returned from the car because she'd shifted the mess into two large trash bags outside our door. One she'd labeled trash and the other, clothes. Now that her desk was cleared of the stacks, I could see that it was covered in spilled coke, and dotted with chips. My feet were positioned to bolt through the door and demand a new roommate. I was by no means a clean freak, but I'd never seen anything like this disaster.

Hanging her clothes in the closet, she inquired, "Where ya'll from?"

"New Orleans," I replied with pride.

"You are so lucky. I love the French Quarter and the food," she responded. "I'm from Lafayette."

I tried hard to think of something good to say about Lafayette, and said, "Oh."

We arranged our room into some semblance of order, as the hours ticked by. Thank goodness my mom stayed to see it through. Dawn's side was still a mess with clothes hanging from drawers and disordered piles on every open surface, but mine was tidy, with bed made, posters hung, clothes in the closet and drawers, and school supplies on the shelves. The only thing left to assemble was my stereo, but I could handle that on my own. As I walked Mom down to her car, she said, "I'm so proud of you. You are going to love college."

"I don't know about this roommate situation," I replied hesitantly.

"You mean with Hurricane Dawn? Oh, you'll be fine. Roommates are always an adjustment. If it gets too bad, just string a sheet between the two sides so you don't have to look at the disaster area." Mom was so hopeful. *Why can't I be that way?*

"Yeah, I guess so," I tried to sound optimistic, but my internal organs were churning at the thought of being abandoned before I had time to acclimate to my new surroundings. The words were sticky like glue as they came through my mouth. "Thanks...mom," I said timidly. "Really, thanks for...everything. I'll (deep breath)...call ya'll tomorrow." As she closed the door to the car and drove away, I heard a door inside slam again. *She can't be leaving me here alone with Hurricane Dawn, can she?*

⸺⸺⸺ ((◉)) ⸺⸺⸺

The most outrageous thing I encountered at college was sorority rush. I enjoyed the challenge of reciting the Greek alphabet before a lit match burned my fingers. I took pleasure in the crazy parties, secret handshakes, and horn honks. I even endured being someone's servant, as it reminded me of the things I used to require of my little sister. But then it started getting kinky, even for me.

The fifth event was a sundae party. I didn't really like ice cream to begin with, so imagine my surprise when the toppings were not hot fudge or strawberries, but cayenne pepper, crab boil, jalapenos, and garlic. One of the sisters fixed it for you, and then you had to eat it.

At the next event all the pledges had to walk a table runway in their underwear, and the sisters circled the fat parts on each body that need improvement. Third in line, I saw them totally destroy the girls in front of me. Marked with red felt tip pens in too many places to count, they sobbed as they stepped off stage. In my underwear, I walked on the stage of tables. Scouring the eyes of the sorority sisters for some shred of compassion and finding none, I quipped, "You are all nuts, truly nuts. You call this sisterhood? Well, ya'll can take this *sisterhood* and stuff it. If what you need to feel good about yourselves is to degrade other people in the process, then I don't want any part of you. No way, no play, today!" With that, I jumped off the runway, collected my clothes and never looked back.

Now, why would anyone endure such humiliation to be included in a sorority? I couldn't understand it. Everyone had enough trauma in life related to being accepted and fitting in. If that was what it took to be a part of a community, then solitary confinement sounded civilized. "Normal" looked pretty sick to me.

My first attempt at a boyfriend was Peter. A friend of a friend, he was the epitome of a gentleman. His mother trained him well, because he pulled out chairs, opened doors, and didn't look at my breasts. Our favorite outings were to IHOP. We'd sit there for hours talking about philosophy, religion, and gossip. I liked the fact that he dropped out of the fraternity rush on the second week too.

"It was the craziest thing I've ever seen," he reported. "Guys quacking like ducks as they walked, drinking urine, and dressing up like babies. When they tried to strip us down and beat us with paddles, I figured I didn't need a fraternity that badly."

"It was the same in the sorority," I said, feeling relief to talk about it.

He smiled. "If that is sanity, then an insane asylum looks pretty good."

"So does a lobotomy," I said giggling.

The most intriguing thing about Peter was that he was a regular volunteer at a soup kitchen. He invited me along to the church that served lunch to hundreds each day. Blocks away, a line formed curving toward the kitchen door. Men, women, and children were packed like sardines inside, waiting patiently to receive their hot meals. Although I was slated to help in the kitchen I ended up herding the children who were running amok all over the place. I coerced them away from the long lines into games of duck, duck, goose, before they got too wild. Once their energy was organized, it went down a few decibels in intensity.

We would cook and play at the shelter, and then head out to eat and talk about what we'd learned. Most prominent on my mind was the realization that helping others kept me from thinking about my problems. Wondering about sex and sexuality seemed pretty insignificant when faced with mothers and children who lived on the streets, or battled rats for their bottles. Being around them, I felt alive and real.

That was until 3 a.m. one morning after an IHOP run. It happened pretty routinely. After a long study session, I called Peter knowing that he never went to bed before 2 a.m.

"Are you up for IHOP?" I begged.

"Sure, I'll come pick you up." We devoured the usual: strawberry pancakes with whipped cream and commented how it hit the spot. We walked to his Ford Pinto, and when he opened my door, he leaned in to kiss me. I looked at him with that deer in headlights look. After his lips touched mine, I thought, *I'm not gagging. There are knives in my stomach, but they're not that bad. I'm not clawing his eyes out.*

"I've wanted to do that for a long time," he shared, as we drove around the lake to my dorm.

"Hmm…" was all my frozen lips could say.

He tried it again when he opened the door for me, and I got out of the car. I let him, to see if this time I could feel something, anything igniting my internal chemistry. I tried to concentrate and even kiss back a little.

Nothing. Nothing at all. Not one little iota of connection, force, or feeling. *But could there be a ray of light from under the cell door? At least I didn't gag.*

Chapter 13
Fascination

Part of the fascination of working with glass is that there are constant challenges and a need to be aware that the material presents a degree of unpredictable behavior. [10]

Dearest Jeffrey,

Wow! I can't believe it is you. You have been in my thoughts and prayers since the day you were born. Yes, you have found the right person. I look forward to finding out about you and your life and sharing mine!

It's hard to know where to start. Where do you suggest?

Blessings,
-Jenna

Chapter 14
Coefficients of Expansion

Compatibility is a major problem when using color: when you add color to a piece of glass you are, in effect mixing two completely different glasses together. You need to know what the coefficient of expansion (COE) of each glass is. The COE may be considered as a measure of how much each glass moves as it cools down. If one glass moves more than the other, stress will be created in the final object and it will almost certainly crack or violently shatter the piece.[11]

Anyone who grew up in New Orleans would find it arduous to live anywhere else. In New Orleans, children grow up, get married, and buy houses in the same neighborhoods as their parents or grandparents. It's the New Orleans way.

Sweet mix, aka *Creole*, is a germane description of New Orleans. From the outside, people used Creole as a derogatory term, denoting mixed races or subservient peoples. But from the inside, Creole took on its own flavor, as it blended the sweet mix of cultures for which NOLA (New Orleans Louisiana) was known. From that "sweet mix" was derived jazz, jambalaya, and even Mardi Gras.

How can you describe a city as ostentatiously resilient as New Orleans? Give us one hundred miles an hour wind and a city surrounded by water on three sides, and we invite the neighborhood over for a party, supply lots of alcohol and juices, and name a drink after it called a hurricane.

Give us the putrid reality of slavery: the auction block, the whipping post, humiliation, degradation, and we create jazz and blues-America's only indigenous music forms.

Unload ships of immigrants from every country imaginable, and we craft a "sweet mix" of food that entices people from all ends of the earth to come savor it. Add some colorful artists, voodoo kings, drag queens, a few sprinkles of alcohol and urine, and you have the recipe for the French Quarter.

So when I awoke in another city with its white bread ways, its mono-toned accent and food, its bars that dried up at 1 a.m., I would scratch my head and say, "What? No turtle soup? It's Monday. Where are the red beans and rice? How do I find the live music or the gay bars for the best dancing? Where are the interesting people?"

Peter did not share my love of New Orleans. He thought it was filthy, lewd, and crazy. We managed pretty well as a couple because he didn't try anything other than kisses and hugs. And those I could tolerate now, although I felt like a piece of lead each time. *Will I start feeling something eventually? Does it just take time to get used to it?*

The monotony of Baton Rouge wore me down. There were blocks of bars, but the people were the same, sorority girls, frat boys, and white straight-laced kids whose idea of a good time was getting crazy drunk until they passed out. At least, at home that same old refrain was among tourists, neon lights, live jazz, rich spicy smells, and flamboyance.

So when my friend, Larry, from New Orleans came to visit, I was ready for a ride.

"How do you like it here?" he questioned.

"It's pretty boring," I replied, "the same old, same old."

"What does that mean?"

I forgot. People from NOLA didn't really have time to get bored. There is no 'same old, same old.' One season was a preamble to the next, like a liturgical calendar of parties. New Year's rolled into King Cake season, into Mardi Gras, into Easter, into St. Patrick's parade, into Jazz Fest, into St. Joseph's alter, into Southern Decadence, into summer crab and crawfish boils, into Halloween, into Thanksgiving, into Christmas, and it all started up again. You could never think of leaving the city because the next holiday was just around the bend. Perhaps that's why New Orleanians are great at having parties. We were trained by the rhythm of our calendars.

"So, where are the best dancing places in town?" he inquired.

"There are no dancing places. People here just get drunk. Sometimes at the frat parties, when they get really wasted they dance, but that doesn't start until around 2-3 AM"

"You have got to be kidding," he added with repulsion.

"I wish I weren't," I shook my head in mutual disgust.

"Well, someone told me about a bar called The Cove," he suggested. "They say it's pretty fun. Let's try that."

We ate catfish po-boys first, crispy cornmeal breading that made your mouth water until you bit in. The hopes of a taste sensation dashed with the first bite, which resembled a salty corn chip sandwich. All the hot sauce in the world couldn't bring the foundational fish flavor it needed. We threw the fiery-sauce laden halves into the trash on the way out, and Larry boasted with the toss, "Some places have it and some places don't!"

We headed to the bar next-door and found it to be exactly as I described. People packed like sardines into every area except the dance floor. It was empty. Bar after bar it was the same. "What is the problem with these people?" he chided.

"I don't know. I don't understand it either. People who don't dance, have no soul. How can you hear an enticing beat and your insides not rumble to get out? Even if I try to hold it in, my foot starts tapping and my body wiggling," I said, doing exactly that.

"I know. They must have some blood or soul impediment. Or they are just too wrapped up in themselves to let their spirit out." We moved toward the dance floor and danced a few but no one followed suit.

We finally headed to the other side of town for the Cove. As we parked, I heard the music, loud, lively, and lit. *Is that laughter and carousing?* The beat was so dynamic you couldn't help but groove. We were bouncing before we even hit the door.

"Oh yeah," he said, his neck swaying to the beat.

"This might be the ticket," I replied, sprinting toward the door. "It's Raining Men" was playing, and the pace was feverish. Within minutes the immense dance floor was packed. Like I had just been let out of a cage, not seeing any one or anything around me, I let loose. My soul shook with the pulse. I didn't agree with Gloria Gaynor's lyrics about how wonderful a world it would be if it rained men, but you wouldn't know it by my dancing. It was impossible for me to dance and frown. With every booming beat, my heart resounded. With every swirl of the disco ball, the knots of my insides were becoming unraveled, like a good long stretch. After about twenty minutes, when I was starting to come down from my rhythmic rush, I looked around to see what we had overlooked in our frenetic passion. We were in a gay bar!

We danced even harder with the realization. It was as if we were home in some strange sense of the word! There were women and men, gay and straight, old and young, and they were all dancing. The best part of the evening was when a tall black man walked in dressed as Prince. *Yes, Lord, I am truly home.*

Imagine my surprise when later, we went up to the bar to order beers, and sitting on the barstool next to me was none other than my roommate, Hurricane Dawn.

"What are *you* doing here?" she growled.

"What are *you* doing here?" I jabbed back.

"I…uh, belong here," she retorted, turning her back to me and putting her arm around the girl next to her. I guess that meant she thought I didn't.

I snickered and replied rather proudly, "Well, I do, too!" That was all it took for her to turn around and whisk me on to the dance floor again. Before I knew it we were dancing with a woman named Angel and numerous men, and we didn't get off the floor until they closed the place down at 1 AM. Larry complained again, as we dragged him out wiping the sweat from his forehead, "What kind of a lame city closes things down at 1 AM when we are just getting started?"

Quickly we were invited to Angel's house, if we'd just pick up some beer along the way. They handed us money and Angel got in the car with us to lead the way.

"So you're Dawn's roommate," she said with a look I couldn't quite read. "I've heard about you."

"What have you heard?" I begged.

"Oh, I'll never tell… Well, maybe I will after a few beers." She laughed and winked.

We got a case of Heineken and headed back to her place full of hippy paraphernalia. Beads draped on the doorways, incense filled the air (or was that pot?), and psychedelic music blasted on the stereo.

Larry was very interested in her, I could tell.

"Do you think she's gay?" he asked when he got me alone. *That's always the question isn't it?*

"You'll never know until you try," I offered with encouragement.

"Yeah, but in the meantime, I could get my face smashed in by her or her girlfriend."

"Well, she doesn't look like the butchy smash-your-face-in type girl. I think you may be safe, but look around for mama, if you know what I mean."

He headed back in the living room, which was filling up with people. Someone changed the music to Prince, and our costumed friend took the floor. After that, it was all a blur of dancing, drinking, smoking, and pure delight, especially when Angel swept me into swing dancing.

We danced the night together, when Larry wasn't breaking in. Knowing I had to start sobering up, I went to the bathroom and drank lots of water. I knew if I went into the kitchen, I'd be persuaded once again to drink a shot with Dawn, or Keith, or Greg, or any number of my new friends, so I headed the other way.

Wiping my face, feeling refreshed and on top of things, I looked around. Angel, who was standing by the door, pulled me into her bedroom, and put a piece of paper in my hands. "Here's my number, I really want to get together with you again." With that, she leaned in and kissed me.

My head rolled back like a bobble head doll. As she turned away and faded into the crowd, I stood there totally confused and confounded again. The places on my hand that she touched were tingling. My heart was beating wildly, and my lips felt as though they were buried in mink. *Why, God, why? Why can't I feel this way when a guy kisses me?*

I was a boomerang, from Peter's arms to Angel's. Now I knew where they got the saying, "Give it the old college try." I tried, but it just didn't work. Intimacy with guys left me empty. Thinking that maybe I just needed to go a tiny bit farther to feel something, I did, with a guy at a party after we danced and kissed one night. Nothing! Actually, that's not true, I felt the knives piercing my insides and gagged all the way through. Even with Peter, there was nothing, nada, nil. How could I manufacture feelings if there were none?

Dear God,

You know I'm trying to walk the straight line. I'm doing all the right things, but let's just face the inevitable, and quit this charade. It's not working. I can't feel what other girls feel-well except for the cute ones at the Cove. I'm not comfortable anymore around straight people. Even church is uncomfortable. I went last Sunday and overheard the assistant pastor saying that everything would be fine if God would just send a flood again to wipe out all the gays. Now, correct me if I'm wrong, but I thought you loved everyone. I thought your house was for everyone, because nothing could separate us from your love. Not angels, demons, past or future, could get in the way of your love for us.

I remember Jesus going to bat for the sinners. Like the woman caught in the act of adultery. He wouldn't let the townsmen stone her. He challenged them to examine their

own lives first. *"Those without sin cast the first stone." I wonder what Jesus was writing in the sand with his finger. Was
he writing all the sins of the people around him?*

*Your church is full of sinners by the Bible's standards:
pornographers, adulterers, liars, thieves, gossips, drunks,
gluttons, and rich oppressors. So, even if it is a sin to be gay,
why is that one singled out above all the rest, separating and
isolating gay people like trash on a heap? Why aren't gays
welcomed, with open arms like everyone else?*

*And what about this hand you have dealt me? Why can't
you make me get all choked up when a guy kisses me? It's not
like I haven't asked 1000 times. Are you listening? Are you
even there?*

*The only time I feel you is when I'm at the soup kitchen.
I know you are there when I'm around the kids. But I get
frustrated because when Peter and I talk, I have no feelings
for him in that way. What am I supposed to tell him later
today when he asks me where our relationship is headed?
I keep putting him off. He wants to talk about it tonight. So
what do I say?*

*I've been able to hold him off, to even pacify him with a
few fondles, every now and then, and granted, I am not gagging, but I get nothing, nothing. Do you hear that? Nothing!
And that has been fine for the past five months, if I just keep
my mind on helping people and schoolwork everything is
fine, right? Wrong!*

*Then you have to lead me to the only place of interest in
this whole redundant city, and whom do I meet? I can't meet
a guy who makes my eyes spin. No, I have to meet Angel.
An angel who crashes me into the glass shattering, and
fire-breathing reality that I am one of those individuals that
pastor Reese was talking about.*

*But you made me that way! Or you keep making me that
way, because you and I both know that I have asked 1000s of
times for you to change me. You and I both know that I keep
longing to be "normal," and even trying with every drop of my
being to be straight, but my hopes keep getting dashed like
glass against a rock. The more I hope, the harder it hurts in*

the end. I'm not straight. We're going to have to face it. And the sooner we face it, the better off we'll both be.

If you are going to deal me this hand, then I'm going to play it. You got that? You can change me anytime you want. Pleeeeeeeeeeeeease change me. But until you do, I'm playing this hand. It's not a pretty one. It's probably not a winning one. But it's the hand I've been dealt.

-Jenna

Chapter 15
Incompatibility of Color

The problem with glass compatibility is that it is unpredictable.
Some glasses will fit together under certain circumstances
and not others, so you will need to watch for signs of
incompatibility such as cracks or checks in the color.[12]

Joining Peter at the soup kitchen made me more confused and angrier than ever. *Why can't I be interested in such a nice guy?* I finally had the nerve to tell him that I only liked him as a friend, which pretty much brought to a halt everything except the soup kitchen. We still laughed, served, and played duck, duck, goose with the best of them. Except I always felt like the goose.

Angel and I started hanging out together regularly. Both of us were in biology, so we scheduled our lab classes together. It started with studying together, then sharing our secrets during sleepovers. It all went pretty quickly, as most women's romances do.

I didn't really go to church much anymore. What was the point? The fractures ran deep. God wouldn't answer me, the church didn't want me, and I had new friends and a community who did want me, whom I could be myself around. Whatever leaked through the walls of my heart, they accepted 100%. Why couldn't the church be a place of refuge like that, tearing down the walls of our hearts?

Instead, church people offered guilt and shame freely to anyone who walked through the door. They talked a lot about the family of God but they boxed themselves in as "holy ones" saying, "You will be loved if you follow these rules. Then you can be one of us, and treated like a family member." When did Jesus' love become a commodity? When did the church get to cherry-pick who was appropriate to sit at God's family table? I know they were doing things God would disapprove of. Would letting us in make them more fragile, or more unstable? Did their fear of us make them any more cohesive or durable?

We longed to hear from churches, "You are welcome here. We may not agree with your lifestyle, but we are all in need of God's grace. We all have our sins: gluttony, cheating, pornography, greed, drunkenness, judgment etc. But we are here together trying to figure out how to live more fully."

But we never did. Instead we heard, "You are filth. You are the scum of the world, degenerates, worthless trash that needs to be removed from this earth."

So the gay parties and bars became our church. When we came out to our families and they rejected us, we consoled each other. We rejoiced together when we were accepted and loved regardless of whether others agreed with our lifestyle. We even sang religious songs together-our personal favorite was Gloria Gaynor's "I Will Survive."

Survival was our religion: survival from the rednecks who harassed you if they saw you in the parking lot, survival from the spit that was spewed on you if you weren't keeping the facade every second, survival from wanting to scream in joy from the rooftops that you finally fit in somewhere, that people actually knew you completely and still loved you. But we were not able to because the police might decide to arrest you if they raided the bar or the house or the group congregating in the street.

The hand I'd been dealt was full of stress. It was not what I would've chosen for myself, but I played it. I started with Aces and full houses. They were the sweetest of moments: reciting Sappho, sipping beer, the cool lake breeze whipping our hair in each other's eyes. Desperately we wanted to hold hands in public, but we knew full well the cost. So we resorted to sitting extra close with electrifying shoulder brushes or playing footsy under the table.

The royal flushes were exquisite. They usually came after candle-lit baths and sharing secrets of the soul. But they didn't last long. Soon the stakes got higher, and the table became filled with not only alcohol to cloud the senses, but a multitude of poker chips. No matter whom I was with, the cost was the same. First, it was free time, and money, and then I couldn't hang out with anyone else. Other times it was walking into a room and hearing whispers, wondering what she told her friends about you. Later came over-analyzing everything you said and did, and having to explain every action or expression. "Your eyes aren't that excited when I touch you. What's wrong? You have a weird tone when you say that. What do you mean by that? You're closing the door to your heart. Why are you locking me out?"

None of that was the case. I was just getting more interested in philosophy and psychology. The more I concentrated on school, the more nagging and overanalyzing I endured. The refrain was always the same, "What's more important than our relationship?" My grades began to suffer because I was either walking on eggshells so as not to be analyzed or having to explain myself when I didn't want or need to explain anything. I just wanted to be left alone.

The loathing and self-doubt about screwing up everything I touched began to eat away at my soul. *Maybe if you try harder with guys, you can feel something.* No matter how many times I played my cards, or whom I played it with, I always got to the same point: *ad nauseam.* Then, when it came to the point in the game when I was either all in, or all out, I pushed away from the table and ran the other way.

I laid so many cards on the table at LSU, that before long, I was emotionally spent, not even able to lug myself out of my room to attend class. Thinking I had found the path, the dream, the community, I was devastated when it shattered to pieces all around me.

Although the professors were teaching as they normally did, I heard them as a muffled conversation from the next room. Dancing at the Cove was like peering into a broken mirror. I could see parts of my reflection in the people I had isolated or rejected.

Dawn and I parted ways. Actually, she left college altogether after partying so much she flunked every class, but not without leaving a trail of bitterness. It ended with her habit of begging for the same thing she always begged for: my study notes. When I wouldn't give her the outlines I poured hours into devising, things got ugly. "If you really cared about your grades, you would've come to the three study groups we had to compile these notes," I seethed.

"If *you* really cared about me, you'd give them to me anyway."

"No, because then you'd keep living this way: party all night, sleep it off all day. Then you come hound others to give you their hard work. It's like we're not even really your friends, we're just your note banks. Frankly, I'm tired of it."

"Well, frankly, I'm tired of you and your holier than thou attitude. You think you're so much better than everyone else just because you're smart and pretty. Really, you're just a calculating bitch. Every girl you have dated says it. You're great at first, and then you turn into a cold-hearted, despondent isolationist. No one knows what to do with you. It's like you're a LUG of the worst kind because you make everyone feel like crap when you're through. You walk out leaving a trail of tears with people thinking they meant nothing, nothing at all to you."

Her words were hot embers, sss-ing as they singed their way down. That pretty much explained the whispers when I walked into a room. But I wasn't cold and calculating. I was just trying to figure out where things went wrong. Why did it all go so fast? One minute you're telling someone you really care for her, the next minute she wants to sleep together, bang down the door of the things you hold sacred, and dissect every breath, every raised eyebrow, every twitch you make. It felt like a violation of the worst kind: being caged in. But I couldn't put my finger on when it went from intimacy to inmate. I ran like hell from each relationship because it always went wrong, but I didn't know where, or why. At least with guys they were oblivious to your expressions and feelings, so you didn't have to overanalyze everything. With women, I'd come in starving for a crunchy fish po-boy, but get a soggy corn chip sandwich instead.

Self-doubt and loathing ate away at my brain each day. Like the hyenas in the science class film, doubt and desolation had an insatiable appetite, which could not be curbed: *You had a second chance, and you blew it. You could have had a normal life, but you chose all the wrong cards. No one will ever be able to understand you because you are a freak. You're always going to be an outsider, always a spectator. You don't have what it takes to be happy, or whole. What Roy didn't ruin for you, you ruined yourself.* I could almost see the blood dripping from the hyenas' lips as my despair grew. Luckily, there were never any sharp objects or pills around.

I isolated. Saturday calls home were my only solace. Mom would describe her everyday life like we were at the dinner table. Imagining her outings with Jordan, I could drop myself right into them, smelling the sweet fragrance of home.

Our Saturday rhythm of phone time didn't compete with the Monday through Friday blues though. Everything started slipping. I didn't even make it through all my exams. I introspected, picked up all the jagged memories around me, and mutilated myself from the inside out, over and over again. Before long, I couldn't even leave my room for fear that some of the internal bile and ooze would leak out from my eyes or my mouth. My mother heard it in my voice. One day in May she raced in her car to scrape me up from the floor, and bring me back home.

I don't remember her saying anything when she came into the room; I just remember feeling Mom's warm embrace. My eyes didn't even have to open because I knew it was her. It was like the feel of velvet in the nude. I snuggled closer to her, and inhaled a nice full breath for the first time in months. A purr-sigh escaped. Her chest shifted with her breathing, and I matched my breaths with hers. I could smell the zing in her coffee cake, the sweet mix of allspice and sugar. I was home.

I have no idea how long she embraced me in her lap. I didn't even notice that she packed my things and loaded them in the car. When she said it was time to leave, I looked around my empty side of the room and shook my head in disbelief. Whereas my first steps were into the chaos of a hurricane, my exit was amidst pine-sol and a pile of boxes.

The transition back to New Orleans took no time at all. I was comfortable there. And after a few weeks of Mom's stewed chicken, meatloaf, and peach cobbler, I was able to see in color again and distinguish my mom and sister's hopeful voices from the maddening hyenas in my head. The heated anguish of my LSU days cooled with the nurture and love of my family.

Fritzi, my dog, never left my side. He growled at Mom and Jordan if they came near me when I slept. It was like having a furry alarm system. But that didn't stop either one. Jordan peered at me with worried mother eyes that I had never seen before. That's when I realized how much she had grown without me constantly harassing her. She was a beautiful young woman now, and I could tell how much she loved me too.

Mom made appointments for me with a therapist, but I couldn't bring myself to go inside. The spiders were too creepy. I'd sit in the waiting room so I could say I went, and then leave before they would call my name.

I took the scary steps of attending Loyola University in the fall. Mom coaxed me with her "get back on the horse and ride" speech, but if she knew what I was into at LSU, she might've thought of a better speech. Renting a shotgun duplex in mid-city, I could walk to City Park, stroll through the nearby Delgado art museum, and even take the streetcar to Loyola. Mom and Jordan would come out once a week and take me out to dinner. Being in the shipping industry, Mom traveled a lot, so I checked on Jordan when Mom was out of town. We'd go on sister outings together and have tons of fun. Why did it take me going to college for us to get along?

The hottest new restaurant in town, Malcomb's, hired me as a waitress four nights a week. Their grand opening was two weeks away, and they were training me to be one of the headwaiters. Mom and Jordan both loved meeting me at Malcomb's. Not only was it a happening place, but it also came with my head waitress discount. One night, waiting at the bar for my mom to meet me for dinner, an alluring accent caught my ears. He spoke in a mix of English and another language that I strained to translate. Recognizing some of the words he spoke to his friend, I asked, "What part of Greece are you from?"

"How did you know I was from Greece?"

"I'm fascinated with accents, and I recognized some of your words."

"You speak Greek?"

"No, but I'd love to learn one day. I know 'Efharisto Poly' means thank you very much, and that's what I thought I heard you say, although I wasn't sure because you sounded a bit angry."

"Yea, that was my lawyer. He's not exactly handling things to my liking. I reminded him that I'm paying the bill, so I'm calling the shots, thank you very much."

"A good lawyer will remember that," I replied.

"He is a good lawyer, who's just trying to protect me. He says I'm a softy."

"You didn't sound like a softy with him."

"It's easier with him. He's not one of my children."

"How many children do you have?"

"Two girls."

"How old are they?"

"Six and eight. Here's their picture." He flashed a picture of two darling blondes, one who looked exactly like him. "This one is Eleni, and that one is Sophia."

"Eleni looks just like you."

"That's what everyone says," he commented as he put the pictures back in his wallet. "Hi, I'm Ari Andropolis, and with whom do I have the pleasure of speaking?" His accent brought a swirl of calm and curiosity to the surface of my intrigue.

"I'm Jenna. I just got off my waitress shift here, and I'm waiting for my mother to meet me for dinner. I'm not sure when she'll get here because she is coming in straight from Managua."

"Your mother lives in Nicaragua?"

"Oh, no, she just travels with her work, and since there is no food in her house, we're eating out tonight."

"You don't live with your mother?"

"Oh no, I have my own house, near Loyola where I go to school."

"A college girl. Your parents must be very proud."

At that moment my mother walked in, sporting her fitted turquoise suit, and gave me a big hug.

"Hello Jenna. Sorry I'm late."

"It's okay, I've been talking to Ari. Mom, Ari, Ari, Mom."

"Hello, Mom," he said as he squeezed her hand.

She giggled her reply, "The name's Kate. Nice to meet you, Ari."

With that, he turned to the bartender and said, "Get these ladies a drink on my tab please." We ordered wine, and he guided us to a nearby table. Mom filled us in on her trip to Managua, and Ari recounted his travels there as well. Owning a business that cleaned the barnacles off ship's hulls, he traveled extensively. His ex-wife moved back to New Orleans, so he was in the process of transferring his home base, to be able to see his daughters on a regular basis.

I was excited when I saw the two of them hitting it off so well. Before we knew it, he was ordering dinner for us: appetizers, soups, prime rib, and more wine. As Mom laughed heartily, I couldn't remember the last time I saw her look so beautiful. Both inside and out, she had a radiance that was contagious.

If ever there were a party or an outing that was excruciatingly dull, we would hear from Mom, "Ladies, you create your own happiness, so make a party wherever you go." I'm not sure if she had a formula, starting with the least boring in the room and nudging them on, or heading for the stodgiest first, but however she did it, laughter and fun followed wherever she went.

As teenagers we were dragged to her company picnics, kicking and screaming. One such event was held in the beautiful Abita Springs Park. Everyone was listlessly sitting around the picnic tables complaining of the heat when we arrived. Harry, who was in charge of the recreation equipment, had not shown up. I was hoping we could eat the ribs and chicken nearing completion on the grill, and then hightail it out of there. Everyone else was probably planning to do the same. Mom assessed the situation and kicked into gear.

"So, did Harry cancel, or is he just stuck somewhere with the rec equipment?"

"We don't know."

"So, he might be coming?"

"Maybe."

"But he might not, right?"

"Right."

"So we better get this party started without him, right?"

"Humph." They shrugged and wiped their sweat filled foreheads.

"Did anyone bring a radio?"

"Harry was in charge of that too."

"So the lesson here is…"

"Don't put Harry in charge of anything."

"Or don't put just one person in charge of all the fun. Have a back-up plan," Mom replied.

"Yeah, right."

With that, she got into her new silver Mustang, turned up the tape deck super loud, and drove over a fluffy green patch of lawn right onto the edge of the pavilion. She rolled down all her windows, opened the doors and parked the car. Pointing to her newly washed, hi-fi on wheels, she said, "Folks, meet your plan B."

Shirley and Lee's "Let the Good Times Roll" was blasting with its solo piano chords. As if to accentuate each note in the introduction, Mom immediately started dancing and singing. Every time she sang, "C'mon baby, let the good times roll," her hands reached out inviting toddlers and parents alike to dance with her. As her fingers curled to beckon others, they were fanning the flame of fun. Babies bounced with their short arms flailing to the beat. Their parents joined in, smiling from ear to ear to see their children react so instinctively.

By the time the saxophone riffs began, others were offering beckoning hands to those sitting on the sidelines. Before long, blacks and whites, warehousemen, and managers alike, were hopping their heels or bopping their heads, loosening and laughing with each refrain. We were singing at the top of our lungs, "Roll all night long." Old timers were doing the twist, and teenagers were wiggling while trying to look cool. Jordan and I weren't sure whether to be embarrassed or relieved that she had rescued us, once again, from an interminable outing, but who could resist such a lively flame as my mother in song? The highlight was when a four-year-old girl grabbed her grandma, the last one sitting, to dance. She couldn't help but let the good times roll either.

Mom was the lead domino in a long line poised and waiting for someone to touch, inspire, and move them into action. And she did. Wherever she went, Mom started a chain reaction of fun and familiarity.

Her boss brought out a dance tape left in their car, so the dance party continued. A Frisbee game started when a warehouse man remembered he had a Frisbee in his truck. When the foil was pulled off the food to eat, one teenager rolled it into a ball and started playing a hot potato game with the little guys, which inspired the creation of a foil football. Using it, we had the most awesome inter-generational game after lunch. Old and young, skinny and not so skinny, tall and short, all aligned as if to say, "Since we are making this up as we go along, I'll play too."

No one wanted to leave that day. We stayed well into darkness, until even the car lights (that we took turns using) were beginning to dim. We lamented that it was ending and laughed hard at its rough beginning. Bonds were forged at that picnic that would last for years. I swelled with pride when I thought of my mother and the influence she had over people. I wished I were like her. But how can you have fun with hurricanes and hyenas lurking around every corner?

After another bottle of wine, Ari gave more details of his life. He traveled extensively to check on his businesses in Mumbai, Tokyo, Rio de Janeiro, New York, Capetown, and Los Angeles. Mom had been to both Rio and Capetown, so that kept the conversation lively with their adventures.

"I thought I had it made," he recounted. "I had a business I loved, and a soul mate to travel with on all my adventures. But soon I found out that she just married me for the money. Once we had the girls, she wanted nothing to do with me. When I came home from my business trips, she was busy with her friends, or she was just cold and indifferent in general. My lawyer hired a private investigator and found proof that there had been another man for quite some time." His voice was shaky, and he didn't look up as he spoke. "How was I so blind? How did I not see it coming at all?"

Mom added out of experience, "Love is blind to things it really doesn't want to know."

"I thought everything was fine, perhaps a little adjustment to parenting and travel...for both of us. But now I feel...like...a failure. My lawyer says she's at fault because he can prove infidelity, but I just want it to be over. She can have her fair share. I don't want the girls to suffer, or to see us fighting about a divorce because then I'll lose them too."

"My parents are divorced," I chimed in. "Even though my father lives in Houston now, and is married again, we still talk regularly." My watchful eyes were happy to see that Mom didn't flinch any more at the mention of him.

"I hope that will be the case for me. But Lana, my ex, is trying to make this all my fault. She claims that my traveling and working non-stop were the cause of the problems."

"It's hard to have a relationship with someone who travels all the time," my mother, the voice of experience, spoke again.

"But she always loved the travel. They all traveled with me. It was great. We showed them the world."

My mom's maternal instincts bolted her up straight in her seat. "But aren't the girls in school now? It's hard to travel with kids in school."

"I know. That's what Lana says, but we can hire a teacher, who can travel with us. Lots of people do it."

"Wow," I replied. "That is one way to approach academics. Being an education major, it's hard to get my head around not having a school experience for children. But I know it happens."

"That's what Lana says. She says she wants the girls to have a normal life, and experience school and neighborhood life like she did, and not gallivanting all over the world like gypsies."

"You would hardly be gypsies," I retorted.

"I know, I know. I even bought a yacht with all the comforts of home for us. But she hated it. Said they felt confined. Everything is a mess with us. That's why she moved back to New Orleans, so she can be close to her family, grandparents, and all that. The kids love all the doting, and seem to be adjusting to their 'normal life' just fine without me."

"They may look like it on the outside," I say, with far too much understanding. "But you never know what's happening inside. You can't replace a father."

"I hope not...I hope not," he said as his voice quivered. "Here, have some more wine. We've got to talk about happier things."

We ended the evening recounting stories of Rio's Carnival, Capetown's beautiful Lion's Head, and how rich an education one could gain from travel.

"Yeah, but nothing beats time and connection with family," I remanded, winking at Mom. "Without my family molding and shaping me, I'd be a broken down mess. To family," I said, lifting my glass in a toast.

"To family" they clinked back.

Chapter 16
Manipulating Heat

Glassblowing has very little to do with blowing and very much to do with manipulating heat. This is why you rotate it so frequently. The heat and contour of the glass before you start blowing is what governs the finished product. [13]

How can one explain the Jesuits? The Jesuits of Loyola University were a stream in the wilderness: men who were not interested in sex, but in the spiritual renewal of their students. They provided cool water for my parched soul in the form of St. Augustine and Physics. Saint Augustine was an African Saint of the highest intellect. Born in modern-day Algeria, he spent most of his life as a non-Christian. With a mistress of 14 years and a son produced out of wedlock, he came to Christianity with a colorful past.

One day he was crying out to God, or whoever was in the eternal beyond, to hear. Full of tears and discontentment, he wailed, "How long? How long will I have to pay for the consequences of my past?" Through his tears he heard God's voice in the form of a child saying, "Take and read. Take and read." So he did. Promptly, upon returning home he read Paul's letter to the Romans, and the rest was Church History 101.

By no means perfect, Augustine was honest. And his words were like poetry to me. When I was confounded with my life, I heard his words: "People travel to wonder at the height of the mountains, at the huge waves of the seas, at the long course of the rivers, at the vast compass of the ocean, at the circular motion of the stars, and yet they pass by themselves without wondering."

When confronted with my imperfections, I heard his words: "This is the very perfection of a man, to find out his own imperfections."

When devastated by what I thought was love, I heard, "What does love look like? It has the hands to help others. It has the feet to hasten to the poor and needy. It has eyes to see misery and want. It has the ears to hear the sighs and sorrows of men. That is what love looks like."

No matter what I threw at the Jesuits, they had a quote from Augustine. "The world is a book, and those who do not travel read only a page."

I researched St. Augustine on my own and discovered my personal favorite:

"O Lord, help me to be chaste, but not yet."

Why hadn't the priests taught me that one? The quote that most inspired me, though, was from *Confessions*. "Enter into yourself. Leave behind all noise and confusion. God speaks to us in the great silence of the heart. Look within yourself and see whether there be some sweet hidden place within where you can be free from noise and argument. Hear the word in quietness so that you may understand it."

My favorite professor, Father Ben, who taught a class in Zen meditation, modeled that quote.

"In order to pass this class and understand Zen, you will be required to sit in silent meditation for fifteen minutes each day."

"Fifteen minutes," I whispered. "That'll be a breeze."

After five minutes I thought I was going to die. My knees hurt from crisscrossing them. My back hurt with nothing to sit against. Everything itched and I couldn't scratch it.

"Breathe in God, and breath out your name," he instructed, seeing our discomfort. "Clear you thoughts. Focus on stillness. Forget any pain. If a thought comes in, let it float by like a feather, and then clear it out again."

I'm allergic to feathers. I hope I don't sneeze when I'm thinking about them.

I could not get my mind off of the twinges and throbs of sitting still for what seemed an eternity. I reckoned if Father Ben could wrap his six foot three frame up like a pretzel on the floor and sit for hours, I could too. And I remembered his words: "God speaks to us in the great silence of the heart."

In time, the class quit fidgeting and our Zen Den was so still we could hear each other breathe. And for the first time in my life I was tranquil, not bouncing off the walls like a rubber ball, but serene as a butterfly on a flower, sucking up all the nectar. I couldn't get enough of its sweetness.

Fifteen minutes at home on the floor would easily become twenty. I could hear the old house creaking and even distinguish the different birds' songs. I could redirect my wandering thoughts like a rake draws leaves to the pile. The silky silence comforted a place in me I didn't even know existed. I was becoming a new creation.

Ignatius Loyola, who dared to start an order named for Jesus, founded the Jesuits. They took vows of poverty and were heavy into social justice, and scholarship. The priests challenged us to wrestle with theories, such as the questions asked of the rich young ruler: Will you give up everything in this world to follow Jesus? So, instead of giving us a summary at the end of the class of what we were supposed to have learned like at LSU, we walked out of class with deep questions, enough to want to remain in discourse, bringing our conversations to the cafeteria or to the bar down the street. We even paired up and researched to have a better platform of proof for the next class discussion.

Physics glued my world together. The more I learned, the more captivated I became. To think that every raindrop had the same prismatic colors running through it, and every force could be calculated. Electricity's bond with magnetism mesmerized me. Scientific formulas knit the physical world to the spiritual for me. The more I studied, the more I knew that this well-ordered world did not just happen by circumstance. Someone had a strategic plan for this masterpiece called the universe.

The Fibonacci Sequence was the basic code in my proof. Who could have imagined that the same ratio could be found in the geometry of crystals, spiral galaxies, sea shells, pine cones, or even in your own hand's measurements? They could all be traced with Fibonacci's Golden Ratio.

"There is no way you can explain this complicated universe just appearing after an explosion of matter. It would be like expecting a hurricane to pass through a junkyard and create a Boeing 747. The chances of that happening would be about the same as one in a googol," I would argue with classmates over beer.

"There was a Big Bang, and it happened," they would retort.

"Oh, I believe there was a Big Bang, but Physics assures me that there must have been a 'Big Banger' behind it."

"Physical formulas don't prove anything of the sort; they're just patterns and observations that scientists have made and tested through time."

"I guess it all just depends on whether you believe the chicken or the egg came first. I believe it was the chicken."

The more I sat in meditation, clearing my mind, silently breathing in God, and out Jenna, the more serene I became. I found a respite from having to figure out my sexuality issues. My desire was to be in Love's quiet presence. Although I fought with myself over having to sit still for 15 minutes per day, once I bent my knees, I was all in, falling into a place far, far away but very close at the same time.

And somehow in the midst of the silence, the meditation, and the scholarship I found a reprieve from the blackouts I still suffered from several times a year. They didn't disappear overnight, but gradually they were less and less common until one year I realized I hadn't had one at all.

With my newfound peace, I began to hover around the chapel every once and a while for mass. It could have been the statue outside Loyola that grabbed me, the one with Jesus' hands outstretched as if to say, "Come on in. You are welcome here." He spoke with his open arms, "Even if they don't understand you, I do." And although a mouth did not form the words, the look of his eyes and hands surely did.

I hovered around the chapel's narthex for the longest time, the hyenas growling and thrashing in my brain. *Don't go back in there. Haven't you had enough of that nonsense?* I didn't want to go in, but my feet inched closer. I wish I could say that I felt God with the Latin and the chanting, like I had back in the Vatican, but I didn't. I wish I could say that the priests, the incense, and the rituals did it for me, but they were empty. It was like kissing a man: *nada.*

But each time I walked near Loyola's chapel with its exquisite stained glass windows, filtering light through the colorful stories of God's people, the peace returned. It was if their legacies were stirring around in my heart. The deep azure of the sky beckoned me to strip down and jump in. The ribbons of white, which spattered around the wings of a dove, brought me peace like an olive branch. Resplendent in beauty, the windows' hope pierced through the darkness of my fear and doubt. I just wanted to sit near them and soak it in.

From the outside, the windows of Loyola's Most Holy Name of Jesus Church were dull and nondescript, but from the inside, one was struck with the magnitude of color and light radiating from beyond.

"These windows are alluring aren't they?" the exotic young woman asked, as we gazed at Jesus rescuing Peter from the sea. Her blonde hair fell like corn silk onto her shoulders, resembling Peter's yellow tunic. "I can't get enough of these blues and reds. Hi, I'm Elzbieta. I've been studying windows my whole life, and these are the most exquisite I've seen."

"They are pretty incredible," I replied, doing a visual memory scan of all the windows I had seen in Europe.

"My Dziadzia...my grandfather, grew up near the windows of the Basilica of St. Francis in Krakow. He wanted to take me there one day, to show me the intensity of the colors, but we never made it. I come here to get a glimpse of what he was talking about. The passion in the art is astonishing."

"I agree. The last time I felt this much connection with art was when I saw the Pieta in Rome."

"But with windows, each one tells a story, and not just in the art-in the science as well. Have you ever noticed how the glass in old windows is thicker at the bottom than at the top? That's the proof that glass is a liquid," she asserted.

"How can glass be a liquid, it's brittle and it breaks?"

"Well, it's a very slow moving liquid. It's called a super-cooled liquid. It's not locked into shape like other solids. Over time the molecules will move and creep with gravity."

"That's bizarre. I've never heard of such a thing."

"Glass is basically made of melted sand or silica. When you add minerals or metals to it, it changes colors. That's what I'm doing here, trying to figure out the right recipe for the intense reds."

"So, how do you know so much about glass?"

"I'm a glass artist. I've blown glass, elbow to elbow with my grandfather since I was a child. When he died, I took it over his studio."

Her accent intrigued me, and transported me back to Venice, and our excursion to the island of Murano. I envisioned the glassblowers breathing air into streams of glass. I'd always wanted to meet a glassblower.

"After watching the glassblowers in Murano, I've wondered, what happens if you accidentally suck in instead of blow out?"

"You've been to Murano?" Her eyes almost popped out of their sockets. "That's the Mecca."

Warmth ran down my neck and down my legs with the memory. I couldn't catch my breath. "It was pretty incredible, that's for sure." Words would never be able to explain what happened on that archipelago.

"If you suck in, you'll just run out of air."

Did she notice my shortness of breath?

"There's no way you can suck hard enough to bring the glass to the other end of the tube," she continued. "At the very worst, some glass will suck a centimeter in and close up the tube. But it won't come anywhere near to your mouth."

With my question answered, I relaxed a little. She hadn't noticed my breathlessness. My heart was still racing with thoughts of Italy. "It seems pretty dangerous."

"Actually the most dangerous thing in the studio is the glass dust in the air. Powdered glass has lead, arsenic, and enough heavy metals to poison the best of us. Even the furnaces, once you learn to use them, are not as dangerous as the dust."

"I find that hard to believe," I asserted regaining my composure.

"Come to my studio, and I'll let you play around and see what you think."

"Really? When?" The mischievous crook in her smile beckoned me like a hook, and I followed her to her studio around the corner. On the short walk over she recounted tales of her grandfather, a great influence in her life, who emigrated from Poland and packed his torch in the one suitcase he was allowed for the trip.

"The more time I spend in the studio, the closer I feel to him," she said with both sadness and joy. "And sometimes when I'm here alone, without the movement of the other blowers, it's like he's here, almost whispering to me through the fire."

She opened the garage door to the studio and I immediately broke into a sweat. The sweltering New Orleans heat was no match for what I found within. Benches were arranged around the room with rails of tools attached: several types of scissors, large tweezers, and a bucket with paddles. Tubes and rods of every shape size and color lined the shelves on the walls, and a steel table was off to the side. I headed straight to the jars filled with colorful pebbles that looked like gems.

"Those are called *frit*. It's one of the ways we add color to the glass."

Sweat pooled and dripped down my face. Elzbieta handed me a bandana saying, "You'll get used to the heat. I have two of my four furnaces going at nothing less than 1900 degrees."

"That's incredible heat."

"Just wait. I haven't even opened the furnace yet. It's set at 2200 to fuse the glass. Soda-lime glass can be worked as low as 1350, but most everything else needs a hotter fire for the transition."

"So if you haven't opened the furnace, what is that hole of fire over there?"

"That's the glory hole. It's the small furnace that stays open constantly for easy access. When I'm working with a piece, that hole is where the glass goes in and out quickly when I need to reheat it. It's set at 1900."

"So, what you're saying is, this heat I'm feeling is the afterglow of only 1900 degrees?"

I had trouble catching my breath again with the heat pressing against my chest. I knew how popovers felt right before they exploded into the delicious bundles of bread I loved to eat. She walked to the back of the room and lifted what looked like a garage door. The heat teemed toward the opening and the fresh air rushed in, but I was still standing in an oven, not a broiling one, just a moderate bake.

"Choose your color," she said, as she handed me a bowl. Every muscle in her hands and arms was pronounced, with ridges and veins like a weight lifter. She opened the frit jars and placed some colored pebbles in the bowl.

I went to the purple and grabbed a handful myself, studying the candy-like bits.

"We add manganese to make purple," she said as she emptied the indigo frit on the table. She took a pipe from its shelf atop the furnace.

When she opened the door to the fiery oven, I felt like my face was about to melt off again. Although I searched for the flame inside, there was none-just intense yellow-white radiance. I strained to look for the glass, but all I could see was a blinding glow. Using the pipe, she gathered, like honey on a dipper, something from the furnace. A molten blob emerged on the end of the pipe. As she closed the door, I couldn't take my eyes off the glowing mass turning more orange by the second. She took the pipe and twirled the now yellow-orange glowing finger low to the ground. It looked so alive. At first, it fell toward the ground, but she wound the pipe around until the blob gathered evenly at the center.

"It's all about the center. If it gets off center, you need to put it back in the fire." She gathered even more glass from the furnace, and I struggled to catch a glimpse.

"How do you know where the glass is?" I queried. "It all looks the same, like light." This time when she brought it out of the furnace, the molten blob was the size of a tennis ball.

"You can't see it; you just feel its weight. That's how you know where it is." Then she twirled it again for equilibrium. Moving quickly, she took it to the table with the colored frit and rolled it atop the pebbles. They clung to the blob like filings on a magnet. Quickly moving to the little open furnace, the glory hole, she put the blob inside for a few seconds and then blew the most beautiful bubble. Mesmerized, I moved closer to the stick of fire. As she continually rolled the tube with one hand, she worked the blob with the other, which was losing its red glow the more she worked. Using her tweezers, she pulled and twirled with a determined look on her face. After a few tries, she placed it on the brick stand. It was a flower with a long stem. I stood back in awe of the ten-minute creation of beauty she had rendered.

"Wow!"

"That's for you," she said as she quickly put it in a big metal drawer. It has to cool overnight, but it will be ready for pickup tomorrow."

"Thanks. It's beautiful. Did you know ahead of time what you were going to make, or were you making it up as you went along?"

"That time, I waited for the glass to inspire me, but other times, I have a plan. Are you ready to help?"

"No way."

"Come on. Choose your colors. You can mix and match this time." She must have sensed my fear. "Don't worry, you can start by just blowing gently when I tell you."

After we laid the frit out on the table, she showed me how to choose a pipe that was ready by the dull orange color at the end. "Now, the most important part-you must keep the pipe turning with your fingers the entire time. While it's in the fire, while it's in the hole, while you're on the bench, the pipe is turning. Got it?"

I nodded.

She demonstrated and then placed the pipe it my hand. "Turn, turn, turn."

I didn't realize the pipe would be so heavy.

"Not with your arms, turn with your fingers."

This explained why I could see every muscle in her arms. She opened the furnace again and guided my hands as I withdrew some of the glow.

"See, how you can feel the weight of it? Now turn it."

My turn was not as powerful as hers, so the glowing glass orb fell like a limp noodle toward the floor.

"Center it, keep it low. There you go. Great job." She guided me back to the furnace to pick up more molten glass and then to the table to collect the color. "See how the table cools it off. See how it gets hard so easily." She took it from me and headed toward the hole. "We put it in the hole so we can work with it again. Never work with cold glass; it will break. If you're not sure, just flash it a second in the glory."

After the hole, she put the pipe on the stand and guided me toward the end of it.

"Now the fun part. You get to blow very gently." She directed my blowing as she twirled the blowpipe. It expanded much easier than I thought it would, much easier than blowing a balloon.

"That's enough. Now you keep it turning." She told me to sit at the bench, and then she rose, took another pipe, gathered some glass and placed the new blob on the end of the blown bubble.

The bubble had a tail. While I turned the glass she took shears and cut the piece from the original pipe and began turning it with the new rod. Then, while I turned, she opened up the newly cut edges into a mouth with the big tweezers she called jacks. The more she rotated and touched the mouth gently with the jacks, the bigger the opening became, resembling a child's hungry open mouth. My arms ached as I twirled.

"Keep it turning while I get the pads." Taking plate-sized stacks of newspaper; she dunked them in the bucket of water. "The wetness keeps my hand from burning, and the ash from the newspaper adds another element to the glass."

It took a while but she used the pads like a hot mitt and rolled and shaped the blob it into a vase. I couldn't believe how that glowing mass of living flame was actually the beginning of art. It was so primitive, so malleable.

"I can't believe you don't use gloves when working with glass this hot."

"Everyone says that, but you need flexibility and dexterity. Gloves just get in the way. Actually, they can do more harm than good. Tiny shards of glass can hide in the fibers, or you think you can handle things with the protection of the gloves that you shouldn't. By the time you realize the object is too hot, you are holding it with burning gloves."

When the glass became difficult to work with, she took it over to the glory and heated it up again. She was in constant motion, a dance of tools and twirls to the blowpipe. A lock of curled gold fell into her eyes while she worked, and she blew it up with her breath. Her crystal eyes squinted until it was back in place. Taking the tweezers, she worked the glowing blob until it resembled a spiraled vase.

Using the biggest scissors I had ever seen, she lopped it off the blowpipe and laid it on a pile of burlap and glass pellets. "*Voila.*" She swiped the pesky blond curl from her eyes with her finally free hand.

"It still has to be put in the annealer, the finishing furnace, to cool slowly-200 degrees an hour-so it won't crumble under heat stress, but that is basically the process. What do you think?"

"I can see why you would say that glass is a liquid."

"My grandfather, the master gaffer, used to say that it is a cooled liquid that lost its ability to flow quickly."

"It flows well in its heated stage, that's for sure."

"Yeah, but at room temperature, where an object's state is determined, it's a liquid that has a rigid shape. That is why we are able to work with it. Its elements are disorganized and still moving as it cools."

I was drawn in. Glass was still moving, still disorganized, even as we saw it beautifully colored and arranged on a pane. I could resonate with its complexity.

I kept moving toward glass that year. It helped bring everything together. Hanging out at the studio watching them twirl glowing fire was like therapy. For the first time since Roy, I could envision something as fragile and complex as my life, being shaped into something beautiful. It gave me the drop of hope that I needed to move forward from the pain. Elzbieta let me sweep, and fold newspaper for the mats. I wonder if she knew how mixed up I was, and how much I needed the studio. She continued to describe the windows in Krakow as though she had seen them herself.

"One of them has the hand of God in golden red flames in the act of creation, every sinew etched in color. The purple and aqua fall in ribbons to the sea. You can tell by God's eyes He is captivated by his creation."

If only I could believe that again, things may turn out right.

Chapter 17
Glass Journal 1

One of the hardest parts of glassblowing is gathering glass. A properly heated pipe from the pipe warmer has a very dull red glow. Orange or yellow-hot pipes are way too hot and the glass will not stick correctly if the pipe is not an accurate temperature. [14]

*T*he burst of hot air from the furnace burns all the way down, from throat to stomach. Pain, hovering like a dream, drives me back with its intensity. When I open the door to the furnace for the first time and see its white glow so bright that my eyes can't focus on any shapes inside, I am mesmerized. It has the aura of a presence and an absence simultaneously.

I know the glass is in there, but I can't see it. The light blinds me. I can hear the roar of the oven, feel its heat singing my skin, and the warmth of the pipe in my hand, but I can't see the glass, only the white-hot glow.

The furnace beckons me to a place where neither line nor space exists, only the infinite. Intrigue cannot begin to explain the feeling I have at this nexus: ultimate possibility. It lures me into a place deep inside myself I never knew existed, like a breath from God, if one dares to believe God exists.

Taking a full breath I dare to enter it. My warm metal blowpipe moves to the center of the crucible and my eyes hope for a glimpse of something changing, moving, and guiding. But my eyes are worthless, because the light from inside overpowers everything around it. My only hope is the pipe, which is heavy from the weight of the glass meld at its end. Like gathering honey on a dipper while blindfolded, I pull the pipe up and turn it several times. I am hooked.

Chapter 18
Chemical Bonds

The atoms in glass are held together by strong chemical bonds,
but in a loosely ordered net-like pattern rather than a crystal.
Therefore, molten glass is viscous (thick, sticky, fluid) enough
to be blown, and gradually hardens as it loses heat. [15]

Elzbieta invited me with her to scour the city for other stained glass windows. Churches had the most prevalent supply, but strolls through the Crescent City yielded smidgeons in old houses and institutions. The hook dug deeper. I'd find one from the outside and dream about the view from within. Eventually, I even started going to Mass just to see the view from the inside.

I didn't really tune into anything the priests said. I was there for the stained glass. The iridescence of some panes intrigued me. Their glow changed with the light. On sunny days, the light spurted in visible wrinkles, a sheet of sacredness piercing through the darkness. On cloudy days, the light was indirect, a pool of color that moved around the sanctuary. I couldn't help but follow it.

Before long, I even sauntered into the Presbyterian Church around the corner, whose windows were small but intriguing. They weren't as colorful, but the sanctuary wasn't as dark as Loyola's chapel either. It was open, airy, and loud with guitars and a piano instead of an organ.

As I walked in, the openness made me edgy and reluctant. I couldn't hide like I could at Loyola. What if the people saw through me? What if they knew everything I struggled with?

But the pink orange of the windows were like a soothing Dreamsicle. In my mind's eye I saw Jesus' outstretched arms.

"Come in. Come all who are weary and heavy laden. I will give you rest," the plaque underneath the windows read.

I could sure use some rest from the gnawing in my head, which had begun again with the memories of Italy. And although I still couldn't believe Jesus, I could feel the weight of his love trying to ease my burden.

Before long, my foot was tapping with the music. People were singing along like they meant it, "Our God Reigns." My mouth started singing as well, and before I knew it, even my heart.

Some strange transformation was taking place because I actually wanted to be near the light at church. Was it because I was hanging out at the studio and felt an affinity for the glass? Or was it because I felt accepted that made me want to go? Either way, people shook my hand, and genuinely looked happy to see me. In the back of my mind I could hear Elzbieta's voice, reminding me of gathering glass.

"You can't see it, you just feel its weight. That's how you know where the glass is."

I could feel the weight of the church's love for me warming something inside my being.

"You know we have a Bible study for young people around the corner from here. The leader is great, and we'd love to have you."

"Do you have a Bible? We have one just for you if you'd like."

Someone asked after worship one day, "Would you be interested in going with me to that Bible study? I hear there are a lot of college students going."

"Sure, I'll try anything, once."

Imagine the awkwardness of ten people, some college age, even a single mother, sitting around a dark bare living room reading the Bible. The passage was from the Old Testament-Deuteronomy 15:7-11. "There will always be poor among you. Therefore I command you: 'Be openhanded toward your brother, and to the needy and poor, in your land. Take care of him, give generously, and do so without a grudging heart.'"

The entire time I thought about Carrie and Ebony's bottle. Who was taking care of her? Who was lending her what she needed for her sufficiency? Where were the churches with open hands giving to the poor and the needy in NOLA?

Before I knew it my mouth released the contents of my heart, "What are the churches doing to open their hands to the needy and poor in New Orleans? The poor and outcast are everywhere. Is the church doing anything?"

People wiggled in their seats.

The leader responded, "Jenna, your question is very valid. The book of

Amos expresses how God is fed up with Israel for not caring for the poor. In chapter 6:21-24 God condemns Israel for their shortsightedness. 'I despise your religious feasts. I cannot stand your assemblies. Your burnt offerings are a stench to me, away with the noise of your songs. I will not listen to the music of your harps. But instead let justice roll on like a river, righteousness like a never-failing stream!'

"Many churches are worshipping God with only sacrifices and songs, which is a stench and a noise to Him. When one person is hurting or impoverished in a community, then the rest of us are as well. We are missing the entire point of his message to us, if we don't see that."

A lanky frizzy haired guy named Mike spoke up about the Basin St. Projects where his social work professor ran a program each Saturday, with recreational sports such as baseball, kickball, football, crafts and crude science experiments. Volunteers from the community came to tutor, help fill out tax forms or other paperwork, or help with legal questions.

"I volunteer there every Saturday. If you want the challenge of worshipping God by your actions, here's a chance. We can always use extra hands. It has definitely changed my perspective on life."

"Do they feed people?" the young woman next to me asked.

"We bring in snacks. And if someone has extra trays of food or items from a restaurant, we distribute it."

"I work at a catering company. We always have leftover food we don't know what to do with. I could bring that on Saturday," said one of the students.

"That'd be fantastic. We are having an honor roll party for the kids who made A's or B's on their report card. We were all pitching in for a cookout, so any extra food will definitely help."

"I have tons of bats and balls from when I was a coach. I can lead a game of softball," another college student said. As a result of our lesson, our entire group took the challenge. Intrigued with the thought of worshipping with my actions, I signed on. I counted the days until Saturday.

It didn't take long before I was a regular too, tutoring and teaching crafts on Basin St. with members of the college group. Kids flooded the gates as word of mouth spread. Running a community program from the trunks of our cars, we met in the Smoothie King on Rampart, planned the games and crafts, and then rode in together. Most people didn't want to be anywhere near the Basin Street projects alone, day or night.

White students armed with bags of chips/cookies, paper, markers, clay, and balls led the delegation. The kids came like ants as soon as they spotted us. One day, I gave a demonstration on making God's eyes out of Popsicle sticks and yarn. "Some people use this as a reminder that God is always watching us."

Little Clyde answered, "If God is always watching, Miss Jenna, then why isn't he doing something about all this mess?"

I took a large breath because I had asked that question every night for years. How could a ten-year-old express it so succinctly? As if their heads were choreographed to turn together, they stared at me for an answer. "What if God *is* doing something, but we can't see it because we are looking in the wrong direction?" I replied with astonishing assurance.

"Well," Clyde chimed, "God sure has a funny way of showing it. Seems to me if He really cared, He'd do something in the direction we're already looking."

"You may be right, but what if God wants us to be on our toes, watching for God not just in one, but in all directions?"

"I'm trying Miss Jenna. I'm trying," Clyde confessed.

"I'm trying too, Clyde." If only he knew how hard.

As the sun descended, mothers came to pick up their children, but several little ones were left behind. *Are they going to let their six-year-olds walk through the projects in the dark?* We waited for a few minutes but the night closed in like a black towel around us. My heart ached to see them alone. But I had no idea what to do. Luckily, some of the older children glanced back and called, "Come on, we'll take you home."

Walking to the craft table I noticed Crystal, a lighter skinned girl, with sparkling blue eyes sitting underneath. She was playing with the yarn wrapped around her arm. "Look, I've made a mitten."

"Yep, you've made a nice one. Is your mother coming to pick you up today?"

"I don't know."

"Who usually picks you up?"

"I walk home."

"Well it's getting pretty dark. Where do you live?"

"I don't want to go home. I want to stay with you."

"Crystal, you can't stay with me. I'm going home too."

"I'll go home with you, then."

"Why don't you want to go to your house?"

"I dunno."

"Is your mom at home?"

"Maybe."

"Well let's go see."

"She may be out with her boyfriend."

"So what do you do if she's not there? Who looks out for you when she's not there?"

"Nobody, I'm there alone," she said, as she showed me the key on a string around her neck. My heart sank.

"Alone? What do you do, alone at home?"

"I watch TV until she gets home. But I'm tired of watching TV. I want to make God's eyes and clay dogs, and do the things you do with us."

"I know. I love making crafts with you too, but we both have to go home now. What if I give you some sticks and yarn, and a few pieces of clay and you can make some on your own at home?"

"Okay."

I measured out some yarn and gave her three pre-made Popsicle stick crosses as a base for the God's eyes. She chose purple and red clay. While putting them all in a baggie we heard a whistle from the shadows. Crystal waved at the figure, told us goodbye, and skipped merrily along on her way home. Mike, my friend from Bible Study and I shook our heads, loaded the crates silently, and put them in the back of my Sentra. My insides were screaming, but I couldn't utter a word. Remembering Carrie and Ebony, I wondered what had become of them. *Ebony would be about three years old. Is she still battling rats for her food?*

Chapter 19
Molecular Nets

Don't be deceived by cooled glass. Although, disordered in structure,
taking on a netlike form, its molecules are still rigidly bound.

A ri showed up at the restaurant about three times a week. I began to
wonder if he ate anywhere else. I kept hoping he would ask for my
Mom's phone number, but he would just share with me his adventures
with his daughters each day. If they were throwing tantrums, instead of
just dismissing them off as meltdowns as he had always done, I would help
him backtrack to what preceded the outburst, and what may have been the
cause. He hated that the girls moped around his house and said it was boring, but told of all the cool things their mother did with them. They had all
the toys any child could ever want, but all they seemed to do was complain
and whine.

"So take them places. Get them out of the house."

"I take them to nice restaurants, but they say they want to eat at home."

"So take them on the Zoo Cruise, or to jump on the trampolines." Since
he had never lived in the city, he relished any suggestions, and even took
notes.

One afternoon the bartender told me that Ari wanted to see me at the
back bar booth. When I came to the table he handed me a box. "It's my way
of saying thanks for all the great ideas of places to go with the girls."

"You didn't have to do that."

"I know but you were right about getting them out of my house to loosen
them up. Even though they have their own room decorated really nice, and
toys from floor to ceiling, they act like they're walking on eggshells. But
when we are out and about, it's like old times."

"They'll loosen up at home too, eventually. It's just hard when you're so
young to get your head around having two houses. Their image of family has

room for only one home. They need time to realign their model of family. It takes a while."

"It's killing me in the meantime, and I leave in two weeks for about a month, so will we have to start this all over again?"

"Probably, but you'll get the hang of it."

"Open it up," he said, pointing to the package. "I want to see what you think."

The package had colorful swirls embossed into the thick paper and a bow made of gold lacy ribbon. It was too pretty to open, but my curiosity got the best of me. Then I noticed the embossing: Neiman Marcus. A weird raspy shriek escaped when I saw it. Its exquisite layers of lightly flowered silk fell into a flowing sundress so soft I wanted to rub my face in it. So I did.

"It's so soft! And gorgeous! Look at that design."

"I hope it fits. The sales lady was your size so she steered me in the right direction. But look underneath, there's more." Stylish sandals were underneath the tissue paper.

"This is where I had no idea. They said most people wear a 7 or 8 so I got you a 7 1/2."

"I wear an 8 but who knows, they may fit. You really shouldn't have, Ari." My stomach was churning a bit about the whole thing. "This is too much. I'm not sure I can accept these."

"It's just a thank you. You'll never know how much it means to feel like you're getting your children back. I was lost, without anyone to talk to in this country. You really helped me, Jenna. Please accept it. Here's the sales associate's name. If you need another size, just tell her and she'll exchange it."

My hand kept rubbing the baby soft silk. The dress was snazzy and stylish. It had been a while since I wore a dress, much less a new one. And those shoes...

"Thank you. They're beautiful. I can't wait to try them on."

"I'm glad you like them. I thought of you when I saw them on the display. Although I went in for perfume or a blouse and flowers, this just looked like you: radiant, hopeful, and direct."

"Hmm...I've never thought of myself in that way. What do you mean by direct? Does that mean I'm bossy? I've heard I'm bossy before."

"No, it means, you speak your mind, and don't hold back. It's refreshing."

"Hmm...is there another way to be?"

"Yes. Some women don't tell you what they think. They're a puzzle, and you have to be a mind reader to figure them out. I'm not so great at reading minds."

"Me neither. It's a real waste of time."

"Exactly."

I thanked him and headed back to finish up my paperwork. As a head waitress, I collected the money each night from the waiters, and ensured that their receipts matched the register. In return, I received a free meal. Several waiters made errors that day, so I was leaving later than I expected. I saw him at the bar.

"You're still here?"

He looked up from his papers, pushed his reading glasses up to the top of his head, and replied, "This is a much better workplace than my house. It's too quiet and depressing there. The girls cancelled with me tonight, something about a sleepover with friends to celebrate something or other, so I can't really face the empty house right now. At least I get them an extra day now, so that will be nice."

"What great adventures do you have planned for them this week?"

"I don't know, I was hoping you could help me with that. Do you think they'd like a picnic? I love picnics!"

"Take them to Storyland in City Park. The park is full of great places for a picnic."

"That's a great idea. I want to hear more about City Park. Have you eaten yet?"

"What?"

"Eaten?"

"No."

"Perfect. Then come out to dinner with me. I was just getting ready to go to La Papillion. I had reservations for three thinking the girls would be with me. You're not going to make a devastated dad eat alone are you?"

"That's a really fancy place. I can't. I'm in my uniform."

His smile and odd turn of the head made me remember the box a few hours earlier.

"But then again, I could go get my present out of the car, and try that cute little sundress on."

"That's an idea."

Something inside told me that would be a really bad idea, but I was tired of listening to my insides. I was feeling radiant and hopeful for the first time in a long time, and we were going to a public place. And besides, who could resist a fancy Italian meal when you were facing a lonely meal at home.

"How about this? I'll get dressed and meet you there in about 20 minutes. That way I'll be halfway home when we're done."

"That sounds great. I'll pack up now, and we'll be on the same schedule. See you there," he said as he started putting papers in a pile.

I took my things to the car and changed into the cutest sundress in the world. The shoes fit perfectly as well. Funny, I hadn't really thought about what I would do if they didn't.

La Papillion was well known around town for its exquisite meals and service. From the tales of customers who raved about it, I was sure I didn't have enough money to buy even a dessert there. My heart raced when I saw that valet was the only parking option. But Ari was waiting for me as soon as I got out of my car, handing the attendant money saying, "This is for you, for later." By the grin on the man's face, it must have been a big tip.

"Wow! That dress fits you splendidly. We were pretty sure it would. The lady was so helpful. I'm going to have to give her a big tip next time I'm in the store."

"Knowing you, you probably already did." I replied, as Ari was known for his large tips. Everyone loved to wait on him.

People scurried like ants when we walked in. The maître de said something about his favorite table and sat us at once. While he was taking the extra place settings away from the table, Ari ordered a bottle of wine, some calamari, and said, "Hopefully, this will tide us over until we look at the menu."

"I'm just so glad to be out of there. Three of Malcomb's waiters made errors in their credit card tips so it was very frustrating. If they would just slow down, they wouldn't make so many mistakes. Actually, two of them reversed some numbers, which made their totals all screwy. I wonder if they are dyslexic."

"We're wondering about that with Eleni. They say it's too early to tell but she gets directions all messed up. And she reverses her numbers and letters all the time."

"It may be that she's just confused with all else that is going on in her life. Just keep an eye on it, but she should be tested next year if it continues. If she is dyslexic, the longer you wait, the harder it will be for her to catch up."

"What would I do without you? Your friendship is a ray of light in this cloudy American world."

The evening was incredible: Caprese salad, osso bucco, pasta with truffle oil, and tiramisu. He was charming, fun, and wanted nothing more than to talk about his kids, and his picnic at City Park. I told him of Storybook Land, the paddleboats, feeding the ducks, the trees with billowing branches so large and low to the ground that several kids can climb them at one time.

Although I tried to talk about my mom and what an interesting woman she was, every indication was that he was not shopping for a new woman. He was pretty shaken by his divorce.

"I don't know if I will ever be able to trust my heart to anyone ever again. I gave it all to her. Everything. And she tore it to shreds, and then discarded it like yesterday's trash. And quite frankly, I don't have anything more to give. It's everything I can do to scrape up enough for my daughters. It's especially hard because Sophia looks just like her. Looking at Sophia rips my heart wide open. I'm filled with love and despair at the same time."

It was refreshing talking to Ari about children. It was a way to bring order to the chaos he felt. Ari and I had a lot in common, actually. We had both given up hope about ever experiencing love again. The whole heart, intimacy, and sex thing had been completely x-ed out of our lives. I figured the way to be happy was to pretend that it didn't exist at all. Thoughts of love, sex, and intimacy were like adding purple to glass-making. The mix was too fragile, too volatile, and too dangerous. So, any time I thought about Angel, or Jacquie, or Peter, or...I would surround myself in the safety of another book, and read into oblivion.

Chapter 20
Jewels of Sand

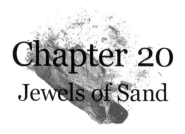

Imagine the first person who stood by a pile of sand and said, "You know, I bet if we took some of this and mixed it with a little potash and heated it, we could make a material that would be solid and yet transparent. We could call it glass." Call me obtuse, but you could stand me on a beach till the end of time and never would it occur to me to try to make it in to windows. [16]

My time in the studio was spent primarily watching the artists, and sweeping. My favorite task to make myself useful was helping to recycle broken shards by sorting them according to color in cullet piles, which could be added to new pieces. Each day I felt a little more trusted, a little more like I belonged. And in keeping with my nature, I had to test the boundaries. "You know what they are teaching us in Physics is very different from what you learned about glass."

"How so?" Elzbieta said as she gathered glass from the furnace. I could tell her curiosity was peaked.

"Well, they are not calling glass a liquid anymore."

"What?" Her eyes popped, as she laid the blob on the marver.

"Now, it's a solid."

"That's ridiculous!"

"Not really, when you think about it. A liquid is a substance that isn't ordered enough to have its own shape but takes on the form of the container it is in."

"Exactly." With a grin, she moved the blob across the table, pressed it, and the flipped it over and did the same thing. "See, it has no form on its own until I shape it with my tools."

I could feel the tension build and the turbulence brewing, so I proceeded carefully. "Yea, but when it cools at room temperature, it will take on a designated shape the glassworker intends or the mold it's cast into."

"So, it acts like a solid, but it is definitely a liquid," she said matter-of-factly, placing the blob on the long pile of shards I had separated the day before. Only the cullet piles with the correct hues of red, orange, yellow, and brown were put onto the marver. Watching her add color was like watching a painter work with a brush of fire. With each roll and flip on the marvering table, the glowing blob accepted the shard's color and form into its own. I couldn't help but think about the effect Elzbieta had on my life, and how her vibrancy had given me hope. Her positive influence, and love of glass had shaped me as well.

Dancing the piece from fire to marver to paddles and back again, her moves were smoothly choreographed. She continued the same motions over and over. I could tell she was frustrated with the progress. Jagged colored edges were stubbornly resisting the fire and when she molded them into the form, the intensity of the color was lost. When she laid the pipe on the rail of the bench, it was a respite from the intensity of rapid cooling and heating. She guided me to sit and turn the blowpipe.

I began again along another path. "Did you know that glass can be traced back to the ancient Roman historian Pliney around 5000 BC? Supposedly, a Phoenician merchant ship near Syria used blocks of nitrate from their cargo hold to build a fire on a nearby beach to cook their food. After filling their stomachs, they fell asleep and the fire burned itself out after a few hours. In the morning, among the ashes they found small round, clear jewels in the sand. The fire had grown so hot that the sand melted to form glass."

"Interesting," she replied with eyebrows raised. "I knew that glass will naturally form on the sand when lightning strikes it, but I've never heard that story."

I had so much to tell her about glass; I couldn't get it out fast enough. Its complexities were a mirror image of our psyches, analyzed through the ages and pages of clinical studies, maneuvered and marvered with each new diagnostic manual. Of course, her never-ending refrain as I spoke was, "Keep turning. Do it until it becomes natural." My fingers, bearing all the weight of the pipe, had lost all their strength; I felt every sinew.

While her movements were fluid as she turned, mine were rigid and painful. First, she took out the jacks (long tweezers) and made a line where it would be cut from the pipe. Pulling the top to a point while I twirled, she drew up with the jacks again until it formed a flame shape. Then she motioned for me to take it over to the glory to warm it back up.

"How do you know it's time for a flash in the hole?" I asked. "It's still malleable."

"Are you asking, or are you telling me?"

"I'm asking, really." And I was. This was the part I still couldn't get. How did the glassworker know?

"That's the part that is the hardest to learn. There is no set answer. It just comes with time and practice. When you damage enough pieces by working too cold, then you know. The glass gets too hard to work with, rigid, stuck in its own form. When it starts wanting to be the boss of the piece, then I put it in the fire. I'm showing it who's boss." As I handed the rod back to her from the glory hole, I couldn't help but resonate with the stubbornness of glass. It did seem to have a mind all its own.

"The more I put it in the fire and see its resilience, the more enamored I am with it," she elaborated. "It takes my direction until it cools and I need to put it back in. After a while I know the piece and its composition so much that I can foresee how it will respond even before it does. That's why I still don't get how your professor can say it's a solid when it reacts to my moves by flowing continually like a liquid," she said, eagerly taking it from me and sitting on the bench herself. I was inspired by her focused conviction. Although she questioned with depth and determination, she never took her eyes off the piece. She took out the jacks and worked the end next to the pipe.

"Actually most professors don't like to be hemmed into a category of liquid or solid for glass because it has tendencies of both," I answered carefully. "It never freezes into a crystalline shape of molecules like solids, but it doesn't flow at room temperature like a liquid, so scientists give it a whole new category all its own."

"A whole new category. You mean there are more than three states of matter now?"

"Well, yeah..."

"What is the new category?"

"Amorphous solid."

"What?" I tried with all my might to read her expression. It had the look of disbelief and rage all at once.

I took my time in replying, "Amorphous means it's a solid without a shape."

"That makes no sense."

"I know, especially when you factor in that physicists don't usually like grey areas at all," I replied. "Everything needs to go into its own neat little box so they can dissect, classify, arrange, and examine it ad nauseam."

"I can see that." She chuckled as she motioned for me to take the piece to the finishing table. "Scientists are so ordered and methodical. That's why I would make a horrible scientist. I can't stand to be boxed in."

"It's the same for glass," I continued. "Glass has been prodded poked and analyzed for centuries. They still can't figure it out, can't box it in. Even after it cools, it never freezes into shape. It's still creeping and moving ever so slowly. As a matter of fact, if you could preserve a window long enough, it might eventually become a rigid puddle on the floor. Of course it might take 100s of millions of years, but since it's not organized into crystalline structures like most solids, it's constantly evolving, trying to get equilibrium, find its center. Kind of like someone on a journey, trying to keep his energy balanced."

I couldn't help but think about my journey through life and how I craved balance. If only everything would line up in ordered little rows. But nothing worked that way. The more I tried to deal with my feelings, and my past, the more everything spun out of control, and the more I tried to keep it all in line, the more exhausted I became.

"So scientists came up with a whole new category: amorphous solid," I exclaimed.

I saw her tiny muscular belly ripple through her bare mid-drift as she laughed, and my eyes couldn't help but notice the parentheses her curves made from her breasts.

"Amorphous solid. I like that." She nodded as if inscribing an end mark with her head. "To think that I work with something that can't be classified in ordinary terms," she said, her eyes curving toward her smile.

She took out the shears and cut at the end near the blowpipe, where she had put the jack line minutes before. The piece came off the pipe and she quickly grabbed it with the mitt. We smiled simultaneously as we admired her flame-like statue.

"Who would've imagined that those broken shards that I so courageously organized by brown and yellow tint could give such a colorful effect?" I said as I opened the annealer.

Elzbieta smiled, putting the piece in to cool overnight.

"In my studio, you have to use what you have. And this month, we had lots of shards."

"I love that you work with what you have," I resounded.

"That's the definition of beauty to me. We are each given different things in life. Sometimes it's sand, other times its coal. Beauty lies in finding a way to turn whatever we have into something that brings joy. Whether it's transforming irritating objects like sand into pearls, ink to poetry, or left-overs from the fridge into gourmet dinners, that's the privilege of art, to create beauty from what you have."

"Yeah, but first you have to figure out what you have. That's where I get stuck."

"You've been given a lot, Jenna. Where's your gratitude?"

"It got lost somewhere along the scrap pile."

"So make a list."

"A list of what?"

"A gratitude list."

"A what?" I questioned.

"A gratitude list. On regular days you list 10 things you are grateful for. On bad days: 20. On really bad days, 50."

"I'm thinking five would be a stretch."

"That's pretty sad. Keeping a gratitude list is how I get through my day. My grandfather was a great gratitude list-er. He kept a running one all day long, even out loud sometimes. A gratitude list helps you to focus on the things you have instead of the things you don't. It puts things in proper order."

"I put things in proper order by studying physics, or volunteering in the projects," I responded proudly.

"You should try gratitude listing."

"OK, but in the mean time I'll keep my physics books handy for ordering the world. That's why I love physics!"

"Shaping that stubborn dribble from the fire into something magnificent and full of wonder: that explains the world to me. And that, my friend, is why I love the art of glass!"

Chapter 21
A Thousand Flowers

Millefiori literally means "a thousand flowers." Mosaic sections of glass are made by pulling strands of glass in to thin cane. Stacking them produces layers and layers of color. When this multi-colored cane is then cut into pieces, it is carefully arranged as distinctive decorations in glass pieces, often in flower-like designs. [17]

As the winter winds howled and hurled around the buildings, it became harder and harder to conduct a program outside. Noses were running, sniffles were snuffled, and the chill chomped our bones. The kids were arriving in droves, but after four days of frigid weather, we wondered how we'd be able to continue.

One drizzly day, while we were unloading the overstuffed crates from the back of my car, a tiny old woman with a feathered hat came our way proclaiming, "I'm Jerome's grandmother. He says you may not be able to come any more because of the weather."

"That's correct," I conceded. "It's pretty miserable out here. But we'll be back in the spring."

She had a star-like sparkle in her eyes that drew you in. "Well, Jerome looks forward to this every Wednesday and Saturday. He talks about it all week. What you kids are doing out here is incredible. Our children need something like this to look forward to. It's what gets them through the darkest of days. So, my apartment is not very big, but if you want to meet inside, you are all welcome there until it warms up again."

The kids were cheering. My hand covered my mouth. Trying to fight back tears, I looked at Mike. He was just as overjoyed, but managed to stammer out, "That...would be...fantastic. When can we start?"

With that, she picked up a crate and said, "Follow me!" You've never seen people scramble so fast. Like the Pied Piper, with fifteen kids dancing behind her feathered hat flapping in the wind, she tromped through the muddy courtyard.

She was right, her apartment was not very big, but it was cozy and clean. Her red brocade couch was long, with a huge coffee table in front, for our craft materials. Apologizing for the temperature, she promised that by Saturday the heat would be turned back on again. "At least you're out of the wind and rain," she offered humbly. The kids cheered and Crystal said, "It's much warmer here than in my house." I loved her for that.

We started by having the kids introduce themselves to her, but she asked us to wait so she could bring out Angela, her granddaughter, and Angela's five-month-old baby, Kayla. "I want Angela to get to know you too, because if I'm not here she'll let you in and get you what you need."

Gertrude told her story. "My husband worked in the oyster shucking plant on Wharf Street. I was a cook at the Kresge's five and dime store. Even though the counter mainly served hamburgers and grilled cheese, I persuaded my boss to let me cook some of my specialties. Within a few weeks people were standing in line for my stewed chicken, oyster stew, and jambalaya. When my husband, Jimmy, died from cancer, I was delighted to have my grandchildren live with me so I wouldn't be lonely anymore."

She told of how she had been richly blessed with a place to live and two beautiful grandchildren, so she wanted to give back whatever she had. "It's not my blessing to keep. Everything I have is from God. I'm just passing on God's blessing!" She was so proud of Angela, who was the first in her family to go to college. Angela blushed and said, "Granny, it's only community college."

"College is college," Gertrude replied. "I tell Jerome every day that he is going to grow up to be just as smart and college educated as you. If only your mother would've gone to college, she wouldn't have ended up in such a bad state." Their mother hadn't been seen in years.

I suggested we continue the introductions but we added a new twist in honor of Jerome's grandmother. After our names we were to fill in the blank: The best thing about grandmothers is_____.

Opening our crates, we took out a variety of colored construction paper, markers, glitter, glue, and Christmas stickers to make Christmas cards for families and friends. Mike worked at the kitchen table with three game boards teaching students the finer points of checkers.

At one point, I had to go to the restroom. As I walked through the hall, I noticed that clothes were hanging on lines all throughout the house. In the tub, another "load" of clothes was soaking. Her home was clean but every inch was stacked and stacked again with things. Plastic containers, folded clothes on every flat surface, figurines, books, canned goods, I couldn't believe how much could fit in one small apartment. I peeked into one bedroom on the way out and noticed that there were two twin beds and a crib. I guessed that was for Angela, the baby, and Jerome. I started scanning the house for Grandma Gertrude's bedroom to no avail.

As far as I could see, there was only one bedroom for four people. Then, as I walked back to the living room I saw it: a closet, shaped from the underbelly of stairs, with a tiny mattress underneath. Someone had taped a piece of artwork to the ceiling. It was a picture Jerome made of himself and Mike playing football while other kids sat at a table. Two of the figures were labeled: Jerome and Mike. This tiny closet was Jerome's room.

What felt like a bare hand clenched around my heart. Perhaps gloves would've softened the blow a bit. In my mind's ear I heard Elzbieta saying that gloves get in the artist's way. Even the thinnest of layers trap some of the sting. But there were no gloves to trap my sting.

I coughed back tears and took a lot of deep breaths before going back to the living room. Taking in the squeals and giggles of the students around me, I could hear Angela helping little ones trace their hands for reindeer pictures and Grandma Gertrude teaching others to make brightly colored tissue paper flowers. The kids could not make enough of them and devised a way to make bouquets by attaching pipe cleaners.

In my mind, I started a gratitude list: Gertrude, these children, Elzbieta, glass studios, my family, laughter, giggles, Christmas, tissue paper flowers, soft beds, and warm hospitable homes. *That wasn't so hard.*

It was an incredible afternoon. Every child and adult in the room made a Christmas card for Grandma Gertrude. Her generosity was so overwhelming that we couldn't help but respond. My card to her was a vision of what I wanted to happen on Saturday when we returned. In the center was a small Christmas tree (which we would provide for her home), decorated with lots of paper chains, myriads of tissue flowers, God's eyes, and a star on top just like the stars I saw in her eyes as she lavished us with her generous gift of love.

On that drizzly day in the outskirts of the French Quarter, in the most dangerous projects in the city of New Orleans, her eyes provided a star of hope that would last for years to come. Grandma Gertrude became famous that day. From then on, when she walked into the Basin Street projects, children of all ages ran up for hugs and kisses. If anyone suspicious came near her house, swarms of people were there to interrogate them.

Did she have any idea that by passing on the blessings she had received, she would make such an impact? That one act of gratitude extended her borders deep into the hearts of every child in our program. And into my heart she brought the fragrance of hope, like a thousand magnolias after a rain.

Chapter 22
Viscosity

Viscosity reflects the internal friction amongst particles and molecules. Glass, which is gooey until it cools into stiffness is said to have a high viscosity, while water, which runs easily and is very fluid, is said to have a low viscosity.[18]

Dear Jenna,

Well, I guess I should begin.

I'm 22, living in Santa Fe currently. Up until Katrina hit, I was living in New Orleans with my mother (my parents divorced 3 years ago). In many ways Katrina was a horrible incident, but I've managed to gain something from it, namely, a great job in a fascinating new place, surrounded by equally fascinating people. In fact, Santa Fe/Katrina is probably the greatest thing to have ever happened to me-by far. This experience has been life-changing. I work in the ultra-high-end audio/video industry, programming control systems for houses and businesses. Basically, imagine what Bill Gates would have in his home, that is the type of thing we install in all the numerous overpriced homes here in the Sangre de Cristo Mountains-huge home theatres...although more 'theatre' than 'home'. I'm the (sole) programmer, as well as IT guy.

I have spent 2 years in college (LSU & UNO), but it just happened to come at the wrong time of my life. I was too busy searching...in all senses of the word. I quit, but am hoping to go back very soon.

I'm a man of many interests, but if I were to have to narrow it down, the top would be anything electronic or mechanical, reading, philosophy, physics, psychology, food, thinking, thinking, and thinking. I love the limited traveling that I have done so far-mostly from this job. Politics, law, and human rights are things I love getting worked up about as well.

I have quite a balance of intro-and extra-version. I love being around people, but love having time by myself to read and reflect. Balance is key, even if it is hard to maintain.

I'm 6ft, 190 pounds, with brown hair with hazel eyes. I'm very open-minded, a big fan of change, and shaking things up a bit. I probably question things too much for my own good, although, honestly, I wouldn't have it any other way. All right, hopefully that will do for starters. Don't feel pressured to write as much as I did just now. I just have a tendency to talk and talk forever. Not everyone can always keep up, ha-ha.

-Jeffrey

Chapter 23

Ding Dongs

Impurities in the sand gave early glass its color. Soon, blowers began to add chemicals to manipulate the color, but their imprecise methods caused darkening or fading over time.

A woman came up during afterschool program one day. Her eyes were familiar behind the inch long lashes. *How do I know her*? Distracted by her skin-tight satin pants and long painted fingernails, I struggled to concentrate when she spoke.

"Get over here, Crystal. You know you weren't supposed to come to the program today. We're going to Ty's."

I recognized those eyes. They were the larger version of Crystal's.

"I don't wanna go to Ty's. I wanna stay here and make things," Crystal replied.

"Get your sorry ass up over here now. Ty's waiting."

Crystal stood her ground, not budging from her place at the picnic table. Her mother yanked her, lifting her straight in the air by her arm. I winced, concerned that her arm would come out of the socket like my sister's used to do.

"You better be on your best behavior today, Ty is taking us to the grocery store. We need lots of things and we don't need any of your foolishness. Maybe he'll get us those Ding Dongs you saw on TV you been bugging me about." Crystal, curling her lip like she was about to cry, looked back at me, pleading.

Grandma Gertrude rolled her eyes as Crystal's mother dragged her back toward her apartment. Passing by a picnic table, Crystal's mom, Tamira, beckoned the two guys sitting on top to follow her. One slid his arm around her and then let it drop to pinch her behind.

"Babies having babies is what that is. It's a crying shame. That girl used to be one of the smartest in the neighborhood. She was real good with

Crystal too, and then she goes and gets mixed up with that man. He is bad news, he and his hoodlum friends. Now that child is hungry all the time, always asking people for food. What she does with her welfare check is what I want to know, because she sure doesn't feed that baby enough." I had never seen Grandma Gertrude so angry.

Grandma Gertrude had been showing up regularly now that we were back in the courtyard. She helped with crafts and read to some of the young ones. Most importantly, she was our inside scoop of information since Charles (the social worker professor who started the program) was making himself scarce.

Charles passed the program on to my Bible Study friend, Mike, his star social work student from the University of New Orleans. But we were always eager to pummel him with questions about the health and welfare of the children when he appeared. One week I told Charles that Crystal's mom sometimes left her alone in the apartment. Later in the month he related back, "I've checked in on Crystal several times but each time her mom or her boyfriend, Ty, was there. I've reminded them that she is too young to be left alone in the apartment for even a moment. The boyfriend got angry and said that we had no right telling him how to raise Crystal.

"I reminded him, that as a Family Services Worker, I could report them and take Crystal into protective custody. Ty got really angry and almost threw a punch at me, but Tamira stepped in and said, 'Take a hike, Ty, she's my daughter, not yours.' She assured me that Crystal would not be left alone again."

"Thanks, Charles," I said, really meaning it. "I was worried about her."

"Well you should be. Her life is pretty unstable now."

The image of Crystal asking people for food haunted me. *Is that why she stays late and helps us clean up?* Usually we gave her the rest of the chip or cookie bag to take home. *Is that all she has to eat?*

Visions of Ebony and Carrie and that empty refrigerator which reeked of hunger and thirst disturbed me, especially when one of my classmates at Loyola bragged about the $10,000 her dad paid for her to be a lady-in-waiting in the Mardi Gras Krewe, Iris. She was just in the court now, but hoping to be chosen as queen of the parade one day. Bragging that her dress for the ball cost $5,000, and the throws for the Mardi Gras parade, such as beads, cups and doubloons were another $1,000, she prated of the $16,000 spent to be royalty for one day. Didn't she know there were hungry children begging for food in the concrete dungeons around the corner?

"Why would you spend that much money for one day?" I questioned. The side of her mouth inched near her eye with a look of disgust.

"What kind of question is that?" Penny grumbled with her friends. "It's the chance of a lifetime to be royalty, to wave at the masses below, and see the city from above on the most amazing day of the year."

"It's a waste, when there are people who are starving, or out of work. Don't you feel a bit guilty, sitting up there on your high horse throne when the castle walls are crumbling all around you?"

"Not one bit! The only castle that is crumbling is the one around the degenerates who don't want to work, and who want to sit and beg for my father's hard earned money. They should feel guilty for being lazy and worthless."

Her words were like a kick in the gut; they inflamed me so. How could someone in college be so bubble-brained? I took a long breath and clenched my fists. I imagined myself with the jewel-studded scepter the queen waves, smacking her right up side the head to knock some sense into her! *16,000 dollars! For one Mardi Gras Day! How many Ding Dongs could that buy?*

Chapter 24
The Hot Shop

Welcome to the hot shop. If you've ever seen a working glass studio you may be shocked by the dangerous movements of artists walking around twirling glowing globs. But, once you learn a few simple rules, you will be able to navigate the studio without being a danger to yourself or others. Move your eyes, then the glass. Look first, then move, and never lead with a hot piece of glass. [19]

Elzbieta couldn't keep up with my incessant questions and still have time for her art, so she gave me a book, *The Art of Glass*. "This will help you see how we move, so you'll be able to anticipate where we are going next, and not get in the way or get hurt."

I opened the flimsy book, let the page fall randomly and read. "Pay attention to the glass but don't focus all your attention in one spot." I couldn't focus all my attention in one spot if my life depended on it, so I liked this book. But then it told me to look first, for the big picture before I moved from one thing to the other. That was a new and intriguing concept.

The more I read, the more I began to see my life as a studio. There were various parts of the studio-tools, benches, and coloring canes, but they were all centered around the furnace. The furnace was what brought it all together. All the glass, all the color, all the complicated moves, would be nothing without the flame. My affinity and connection to glass broadened. I began to see not just the glass, but the intricacies of the studio as well. Instead of just watching my piece, I saw how Elzbieta and the other artists were moving, and how I could fit in. I began to study the studio and the artists, searching for my place. I noted how beloved each piece was to the blower, yet how fragile. Could it be that we are that beloved by God? While I observed, I made lists: lists of observations regarding color and fragility, lists of combinations of form and color I'd like to try one day. I even began lists of gratitude for how art, glass, and science were converging and helping me to understand a world that had once been frighteningly foreign to me. I made lists of lists, and could finally see things worthwhile enough from my life, which could be made into art.

I am thankful for glass, for the power of the furnace, for Elzbieta, for the stained glass windows that brought me here, and for my curiosity. If I didn't have that, I would've never continued to come to the studio. As a matter of fact, that curiosity is part of what makes me who I am. I love to learn how things work, how they fit together.

All of my life, when a workman came to my parents' house to fix or install anything, I was right beside him.

"What does that do? How does that work? What is that called?" Watching with eager eyes, and asking a million questions, I would sometimes get to help him hang wallpaper, prep for painting, lay tile, fix light switches, and refinish furniture.

So while making my second gratitude list, I got the brilliant idea to ask my landlord if he would reimburse me for renovating my half of the shotgun duplex on the edge of City Park. When I did, he almost jumped out of his skin with excitement.

I took off work for two weeks and began my artistic endeavor. After I added a new coat of azure blue paint in the kitchen, some of Elzbieta's artsy light fixtures, an Italian tile countertop, and a wallpaper border, my dilapidated apartment became my first opus. My second masterpiece was an old painted hutch I found in the basement that I decided to refurbish. As I sanded and scraped that piece down to its bare wood, I discovered the intricate carving and molding that had been hidden by years of paint and dirt. With each wipe of the stain-soaked cloth, I felt like an archeologist, bringing forth the luxurious grain that had been buried for so long. Steelwooling it before its last coat of polyurethane, I wondered how many other gorgeous things were laying dormant out there, waiting to be uncovered with a little TLC.

"Look first, then move. Be aware of your surroundings." That was the bottom line of studio movement, which was beginning to translate into my life as well. So I began looking everywhere for things that needed a little human care and concern.

While studying the creation story one day, the kids and I talked about how Adam and Eve were caretakers and how it was our job as humans to leave this world a little better than the way we found it. One student looked over at the abandoned park nearby. It had long since been taken over by the drug dealers. Its basketball courts were littered with broken glass bottles, the nets disintegrated, and the hoops were barely attached to the backboard. Men were rustling under the nets but no basketball was being played. Their game had much higher stakes.

Little Demetrius said, "What about that park? Could we leave that park better than we found it?" Those who couldn't see stood up to get a better look. *Look first, and then move.* Their curiosity was contagious. I noticed that with all of us standing up and ogling at the drug dealers in the park, they started looking this way and that, and then back at us. A fire ignited inside my gut, and its power propelled me from my seat. I walked over to survey the situation and the children followed. You could sense the tension in the men as we walked closer to their turf. But we weren't interested in their dealings: we had a mission. We were scoping what was necessary to clean it up. *Move your eyes and then the glass.* As we started picking up trash, they relaxed a bit. I sent a student for a notepad and pencil and together we made a list.

- Clean up the glass bottles
  Pick out the weeds
  Repair the basketball hoops
  Fix the benches
  Put new seats on the swing sets
  Paint the benches
  Paint a mural on the wall

I called the city of New Orleans; told them our plan, and asked what resources they could offer. They were very helpful. When we returned on Saturday, we found the kids jumping up and down. Grandma Gertrude, the counselors, and the kids were waiting on the street to help us unload the goods from the trunk. They couldn't wait to show us how the park had been cleaned and repaired. The city had even donated paint supplies.

The dubious men were hanging out and talking about the cleanup, scratching their heads in disbelief. When Grandma Gertrude saw one of the men smash a beer bottle on the newly cleaned pavement, she marched over with the fury of an ant whose hill had been tromped.

"These young people have invested their time and energy to get the city to clean up this park. And these children are about to paint and spruce it up. Do you gentlemen see the condition of this park, now? You're not planning on messing this up for these kids are you? For once they have something nice to look at, and something to feel proud of. Do you remember what that feels like? It's time we all start sacrificing some today, so our children can have a better tomorrow. Now if you want to be a part of this, we would love your help with the painting but if not, kindly pick up your broken bottle and skedaddle. It's time to give this park back to the kids!"

Our mouths could have caught flies that day they were dropped so in amazement. How could so much fire come from such a tiny old woman? I was terrified that they were going to pick her up and toss her into the nearby trashcan but they just shoved her off with the flip of a hand and walked away. Surprisingly, one of the gang stooped down to pick up the bottle pieces before he left. And he wasn't even the one who dropped it.

Soon we were underway, painting the benches and rails. An artist friend and some neighborhood parents helped sketch out a mural on the wall. It read: Leave your handprint on your community: CARE. Each child left his handprint on the mural and chose a stencil such as a flower, heart, or leaf to paint.

The amber sun set on a totally different park that day. People came out of their apartments to look at the newly renovated playground. Kids showed their relatives the handprints, benches, and walls they painted. One grandmother came out with Popsicles and popcorn and said we needed to celebrate the playground that "popped up" overnight. We couldn't believe our eyes.

The best sight though, was when we returned on Wednesday. From the interstate, before we even pulled into the lot, we saw dozens of children swinging, playing jump rope and playing basketball on a playground that had (for years) been the center of drug activity. But even better than the sight of laughing children, was the sight of parents, siblings, aunts, and grandmothers cheering them on from the sidelines and sitting on the benches talking to each other.

Chapter 25
Exercise vs. Production

Many students are dismayed at the number of non-glass exercises required in glassblowing because they do not yield any physical objects. Perform the exercises and your ultimate production will improve greatly. [20]

Back at the studio, I gained the courage to ask Elzbieta the question that had been on my lips for weeks. "You know, I love being here, separating shards, sweeping, packaging, and helping out wherever you need me."

"I know. Everyone loves having you here, Jenna. You are a great help."

"I was wondering if I could start working the glass on my own sometimes, to learn the art?"

Her crystal blue eyes scanned something off in space, and she shook her head a wee bit as she smiled. "I was wondering when you were going to ask. Most helpers are eager to jump in after a few weeks. How long have you been here?"

"Almost a year."

"You're a cautious soul, aren't you?"

"Hmph...I guess that's one way to put it," I hung my head as I responded.

"Caution isn't really a friend of art," she said as she threw me a pipe. "But if it's what you have to offer, we'll take it and see where it goes. Turning this pipe is where it all begins."

Elzbieta had me do the exercises I read about. I balked because they seemed pointless. She consoled: "The trickiest part of glassblowing is your turning techniques. That's what takes years of practice. I can compensate for any blowing if I turn it right.

"You have turned for minutes at a time, relieving us. But if you are to be a glassworker, you will be turning all day long. So you need to condition yourself. It is a totally different proposition. Now, take this pipe and rotate it continually, at the same speed, like this. About one turn per two seconds is fine. It's not the speed really, but the consistency." The well-chiseled lines in her arms rippled as she turned. "Take it home and practice. My grandfather made me watch TV shows while rotating the pipe. My pipe was like the football some athletes carry around wherever they go. My pipe and I are one."

I was sure it would be easy, but after ten minutes, I felt every synapse sending pain. As it moved from elbow to forearm to fingers, the burn of muscles matched the burn of the furnace, and sinews I never knew existed in my hands began cramping. It helped that there was an apprentice in the studio who encouraged me. "Keep turning. When you turn consistently and unconsciously, it makes everything else easier to learn."

Another blower added, "I didn't spend enough time with the pipe, and it took me twice as long to learn everything else. So spend time at the front end, when you're not messing up glass every time you hesitate in your turning."

But the most helpful comments were, "I know it hurts like hell. It's hard, but you'll get through it. Just keep turning until it comes naturally. It'll pay off in the end." I guess misery really does love company.

When I was at home, I turned. When I rode the streetcar to school, I kept a heavy metal pipe with me and I turned. When I was at work, I found myself turning anything that resembled a rod, such as the silverware in napkin rolls. If it was shaped like a cylinder in any way, I instinctively turned it.

I added my own layer to the revolutions. When I could remember, I added prayers along with each turn. Sorry for hating Roy so much and for running away from feelings. Thanks for glassblowing and how it helps me sort things out. Thanks for school where my mind can grow. Thanks for no more blackouts. Please help Crystal and all the others at Basin Street. Please help me to be honest with myself so I can find my way through the darkness.

And eventually, turning did become second nature. Whereas, each tendon in my hand and arms once screeched in pain, one by one they became silent. But they were not to be ignored, making themselves known through my tank top.

And somewhere along the path of turning and prayer, I gained confidence to gather from the fire. Gathering my first blob of glass without her help had the exhilaration/fear factor of taking the wheel of a car for the first time. Now I was aware of my surroundings. I was humbled and awed by the glow of the furnace. I was entering holy ground.

Gathering the light was like gathering a wad of Spanish moss from the trees. When Elzbieta guided me to the frit pile, and I rolled the glowing orb for a second in the green pieces I had selected; they stuck like glue. We moved over to the marver, and I was amazed at how easily it took on the smooth flat edge. I flipped it over, and the blue frit slipped right into the form, like being curled into a wave. I kept rolling it until it became a cylinder shape, more stubborn with each roll. I bit my lip so hard it hurt. She must've seen the frustration in my face. "It's harder to work now, right?" I nodded.

"When it feels like it's resisting you, then it's time for the glory. But think about whether you are going to blow or shape it after that. That will tell you how long it stays in and in what direction you move."

"I'm going to put in my jack line." Her eyes registered confusion, and I hesitated. Wasn't that the next step?

"Okay, just a second in the hole and then move with your eyes, not the glass." I did just as she said. I went to the bench and chose from the many shaped wooden spoons. My hands turned while I used the wooden spoon to shape it into a bulb noting how easily the glass nestled into its rounded form. And then before I knew it, it got stubborn again. "When it's hardening, it's brittle. Stay close to the glory." I put it in the hole again. When I took it out, I couldn't help but notice how pliable, how ready and willing it looked. My heart skipped a beat at how vulnerable it looked waiting for me. *If only I could be that way, perhaps God could do something with me.* I squeezed the jacks gently to put in the jack line.

"Now blow if you want." I blew and it expanded to a small bulb. Turning all the while, I blew again and it became a bigger bulb. Now was decision time. Was it to be a vase or a drinking glass? My next step needed to be precise. Do I open it up or flatten the bottom? Every second was a second closer to shattering.

I glanced at her for direction, and she was looking at me with the same look. It was clear that I was in charge of the piece. A drinking glass would be more useful, so I reached for a block to flatten the bottom before I made the mouth. When I flattened it, it squished into half its original size.

"Easy. Easy. You don't need that much pressure, just guiding touches at this point. Its heat makes it susceptible now to shaping." To open it up, she directed me to get a punty attached so I could work on the other end. For the first time I realized Elzbieta had not touched the piece at all. I held it by the punty and removed the blowpipe. Then I brought out the jacks so I could open up the glass's mouth. Did I have enough finesse to twirl and shape simultaneously? My heart pounded and muscles ached as I concentrated on both. I didn't want to lose the piece so far into the process. It drooped to one side.

"Gravity is the cheapest tool you have, so use it," she encouraged.

So I quickly compensated and centered it with one twirl, all the while keeping the pipe down. When I sat back at the bench and stuck the tweezers in to open the mouth, I couldn't help but think: I didn't have to take gaffer direction. I could've gone it alone on my own. But I chose to accept her directions.

The glass is taking my direction too. Although it has its own weight and disposition for gravity, it moves how I move.

To be that directly involved with the growing, changing force in front of me made my heart race. I moved toward the shears, and she nodded in approval, talking me through how to cut it from the pipe. "See the jack line you put in earlier. That's your guide of where to tap." She pointed toward the burlap pile. I took a deep breath before I tapped. It could all be over now. If it's too hard, it'll shatter; too soft, it will collapse off center when I stop turning. My hands ached from the pressure of turning and deciding. But I tapped, and held my breath. It fell with ease into the burlap: a complete un-shattered piece, before it quickly went in the annealer. "There you go," she said proudly, patting me on the back. "How does it feel?"

I stood looking at the odd shaped irregular glass for a few seconds, turning my head from side to side to etch its glowing image into my mind. As I popped it into to the annealer, I remember thinking that it may have been a little crooked and a little off center. It may have been a little small to be useful for as much as I drink in a day, but it was my first glass creation, full of me, all of my fear, doubt, caution, and pride. My first solo piece was full of soul.

Chapter 26
Glass Journal 2

When glass is first gathered from the furnace, it is taken to
the marvering table where it is pre-shaped while still on the
blowing iron. Rolling the glass backwards and forwards across
the cold table gives the approximate shape desired.

When I pull the pipe out of the furnace and see that little glowing gooey orb at its end, I cannot help but feel elation. I am taking sand, the rawest of materials and expecting to transform it into a work of useful beauty. But there is the equal force of gravity pulling it downward. The more glass I gather, the more I feel the force against me. Even though I fight with all my might to keep it centered and balanced on the pipe, sometimes gravity wins. All the while, I turn as if my life depends on it. The glass has a mind of its own, demanding I keep a watchful eye for the color changes, and how fast it cools and hardens. Because if I dawdle a little too long, or forget to turn my pipe even for a second, my orange blob can become so misshapen that it is fodder for the shard pile.

Chapter 27
Touch the Reflection

When gathering glass, touch the reflection. The white-hot glow makes it difficult to see in the furnace, so look for the reflection of the pipe. Lower the pipe until it touches the reflection (usually about half an inch) then go no further. Keep the pipe turning.

Tamira smiled as she spoke, "Thanks for the things you gave my baby. She talks about you all the time." Her eyes, minus the fake eyelashes, shined like diamonds in the sun.

"You are very welcome. Crystal is a sweet girl and very bright. She helps us clean up every week," I bragged.

"She taught me how to make those God's eyes, and I got some more popsicles, but I don't know where to get the yarn. Can we get some more of that? We've been decorating our house with God's eyes since you taught her how. We even used twigs from them trees, but they break," Tamira shared.

"Sure, I don't have any now, but I'll get some extra next time I go to the craft store. I need to go soon anyway."

"I'd really appreciate it. Is there a craft store around here?" she asked.

"No." *Why is that?* I couldn't help but think to myself. "I've checked, so I go to the one in Metairie."

"Thanks for everything you are doing for our kids. They look forward to coming to your events all week."

"You're welcome. We love every minute of it!"

As soon as Tamira left the picnic table, Gertrude informed us about Tamira's breakup with Ty. She relayed, "After Ty stole some of her welfare money, she threw him out. He banged on the doors for hours. Tamira called the cops, but they never came. Finally, he left, but not until he called her every name in the book and threatened to kill her.

"Now, Tamira plays with Crystal a lot. She goes to cooking classes at the New Orleans School of Cooking in the French Quarter, just a few blocks from here, but she goes while Crystal's at school. Tamira worked out a deal with the owner that she would help with his catering business for a reduced rate on her classes. Once she broke up with that tramp, Ty, Charles made sure she got help for school through the DCFS programs. Now she picks up Crystal each day from school and they share with each other what they learned. I'm so proud of her. She has finally realized what I've been preaching to them since they were children: The greatest legacy we can pass on to all our children is not material possessions, but the legacy of good character and faith."

I couldn't believe my ears. I had noticed that Crystal looked like a different child. Confident and courageous, she wasn't begging for food anymore. Actually, she was sharing some of her goldmine with others. And Tamira looked healthy too. Gertrude continued, "She and Angela, my granddaughter, have started hanging out together again. Tamira is teaching Angela how to cook and Angela is teaching her the economics and finance she's learning at community college. They are dreaming about opening a restaurant together, or at least a little sandwich shop. Angela will do the books and advertising, and Tamira will cook her famous pot-likkered roast beef po-boys and muffalettas. You should taste them." I was inspired to see that Tamira had rearranged her hardships into healing and began working her strengths for the good of all.

The following week Charles gave Tamira money to cater a volunteer banquet in our honor. Tamira beamed as she brought little samples of her concoctions. Word spread like wildfire and people came out of their doors and made a line in two minutes flat. While they waited they expressed their gratitude for our presence in their courtyard.

"Thanks for all you do for our children. When you're around, there is hope again, and the neighborhood feels safer." The reviews didn't stop with our program but moved on to the food.

"This is incredible. Girl, you have a gift!"

"I didn't know you were such a great cook."

"Can you cook for my son's graduation party?"

Her Creole pasta with shrimp and pink sauce was the neighborhood favorite. But they were branching out and trying her new creations as well, such as spinach and artichoke soup with mushrooms. She used it as gravy, a filling for chicken or fish, or thickened as dip.

Tamira, on such a high from all her rave reviews, volunteered to show the kids how to make praline pretzels during the afterschool program at Grandma Gertrude's house one day. "First, you start with three cups of pretzels," she began. The students helped each other break them into little pieces. Each child got a chance to read a step on the recipe.

"Measure out one cup of sugar," Crystal read proudly.

Was this the same student who couldn't sound out a word a few months ago?

I was amazed at how much they had progressed. Just a few months before, they fought and yelled over whom was next in line to help. Now they waited patiently and cheered each other on when doing a good job.

After each batch, we did a taste comparison and suggested creative things to add: vanilla, nuts, and sprinkles. Each child got to take home a bag of praline pretzels for his/her family. Their faces could not fully contain their smiles.

"Now I see why you don't want to miss the Saturday program," Tamira said to Angela as they were cleaning up the kitchen. "At first, I thought you and your mom were crazy for letting all those wild children in your home, but they're not so wild after all."

"Oh, they were pretty wild at first. You couldn't compliment one without the others getting mad. Ms. Jenna is constantly telling them to share in each other's joy instead of stealing it, because in God's world, there is enough joy to go around. It's all worth it when you see the look of learning in their eyes and know you have something to do with it, isn't it?" Angela asked.

I smiled because that was exactly what kept me coming back.

"I wish we had something like this when we were little. Maybe I wouldn't have gotten in so much trouble." Tamira sighed.

Angela's eyes brightened. "You know, I was just thinking that same thing. What if we ask the teenagers to start helping us with the kids? That might keep the teens out of the trouble you and I both know they are headed into!"

"The teenagers could be like counselors," Tamira replied with such excitement she began to pace. "We can even use Grandma Gertrude's words to recruit them: 'Sacrifice today, so our children can have a better tomorrow!'"

"With their help we might be able to add another day to the program. The kids would love activities three days a week. What do you think, Miss Jenna?"

"Ya'll are incredible!" I added. "The kids and the parents will love that. You two are the best advocates for this because you have been through the fire of living here, and know all the pitfalls. You're turning those pitfalls around and can sell this program to anyone." I don't think Mike and I can come any more than our two days a week, but I'm sure we can get supplies for you. We'll do whatever we can to help you!"

My mind was racing with ideas, but it was not the time for planning and concocting. It was the time to celebrate the fact that both of them had been through hard times, and were not broken by them. They were strengthened enough to want to help others not make the same mistakes, to pass on the blessings to others. And what better way to celebrate that than with a gratitude list. This time I rattled off 15 things without a hesitation: children, Tamira, Angela, teaching, praline pretzels, hopeful lives, people who want to give back, teenagers who want to do the right thing, a legacy of character and faith such as Grandma Gertrude's, Basin Street, the stained glass windows and the church who brought me here to this special place.

The extra day was a success. Their energy and extra hands meant we could reach out to more children. And soon, we had joint programs in Grandma Gertrude's and Tamira's house. Usually, in her apartment, Tamira made some cool recipe with the kids like marshmallow treats, apples with caramel dip, or veggies and spinach dip, with donations of food people brought to her. Angela and a group of the teens were homework tutors who quizzed the children on their math and reading facts after their homework was completed. We wrote a poem together that became our motto. The children recited it each time we were together. Tamira was consistent with the recitation, even though sometimes I'd forget. She said it helped them to remember who and whose they were.

I am God's Project

I am God's Project
I'm different from all the rest
He made me; He loves me
He wants me to do my best.
I will give Him my every thing
I will try to grow and learn
I will not waste one moment
On earth I get one turn.
And when I've had a bad day
And my temper's not at its best

Please, be patient and forgiving
God's not finished with me yet!

With a daily reminder that there are bumps in the road, but God's work continues in their lives, and with a double dose of doting love, fusing the bonds of their community, the students responded beyond expectation. The younger children and teens quit missing school. Their grades improved because they had people to ask them about their assignments and quizzes. The afterschool program became such a hit, that professor Charles used it as a model for programs in other projects. If Basin Street was a hot shop, I'd say it was producing some pretty incredible glass. It was amazing what a little internal renovation could do!

Chapter 28
On Being Woman

Moil is overblow. It is the unwanted bit of glass, left at the neck of a bottle or glass after shaping. It can be torched down or broken off and returned to the glass production cycle as cullet.[21]

The air was crisp that Saturday morning. Crystal met me at the car and showed off her purple fingernails painted at Angela and Gertrude's house. Angela and Kim, one of the other counselors, invited the girls who made straight A's over for a sleepover.

I couldn't stay the night due to my work schedule, but promised to come in early to help them make butterfly pancakes. The girls were so proud of their hairdos and fingernails. We mixed the batter and I demonstrated how to pour it, spoon by spoon, into the shape of a butterfly. After topping them with cool whip and sprinkles, we stood back to admire our incredible edible artwork.

We were eating our second batch of butterfly pancakes when we heard the booms. I thought they were firecrackers, but when the kids scrambled, screamed and ran for cover, I knew something was wrong. They had a lot more experience than I did with explosive sounds. Another cultural chasm: I thought fireworks; they thought gunshots.

Running with her baby, Angela corralled the girls to the bedroom. We tried to calm them down as Gertrude peeked through the window. Neighbors were filling the courtyard, yelling, "Call the police. He's getting away."

I followed Gertrude, who was inching toward the door. As she walked outside, a man clad in black pushed her aside like a barrel. He continued toward the gate. Crystal escaped from the bedroom, peeked out the door to look for her mother, and screamed, "Ty?" as he ran by.

That's when it hit us. It explained why Tamira didn't come back in time to make butterfly pancakes. Before anyone could get to her, Crystal ran in the opposite direction toward her house. I stumbled behind her as Jerome helped his grandmother up from her fall. When we got to Tamira's apartment, the door was open. The neighbor inside saw Crystal and screamed, "Get her out of here."

It was too late. Crystal, seeing her mom splayed out on the floor, leapt over the strewn remnants of her mother's purse, the pile of broken glass and furniture, and clung like a magnet to her mother's blood-soaked body.

"Momma, Momma," she screamed as if a siren was in her mouth. Kissing and hugging her mother's bloody face, she was met with a vacant stare. Near Tamira's right hand was a kitchen knife proving she did not go down without a fight. But it was no match for the hole left in her chest. Crystal didn't notice; she just kept kissing her mother's face and saying, "Wake up, momma. Wake up."

It took two of us to peel her blood-drenched body off Tamira so someone could check her pulse. Her screams still haunt me. "Momma, Momma, nooooo...please, Momma!"

Thirty minutes later, the police arrived. The residents told me that it was record time, the fastest they had ever responded to any Basin Street call. But it was the longest half hour of my life, rocking a bloody, crying child whose small world had just been blown to pieces.

Sirens, flashing lights, walkie-talkies, and lots of badges intruded our lives for the next few hours. The police pronounced Tamira dead on arrival. Everyone knew who pulled the trigger, so witnesses lined up around the apartment and investigators used all available rooms to question the neighbors.

The story played out the same as it had almost every other month since Tamira had broken up with Ty. He showed up when her welfare check was due, banged on her door and she told him to go away. He pleaded for another chance. She threatened to call the cops, except this time, he broke the window, broke through the chained door, and this time he had a gun. The neighbors heard screaming, glass breaking, and had even called the police.

Some neighbors led the police right to where they knew Ty would run: to the nearest dealer's house with his new wad of cash. They quickly retrieved him, complete with smoking gun. When a social worker talked to Crystal, she asked, "Do you have a grandma or an aunt that you can stay with for a while?"

"Grandma Gertrude," she responded.

"Is she your mom's mother?"

"No, she's Angela and Jerome's grandmother."

I interjected, "She stayed with Gertrude last night. The families are very close. Can she stay with her again until you hear from her relatives?"

"That's impossible," the tiny caseworker replied. "The state's now responsible for her well-being."

Crystal clung to me as the social worker tried to contact any living relative, but it was of no use. After being ripped apart from her lifeless mother, she was now being torn from my arms.

At that moment Charles, the social work professor, walked up with Mike, whom I had called while we waited for the police. Charles knew the caseworker, and they had some words before he took her to speak to Grandma Gertrude. Drying Crystal's eyes, I tried to get her mind off of what just happened.

"Show Mike your fingernails." She proudly displayed them.

"We painted them last night at Grandma Gertrude's sleepover. Then we had butterfly pancakes, and, and ..." she gasped for breath. The tears flowed so he lifted her into his arms and hugged her closely.

Charles came back and said, "Pack her a suitcase for a few days. She is going to stay with Grandma Gertrude for a while."

"How did you manage that?" Mike asked.

"It's a long story," Charles relayed, "but this child does not need any more trauma right now. This will buy us some time until we sort things out for her."

We all sighed so mightily it felt like a breeze went through the house. Packing, Crystal chose her favorite turquoise shorts and tee shirt, her stuffed animal, and of course her blanket. I threw in a picture of her mother and her that was next to the bed. She clutched it to her heart and wouldn't let go.

Gertrude, Angela, and Jerome gave Crystal a warm welcome, and Angela's first words were, "Let's go put your things down in my room. You are sleeping with me tonight." Crystal crawled up into her arms like climbing a tree.

"Can we make butterfly pancakes too?" Angela nodded and they were getting out the bowl to make the batter as I left.

Although it was only 2:00 PM, it felt like midnight. Mike wrapped his arm around me and asked if I wanted lunch. I cried and cried as I nodded. He walked me to his car, and we sat there for a long time until I could get my breath. In between sobs I blurted out details.

"Her blood was sprayed on the walls like a spin art painting, and pieces of organs were on the ground around her. Crystal was covered in her mother's blood kissing her face. When we saw him run away, we knew why she didn't come for the butterfly pancakes; we knew what the shot was."

After being Crystal's human towel for the last three hours, there was no way I could enter a restaurant covered in blood, so we got po-boy sandwiches from the local stand around the corner and sat in his car. Or at least we tried to. After a few bites, we both wrapped up our sandwiches and just drank our drinks. At first, the cool liquid burned down my throat but it filled a void in my empty stomach. He explained what Charles had told him while I packed with Crystal.

"Before Angela and Jerome came to live with her, Gertrude was approved to be a foster mother. She had one placement for about four months, and it worked out great for both of them. She wasn't as lonely for her husband, and the toddler just needed some loving arms until her mother was released from the hospital after a fall. Charles was the acting caseworker at the time. All Gertrude had to do was show the caseworker her license. She can keep Crystal as long as needed."

We talked until the sun went down, then he drove me back to my car and followed me home. He asked if I wanted him to come in, but I said no. All I wanted was take a bath and cleanse the blood and memories off of me. What I had witnessed, brought terror back into my chest. I gasped for air. I shook uncontrollably, and I could barely make it to the bathroom before the contents of my stomach exploded through my throat and all over the sink.

As I peeled off my soiled clothes, and eased into the scalding tub, I remembered all too well another time when I couldn't wait to scrub the repugnance that a man had inflicted on my body. But I never could.

And so, with the incessant visual tapes running through my head of Tamira's innards on the floor, that night I made a pledge: If being a woman meant that men had the power to mar and mutilate you so severely, then I wanted it no part of it, ever, ever again! It was time to rid my life of all the moile, forever!

Chapter 29
Trapped

A trapped air bubble in glass will continue to increase in temperature, but instead of increasing in volume it will increase in pressure, which can force up the top layer, creating a bump. Depending on circumstance, the glass can become so thin that it ruptures and a small hole is created.[22]

The walls began to close in on me and even breathing was contrived. Breathe in: two, three, four. Breathe out: two, three, four. I dragged myself back to Basin Street, telling myself that if the kids had to get on with life then so did I. But the breathing didn't get any easier, just more regulated. The gut wrenching claws that had hold of my insides made the simple act of getting out of bed seem like running a marathon. I was full of rage about everything: Ty, the police department's sluggishness, and men in general. It boiled over into everything. But then I saw Grandma Gertrude and Crystal together.

There was a slowness, a guarded way in which they moved together. Tears came and went as Tamira's name was mentioned, but there was a remarkable stillness, a calm that we felt far down in our being-in spaces you didn't even know existed. It was an eerie feeling and somehow it squelched the rage inside.

When at home on my own, the rage returned, but at Basin St., in community, it was reduced to eeriness. Since there was no money for a funeral, or even a decent burial for Tamira, donations were being collected to help with the costs. Grandma Gertrude's pastor agreed to conduct the service, so children and parents alike were taking collections. It took the full two weeks (before the city would just cremate her) but a wooden box was procured and a service planned.

People seemed to be like machines on the day of the funeral but dressed to the hilt. They prayed, sang hymns, and spoke of God's touch that could heal all things, like this was a routine thing. The pastor preached about hopefulness and how perhaps her death could be God's way of gathering us, uniting us, and shaping us into who we were called to be as the community of Basin Street. Grandma Gertrude gained enough composure for a eulogy. "Tamira learned to live like all of us should: To live in such as way that when your children think of patience, love and generosity, they think of you. All the children of Basin Street will think of Tamira that way, because to Tamira, they were all our children." Crystal sat up straight when Grandma Gertrude spoke so lovingly of her mother. But I was a mess especially when they wheeled her bare wooden casket into the hearse and took her away. That's when it hit me, the emptiness of it all.

Why is it you never have anything to say, God? Your people pray all the time and what do they get? Nothing. I don't even know if you exist anymore. I don't know how anyone here can still believe in you after everything that happened. I just don't get it, and frankly I'm tired of trying. Exhausted, really. I'm over it.

In my mind's eye I saw Elzbieta, and I could hear the roar of the furnace as she opened it to gather the molten blob on her pipe. At the marver, she pressed, flipped, pressed and flipped. I could feel the cool of the steel all around me. *If I could only feel you, the weight of your presence, I could believe. Then maybe my heart could melt. For now, God, all I feel is icy chill when I think of you.*

Chapter 30
Broken Things

During the fining process, agents or chemicals may be added to help
release the large bubbles from the melting glass, which can cause
fracture or impurities in the glass. The large bubbles rise and collect
the smaller ones along the way producing a purer homogenous glass.

Muddling through the motions of school and work, I somehow managed to continue showing up at Basin Street. I tried to hover around the fires of the studio, but I was living in a thick, insolated cloud. The lines were fuzzy, and I couldn't tell if I was going to, or coming from somewhere in my life.

If you are really up there, God, how could you let this happen? When Tamira was finally getting her act together and just when I was beginning to have hope again? Why are men monsters? Why didn't anyone see it coming? Where were you?

I wanted to believe God existed, but all evidence proved otherwise. I didn't feel safe anymore in my own skin. The sweet delicacy I once found in food was replaced with a foul taste that affected my ability to smell as well. No matter how much I concentrated at the studio, all I seemed to do was break glass and get in the way. At school, our discussions were meaningless nonsense. Even walking in my neighborhood was a nuisance. Instead of noticing the beauty around me, and counting the blessings as I had done in the past, I was counting how many steps I had until I could get home to my bed.

One day, I wandered by the church. Caught off guard by the stained glass windows, I felt a tug, and the struggle began within. *Remember the light that used to soothe, the resplendent colors that used to inspire? Before I knew it, I was back inside.*

Decatur St. Church had a different way of doing just about everything. That Sunday, we were to reflect on the Lord's Prayer, the part of the service that was rote in my childhood church. We were told to emphasize the words that meant the most to us. As we recited it, it was like saying it together, but in different languages.

They made a big deal about offering that day, as if it wasn't all about money. *Are they just trying to manipulate us to give even more?* We were to take silent time in our week to reflect on the greatest gift we could offer to God. That was what we were encouraged to give, more than even our money to the church.

What would be even more crucial than money to a church?

"Only you know your heart," Pastor Joe explained, "and God asks you to give those things inside that get in the way of loving God and doing God's perfect will. So today you'll get a large index card with your envelope. This week you will pray, and then write on it what special offering you will be giving to God in the future. If there is money in the envelope when you turn it in next week, we will take the money out, but we will never read the card. That is between you and God. Some of us have shared with you our offerings of the past: our addictions, our relationships, our need for control, and our career paths. But you may put in anything as you feel led."

Are they for real? The most important thing is what's on the card. Yeah, right.

But I was intrigued that week, sitting alone with an empty card. *How can I narrow it down to just one thing? There are lots of things that get in the way of you and me, God: Tamira, my sexuality, and Roy, to name just a few. I've been trying to forget about them because they are the shards that mangle me. There has been enough butchering, enough blood on the rocks. And besides, this card's not big enough, this pen not filled with enough ink to write them all.*

The silence seeped in. It stirred and swirled with the painful memories until they all collected as one. A splintering of agony burst like a bomb exploding inside of me. I tried to cry for help, but there was not even enough energy for that. A silent abyss was before me, and I sat with it. Before long, a pattern of breathing emerged, and then a tune fluttered in, filling the crevices of my mind. As I tried to reconstruct the lyrics of Julie Miller's "Broken Things," words fell, with tears on the empty card.

Broken Things

You can have my heart
Though it isn't new

It's been used and broken
And only comes in blue
It's been down a long road
And it got dirty on the way
If I give it to you will you make it clean
And wash the shame away?
You can have my heart
If you don't mind broken things
You can have my life if you don't mind these tears
Well I heard that you make all things new
So I give these pieces all to you
If you want it you can have my heart
So beyond repair
Nothing I could do
I tried to fix it myself
But it was only worse when I got through
Then you walk into my darkness
And you speak words so sweet
And you hold me like a child
'Til my frozen tears fall at your feet
You can have my heart
If you don't mind broken things
You can have my life if you don't mind these tears
Well I heard that you make all things new
So I give these pieces all to you
If you want it you can have my heart. [23]

I wrote those words on the card with more clarity and passion than I had ever written anything in life. I signed Julie Miller's name and then mine underneath. *What more can I say?*

Chapter 31
Murrini

Glass cane can be made by stretching out long lengths of colored gathers on a punty rod (and laid to cool like glass strands on a ladder). Bundles of cane are fused together and stretched out again, creating intricate multicolored canes, called murrini.[24]

In the New Orleans summer heat it was prudent to keep the studio closed in the day, and work late into the night. Since I couldn't sleep well after Tamira's death, the summer schedule worked great: school in the daytime, sleep and study for a few hours, and studio work at night. The studio's pull on me was even stronger after the funeral. Every time I entered it I could feel another presence with me, much like Elzbieta's feeling that her Dziadzia, her grandfather, was there whispering in her ear. The presence was especially strong in the wee hours, when the stillness moved in.

One night, Elzbieta invited me to work on a special project but gave no details over the phone. As I walked in, the hum of the furnace wrapped me in a blanket of security. She immediately grabbed a blowpipe and smiled. I moved near and started to talk, but from the look on her face I could tell she wanted silence.

She whispered, "Grab the biggest jacks. We are going to make canes for the murrini."

In the middle of the room lay a ladder with rungs closer together than usual. Elzbieta began by dipping into the top-open furnace filled with pots of colored glass to marver. Then she handed me the pipe while she walked backward with the large tweezers and pulled the blob (like a string) into a long cane of about ten feet. She laid it gently on the ladder rungs. As it began to cool, I could see its rich aqua color emerge. The cooling process didn't take long and after slicing off the ends of the canes with shears, she cut the canes into ten one-foot sections and laid them on a table.

We made colored canes the rest of the night, following the same process. Sometimes she would put the little molten finger into a mold after layering color, other times she would stretch and twist, but the process was generally the same: layer color, marver, mold, or twist it, and then stretch it into cane before laying it on the ladder to cool. We continued for hours: same process, but different molds and different colors.

When she saw my attention dwindling, she let me choose the colors and I, of course, chose my favorite: azure blue. I had been playing with the recipe of blue, purple and white for a while now and had it down. After I rolled it into a cylinder, she took the pipe and asked for my next color choice. I chose yellow for the blare of the furnace, and she asked if I wanted a mold. At that instant I could feel the presence in the room urging me on. I remembered Grandma Gertrude's sparkly eyes, so I pointed her in the direction of the starburst mold. She explained step-by-step about the colors, how some would need extra layers or thickness to withstand the mold. We finished off with a layer of blue for Tamira's crystal eyes, purple for my favorite color, and red for the depth of emotions I was feeling in the studio with Elzbieta. I could almost feel the presence of a smile in our silence. *Was that her grandfather?* I gave the glass a twist before caning it.

"When my Dziadzia came over to this country all he had was his torch, so he had to buy the pre-made murrini for his creations. I remember him saving every penny he could get his hands on for his first furnace and pots of color. The joy in his eyes when he...when we...pulled the first cane for murrini, it was the same joy he had when they brought home my baby sister."

Her words were a special bond, like she was sharing one of her most precious memories and inviting me to interact with it, to create a future representation of it. Like a glass thread of cane stretched from one point to the other, the creative process leaves a sort of legacy from where you were in a particular moment in time, to where you are in the present.

I could feel the dangerous territory this moved me toward (special bonds) but somehow I felt safe with the hum of the furnace reminding me of redemption, and a power greater than my understanding.

Although we worked in silence early into the dawn, I began to understand her moves. I knew how long to stretch the cane and whether to twist, mold, or pull it. It became like a dance: trying to intuit each other's steps and respond without words, and I felt alive and rejuvenated. By the time we finished, we had hundreds of canes of color.

It was a labor-intensive process and I didn't fully appreciate the task we had completed until hours later, when she asked me to sweep the ends she cut off into the shard pile. She could tell by my hesitancy that I was confused. *How could she reject pieces so intricate and beautiful?*

"I discard them because the color mixture is too inconsistent. What makes the murrini so vibrant is the consistency throughout."

That's when one caught my eye. The end piece revealed indigo, aqua, and orange almost bursting out of its yellow glass cage. I stuffed my pockets with several of the larger end pieces and could imagine them displayed in an artful arrangement on my dresser at home. She began to say something, but then bit her lip with such a mischievous quirky smile that my curiosity was peaked. *What was she about to say? Was she worried about me taking the end pieces? Was she troubled that I was stealing some of her designs and sharing her secrets with others?*

She had told me that in Murano you would be disowned for life if you gave away the family secrets to designing the intricate canes. Concerned that I should put the pieces back in the cullet bin, I put my hands in my pocket, and felt a pop from inside, and then another. I grimaced and removed my hand quickly, seeing tiny drops of blood forming from where splinters of glass pierced.

"I was about to warn you," she said with a knowing nod of her head. "But some things are better learned on your own."

"What happened? Why did it shatter?"

"With some of the glass combinations, if it doesn't have time to set, or anneal, properly, it will crack. You never know if the cracks are enough to split it, explode it or just give deep dimensions within it. That's the unpredictability of glass."

"I could've lost my hand."

"No, it was in a confined space, and only a little piece. It's better to let you weather a scrape now, so you won't lose a hand later."

"I suppose."

"It'll stop you from cutting corners on annealing, and teach you to be mindful of pieces with cracks. You never know when they'll splinter. It could be today, never, or in years to come."

"Thanks...I guess." Beginning to remove the colorful shards of glass in my hand, I wondered if the present discomfort was truly worth the pain saved in the future. Only time will tell, I guess, if my brain could retain the memory. I covered my hand with a cloth and vowed never to forget. The sting has followed me ever since.

After hours of making cane, and cleaning up the studio, the process was still not complete. I had to come back the next night for the final step: using a tile cutter to cut the canes into little discs called murrini. Fortunately, several canes could be cut at one time depending on their thickness. It wasn't until this simple step that the grandeur of our mission was revealed.

When she cut the first pieces of murrini and the patterned layers of azure blue, yellow, purple, and red appeared, I fell off my stool. From the out-side, the cane had no beauty or appearance that anyone would notice. Its red exterior was not any brighter or deeper than any other red. But once cut into cross sections, the richness of the red casing looked like a velvet glove hold-ing the layers of yellow, blue, with a purple starburst inside. The repeating patterns and colors were so deep and expansive they drew me in. One had a stark, vibrant yellow bursting from the purple outer lip, announcing the tiny worlds that lay within. That's when I realized it was mine: a starburst of azure blue summoning you to strip down and jump in. And there were hundreds of other discs that looked just like it coming from the same cane.

It took my breath away that cane, and every piece of murrini we cut that night. For it explained the world to me in a way no words could contain. When your eyes stop at the outer layer of the world of people and faith, you see a variety of ordinariness. It is only when you learn to look inside that you see the reflection of what the creator sees: the layers of color, molds, and stretching that it takes for each intricate design.

"Earth's crammed with heaven, And every common bush afire with God; But only he who sees, takes off his shoes – The rest sit round it and pluck blackberries." [25]

Chapter 32
Fire and Fury

Fragility is the maze of intrigue, which fuses one's heart to glowing glass.

You would think that a bloody hand would deter me from hanging out in a glass studio, but it actually has the opposite effect. I am more determined than ever to figure it out, to know its unpredictability and what makes glass tick. The fact that something so beautiful can be so fragile when it looks so sturdy helps me see myself from the inside out, walking the tightrope of chaos and order.

I go through life so determined to find the right path, but sometimes the science, the fate, the unbalanced mixtures, and the struggles of life are too stressful for me to hold it together. Sometimes the passion, the color, the intensity, and the fire are a recipe for disaster. The intrigue is not knowing which is which, until it falls apart right before my eyes.

The more I learned about glass, the more I found bonds and systems of complexity in the world. This was not always a pleasant thing as it unearthed a world of offenses that I never knew existed. Another season of Lent was upon me, and that was not to be taken lightly in New Orleans. Everyone asks, "What did you give up for Lent?" Usually, I joked and I replied, "Mardi Gras parades". But this year instead of boasting that I was Presbyterian, and not hedged in by Lenten abstentions, I took a good hard look at the season and myself. Why had I always denigrated it? What's wrong with a little self-reflection?

I began to see that Lent, much like the Jewish Yom Kippur, was the curious time in our calendar when we peered inside the garden hose of our lives to ponder the mire we had let settle inside, praying for a clear stream to flow when attached to the life giving source. How could I joke about that? Why didn't I give it a try?

When I attached the dirty hose of my life to the faucet, all I kept getting was murky slush. Could it be because I never really looked beyond my sex- uality issues? What if that wasn't the thing that most needed my attention?

In order to have a good hard look at what was inside, I had to begin somewhere, but where? Everywhere I looked was ground waiting for the plow: hatred, selfishness, self-absorption, hidden motives, lust, gluttony, anger, and resentment...what needed to go first?

One day, Ari invited me to take a trip with him to a nearby plantation for a tour and lunch. Being raised in Greece, he was especially intrigued with how the Hollywood movies portrayed plantations and he wanted to see one up close. He could tell I was not that comfortable with the idea, but my curiosity was peaked.

It was a beautiful spring day, and the grounds of the Oakwood Plantation were impeccably kept. We arrived too early for the tour so we strolled along a path of majestic oaks draped in Spanish moss. We continued on a trail through a forest of magnolias and the smell, like perfume, wafted down the path causing squeals of delight from walkers. Each time I inhaled, I could feel the sweetness expand in my lungs and relax me. So I was caught off guard when Ari started the inquisition.

"Thanks for humoring me, Jenna. I've seen these plantations in the movies, and wondered if they could be that grand."

"Don't get your hopes too high. You know things are never as good as in the movies."

"Some things are better, Jenna. Like Venice, nothing on film can com- pare with its magnificence. Mykonos, it's better than ever depicted, too. Have you ever thought about traveling the world?"

"Of course...I'd love to travel...once I get out of school," I managed to stammer out once my heart got over the mention of Venice.

"That's next year isn't it?"

"Yep, next June, I'll be done."

"Why don't we take a trip then?"

"What?"

"We could fly to Greece, pick up my yacht and sail off from there. Or we could just hop on a plane if you prefer. You name the destination. It'll be your graduation present."

"That's quite a present," I said as my stomach began to gurgle.

"Where have you always wanted to go? Paris, Venice, Morocco, Istanbul? The world is your oyster..."

I'd always heard that saying, but I wasn't thinking oysters at that moment. Oysters were luscious, sensual, dripping fruits from the sea. But instead all I could smell was rotten, rancid fish, and my insides were churning at the thought.

"My girls could join us for a portion of it if you would like. We'd have quite an adventure. Just think about it."

My breath escaped me. I hadn't even met his girls. *How would we go on a trip together? What was he thinking? What did this mean? Why did he have to go and ruin things? Why did men always have to go and ruin everything?*

The tour director called us into the house and the beauty of the classic china and exquisite brocade fabrics rescued me. As we walked to the kitchen house with ovens, stoves and long tables stacked with every type of jarred fruit and vegetables, I had to admit, it was pretty impressive, even the fields.

Ari was most enamored with the rows of planted cotton and the weighing room, which had blackboards to calculate the net worth of the haul each day. He was intrigued by the big business of the plantation and how such production came from one family.

"Well, it wasn't exactly from one family. The slaves were not part of their family, and that's who did all the work."

"Not all the work, Jenna. Don't oversimplify. Much expertise went in to running a plantation, harvesting the product, getting it to the right market in a timely manner, and selling it for profit. That part was not done by slaves." Of course he, a businessman, would see things from a different perspective.

The more we strolled away from the fields and closer to the slave quarters, the more I seethed. Row after row of tiny cramped clapboards houses, which housed 10-15 people in one room, encircled a pump and a fire ring. The tour guide showed us dolls that the slave children played with and a room full of shackles and whips. My head filled with their cries, screams, and gurgles as I scanned the rooms, so I kept moving.

The tour director boasted of the plantation's history. Once they were ordered to free their slaves, the owner was surprised to find that many wished to stay on as sharecroppers. In time, the master's daughter, Reva Pittman, took over the property and started a plantation school where she taught reading and math to the former slaves. Teaching them to calculate prices and read contracts on their own (and not to rely on the honesty of others) she was the catalyst, and eventually many of them became profitable business owners.

But in the south, contempt ran in streams for those with dark colored skin. The tour director read intriguing passages from Reva's journals:

"How can the slaves be treated so cruelly, just for being who they are? Through no fault of their own, God chose their skin to resemble the shiny mare: dark, deep and muscular. Was that the problem? Their unfathomable strength, when combined with knowledge, frightens my neighbors? I am caught in the crossroads. Called, unequivocally, by God to bring his word to all: How can we do that if they can't read it for themselves? Hatred must be clouding minds because it is written so plainly in the Bible-the book we all profess to live by. Perchance the scriptures my fellow citizens are reading are different from my own. It is clear as light to me."

As the tour guide read, I came alive. I could hear her former slaves squeal with glee upon reading their freedom papers. I could feel the pen in their hands signing their names on the documents for the very first time. Education eradicated the powerlessness they had felt for years, and offered them a freedom no shackles could ever bind.

"Before long, word got out and the townspeople were incensed," our tour guide continued. "They tried to shut her down. She worked for years praying, hosting women's guilds and attempting to change the hearts of the people, but one by one her friends abandoned her and she stood alone with her convictions, resolute to the end that she was doing what God called her to do."

Reva Pittman was so despised, that some even tried to burn her plantation, but her sharecroppers worked for days putting out the flames. Then they devised a schedule to guard the grounds round the clock. She armed every man, woman and child on her property with a gun and instructed them, "Do whatever necessary to secure your land and learning." Eventually, the townspeople gave up trying to burn her out. But they moved to boycotting her crops and refusing her credit. Her last days were spent in depression, seclusion, and fending off bankruptcy until she fell exhausted into death. She left the house to her workers, as a living legacy of the hatred that can kill a dream before its time.

I seethed with anger against the men whose bigotry destroyed her, so I could not even finish the tour. There was fire in my eyes, and I could barely get a breath deep enough to get oxygen. I found refuge under a large oak waiting for Ari's return.

"A little passionate about all this, are we?" he jabbed as he sat next to me under the tree after the tour.

"Just a little. She could have done so much. She had such vision."

"What do you mean she could have? She did do much with her vision. Think of all those former slaves and the world she opened up for them."

"But if it weren't for man's bigotry and hatred, she could've opened schools for everyone, and changed the course of history."

"She did change the course of history, just not in the visions of grandeur you have for her, Jenna. Not everyone is called to be grandiose saviors of the world. We are each just supposed to do our part. She did her part. If you would've stayed to the end, you could see all the relatives of those slaves who went on to be pioneers in the black trade movement, some even becoming lawyers. They were actually the ones that helped to preserve this trust in her honor."

"But she could've done so much more, if the world wasn't so against her!"

"Times were different. Lives were different. Fear was rampant, and with that, hatred ensues. You can't read history through your present lens. She was a major crusader, and a very brave woman. Don't belittle what she did because it is not grand enough for your imagination."

"I'm not belittling her, I'm belittling the small-minded and hatred-fueled demons who destroyed her. Their fear and loathing robbed us. Imagine where we would be today in the world, if her vision of education and liberation would've taken hold back then. But no one stood up for her."

"Hatred robs all of us. That's exactly what happens when good people do nothing. The evil of hatred is allowed to deprive and destroy everything in its path." The rage within me was too much for my arms and legs to bear, and the only way to keep my blood vessels from exploding inside me was to walk. Ari had to skip to catch up with my brisk pace.

But then he began gaining speed too. The faster my pace, the more he led in conversation and stride saying, "When good people do nothing, the passion of the ignorant gains fervor and momentum, filling everyone's head with lies."

"But people were standing up to it," I added. "Lincoln was. Congress was when they freed slaves legally with the 13th Amendment. Where was everyone else?"

"The bonds of oppression are deep and dark, and woven into every fabric of life. It was a way of life in your South. At least that is what the tour guide said. It was not going to go away easily because it directly affected their economy and culture. Slavery may be the embodiment of hatred, but really it starts with fear, racism, classism, sexism, poverty, and judgment. If no one stands up against those, it festers into oppression, and eventually war."

"It's like hatred is the potion we hand out to others, poisoning ourselves instead."

"That's good, Jenna. Say that again."

"That *is* good, isn't it? Hatred is the potion we hand out to others, poisoning ourselves instead."

We feasted on that nugget all through the day. Lunch was served at the plantation house, and yes we ate it, but for the life of me I couldn't remember one single bite. The conversation was so deep and luxurious the food paled in comparison. Our appetizer was Hitler and his pestilence of fear and hatred that almost destroyed civilized society as we know it. Germany was saved by the courageous who stood up to his evil, even pastors were in an ethical dilemma with a plot to execute Hitler. Our main course was Gandhi, JFK, Mother Theresa, and anyone who had their name attached to conquering hatred, judgment, oppression, and fear while upsetting the social order.

"The main thing I learned from sociology and philosophy," I purported, "Is that people are very tolerant of ideologies and theologies, until it upsets the social order. Jesus was fine until he started blessing the poor, condemning the rich, and preaching freedom for the oppressed. And Martin Luther King Jr. was fine until he started talking about poor whites and blacks being under the same movement."

"Exactly," Ari replied. "'God and country are an unbeatable team: they break all records for oppression and bloodshed.' At least that's what my favorite filmmaker, Luis Bunuel, says." As he paid the bill I wondered how much he paid for a meal I couldn't recall.

On the way home, I noticed the fields of flowers in bloom. Where were they on the ride in? I opened all the windows to smell the fragrance in the air. The wind blowing through my hair was fresh and breezy. I didn't even mind when he put his arm around the back of my seat, letting his fingers rest on my shoulders. It was the first time he had touched me.

Even the rain was beautiful, making a rhythm with the windshield wipers, though we had to close the windows as it streamed in. We laughed at how quickly it came from nowhere once we entered the town named Jena. Lightning, like fingers, spread though the sky and thunder roared, jolting the car as we traveled.

The trip back home was brief, full of engaging conversation the entire way. Upon entering the city, though, he ruined everything. "So, have you thought of where you want to go for your graduation present? Seriously, get out the map and dream. It'll be summer, and I have the girls for most of it. My yacht has three bedrooms so you can have your own room. You just need to choose the destination. No strings attached. We can go anywhere, and my captain is standing by with sailing orders. Where will it be, Jenna?"

Bubbles started welling up in my stomach. Was it something I ate? "Hmph...hmph," I coughed. "Sounds...like...quite a...trip."

"We do it every summer, kind of like Dr. Dolittle. Spin the globe, put your finger on a spot, and travel there. It is my consolation prize now that the girls go to school."

I fidgeted around in my seat.

"Is your stomach upset? Mine is feeling queasy. Could be the..." I tried to complete the thought, but couldn't remember any of the meal. What could it have been?

"It was probably the chocolate buttermilk cake. It was very rich," he said, completing my sentence. "I can't believe you ate it all. I couldn't finish mine."

"Remnants of living with my dad who said I always had to clean my plate." I ran out of the car when we neared my house, thanking him for the plantation excursion. Words escaped me as I tried to describe it: eye-opening, educational, splendid, wretched, stomach churning. I ran away thinking, why do they always do that? Why do men have to go and ruin a perfectly good...everything?

The churning continued even after my trip to the bathroom. But I couldn't stay inside. The walls were closing in. *Why couldn't he leave everything so...convivial?* I left my house but had to stop mid block for the sea of green moving toward me. I had forgotten that it was St. Patrick's Day. The parade caught me by surprise. In desperation I sat on the edge of the curb, turning away so I didn't have to see the joy and merriment of the masses in direct opposition to what I was feeling. Holding back the dry heaves, I looked up and called out to God, "Why does everything have to be so complicated? Why do you make things wonderful one minute and then terrible the next? There we were having one of the greatest conversations in time, and the next minute I never want to see him again, can't stand to even look at him."

That's when I heard a thud. I looked to see that a clump of beads and a head of cabbage had landed right next to me thrown from the St. Patrick's Day parade. The cabbage split into pieces as it was hurled from the float to the pavement. I picked it up, angered that I was not in the mood for a parade. But I *was* in the mood to throw things. The rage over Roy, and Ty entwined with Ari, and the resulting emotion was so overpowering I smashed one of the cabbage pieces as hard as I could to the pavement. *What is wrong with men? Why do they have to wreck everything?* Another piece I chucked shattered in bits around me. *Why do they have to twist and mangle everything into a grand scheme to get people into bed with them? Is there any other thought in their brains other than sex?* I was running out of pieces to throw but it was feeling so good that I stomped on the fragments until they were decimated. *Why are their brains controlled by their genitalia?* Another stomp, so hard that the green of the cabbage piece was beginning to meld with the dirty concrete. *Don't they have enough blood to control both at the same time?* Stomp, stomp, stomp.

There was nothing more to stomp or throw so I walked toward my house. *Why did you create such wretched creatures, God?* I found an aluminum can along the way and threw and stomped on it to the ground. *Why do you allow them to keep living and spreading their evil around? Why? Why? Why?* By the third why, I was growling and looking straight up to heaven shaking my fists. My hands were outstretched waiting for an answer.

That's when I saw it coming straight toward me. The cool March rain slapped me right between the eyes, sliding down my nose and chin, heading straight to my neck. The sting of the rain brought the realization of what I had just thought: *Why do you allow them to keep living and spreading their evil all around?*

Jolting back, I hung my head and let that thought puddle around my feet. *How is my hatred any different from the hatred and bigotry that I despised at the plantation? When did I become so filled with rage, and fear that I would desire the destruction of not just one, but many others?*

Seeing the decimated brown cabbage leaves and the aluminum can in my wake, I was taken aback. *Why did I take out my anger on a poor head cabbage thrown to celebrate peaceful St. Patrick? What damage would I have done if I had had a gun, or a knife, or any type of weapon nearby?* Then I heard my very own words; "Hatred is the potion we hand to others, poisoning ourselves instead."

It was a bitter realization, and swallowing it was like gulping guilt. I found myself pleading with God to break hatred's hold on me. No, I wasn't responsible for the horror inflicted on me by men, but I was responsible for what I did with it, and how I distributed it through my life. How many times had I unwittingly let that hatred spew forth from me? It was time to take responsibility for my healing.

I spent a good portion of the evening walking around my apartment, crying out to the God I was partially believing in, and praying the best prayers I've ever prayed. "Sorry, God. I can't believe those thoughts were flowing through my head. Please help me break the chains that have bound me to this hatred. Help me see other areas of my life where I am just as bad as the people I loathe. Please help me to keep lifting my eyes and heart to you so I will know the difference. Help me be truly honest with myself, and not such a stubborn imp, resistant to change. Please don't give up on me. Thank you for being there, no matter where I find myself."

The eerie presence I found at the studio moved into my room that night and nestled like a cuddly dog at my feet. Its warmth and comfort brought healing. I could almost feel a breath whispering hope into my ears. I didn't move around much because I was afraid it would leave. So I stayed perched on my lounge chair and wrote furiously in my journal. Before long, I wasn't afraid anymore to sit alone in silence and meditate like Father Ben had taught me. The fear and fury that had kept me in motion was overtaken by the thought of fur at my feet. And the more I sat in stillness, the more I believed that something or someone was there.

Chapter 33

Out of the Furnace

Where there is ruin, there is hope for a treasure. [26]

I am mesmerized by the furnace's glow, and its power to overpower any other thought in my head or heart. I am awed by its ability to correct and meld. It draws me in. Yes, I know the fire that warms and charms is also the fire that burns, but I can't help but hover anyway. Hope, starting in the back of my knees with a wobble, dares to believe that the trifle breath of creativity that I so feebly offer can be fused into something useful or inspirational: that the formula for color, temperature, and wonder that I have, will produce something-anything of value.

The more I learned about glass, the more certain I was of my vitreous nature, except I was lacking one important property: transparency. Constantly hovering between jello and a brittle hardness is not unusual for a person with my past. I learned from educational psychology that the normal tendency for those experiencing trauma and shame is to flee in fear of transparency and its dangerous by-product: intimacy. At 22 years old, my baby steps toward self-honesty, though, were helping me see things more clearly. I became obsessed with the question: Does transparency give a material its strength or its fragility?

In class we learned how photons (carriers of light energy) transferred energy with other materials. But with vitreous materials, protons passed through unchanged because they don't interact with any electrons on their journey. Usually, electrons reside together in energy bands, but vitreous materials, have giant band gaps, where energy levels for electrons don't exist at all. Hence, light is transmitted instead of getting stuck transferring energy in the bands. I began to model the electrons I studied which wanted to achieve equilibrium and conserve energy simultaneously. Hence, when given a choice, I moved quickly toward places that gave energy rather than drained it.

Studying, writing, and musing gave me energy. Bible study did too, most of the time. Sometimes I'd leave angry and even more confused. Self-examination was a painful task. One night, I had a physics assignment that needed attention, but I remembered Elzbieta's lesson about turning the pipe: *Do it until it becomes second nature.* I knew I needed to keep putting myself in places where that trust and peace could envelope me, even if I didn't always want to go. Some things you had to work at to get right!

So as our Bible study group listened to the sounds of thunder and lightning battling their way through sheets of rain, we completed the study and took prayer requests. Tired of sitting there each week and listening to everyone else's supplications, I tried for the first time to jump in with my requests, "It's been a more than a year now, after Tamira, and now that I'm almost put back together, I've been wrestling with going to graduate school, but I'm not sure what to major in."

"I thought last month, you said you were going to graduate school in science," the leader, Dan, said.

"I know. But now I'm thinking about psychology, or even going overseas to be a missionary. When I was in high school my principal told me I would be great in the Peace Corps with my love of cultures. I'm wondering now if I should give it a try? I'm having trouble figuring out a process to determine the right path to take."

"Process?" the young single mother questioned. "I just go for what feels right?"

"I'm not good with feelings. Don't really trust them at all."

"Then you need to pray to get in touch with your feelings." Dan prescribed.

"How do you do that?" I sincerely wanted to know.

"Pray for feelings, and honesty. Then take each feeling out as it comes, little by little, sort it, analyze it, journal about it. What do you resonate with? What do you resist? Trust its ability to reveal something to you." The others nodded to Dan's advice. *My first feeling stung me before I even asked: Trust.*

"I hate to trust. There's nothing about trust I like. It makes you vulnerable, weak, and powerless."

"Yes, but it teaches you patience. It teaches you something else out there might have your best interest at heart."

"Yes, but it shows pretty glaringly when it doesn't. Most don't. They only have their interests at heart. I have issues with trust."

"You have to trust, Jenna. You trust God, don't you?"

"Uh...I'm trying, but no, not really."

"Surely there's someone you trust about something, even a little bit?"

"Hmm...Uh....I guess my friend Elzbieta...I trust her...her knowledge of glass."

"See there. How did you gain that trust?"

"I'm her helper, so I work elbow to elbow with her. If I want to learn her art, I have to trust her ability."

"Okay, so what are the things you most want to know from God?"

"Who I am. What am I supposed to do with my life?"

"Then you have to trust. If you want to know God's plan for your life, you have to trust God. We can't look at the world the way God wants us to until we see ourselves the way God sees us. And that comes by spending time-I like your image, elbow-to-elbow time with God. By listening, by reading, by not being afraid of who and whose you are."

"But what if I don't like who and whose I am?"

The room had no more air. People looked as if they had stopped breathing.

"God loves you, Jenna, and you are God's."

"I don't know about that."

"What is your hesitation about God loving you, and claiming you as God's child?

"If you really knew me, you wouldn't need to ask that question."

"I know you, and I know God loves you."

"You don't know the real me," I said tightening up inside. "I keep a lot of things inside."

"We all do. Why is that?"

"Because things are safe there. If...I...told...," the tears started leaking. I felt an arm around me, and a silence beckoning.

"All of us keep things inside, Jenna. I don't know why, but we do. We show off only our best sides, but when we do that, we rob each other. Especially when we are safe among people who love us, and want to know us. You're safe here. What you say here stays here."

"Like when I told you of my battle with drug addiction," our newest member, Alfred, added. "You still loved me and accepted me here. And because of that I got my three-month chip in NA last week." There were shrieks of joy and claps for him.

"I know, but my issues are different. They can't really be changed."

"All of our struggles, though unique, are the same in how they put up walls that separate us," Dan added. I envisioned that stubborn piece of glass on the marver, and felt its unyielding hardness.

"Yeah, well...I like women. I mean, the only people I can be attracted to sexually are women, so I try not to think about it. I try to put it out of my mind but when I do, everything gets all messed up. I think I'm supposed to be following God, but how can that be if I'm having these feelings? So when you say I'm supposed to get in touch with my feelings, well that's what I'm feeling...that's why I'm confused."

It was the same stillness we shared after our concert in Rimini, before the big applause. The same heart pounding silence after Jacquie sang her song. The world hushed as if taking its last breath. I don't know where I got the courage to look up, because all I wanted to do was hang my head in shame, but as I scanned the room, I didn't see disgust at all. Alfred was crying, and the woman next to me reached out and embraced my hand. She whispered, "You are a brave soul, Jenna."

It seemed like an eternity before I inhaled my first breath. I couldn't help but breathe in God, and follow with an exhale of Jenna.

"That is powerful, and honest," Dan offered. "Thank you; thank you, Jenna, for sharing your soul with us. You can't imagine what a treasure that is. You are very much loved here. And God promises that there is nothing in all of creation that can separate you from that love, not death, nor life, nor angels, nor demons, nor present, nor future, nor powers or principalities, neither height, nor depth, nor anything else in all creation, can separate you from God's love for you through Jesus. That is a promise directly from Romans 8:38. How can we pray for you? What is the best way for us to support you at this time?"

"I don't know. I don't know. I just need you to know me, and what I struggle with. What I try not to struggle with. Why I can't, don't, won't feel."

Like a blob, I fell into the arms around me. I could almost see the electrons inside sparking, and I could feel the connections as myriads of atoms danced within. Before long, I heard them closing in prayer. I could only catch bits and pieces in between the soul releasing sobs. "Pray...Jenna feels your love...love in this room, the love that stems from you...love that doesn't hold back, and has no boundaries. Give her strength...Thanks for her courage that touches us all."

Chapter 34
Fusion

Fusion creates a homogenous liquid mass by melting together different materials. It is aided by the release of bubbles, which rise to the surface and provide a stirring action, bringing more of the particles together. [27]

Nights with Elzbieta in the studio were so much more than techniques. Elzbieta could tell if I'd had an intense day, because she'd speak a little more than usual. "Easy, easy. Don't bring all that outside junk in here. Slow down. Find your peace. Wait at the door and discern if you're ready to come in. Watch the glow. Honor it, and feel its groove. Then come in." When I did, I'd immediately calm down. Sometimes, she'd put on classical music to get me relaxed enough to work the glass. I came to realize that studio time was another dimension all its own. "One day you'll learn, Jenna, that the more you rush through things, not feeling them out, not allowing time for adjusting the energy, the more messes you make."

"Are you talking about glass or life?" I couldn't help but ask.

"I'm talking about glass, but to me, glass is life. Everything I learn from this studio, I take into life. You can't be this close to fire, this close to chemistry, creation, and creativity and not be changed, and not be linked on a very deep level to the transcendent. It's the ultimate connection. It's the transparent medium that brings us to the thin, fragile places in life where we, like our pieces, can be transformed."

"I'm beginning to see exactly what you mean," I replied.

As our eyes connected, a warm smile started down in my toes, and lifted my spirit as it moved throughout my body and spread to my lips. Elzbieta exuded balance and confidence. To her, the studio was a combination of attention, time, and movement choreographed as a ballet. Even though we were working silently on our own pieces, with rarely ten words between us, our movements were fluid, our steps in a rhythmic pattern, as we nodded in acknowledgement and made room for each other at the bench or in the glory. Sometimes classical music blasted and other times the roar of the furnace was our inspiration.

Between the studio, Bible study, the combination of Zen meditation and quiet time, I felt like I was exercising on every front. But it was in a concentrated laser point way. Before long, the world around me began to settle, and the endless haranguing about my sexuality faded away. Not necessarily the feelings, but the endless haranguing about my feelings.

With the settling came an ability to pay attention to the world around me, to hear the trees rustle and the birds chirp at a good strong 24.50 Hz frequency-G.

It didn't happen overnight. Elzbieta was right: it was all about consistency. The more consistently I practiced quiet time, journaling, and centering meditation, the more serene I felt, even when the world got confusing around me. I started hearing the same words Augustine heard, "Take and read." Those words inspired me to pick up my Bible more than I ever had before, and to use it as a sort of road map to chart my course. I started with the words of Jesus that were printed in the red letters in my Bible. I never knew Jesus to hurt anyone. So I trusted him. And the more I took and read, the more I felt an affinity for the creator, the shaper, and lover of all. And the more affinity I felt, the more I wanted a conversation and a depth of connection.

So I found myself saying, "If you're really out there, you know everything I'm thinking and feeling, so I really don't need to say much. But you know what a rough road I've had. I'm tired of trying to figure it out, trying to do better. Can we just call a truce? I'll promise not to give up so easily and believe in you, if you promise the same thing. Is that something you can live with?"

It was at that instant that I finally understood a quote by a great writer/philosopher that I had loved since reading her books as a child:

"I have to write every day whether I want to or not. I have to pray every day whether I want to or not. It's not a matter of feeling like it, or waiting until I feel inspired, because both in work and in prayer, inspiration comes <u>during</u> rather than before." [28]

Chapter 35
Close to the Fire

The properties of glass-its fluidity, transparency, fragility, and
defiant durability-make it a fascinating medium that combines
predictability with serendipity, technical properties with creativity,
the artist's intellectual intent with his/her liberating breath.[29]

*There is nothing that can compare to the fire. It's the bass line of all that is
blown. Although it is my breath, my movements, and my choice of color
that I am shaping, I never forget that the flame is the source of connection for
all elements. Whether gathering from the furnace or reheating for a second in
the glory hole, I am drawn to the intensity of light. Captivated by its radiance,
I cannot look for long without being reminded how insignificant I am next to
the raging power of 1900 degrees. Like gazing deeply into the darkness of my
imperfect existence, I bask in silence as the awkward thin space envelopes me.
My chest tightens. My senses heighten. My eyes know their proximity to power
and demise, for all I can do is blink or look away.*

Creation brought elation. I felt electricity rushing through my veins like
never before. I could almost count the electrons lining up in a neural
path from my head to my heart as I spent time with Elzbieta, Professor
Fusee my physics professor, or Father Ben. As the conductors on my new
journey, Professor Fusee made the world ordered and beautiful, and Father
Ben encouraged me. "Your soul and your passions are so deep, Jenna. Have
you ever thought of being a nun?" I covered my gasp, knowing he meant it
as the ultimate compliment. But I didn't wish to become one. I did fantasize
about majoring in religion, though. I had a decision to make and it was not
an easy one.

Whenever in the lab, I was sure I was to be a scientist. Filled with
endless questions, and hypotheses for new experiments, I considered and

calculated into exhaustion. I was energized by how the equations balanced and were precise instead of nebulous. Until, of course, I couldn't get them to balance, and then I dreamed of stomping my books and lab equipment into oblivion.

In the studio, I prepared to be an artist, driven by deep questions from Elzbieta. "How do you perceive the fire? Are you afraid of it, inspired by it, or equal to it? Jenna, listen carefully. How you see the fire determines everything else. It determines how you will interact with everything around you." *How did I view the fire?*

I pondered that question for months. I was flabbergasted that she would not tell me the right answer, or how she viewed the fire, but made me wrestle with it on my own. *How did I see the fire? Why did that determine everything?*

I was very afraid of the fire, but my fear was more of awe, a curiosity as to its depth, and power. Pure power. It was intriguing. Fear and power. Power and fear, and perhaps a little bit of awe thrown into the mix-that's the best I could do for an answer. What did that say about me? What did that say about how I dealt with everything around me. If something was powerful, weren't you supposed to fear it, and be in awe of it? I didn't get it. Was I supposed to be equal to it? Overpower it? Use it? Conquer it?

It infuriated me that she wouldn't answer me. She just came at me with more questions: "At what point does the fire move from being beneficial to detrimental? How can you be sure it won't destroy your pieces? How do you know when you're close enough, or too close?" I was answering about the fire, but it became more and more obvious she was speaking of something else, something profounder than I was able to understand.

She was leading me on a journey. The more I integrated my studio life with my street life, the more it brought renewal. Before I walked into Basin Street, I adjusted my energy, and saw myself as that molten blob, in the thin space, awaiting the nudge or stretch from the gaffer. Hence, my times were spent focused on enjoying and getting to know the children even more. We talked about anything and everything, even Tamira and Crystal and the impact they still had on us.

I took out a student subscription to the New Orleans Symphony-buying season passes for two. I started inviting kids, and fellow volunteers with me. Music took up space again in my heart. As I listened, I was intent on determining how the composer could envision all the parts coming together. Like the gaffer with canes for murrini: how did he figure what note the cello would play to affect the mood he wanted? And if he decided on another note, and ran down that rabbit hole but didn't like how it played out, did he just try a new one? How did he know which notes were rabbit holes and which were inspired? How can anyone know? Life is full of rabbit holes-scary, dark rabbit holes.

All I knew was that music renewed me. And so did prayer. Instead of the long lists of things I used to hold before God in prayer, I started to focus on the things I learned in pre-school: sorry, please, and thank you. Sorry, please, and thank you-so simple, and yet so profound. All of the unwanted junk in my life started to fall away: fear, doubt, hate, and self-loathing.

I didn't really have time to think about any of them because I was too busy looking forward and becoming curious again. I began to wonder about Ari and how he was taking me not talking to him and basically wiping him out of my life forever. I began to have a need to explain to him. But what could I say? For months, I just claimed to be too busy with school and work. And that was somewhat true, but how could I explain what was really going on?

What could one do with a lifetime of hatred? Like an onionskin, I knew it would have to be peeled back, layer by layer before I could expel it completely from my life. Was it a rabbit trail or the real deal? Did I really have the energy right now to unpeel it? Did I really have to deal with that now that I was trying to figure out what to do with my life? Or was that why I was having such difficulty choosing a career path?

How was I to know which career path was a rabbit trail, and which was my destiny? I began again to listen for God in Augustine's stillness of the heart. Being still was the hardest task I had ever encountered. It was and is the real work of life. I could move and dance and study and analyze, blow glass and teach and philosophize about my struggles, and even dream. But the harshest path was to sit still and empty my mind. Blaise Pascal knew what he was talking about when in his work *Pensees*, he said, "All of humanity's problems stem from man's inability to sit quietly alone in a room."

Working glass helped because I could imagine the furnace. The fire was so blinding that it wiped out all thoughts of anything else. I concentrated on that overpowering light.

If my mind meandered to the 1000s of directions it wanted to go, welcoming the hyenas and their friends to the brainy feast, I always resorted to Psalms 46, spending time with each sentence and deciphering what each meant. "Be still, and know that I am God. Be still, and know that I am. Be still, and know that I... Be still, and know that... Be still, and know... Be still, and... Be still... Be."

By the time I got to "be," I truly was a human being instead of a human doing. I was not plotting or planning or figuring or analyzing. I was *being*. Just like the glass in the furnace, I was hanging out until the gaffer took what she needed and shaped it into the dream dancing in her head, working it into something useful or beautiful. I was still, ever so still, waiting on the master, and fully content with where and who I was.

⸺ ◈ ⸺

Winter in New Orleans meant that one day it dipped below 40 degrees, and the winds moved in. The leaves fell off the trees without warning. There was never color change: no fall, and no transition at all. The only distinguishing feature was that the humidity and temperature drop a bit in the mornings and evenings. Hence, the studio could be open during the day. This made it a little less intense. I would attend school in the mornings and then hang out at the studio on my days off from work.

Elzbieta's mood and energy level changed depending on whether she was at the torch station or the furnace, or whether interacting with the other blowers. One day, I came in to a silent studio. The roar of the furnace was so noticeably absent it was eerie. No other blowers were there either. I walked over to her at the torch station and asked, "Where is everyone?"

"I need a break from the furnace for a while so I gave everyone a few days off."

"Do you want me to take a few days off too?"

Her eyes sparkled as she took out the most beautiful indigo, red, and turquoise cane. The colors were so spellbinding I was hoping she didn't want me to leave.

"No, you're fine, I just need a little peace. These are for our millefiori. It's been too busy to make any cane lately, but I need to work the torch for my sanity. I'm exhausted these days for some reason." Recently, I had noticed that she needed more help lifting the heavy pieces. She was taking more breaks, and retreating to her office a little more than usual, but I hadn't said anything.

"Is everything alright?"

"Everything's fine. I just need a little less intensity, a little variety. Sometimes I feel that if I keep working so close to the fire I'll get overcome by it, or worse: start to forget its power. So I work a little cooler at times, just to slow things down a bit." Blowing glass with a torch (also known as a lamp) was not only Elzbieta's preference but also what distinguished her work from her grandfather's.

So, at the torch station, with the pieces of murrini we had cut last week laying all over the table, she was creating paperweights, pendants, and ornaments. Placing some of the murrini into small metal rings about the size of an orange, she used tweezers and positioned each one with the intensity of a jewel crafter with a big lens attached to her head. Although she graciously explained her method, twisting, turning, and attaching with the torch, I was a mere spectator. Her creative arrangement required too much precision for a novice. I moved the metal plates holding the paperweights to the back of the table once she had finished.

I knew for sure I wouldn't be able to achieve that level of attentiveness, so I was relieved when she had little expectations of me. But after hours of admiring her work, I was excited when she let me use her leftover murrini pieces in my own design. Of course, mine was a hodgepodge, like a dinner of leftovers. I tried to make the pattern as consistent as possible with the remnants I had, but it still looked liked leftovers. I inundated her with questions at lunch.

"How do you know which cane colors will work together?"

"You don't, until you get them next to each other. Some work, some don't. Some clash, some accentuate. Some blend in color but don't fit in shape or size. It really runs the gamut."

My musings leaked from my mouth. "I wonder if that's how God feels about us? Does God ever know until we are put side by side, clashing, accentuating, or complementing, how we'll fit together in God's masterpiece?"

She poked her tweezers at me with a smile, "Or does God just play around, moving us here and there until we take hold of each other?"

I plucked my fingers like tweezers right back at her, and said, "Perhaps that's how God plays. Like putting together a puzzle. I love puzzles."

"Me too."

"When you are making the canes, do you envision which ones will go together?"

"Sometimes. Other times I try to stick with the color wheel or I just go with my inspiration. The color wheel works, like a guidebook. I think it may be laid out according to the wavelengths of light or something like that you nerdy scientist types understand. But, the closer I adhere to the wheel, the greater percentage I have of success."

After lunch we continued at the torch station. It was so much different than the furnaces. The furnaces require physical strength and teamwork for the useful pieces. The torch station was all about finesse and precision. Gathering just the right sized tubes of glass for the size of ring, I watched as she heated the glass and eased it over the murrini. With some she blew a bubble and then rolled the murrini into the ornament, which adhered like tiles in a mosaic. Unlike the furnace (where you had to trust that the colors would emerge more vividly with time because the blob's heat prevented you from seeing as you went) with torch work, you saw the color instantly. The blob was never too hot to see the colors emerging.

The millefiori were beautiful from beginning to end. Encasing them in a cage of clear glass only intensified their color. She gave me an orange crayon to put my initials on my pieces so I'd know for sure which ones were mine, as if I'd forget. I loved how you didn't have to put all the torched pieces in the annealer. Since they weren't worked at high temperatures, they could cool to room temperature without cracking. What a different process lamp-working was.

"So you layer color on the cylinders, stretch them into canes, cut them into hundreds of pieces, arrange them into metal rings, or onto a glass bubble, place glass on top to accentuate and encase them. Let's say, after all that, the colors don't work. They clash, or they're too weighty. Isn't it a lot of wasted time? Seems like a lot of work for such a gamble of art."

She chuckled, and I saw a euphoric sparkle in her eyes, a reflection of something so deep and wide that I was mesmerized. So enraptured by the passion exuding from her eyes, I hungered for the same. "Yeah, you say that because you haven't produced your first piece of millefiori yet. Just wait, Jenna, and you tell me. You tell me if it's worth it."

<hr>

I tried to capture that spark, that flame of fervor I saw in Elzbieta's eyes. I decided I needed a break from the intensity of the furnace and my street life too. Taking a blanket, my journal, and lots of pens, I hung out under my favorite tree in City Park to write and gain clarity on the many decisions weighing heavily on my mind, namely my career path and Ari's gift of a yacht adventure. Elzbieta's question of worth intrigued me, so I decided to take Pastor Dan's advice and pull out some feelings, analyze them, and see where they led me.

After my eye-opening plantation experience, with Ari, I had to figure out what bothered me so much about him and his offer. He was responsible for my eyes being opened to my own hatred. Recently, he had come to the restaurant to tell me that he and the girls were back on track. They were asking if there friends could have sleepovers there as well, which he took as a sign that he was "making it" as a dad. I was happy for him, but not with him, because he still hounded me about the trip.

How could I pass up a trip to anywhere in the world I wanted to go? I earned it didn't I, by working a restaurant job while completing my college degree? Why wouldn't I go? Other than the fact that a man was asking me, it sounded like a dream vacation. I remembered going to my mom with my doubts and fears, and her response was quizzical.

"Isn't he the guy that is filthy rich?" She was obviously very enamored with his charisma and his money. "Think of all the possibilities it could bring for the future."

"Mom...I don't have any feelings for him at all, and I don't want to encourage any either. And I especially don't want to feel beholden to him for a trip." She looked confused and even shaken (a look, I don't think I'd ever seen from her).

Her hand scratched and then rubbed her forehead as she replied, "Jenna, a butterfly can just as easily land on a diamond as a turd."

Diamonds and turds. What kind of wisdom was that? Was she hoping that I would go on the trip, fall in love with him, and then she wouldn't have to worry about me anymore? Was she thinking about her future instead, traveling with me around the world on that yacht? Stop it. Why are you so cynical? My pen answered for me in my journal:

A diamond or a turd, are those my only options? What about a piece of pizza, or a muffin? Can't a butterfly land on those, too?

Once again, I feel boxed in by someone else's "either/or" categories. But I am at least, beginning to recognize how I balk, resist, and defy, anything that tries to cage me in. Can there be anything worse than being on a boat in the middle of the ocean with a man and no way to escape?

Is that what is freaking me out? Or is it being with him? Going on a plane somewhere does not worry me as much, so I better go with that. Work that angle. Why is there no problem there? I could get away, could see new things, and would have companionship. Perhaps that is all he wants too, to share in his great wealth and enjoyment of what life has to offer. What is so bad about that?

I still get sick to my stomach thinking about it. If a woman would ask me, I wouldn't hesitate for a moment, but a man, who could trust a man? Diamonds or turds? How does one decide?

The more Ari pressures me, "Come on Jenna, how can you turn it down? You deserve it with all you've done to help me. It's just my way of saying thanks," the more rigid I become. I can feel my exterior hardening like glass on the marver. I try to focus on the adventures just to entertain the thought, as my mom instructed, but all I can see are the shards of glass lying in pieces on the floor. I may live to regret letting such an opportunity slip through my fingers, but at least I'll still be standing, still be sane, and not a female pate' splayed on some wall like Tamira.

If I take the best and the worst scenarios, examine the fears and unravel them and their power over me, the worst extreme is that he would try something. I'd go ballistic in some remote place and be stuck without a way home or a friend on that side of the world. The best extreme is that I would fall in love with Ari, and be stuck with a man who already had a life, already had a family, already had a dream and the means to procure it, and I would be his ornament. I would be a beautiful ornament, a pampered and well-fed ornament, but an ornament just the same.

Like starting with glass tubes and torch-working rather that gathering the glass from the fire, it is still glassblowing. The pieces are still beautiful, but it is like starting in the middle of the process, and playing it safe. And for some, that might work. But for me, the chemistry is the captivating part.

Building everything from scratch, its mystery, mystique, and yes, possibly even failure while working on a masterpiece together is what the art of fire and life is all about. And I am no longer scared of the fire, or scared of getting burned; I am more scared of living without the flame. With no chemistry, no dance, and no risk, there is no intrigue. And that applies to my education too. I am beginning to see science as starting in the middle of the process. If I really wanted to create a masterpiece, perhaps I need to begin at the real beginning of it all and study God. Stay close to the flame! I can always read science on the side for fun.

Chapter 36
Centering

The most important thing to do as the blob leaves the furnace is to center the mass over the pipe. Centering the mass should be done quickly before the heat of the new glass penetrates the core and softens it to the point of weakening. [30]

Someone must have believed that New Orleans, the Big Easy, chocked full of every type of sin imaginable, needed a double dose of seminaries to train its priests and ministers. The most notable was the majestic Notre Dame Catholic Seminary, a red brick gothic masterpiece in the heart of the city. But tucked away on the East side, under the Greater New Orleans Bridge was the more diminutive Conservative Theological Seminary (CTS). The more I was urged by Father Ben to be a nun and Augustine to "take and read," the more I was intrigued. I loved the warm furry comfort I found in prayer, once I had stepped up to the plate and called it prayer. And seminary seemed to blend most of my graduate school longings: psychology, religion, and education. Since I was neither Catholic nor male, my seminary option was CTS.

Starting seminary was exhilarating. With hopes of being the next Mother Theresa (except in Africa) my first course, Missions, was welcomed. But coming from the rigor of Loyola, with its intensely trained Jesuits, I couldn't believe the low level of academics that was pawned off as graduate school. One professor even gave the answers to the test the day before. On the most well attended day of each week, he literally put 1A 2C 3E on the board.

Although I went to my Theology class with an open mind, I was horrified to find more of the same: true false theology tests and people that were afraid to think out of the box. *Is this a seminary?* There was only one class that could be anywhere near be called a college, much less a graduate course, and that was Ethics.

The people in seminary were so uptight. All the men were clean-cut, short haired, no beards or mustaches. They all wore dark pants, white shirts, with briefcases in one hand and usually an umbrella in the other. The women were overweight with skirts, hose, and blouses buttoned up to their chins (some even with little ribbons tied at their necks).

I figured that fitting in was not going to be an option with my sweaters and jeans, but what else was new? Quickly, I was becoming disillusioned with the academic choice I'd made.

I'd embraced Augustine's belief, "absolute abstinence is easier than perfect moderation," so I'd given up the encumbrance of thinking about men or women sexually for life (a small sacrifice, I thought, for a life of service to God). Hence the focus of all of my passions had gone into food. My menu suggestions at Malcomb's were getting rave reviews, and my creativity was heightened.

Since food was such an excellent substitute for thinking about sex, I was gravely disappointed with the selections in the seminary cafeteria. The line consisted of a heart attack waiting to happen: fried chicken and fish, mashed potatoes, macaroni and cheese, pinto beans, and green beans covered in bacon. The only thing that resembled a salad was green jello with fruit cocktail in it. Growing up in the South, I should have been comforted, but New Orleans food was not really Southern cooking. *Where are the red beans, the dirty rice, the stuffed mirlitons, and stewed okra?*

The lack of imagination and flavor was evident everywhere I looked at CTS. And if I needed substantiation of the effects of the cafeteria menu, I just needed to look at the hefty bodies on every graduate school chair. I made a quick note to self to bring my lunch from then on.

After paying for a Diet Coke, I sat at a far table by the door. Perusing my ethics syllabi, I looked up to find a bearded man with a beautiful smile coming near me. *A bearded man at seminary? That's odd. What's he hiding?*

"Did you get a syllabus for that ethics course?"

"That's what I'm reading now," I replied.

"I was thinking of taking that course, so I sat in on it today. Quite frankly, the rest of my classes are pretty uninspiring, so I thought ethics might be a bit more stimulating." *Is he reading my mind?* I showed him the syllabus, and immediately we started talking from the heart: low level academia, ethics, horse racing, drinking, travel, and my experience growing up in NOLA. *Who is this man?*

The only clue was that he was wearing a wedding ring. Great. He was safe. We talked for about ½ hour and he left me with the same mantra I had been hearing since I was a teenager: "All the good ones are either gay or married."

He peaked my interest though. At least there was one other person there I could relate to amidst the sea of bulges, briefcases, and barely thinking graduate students. *I will definitely look for him again for another good conversation.* I was always up for a good conversation.

Bouncing into the cafeteria the next day, he wore a tee shirt, overalls, a backpack, and toted a coffee thermos. Obviously, he did not get the dress code either. Intrigued by his non-conformity, I asked and found out his name was Matt Malon. We talked briefly about the oddities of the seminary, and when he turned to go, I noticed the wedding ring was on the other hand.

Later that week, I saw Matt in ethics class (I guess he decided to take it after all) and was astounded to find him challenging the professor. Some would say that he was just questioning him, but I thought it pretty bold since I had seen little compelling discourse in my first week of seminary. Unlike Loyola, the CTS students rarely questioned anything and seemed to file in line with the professors like sheep to be sheared.

After class, I watched the professor move toward him with a smile, so I hustled for a place in their conversation. They were speaking about my favorite subject, Augustinian ethics, so at one point I couldn't help but interject. "If we prescribe to Augustine's extreme intentional ethics, then if you think about doing anything sinful, you should just go ahead and do it because just the thought of it is already sinning. Right?" I asked it with a full smile since I loved every minute I studied the African saint. Matt grinned as he replied, "I guess that depends on whether you really want to do it or just think about it?" We all laughed.

My professor rightfully corrected me, "That's one interpretation, but I think Augustine is directing us to an intense self-examination of our thoughts and motives. He goes straight to the heart of the issue when he compels us to clean out our thoughts in order to be truly pure down to the core. What better way is there to center us to God? Where your thoughts begin, sin enters in." *I think I'm going to like this class after all.*

Chapter 37
Without Title

Fire and smoke pour out in great quantity as molten glass melds and burns into wooden forms. The heat is almost unbearable. As this modern replay of a prehistoric ritual unfolds, you feel that a mystery is being celebrated with each herculean effort made by the glass artist. [31]

After class, I saw Matt get on a motorcycle and ride away. *Is this guy for real? He rides a motorcycle!* I was sure there was some conservative rule amidst the "I don't dance, and I don't chew, and I don't go with girls who do," somewhere among the long list of things you must avoid like smoking, gambling, drinking, and having fun that said you couldn't ride a motorcycle either.

Sitting together in the cafeteria the next day over fruit, nuts, and great cheeses my mother brought back from a work trip to Amsterdam, I asked about his bike. "It's actually what made me come to New Orleans. As the son of a preacher, I've had enough of religion, but I got a scholarship to the seminary and New Orleans has great weather for my motorcycle."

I couldn't fully take in his words because while he was talking I noticed the absence of the wedding ring. Mustering up my nerve I asked, "Are you down here with your wife?" He choked on his coffee with the question. "What makes you think I have a wife?"

"When I met you, you had a wedding ring on. Now you don't. What's up?"

I was confounded with his response, "It's my girlfriend's grandfather's ring. I just wear it because I like it." It was by far the lamest excuse I'd ever heard. I doubted his intentions and figured he was married, until later we met up with his dorm roommate on campus who confirmed he was single.

He's still safe. He has a girlfriend. Or he could be lying through his teeth. Somehow my thoughts went toward him, more and more. *Is he serious with his girlfriend? Why is he in seminary if he's sick of religion? Can I believe a word he says? Red flag, red flag. Stay away!*

I never sought out Matt but he always found a way to serendipitously bump into me on campus. Sometimes Matt would even find me as I got out of my car, and we began talking and walking to class together. Soon the seminary hosted an art show featuring prints from all styles: classical, impressionist, and modern etc. Sauntering through, we shared our thoughts and criticisms about each one.

"I get bored if the picture looks too perfect, too much like what it is trying to show. For me, there must be something supporting, or penetrating it, some mood or color that is trying to escape," I offered.

"My favorites are the impressionists. Look at this; see how Monet brings out the colors on the beach. Or Van Gogh's indigo sky tries to tame the stars."

Matt saw effects and themes that I didn't see. And his connections fascinated me, giving me a secret tunnel into the inner recesses of his mind. It was if he could delve right into the artist's complexity and bring it out for me to understand. "Van Gogh's stars have a passion that can't be contained by the indigo sky," I asserted. "It overrides everything. It's so hopeful. If only Vincent could've transferred some of that hope into his own life. Look how disheartened he looks in his self-portrait." *Now, there's a look I can understand.*

Purchasing Kandinsky's *Without Title* print, I asked about the name. "How can you create something so beautiful and give it no name?"

"Perhaps he cranked them out so fast, he didn't have time to name it," Matt conjectured.

"Really? How can you labor over it, work its angles, and design the colors, pour your life and soul into it and then give it no name?" The print deeply captured the violent maelstrom that was churning through the grey matter in my brain. The peaceful colors and hopeful forms were paralleled with the ugly, sharp fragments that kept rupturing through the veil of my reality. I could understand everything about *Without Title*, except the name.

Hope was trying to win the battle within me, but the fragments that ruptured through were the grunts, the "you know you wanted it" lines, and the rat-chewed baby bottles. Those were what floated to the top of my thoughts. No matter how much I begged the hyenas of doubt and loathing that ate away at my brain to stop, their insatiable hunger had a mind of its own.

Most of my thoughts were painful emotions splattered spin art style on the walls of my brain, but some, like Van Gogh's luminous stars, were rich with optimism, their intense light piercing the darkness. Before I knew it

I'd find myself imagining deep theological conversations, a picnic blanket in the sun, and belly laughs.

When it was time for our first ethics test, Matt suggested we study together during lunch. Scouting out an empty classroom nearby, I tried to muster up the courage to ask him about his girlfriend. Eating my packed lunch of crab and artichoke quiche, I offered him some. He opened up with each bite. "We are having difficulty at the moment. Linda's a third-year law student with very little spare time. I really loved her in college. She was the laissez-faire free-spirit, but now, things are really different. She goes to bed every night before nine, and I'm in seminary, trying to work through some heavy issues of life and faith. I need a little more from her than she can give right now. And she needs me to be more understanding about the rigor of law school. We'll have a natural separation though, next week. Her studies are taking her to France for the summer. Neither of us have much hope of it lasting through our separation, but neither of us wants to be the one to end it. It's weird."

With no experience in a long-term relationship, I didn't have much to add, so I just listened. I admired the way he spoke of her with such reverence and respect even though I could tell he had conflicting feelings.

The ethics test was comprised of everything we had learned. And it was full of Augustinian applications. I was challenged and confident. We compared notes after class. "I know we aced that test. Teamwork, that's what it's all about. So do you want to get together on Saturday morning to celebrate?" Matt asked. "I'll have a little more time on my hands once Linda leaves."

My stomach started to churn a bit at his offer. Like a deer in headlights all I could say was, "It does seem like we studied all the right things for our ethics test." I surveyed the area for an exit route but couldn't find one. And the thought of running actually unnerved me. My lips answered before my brain could think it through. "I guess we could. I don't have to work until 5:30 that night. We can meet at the Pavilion at City Park and walk through it. It's right by my house."

By Saturday, I wanted to cancel but didn't have Matt's number. I had been up most of the night in a Charity hospital waiting room with my mom. One of her close friends, who had come out of the closet to his parents the week before, had tried to commit suicide because his parents (not taking the news very well) told him, "As far as we are concerned, if you are gay, you are dead to us." I remember seeing his usual jovial face sunken and drawn, and his skin almost grey. The giant bandage on his forearm was a visible reminder of his darkest night. He didn't look up the entire visit, but down at the floor like he was studying cobwebs. We used to kid him about how his low-pitched laugh could warm even the coldest of rooms, but there was no warmth or smiles in that ward, just row after row of forlorn faces staring blankly, or diminutively at the floor.

Matt was at the Pavilion as I came straight from the hospital. I was still a bit shaken, but we decided to continue our plans and walk through the park. City Park was a thriving artistic creation right in the middle of New Orleans. The reddish brown trunks of the live oaks split in humanlike form. The weeping garlands of Spanish moss that bearded the majestic trees swayed in the wind and whispered the eerie secrets of the city, which relaxed me in the secret places of my heart.

I told him about Chuck and his family disinheriting him with disdain because of his homosexuality. Livid that anyone's narrow-mindedness and lack of grace would almost kill a friend of mine, I forgot that Matt was a preacher's son. I ranted and raved for nearly an hour when Matt very sympathetically said, "How can parents not love their own son or daughter just because he or she is gay?" *Was he for real?*

Perhaps it was the bayou that meandered through the park, pooling in the shadows of palmetto bushes that invited tales of the untold. *There are a lot of skeletons in my closet. How much do I tell? Do I really want to end this by telling him anything?* The musty smell of water-soaked-logs lingered on the nostrils, causing me to stride near the murky muck of my soul, where the pirates and voodoo queens lie. A faint metallic ding chimed through the distance, drawing us, like sirens, to the arched stone bridge.

From the bridge, we saw the vendor at the pavilion selling hot dogs and French fries and we ordered lunch. The chime pa-pinged again. I looked toward the bridge to see the shimmering water and the source of the peculiar peal: it was the ring of a stringed bell dangling from the front of a boat pulsing to the ripples in the water. Tiny boats were rented for passengers to glide through the lagoon, and as another floated by, it sent the bell on a new rapid cadence: pa-pa-ping, pa-pa-ping.

My heart raced to keep up with my feet as I ran below the bridge to find the rental booth. My hands juggled the food to search for the required fare from my pocket. The coins jingled but not enough for a tiny vessel. Matt was there, with the rest of the money pointing toward the paddleboats.

As we climbed on the tiny craft, and positioned our hot dogs and drinks, I rolled up my sleeves to provide some relief from the scorching sun. Away from the crowds and into the back ravines, we talked honestly about our families.

"My mom and dad are still so much in love that sometimes when she is in the middle of washing dishes, she just blurts out, 'Oh Charles, I love you,'" he stated with a dreamy stare.

"My parents have just the opposite relationship," I compared, tossing a piece of bread to the swans swimming nearby. "I remember one night walking into the kitchen and seeing them screaming at each other, 'Why have a dishwasher if you feel the need to wash each damn dish off before you put it in? I forbid you to waste our water anymore!'

"My mother replied, 'I don't care what you forbid me to do; I am going to follow the directions in the manual!' she yelled defiantly. With that, he slammed a plate against the wall shattering it, and then another. Mom quickly corralled my sister and me. We escaped from the house and his plate-throwing tantrum. They got a divorce pretty soon after that. He never hit us, but I guess it was too close for my mother's comfort. Actually, my sister and I were somewhat relieved when they said they were getting a divorce. The constant fighting was intense."

As the swans followed our paddleboat around the lagoon, I couldn't help but think of the gondolas of Venice. We were lured down the canal by the sweet spicy fragrance of the magnolia tree at the edge of the lawn, sagging with hundreds of glossy green leaves. The closest thing to snow New Orleans ever saw was the ground littered with the enormous white magnolia petals that fell as the flora faded.

Oaks, elms, magnolias, and cedars were the signature of City Park, caressing and embracing its children's curiosity and sense of adventure. I was high on a sense of adventure by that point, and with the white snow-like petals on the ground reminding me of the comforting fur of a dog, I recited a few of my poems. Some were deep and dark, about bones locked in closets, and death with great strong arms of light. But I ended with the one that I had penned the day before in one of my boring classes.

Butterfly

The most perfect smile
Illuminates a radiance of gaiety and song
Warming my untouched heart

Taking me by surprise
I laugh again like a child in spring
Chasing butterflies and life with a renaissance spirit
He flies with a form of his own
With wings painted by God
A classic creation
I run wildly after
Lost in time
Longing just to touch him if I can
He flies higher and higher
Round and round
In my dizziness I smile and fall
I cry
Surely he has left me
To dance in the wind with the leaves and trees
For I cannot fly
His soft kiss opens my eyes
To a rainbow sitting on my nose
Face to face we meet
Yet I am afraid
For his tiny eyes
Hold a world of knowledge
That I do not know
We spoke without words
Touched without reaching
And loved without knowing
In that moment without time
And as quickly as he came
He left
Once again to frolic in the blue
And I after him
More feverishly than before
My heart pounding
Skin tingling
Running to be with him
But not catching
So as not to make our time
Any shorter than it has to be

At the end of poem, on that floating picnic blanket in the sun, it happened. Matt leaned in, bringing those sparkling eyes and beautiful smile next to mine, and said, "I'd love to kiss you now, if that's okay." I didn't back away. I moved in, on the edge of adventure, knowing full well that everything could crack, splinter, or shatter right then and there before my eyes. But it didn't. A stillness lingered as his lips touched mine. It was the most amazing soft, slow, velvety, tingly kiss of my life!

When the kiss was over, I literally saw fireworks. *Are those spiders creeping in or is my skin tingling?* My body did a shakeout like a dog after a bath. The kiss was so mind-blowing that every inch of my body was singing its praises, just like I had once imagined it would be after a kiss. *How can this be? I'm not gagging, or hurling. When can we do that again?*

Chapter 38
Defiant Durability

Few materials move the craftsman as deeply as hot glass. Molten glass glows with inner light. It's hypnotic and seductive to watch and it demands of the blower a conduct so precise, so in tune with the material's nature, that any slip can invariably result in failure. [32]

I cannot help but resonate with the glass at the end of the pipe, seemingly helpless when paired with the fire. Nothing compares to the roar of the furnace. But the glowing growing orb, the molten orange blob that clings to the pipe like a halo is a force to be reckoned with; therein lays the promise and the pain of passion.

Its defiant durability pushes back at you from the marvering table as if to say, "Notice me. I am not like the others." For each bit of color added, adjustments have to be made. The wily darks hold the heat more, so you don't have to work as fast. But you never forget that every second you teeter the edge of destruction and creation.

And just when you get the hang of working with one color, you add a lighter one, and the chemicals and coefficents are so different that you have to compensate, and bear harder on the marver, or turn the pipe more quickly to keep the piece balanced. Otherwise, it flops, or cracks, and the shard pile increases.

Chapter 39
Error Correction

You may want to view the entire process of glassblowing as continuous error correction. From moment to moment, you must constantly re-balance and repair the piece of glass in your care. Learn to fix what is wrong, and what's right will take care of itself. [33]

After the paddleboats, Matt and I spent every waking minute together. It was uncanny how similar our interests were. We both loved to read. Poetry was a particular favorite, so many evenings we recited to each other from anthologies. I was fascinated with American works such as Emily Dickinson's "Dear March-Come In" and Robert Frost's "The Road Not Taken," and he of the British such as Gerard Manley Hopkins' "Pied Beauty."

It was all too congruous to believe, so of course the hyenas of doubt and fear eating away at my brain were ravenous. *You know this is not going to work. He wants something. Remember how much men mess you up. Remember Tamira. Remember Roy.*

I'd see or hear something that started my memories, and my body would clench with anger, thinking of Tamira and the horrors of men. Then I'd hear Matt's laugh, or envision how his eyes squinted and sparkled so radiantly when he smiled and something inside would melt. My body and breathing would resume to normal and all would be fine. *Was I manic-depressive? Naïve? Optimistic?*

We both delighted in cooking and eating, so I made him barbequed shrimp-a New Orleans favorite that has nothing to do with barbeque sauce and everything to do with shrimp, butter, garlic and loads of black pepper, basil, parsley, red pepper, and a few other secrets. It was probably the night he fell in love with me.

Growing up in NOLA, I put shrimp in the category that most people put the common egg. The question was not IF you were going to have shrimp that week but HOW you were you going to have shrimp that week. So I ate a scant amount and then sat back and watched him relish it. He couldn't get enough, sopping French bread into the buttery mix.

But it was excruciating to watch non-New Orleanians eat crustaceans. Interminable. How could shrimp take forever when it required two pulls? You peel off the section nearest where the head once was, and then you pinch the tail. One, two. It comes off in two pieces. But he was taking it apart millimeter by millimeter. I could bear it no longer, so I started peeling his shrimp for him. His eyes bobbled more in ecstasy with each bite, and I literally had him eating out of my hand by the end of the night.

The first time we ever fought was when I came home from a beer run with Bud Light in hand. When I lifted it from the crisp brown bag, his vibrant smile drooped to the ground. "I thought I told you Budweiser."

"You did, but I thought Bud Light would be better."

"Are you telling me I need light beer?" His body tightened and tension built in the air, making it hard to breathe.

"You don't want to get fat do you? You drink a lot of beer."

"Are you telling me what I need?"

"Yeah," I said with full assurance. "With as much as you drink, you'll have a beer belly like your friend, Kevin, if you don't watch it."

"I think I can determine what I need and what I don't," he replied curtly.

"The heart is deceitful, above all things and beyond cure. Who can understand it?" I added with my most charming smile.

"Now you're telling me I have a deceitful heart?"

"Just quoting scripture: Jeremiah 17:9." My energy sagged as I saw his response.

He looked straight through me, like he was reading something on the wall behind me. The silence between us was chilling. Our heavy breaths were not in sync. Then, like a car sputting in a stubborn attempt to start, he chuckled. "You...are...unbelievable, Jenna. Unbelievable!" His voice was loud and terse, as he swung his head from side to side.

"I know. You keep telling me that," I said as I kissed him and gave him change from his ten dollar bill. He continued shaking his head in disbelief. "How about...you don't ever get me a light beer again, okay?"

I gurgled back without a reply, but exhaled with ease one he smiled. *That was a close one.*

The closer we became, the more I was plagued with fear that once he knew about my struggles with sex and sexuality, our relationship would be over. So I shared tiny bits at strategic times. If he took the bait and responded in the gentle and affirming manner I was accustomed to from him, then I would give more. I started with Roy. As I inched out my story, I saw tears form in his eyes.

"And you still have such a deep faith, and love for the church?" he asked. "Most people would have rejected the church after that."

"I know. It's weird. That's what the psychologist said too. But I always felt at home at church. There were people there that were trying to figure things out, deep things, like why we were created, and what difference one person can make in life. My family didn't really care about those things. Nor did anyone I knew at school. But at church we talked about those things all the time, and they treated us like adults. At home, I was treated like a kid, a weird kid because I had so many questions. But at church they loved my inquisitive nature."

"I love your inquisitive nature too," he said as he snuggled his face in my neck.

I recoiled in ticklish laughter. *You know he's just saying those things. You are damaged, and no one wants damaged goods. You'll never want him either. Once he gets too close, you'll start gagging and hyperventilating. Why don't you just stop this charade?*

Our motorcycle rides whelmed the hyenas. Weaving in and out of little streets, with our bodies shifting and turning, I pondered the centrifugal force and theorized about the decibels in the rumble underneath my legs. When we'd soar through the interstate, the wind blasting hair and clothes, natural air conditioning on an otherwise sweltering day, all my calculations and concerns were blown to smithereens with the excitement.

Matt loved my stories of Grandma Gertrude and the Basin St. children. I kept thinking I would bring him to meet her and the kids, but then life got really complicated with school, work and the glass studio. Trying to balance it all was just too overwhelming. When I started snipping at the kids, I knew I had too much on my plate so I dropped down to only one or two days per month. But every time I was with Matt I could hear Grandma Gertrude's words ringing in my heart, "Let your hopes, not your pain, shape your future." I was letting hope creep into my soul and that always ended badly. But somewhere I felt that if I could try just one last time, maybe...

Part of the reason Matt and I got along so well was because he really didn't pressure me about sex. He was very romantic; full of cuddles and kisses that left us breathless. But then he'd pause, look up, and leave me wanting more. One night, after a few months of dating, things were heating up, and I felt a new intensity in his kisses and movements.

I ran my fingers through his hairy chest and felt a heat run through his body I had never felt before. His hands were not just caressing but with a seeming destination. The kisses were more frenetic instead of in discovery. When it started to go to another level, I clammed up, just exactly as I always had before. Rigid and stiff, fearful and frantic, the hyenas were salivating.

Hah! Here we are again. I told you it would happen.

But he sensed my discomfort. I didn't even have a second to respond to their taunts, before he said, "I can see you are getting uneasy, so let's just slow it down." I had never heard anything like that before from a male. Usually, the comments were, "What is your problem? Don't you dare throw up on me."

Instead, Matt inched to the other side of the room. As I sat in the opposite corner watching that gorgeous smile, those concerned eyes and that thick mane of curly hair, I felt my heart melt into complete and utter love for the man that put my needs and wants ahead of his own. I never imagined a man like that existed.

Matt left that night, with the same soft embrace I had known before. His satiny kiss lingered long after he was gone. But when it faded, the walls started closing in around me. Something inside me burned, not a stomach churning burn, but an inside burn that I couldn't figure out. It was fecund soil for a harvest of despair. So I put on my running shoes and took off.

See, it happened again. You went crazy when it started heating up. You are sick. When are you going to get it through your thick head? It will never be right with a man.

Stop it. It is real. He stopped. He noticed how I was feeling.

Hah! You know this is not real. He probably remembered that you are damaged goods from Roy. You are one sick puppy.

The battle raged with each step on the street, but the more energy I expended, the stronger I felt.

I am not sick. And he is different, really, really, different. He's pure and right and noble. And I'm tired of listening to you anyway.

You have to listen to me. I've been with you through it all. Use your brain. He's a man, and you know the horrors that will bring. You don't know what he's really like. He could be doing things on the side to kids just like Roy!

My shins ached, and I struggled to catch my breath. The streetlamps lit an endless path so I scanned for a pattern to help me through it. Inhale 2,3,4, exhale 6,7,8.

I don't have to listen to you just because you've been with me through it all. You're part of the problem. I've been listening to you too much.

The swing of my arms propelled me forward and I picked up speed turning on to Esplanade Avenue. Noticing my clenched fists, I wriggled my fingers a few times, releasing the blood flow. It felt so good I had to do the same for my arms. As I hugged the air a few times, a wave of freedom and energy pulsed through my body. I kept my octave breathing.

Besides, I like being hopeful instead of listening to your crap. Hopeful is building and encouraging. It helps me grow. I'm going to let that shape me for a while, instead of the pain you keep reminding me of. That's what I'm going to think about from now on: being hopeful and encouraging. You're the opposite. You're from somewhere else. And I'm not listening to you anymore!

I ran and ran until I couldn't run anymore. I found myself one block away from the place I needed to be: the studio. Longing for the roar of the furnace to block out the expected chorus of the hyenas, I sprinted to the door. I ducked under the half-opened garage door and let the sweat cleanse my fears. I needed to trust, and the place I saw trust in action each day was the studio. The gaffer trusts her own creativity to move and flow where the piece needs to go, and she trusts the piece to endure the stress of her pulls, but more than anything, she trusts the flame's redemptive power over all.

It was my sanctuary of solace. I knew Elzbieta would be there because nighttime was her discovery time, with the whispers of her grandfather guiding her creative spirit. I felt her motion, before I saw her. Energy was radiating near the furnace and I saw her examining the pipes in the warming shelf. I had put in countless hours of non-stop turning and observing studio activity, so I could read her movements and sense her next steps. Her glance to the left meant she was going to turn. If she positioned her feet for balance, a strange contortion with the pipe (to center the glass) would soon follow. So I stayed a few feet from her as she collected and twirled the living flame with ease. She didn't even turn around, and gave no acknowledgement of my presence, but somehow she knew, for she spoke…

"Make a pile of yellow and purple jimmies on the table. I'm going to try something." I hustled to her commands as she centered the gather before moving it to the marver. She moved the blob over the table and the yellow pebbles collected on it. After marvering, she put it in the glory hole. By her glance, I knew she was headed to the jimmy table so I stepped back from it. When she touched the blob to the purple jimmies they gathered like glue to the base. The purple added a vibrancy and depth to the cheery yellow. Then she brought it to the stand. "Keep turning the pipe while I shape."

Cocking her head, she fashioned it with the wooden spoon, as if responding to its own scream of identity. With one piece she was focused and deliberate, each pull calculated and rigid. With another she was smooth and fluid, like dancing with a paintbrush attached, then looking back to see the designs. No two were the same, pieces or processes.

"I love working at night. During the day, most things have to be perfectly uniform, like stock orders for light fixtures to meet code specifications. Don't get me wrong; I don't mind using molds, or following patterns, but at night, everything is free form." She shook the curls from her eyes. "What have you been up to lately?"

"I've been working some free-form myself."

"Yeah, how's that?" she inquired.

"It's a long story."

"I've got time. Grab a pipe and do tell."

"I've met a guy, but I've sworn off men for life. So I'm pretty confused."

"Really, now. I never would've noticed." She chuckled, so I knew she was joking. "Many people come to glass blowing from confusion. Somehow the mixtures and the heat seem the perfect antidote."

"Makes sense," I replied.

"You've sworn off guys for life too, huh?" One of her eyes squinted with a questioning look like she didn't believe me.

"Well I had until lately. But he is not like anyone I've ever met."

"Yeah, they all start out that way."

"I know. I know. I'm finally starting to get my life back on track after a lot of man pain and I really don't want to get all messed up again. So I'm just gonna hang out here more, if you don't mind."

Her eyes smiled back with a glow that I usually saw only when she was creating. "I don't mind at all."

⸺ ◦((�))◦ ⸺

Matt called and called, but I couldn't speak to him. Everything was all jumbled up again. I would see him at school if I had to, but I tried my best to avoid all of our regular meeting places. Since we didn't have any classes together after the ethics semester, it was easier to make myself scarce. I really didn't know what to tell him. I can't hope anymore. It only brings pain. I need some studio time, especially if Elzbeita has sworn off men too. Perhaps she can be of help in this maze.

The more I thought about Elbieta, the more I realized that Matt didn't even know about the studio. How could I keep something so important from him? It was like I was compartmentalizing my life, but why? Was I ashamed of him, or my hope? Why didn't I ever find time to introduce him to Grandma Gertrude and the gang? Did I know it was not going to last?

I began to feel suffocated at the seminary. The charade of academics began to sicken me. Was I just confused about Matt or were my feelings about the seminary real? They passed out "Christian Faith and Message" tracts as our textbooks in Theology. Putting God in a box, explaining it away, and delivering a one size fits all message of salvation for everyone made me squirm. That was not how I experienced God at all. How could their one dimensional flat God be the same as the one I experienced in my quiet times? I wanted to talk to someone about it, but who would understand better than Matt? Elzbieta?

What is going on? Why am I so confused? I thought the hyenas were gone. But these questions did not feel like hyenas eating my brain at all. They were not self-loathing or derogatory. They felt like real questions and longings that needed to marvered, fired and shaped.

I kept feeling drawn back to the glass studio but that brought confusion as well. The more time I spent there, the more I began to wonder if I had feelings for Elzbeita. There was a connection between us. She was starting to get more personable with me since I shared about Matt. But is that a spark? And times with Matt were not sparks; they were full out electricity. I never knew electricity with a man was possible. Why go backwards? Why go anywhere at all if I'm not ready. My heart palpitated every time I thought about possibilities. The only real place to go to sort things out was to the studio. So I spent my free time there.

One day, I walked to the warming shelf and picked up a glowing pipe, finding the right shade of orange. Elzbieta noticed my entrance and gave me a wink. *I'm reading way too much into things. And I'm not thinking about possibilities anymore.*

"I've noticed how you're different with different pieces. Why are you so rigid and focused with some and fluid and gentle with others?" I had wanted to ask that question for the longest time.

Her eyes lit up as she spoke. "I can tell by the gather and marver how it's going to be. Some pieces resist more, depending on the mix of materials. If they resist my nudges, then I have to be more focused and direct for them not to crack under stress. Some are pliable and easy, so I can let loose, and play with them. With those, I'm not worried about whether they'll break or crack. I can relax and enjoy our time together. Sometimes I hang back and listen, taking my lead from where the glass wants to go. That's when it's pure joy."

"So, how do you know you're not going down some rabbit trail?"

"You don't know," she replied. "You just feel the movement of the glass, get an idea, run with it and see where it goes."

"You could waste a lot of glass that way."

"You could waste a lot of life worrying about the glass you might lose."

"If you go down every rabbit trail a piece of glass wants to go, you may never finish anything." I knew that truth first hand.

"Yes, but on some occasions, when you are truly connected, when the timing, temperature, touch, and technique are just right, you might just have a piece that brings delight for years to come."

"Yeah, but how often does that happen, really?" I quizzed.

"More often than you might think. You never know what piece may inspire another. And what's even better than that is teaching someone else and seeing his or her eyes light up with creative spark and connection."

"I bet. I remember the day we made murrini and when I made my first piece alone. You looked as happy as I felt."

"When you create something with another person, there is a connection beyond words, thoughts, or feelings. It's transcendent. Like my grandfather's touch, my grandfather's spirit is still moving through the glass. All that attention, all that trust, all that transparency and joined vulnerability binds you together in a way that can't be explained."

That was when it all began to make sense, the trust thing. I felt little pieces of it attach to the insides of me. I could feel it transition from a burn to a fire in my belly, and then take shape just like one of the glowing fingers in the studio. It was like being poked in the belly by some transcendent force bonding fear and vulnerability, trust and intimacy.

When other glassblowers were there, they trusted Elzbieta's expertise as the master gaffer. They had to trust and respect each other's space as well. The artists had to trust in themselves enough to keep growing and creating. And somewhere in the dance of trust and vulnerability, creativity ignites a flame of inspiration that cannot be quenched.

Every once in a while you could hear the ping of breaking glass, but rarely from Elzbieta's corner. I expected her to be angry, because each broken piece was essentially wasted (though some could be thrown into the shard pile). More glass had to be fused to replace it. But instead of anger, her eyes were bolstering as she gave directions. "Were you working with a bubble?" or "Use the pad first, until you get the hang of shaping it." I felt sorry each time someone broke a piece, but they didn't look as concerned as I did.

While others in the studio resembled fire dancers with swift, smooth circular movements, I felt like a robot, stopping and starting with abrupt shifts and rigid lines. Frustrated, I wondered how long it would take for me to move with fluidity. "It could take years," Elzbieta consoled. "Although some people never get it. They are rigid their whole time. They are afraid of working too hot, afraid of messing up, afraid of the art. It's painful to watch them, really."

Deciding at that point that I wanted to be a fluid glassblower, I surmised I needed to work to the edge of my brittle abilities, challenging myself, and the strength of the glass (and my life) to withstand the fire.

Chapter 40
All My Tears

Don't tell me the moon is shining; show me
the glint of light on broken glass. [34]

The day after Thanksgiving I answered the call. I hadn't been around
Basin Street much since starting seminary, but Michael knew to call me.
Gertrude was carrying groceries into the house and collapsed at the sink while
pouring a glass of water. Everyone was home. Her family was all there with her
as she died and had time to declare their love while waiting for the ambulance.

I crumpled to the floor and felt spiders begin to crawl up my arms. I
didn't even have time to think; I just picked up the phone again. "Please...
come...over," I cried. Matt was there in minutes and held me while I sobbed.
He heard story after story about Grandma Gertrude. And when I finished
with her, I even told him about Elzbieta and the glass studio. He listened
with the kind, attentive eyes I'd come to miss the past few weeks.

The service, held in her little African Methodist Episcopal church five
blocks behind the projects, was packed. Matt sat close to me as we watched
over forty children file into the pews. As a result of her after-school ministry,
most of them were regulars at church and sat up front behind the family.
My heart swelled as church members called the students by name and gave
them hugs. Even Crystal, who was now living with her great aunt, was there
and seemed to be recognized by all the members.

I could barely see for all the flowers, thousands of different colors,
shapes, and sizes, like the people in the pews. The aroma was overpowering but sweet. We were beginning to swelter, so ushers were passing out
fan-bladed Popsicle sticks.

The preacher spoke of hope and new life. "Gertrude is like a ship that
has sailed. And as we are sadly watching her sail over the horizon in our
view, there is someone on the other side smiling with pleasure that she is
entering His sight."

What a splendid image of heaven.

The preacher continued, "Today, God will gather Gertrude in his arms, and as she settles into his lap, he will tell her that tears will be no more. Psalm 56:8 says 'You list my tears in your scroll. Are they not in your record?' Some Mediterranean countries take this Psalm to heart and believe that God has been collecting all our tears in a bottle. So, in heaven, God will hand each of us his or her bottle back, saying, 'I counted each one.'

"We all know Gertrude had lots of tears: the tears she cried for her daughter lost to drugs, for her husband lost to cancer, for Tamira, for all the children she couldn't help. Today she is getting them back, all counted and collected in love.

"And God is counting our tears as well. And one day, God will intimately embrace us too, and hand us our own bottle. All the tears we are crying today because we have lost her. All the tears we will shed from anguish, disillusionment, failed relationships, disease, or death, will vanish, forever. The tears we have cried for the children who are lost to drugs, or depression, children who are sacrificed on the altars of our greed and power, and for the marriages that are discarded like yesterday's trash.

"It's hard to envision heaven because our eyes are clouded by pain. But God calls us to put on new eyes that seek Him. This puts the rest of our lives into perspective. All of us are like flowers, borrowed from God. If the flowers die or wither, we thank God for a summer loan of them.

"Remember, no matter how grievous the pain that we are enduring at this time, God's spirit is interceding for us and in time, He will wipe away all our tears, too. Reach out to him, today. He is waiting. Amen"

There was not a dry eye in the house.

The funeral continued for about three hours as they opened the microphone for students, members, and anyone who wished to tell what Gertrude meant to them. The most heartwarming stories were from the teenagers. One boy, Lonnie, could barely get through his speech. "Grandma Gertrude's house was the first house of warmth, welcome, and hope I knew. Most people treat black teenage boys as criminals, walking faster when we're behind them, or locking doors when we go near. But Gertrude treated us like helpers, like leaders, and in time we started to believe we were too. We even started to act like it...well...eventually. We began by making better decisions because we could remember her voice saying 'The little ones are watching you.' And when she invited us to come with her to church, we wanted to see if church and that Jesus guy that she loved so much, was what made her so special, so loving.

When we came here, we found that church was a part of it, but Grandma Gertrude was special all on her own. I believe she is one of God's spectacular flowers. My brother and I always said that she was an angel. And if you ask anyone around this room today, you'll probably hear the same thing."

I had to say something. I could feel it pounding in my heart. My words collected strength as I walked to the podium. "I'll never forget what I learned from Grandma Gertrude. She always said their were two types of people in this world-those with closed, shielded arms, protecting themselves from life, trying to keep safe what is inside, what is theirs. But then there are others with outstretched arms, those who see that the world belongs to all of us, so we need to work together to create something even better than what we have found alone.

"I'm glad she was the second type of person who pulled me in with those outstretched arms. She taught me how a community is built. Although the road is rough and rocky, and you will most likely get bloody on its path, I'd still be out there afraid of the world if she didn't show me the way. She would say, 'Children, let your hope, not your pain shape your future.' What a light, what a lantern, what a firefly of God's hope and love you are Grandma Gertrude! We are a community because of you! Our lives are forever changed, because we finally know what love looks like, sounds like, and feels like. We will never forget your generosity, your fire in the face of evil, or your love. And we will forever hope because of you!"

No one could've provided enough tissues for the tears. Our sleeves were saturated with the outpourings of our heart. *Are there enough bottles for these tears, God?*

When it was all over, the preacher closed us in prayer:

"Thank you, God, for this glimpse of heaven you created in our sister Gertrude. Help us to remember how passionately she lived her life loving others because you loved her. She passed on your blessings because she believed they were not hers to keep. Now, it's her turn to spend eternity embraced by your love. Eventually, it will be our turn. But until then, help us to focus on our hopes instead of our pain. Help us to be there for each other in these thin spaces of our lives where we have an opportunity to get closer to you. Help us to reach out, risk, comfort, and share your grace, mercy and love, just as our dear sister Grandma Gertrude did. Amen."

I had never attended such a joyous funeral. But then, I had never lived in the presence of someone whose internal light shined as brightly as Grandma Gertrude's.

Chapter 41
The Garden

Volatile and intense: the most apt description of the art of glassblowing.

Matt and I spent most of the day crafting a garden in my backyard. Buying plants and seeds soon morphed into an intricate diagram, with labels for where each plant was to be placed. Renting a roto-tiller, we unearthed loamy black soil and mixed it with many bags of manure. Although emitting the foulest of smells, they promised rich returns. Their pungency activated my senses. Since I had never a planted a garden before, my imagination ran wild. With each 50-cent plant positioned in the $5 hole, I could taste the spicy peppers, the crunchy sweet green beans, and the succulent tomatoes. I could hear the okra sizzle in its cornmeal batter, saying, "Soon, and very soon."

Lifting plants from containers, I mused at the symbiosis we shared with each other. As I inhaled its oxygen waste into my lungs, I knew that the carbon dioxide I exhaled was exactly what the plant needed for survival. After we watered each carefully planted row, Matt and I were covered in mud from head to toe. We giggled as we took turns writing our names in the grime on each other's limbs.

That afternoon as I looked down from my second-story porch on the neat and orderly rows, I felt like a parent. Elzbeita was right. Creation was elation, especially when it was shared. Each breath I swelled a little more with pride. With my love of food, my garden was a candy store: sweet, colorful and enticing.

Later that night, after cleaning up, Matt and I sat on the back porch's fluffy couch gazing up at the stars. My new connectedness to the earth brought the humble reality of how small I was in relation to the immensity of the constellations. Matt pointed out Orion's belt and Cassiopeia's chair, which I had never seen before.

"You know those stars were burning thousands of years ago and we are just now seeing them, right?" Matt inquired.

"I know, it's pretty cool, that space/time continuum thing, and that the sky is infinite. I try my hardest to envision infinity. Can you do it? Can you picture it in your head?"

"No."

"No matter how hard you try, our imaginations are only capable of finite things. It always ends with a corner somewhere." I laid my head on his arm. It felt good to be close again.

"Do you think that's how it is with God? If we can really understand God, then perhaps it is just our finite minds trying to box God in," he asserted.

"Exactly. What if God is so vast, infinite and unimaginable, that we only limit God by trying to understand God instead of just being in awe and in service?" Snuggling into his open wing-like arm, I turned sideways and encircled my other arm around him. He caressed my hair gently with his fingers.

"So I wonder if God just laughs at us most of the time," he said with a smile.

"Hmm...I've never really thought about God laughing at us. You mean because we try and think we have God all figured out?"

"Yes, and in the grand scheme of things such as universes, planets, and galaxies that God created, how miniscule our petty differences must be to God."

"Yeah, I guess compared to super novae and black holes, or even the complexities of the human mind, whether we are homeless or rich, white or brown, gay or straight, our differences must seem pretty trivial. You think God is laughing at how big of a deal we make of superfluous things. What if God's crying?" I held my breath as I spoke.

"You know, I've never thought about it that way," he responded. "God could be crying. Hmmm...I wonder if in the vast design if it really matters to God what drug or weed we choose to numb the pain or even what gender we are attracted to? God's seen many pious ones go down with power and greed, just as much as sex, alcohol and drugs. What's the difference really? Have we messed everything up by concentrating too much on these and too little on God?"

That was all the bait I needed. My heart raced as I inched out my story. Matt turned in closer as I spoke. He was listening with every hair on his body. I told him everything about me, the gondola ride, the card games, me begging God to change my desires, then giving in to being asexual.

He chuckled. "Well, now, that explains everything, doesn't it? God creates us to be sexual beings, Jenna. How can you just give up that part of your life?"

"When I'm connecting to the infinite love, and desiring God, it is much more powerful than any desire I've ever had for sex, so I don't have much of a problem with it."

"Really?"

"Well...Pretty much."

"Pretty much? What do you mean by pretty much?"

"Until..."

"Until...?"

I nuzzled my face up and down his wide chest. "Well, I really like kissing you and I never thought that would happen. Mmmm...And you are so...responsive and attentive...and you don't push yourself on me like others have."

"That's because I love you. You are incredibly special, and I'm waiting for you to want me." His words wiggled their way in through my tense exoskeleton.

His ability to recognize my uneasiness, his responsiveness to me, and his willingness to wait for me, melted everything right down through to my toes. The blood began to pulse and heat up like sizzling butter, burning and tickling at the same time. It was both exhilarating and scary, not something I was used to. Perhaps it helped that I had shown the hyenas I was boss. Perhaps it helped that he was an amazing gorgeous, wonderful, and attentive human being who shared the same passions that I did.

Flashes of his hairy chest lured me to unbutton his top button and run my fingers through his thick dark forest. The creamy center of my insides got gooier and gooier. He rolled over and gave me an exquisite kiss, and starry eyed, I was lost. My great ability to manipulate heat like the glassblowers in the hot shop went by the wayside.

Somehow that infinite love of God I so easily espoused crossed over into the lines of passion. And beneath the stars of hope fighting desperately through the indigo sky, on that enclosed back porch, overlooking the embryonic garden we had just created, we started something we couldn't stop, something a lifetime ago, I'd given up hope that I would ever enjoy.

I didn't have birth control, because I never thought I'd have to worry about it, never believed that I would be the one that never, ever, ever, ever wanted to stop. But oh, those stars, oh, complete and total honesty, and oh, those newly planted seeds budding along with the sacred intimacy of our love. And oh, Augustine, I really understood you now:

    -Lord, help me to be chaste, but not yet.

Chapter 42
Mold-Blowing

Mold-blowing is inflating hot glass in a mold. The glass is forced against the inner surfaces of the mold and assumes its shape. [35]

Dear Jenna,

Since I have already given you an overview, I guess I should actually give some background. It might not be the most pleasant story, but, like everyone else, the bad things helped mold me into the person I am today. I was never one to take advice-I always had to learn things the hard way, for better or worse.

I was always a very curious child, in fact, I forced my mom to teach me to read, write and do math at 2-3 years old. I've always loved taking electrical things apart, even at that young age. Sometimes it was because they were broken and sometimes just out of curiosity. As far as I can remember, I had an unquenchable desire to figure out the "hows" and "whys" of everything around me. Everyone in my family just seemed content without thinking about the grand mysteries of life...living almost robot-like it seemed to me. I, on the other hand, would spend countless hours theorizing, whenever I looked at something...using nothing but pure logic.

I was a quirky kid, always doing eccentric things. Somewhere around 3rd grade, I had a religion teacher tell me how I was such a horrible, worthless little child, who ruins everything and will amount to nothing. After that, I got depressed. Did even worse in school (still a B-C student though) and was more apathetic.

I got real depressed, did absolutely horrible in school... and had no interests in things. I was trying my hardest to fit in...and although I was so much better than I had been...I still didn't fit in...and things just didn't feel right at all. Like putting all your breath into a horn yet it doesn't play. My 'friends' really weren't friends. I didn't connect with people on a real level, and I was just miserable. Looking for happiness in all the wrong places. I had nobody that really shared interests with me.

One thing that I did enjoy though was computers. I always had the internet since about 1995 which provided me a way to learn about all the things I was interested in... anything was within reach, thanks to search engines, (hell, me being good with search engines is how I found ya'll in the first place, and learned a little bit about ya'll.)

Eventually found myself at LSU, because I wanted to party, and it was a major venue for other superficial people like myself. Basically failed out every semester. I read more than I've ever read before...about things I had never previously been interested. Psychology/neuropsychology mostly. And then there was Nietzsche-my entry into philosophy. It had come so randomly. I stayed up all hours of the night reading and learning about everything imaginable, and blowing a lot of hot air. Waking up too tired to attend classes, or even socialize much. And that is how learning ruined my education. Funny how that works.

In '03 at the age of 19, being depressed as always (I'll get into the big reason why next email) I hung around a really bad crowd and got into bad trouble. For many people my age, drugs are the bad illegal thing, but not me...I've never been a fan of the stuff. Tried a few, didn't see what the fuss was all about. It was fun, yes, but just not my thing.
...more to come.

-Jeffrey

Dear Jeffrey,

You may find this hard to believe but I have prayed for you for 22 years. I have even searched for information about you on the Internet, but I thought they said your name was going to be Gerard, so I was looking for Gerard or Jerry Brisures to no avail. I am sorry to hear that your parents divorced. I am a child of divorce and I know how hard that can be. But it seems that you have come through it strong and able to learn from mistakes (which is a major factor for success in life).

Matt and I smile reading your emails because of the similarities in our lives and in the lives of our children. We have two other boys: Taylor (17) and Dylan (15). They are great too! They are very much individuals that share some passions with you such as music and mechanics (my side) history/philosophy debate (Matt's side) and independence (everyone.)

I too was a very curious child-taking things apart around me, but that was no good for a girl growing up in the 60's. I was supposed to play with dolls (which I did) but I really got excited when my dad got out the toolbox, and I followed him around asking a thousand questions. I still do it to this day with every contractor, plumber, electrician etc. that comes to install or repair things in the house. One day they are going to start charging me extra for the training they give me.

My two great, but very young (19 year old) parents dropped out of college because they got pregnant with me. Neither of them ever finished, but they created a fun-filled life for us until they divorced when I was twelve. I was devastated when dad left so I basically locked myself in my room and wrote poetry for months. My mother was amazing, making sure I kept up my grades while engaging in many extra curricular activities: piano lessons, drama productions, and youth group. She kept me busy because if she didn't tire me out, I was bouncing off the walls. I'm the same way today.

I did get into some trouble in high school but never over the edge because I was the chief cook and baby sitter for my little sister. I had to have dinner ready when mom came home. Keeping our little world together was a huge factor in my life and forged me into the conscientious person I am today.

I went to LSU my first year and got drowned by such a big school. I transferred to Loyola and received an amazing education from the Jesuits. I was raised Presbyterian so the whole Catholic thing was new and exciting to me. I loved their passion for philosophy, meditation, and I even had a priest teach me Zen. Loyola was a perfect fit for me. I worked at Malcomb's Restaurant while attending school full time for a degree in Elementary Education. I also enjoyed renovating an old shotgun house on Toulouse Street (by City Park) all by myself. By the 80's, it was cool for girls to change plumbing/lighting fixtures and rewire electrical outlets. That is probably enough to start with. I'm eager to hear more about you.

-Jenna

Chapter 43
On the Edge

When adding glass, the main piece needs to be cold enough to resist
the natural heating that occurs when the new (hot) bit is added,
but not too cold or it will crack. Living on the edge of thermal self-
destruction means that timing is critical. When the piece is cold, you
may have only 20 or 30 seconds before it is in danger of cracking. [36]

"**S**o how are you with everything that happened last night?" *God, I love his transparency.*

I chuckled, "You know, I thought I would be much more freaked out than I was. How is it that something I dreaded for most of my life was actually enjoyable?"

"It is supposed to be, you know?" he explained.

"I know. I just can't believe that I let myself go."

"I guess all the exuberance of our garden creation just spilled over," Matt replied with a smile.

"It was more than that. Losing Grandma Gertrude hit me really hard. I was confused, really confused after our..., and her death just put me over the edge, like I'd lost connection to everything good and tangible in my life."

"That's what you looked like when I found you on the floor."

"And you were there, even though I had pushed you away for so long. I really needed you. I've tried my whole life not to need anyone, but I really needed you. And then, in the garden it was like Gertrude's legacy of hope and faith found its way into me, making me stronger."

"And perhaps a little of my love for you found its way in too?" he winked.

"I could feel it. I could feel all of it: the pain and confusion melting away. The more we kissed, the more I fell into hope and love."

His eyes were question marks, "Are you saying what I think you're saying?"

"Yes, I am. Matt. I love you from the bottom of my broken heart."

"And I love you more than you'll ever know."

"It's not going to be easy, you know. I still have lots of issues to work out."

"We all do. But together, we can handle anything," he said, moving in for another long kiss.

⸺ «(◦)» ⸺

Mustering the courage to go back to Basin Street after the funeral was very difficult...until I saw the kids. They were on me like a swarm. "Miss Jenna, come see." They took me by the hand to a large community room with a makeshift sign over the door: Gertrude Green Community Room.

"No one knew this room was in the original plans," Angela explained.

"We get to decorate it with all of her pictures and sayings," Crystal added with a confidence I had never seen in her before.

"Apparently, the management office had an apartment next to it that was designed to be a breakout room for a community center when needed. The plans were there from the beginning, the housing authority just used it as storage instead," Angela continued. "They moved the management office to another building, cleaned out the storage area and gave us both sections. Can you believe it?"

"No I can't. When did all this happen?"

"The best part is that Grandma Gertrude knew about it. She wrote them with pictures of us cleaning up the park. She asked if they could find us a space because we had outgrown her apartment," Crystal beamed more with each word.

Lonnie gave more details, "That was right after the time that Tamira was killed. She proposed that it be named after Tamira. She wanted it to be a constant reminder 'that gardens of love and hope can still grow from pain.'"

"That's so like Grandma Gertrude isn't it? Pointing the praise to someone else instead of herself." I began to tear up. "What are we going to do without her?"

"That's just it," Crystal replied. "We are not without her. We get to choose what sayings and pictures of Grandma Gertrude that we want on the walls. My mother would want it named after Grandma Gertrude. She was the inspiration. She was the hope."

"We all want her legacy to be remembered," Lonnie pointed to the sheet-rocked but not painted walls, "So we have written her quotes on the walls with markers. When the housing authority completes the room, we will choose the best ones and make them permanent."

"Like a wall of remembrance?" I asked.

"Exactly," Crystal said handing me a marker.

I wrote my favorite Gertrude quote: "Hope is a powerful choice which can never be taken away from you."

I could tell by his eyes there was something wrong when Matt picked me up from work after borrowing my car for the evening.

"What's wrong?"

"We'll talk when we get to your house."

I walked into the kitchen with hesitation, but then I saw the flowers, and the table set.

"Something's up."

"Yes, something has come up, but I'm sure everything will work out well."

"Uh, oh. I knew this was all too good to be true."

"It's nothing that we can't work through," he said bringing the pot roast and veggies he had cooked to the table.

"What is it?" The hesitation was killing me. I can concoct lots of terrible scenarios in my head in 5 seconds flat: cancer, he's married, he's being sued, etc.

"Well, you know I've been struggling with the low level of academics at the seminary. You were really the only thing keeping me there."

"I know. I'm struggling too. You won't believe what happened today in class when I brought up women as pastors."

"Exactly, well, when you...were not...around for a while, I applied to Princeton Seminary. Actually, I started the application before I met you and then sent it in when we weren't..."

"Wow, in New Jersey?"

"Yes, and today I received my acceptance letter."

I choked on the delicious wine he had just poured me and took a breath before saying, "It's a great honor to get into Princeton."

"I know. I visited there before coming here. I came here to be near Linda."

"So what does this mean?"

"That's what I'm hoping to figure out together. I only have a little over a year there until I graduate. Most of my credits will transfer."

"So you are going?"

"I'd like to. You can apply too. I brought you a brochure."

I fully understood Matt's dilemma. I couldn't bear another year at CTS either. Albeit miserable, I didn't know which direction to turn. Matt promised the Presbyterians would not put God in a box, but instead challenge our theological understandings. How could I be sure? And how could I leave New Orleans? No one ever leaves New Orleans. I could go back to school for a Materials Science degree, or get a Masters in Education? Or perhaps I could get more work at the studio? The decisions were daunting. And I was paralyzed. I was definitely not going to be rushed into a decision for a man, even Matt.

When Matt was leaving for Princeton, I was more excited for him than devastated. How could that be? By some miracle, I had serenity through the entire process. Perhaps it was the lessons I was learning at the studio. I felt closer to God more there than anywhere else. It was not that God was absent everywhere else, but the presence of people who spoke theology and doctrine, interfered in my God transmissions. In fact, when I was alone, I was at peace about everything. My interior space was open and ready to be filled with whatever the Spirit put out there. It was when I was with people, that things seemed to get muddled and cloudy. When I was alone at the studio I heard: watch, trust, dance, and hope.

Matt and I parted in dignity, in full acknowledgement that it would be hard to have a long distance relationship. *Didn't his last relationship end that way?* We weren't planning on keeping it up, but we weren't planning on ending it either. We would play it by ear.

But sitting at the piano after Matt left for Princeton was the loneliest I had felt since Dad left. My only companion was a dead fly on one of the keys. The faint memory of the chords I once knew caused my fingers to span the ivory. It helped ease the pain of uncertainty that was spreading miles between us. Matt and I had a long amazing kiss. He said he would call, and he drove away. My hollowness fell onto the keyboard and the pain poured gracefully into a song.

My Love

Where are you tonight my love?
Holding me tightly my love
But you are far away
Please say you'll stay with me
Kiss me each morning with dew
My love
Ours is what no others see
Or feel, or hear
Wind playing music we only can hear
Daffodils are dancing with the trees
And you and me in romantic song
Sound like a symphony
And we as one, on a night made for two
Write sonnets to the white light above
She smiles, and sighs, and even cries
It's been a while since the moon's been loved
She sings
Where, oh where, are you tonight
Are you tonight, my love?
Holding me tightly my love
While you are far away
Take me away as only your love can do
My love

Chapter 44
Artwork

Glass and rubber are structurally similar. The chief difference between the two is the ability to rearrange molecularly at room temperature. [37]

Elzbieta's questions, etched deeply in my brain, helped divert me from thinking about Matt. "How do you see the fire? How do you see glass? Once you figure out how you view the flame, then you can move on to how you see the glass." The more I wrestled with these questions, the more I developed in glassblowing and in life.

I was mesmerized watching her with the torch, crafting glass tubes into ornaments and figurines. It was so much less intense than working from a burning furnace. It was beautiful, peaceful and serene. Just as with furnace work, her method was adjusted for each piece. It was not a one size fits all equation. Purples and yellows were the wiliest. But no stubborn piece of glass could match her tenacity. She was always exploring new techniques and mixtures.

Her attention, her hope, and tender care for each piece was as if it had the possibility of becoming a masterpiece. Her optimism was reflected not just in glass, but in each person in the studio as well. Elzbieta exuded patience, care, correction, and connection with all that she touched, even as she danced with the flames. Was it because she danced with the flames that she had such patience and attention to detail? Or was it because of the attention she gave that she was able to dance with the flame's creative spirit?

If only I could have the same hope in others, in myself, in the pieces with which I worked, then perhaps transformation could occur. But hope brought pain. Matt was another reminder of that. Just when I had hoped, he left. If I could have even a flicker of optimism that something I touched could be the murrini in a millefiori masterpiece it would turn my world downside up. Even the pain would be worth it.

⸻ ((◉)) ⸻

Sitting in the doctor's waiting room, I wondered what his choice of art said about him: a colorful South American scene with active women, children, merchants, and animals at an outdoor market. I could feel the dogs jumping on my legs begging for the crumb of bread or taste of fruit that dropped from my hand. The babies babbled and the mothers bargained. And the azure sky was so deep and rich that it begged me to strip down and jump in. Did he serve in a South American medical school?

The well-groomed, dark haired doctor towered over me as I stood to read the charts on his examination room walls. I came in because I was getting dizzy and weak-kneed again. The blackouts had been long gone and I didn't want any reoccurrences. It was time for a checkup anyway. He smiled and reported, "Your blood work and tests came back and we may have a reason for your symptoms. Your pregnancy test came back positive. Congratulations!"

I sighed. Motherhood? I was not prepared for motherhood. My heart began to pump wildly, like a marathon runner after a race, but I wasn't quite sure whether it was from fear, excitement, or both. It was not something I had time to imagine for myself. Womanhood was still a pretty elusive term for me, so my head was in a fog as they set up my next appointment. I walked out of the door in such shock that I didn't even realize they had given me a bag of neo-natal vitamins until I got home and they glared at me with the stark reality of what was occurring inside my body.

"Poor kid," I said to my stomach. "You can't choose your mother. You're stuck with what you got!" I could've sworn I felt a kick of acknowledgement from inside, but I was told that at six weeks the baby is so small and pro-tected, I shouldn't feel anything for months. It jostled me, though. That kick was a connecting point, alerting me to the fact that something real, alive, and spirited was inside of me, and I was absolutely responsible for how it turned out.

What I ate, drank, or smoked, ended up in its little body. That extra bag of Lay's original, made its way to its arteries. If I danced, he or she swayed to the music as well. If I stayed up all night-he/she suffered the consequences of my actions.

No matter how empty and confused I'd felt in the past, there was something crystal clear, filling me up, and giving me a reason to lay everything on the table and sort things out. I kept telling myself that I'd survived the horror of my past, so I could survive this as well.

The weight I felt was heavy as cement. Would this be what drives me over to the edge of destruction? Or could this baby-making thing be like creating a work of art? I guess it all depended on how I handled it. My track record with handling difficult things was not the best. But how could this be happening to me? It was only that one time.

Chapter 45
Punty

A punty is a temporary connection for a piece of glass. It is a glass glob made and attached to the end of the piece, so while still attached to the rod, the other side can be opened up as a vessel. [38]

Matt called regularly, from Princeton. We didn't talk about anything in particular, but just picked up where we left off. Every conversation we toyed with the idea of my moving to Princeton, since it would be cheaper than me paying the $200 phone bills each month. I also knew that if Matt could get into Princeton, I could too, because my grades were equal to his. So I applied, and received my Princeton acceptance letter as well.

I called Matt with letter in hand. When he heard the news of my acceptance, he blurted, "Great! Now you will be coming to Princeton with me!"

"Well…" I hesitated, "things have gotten complicated." Dead silence screamed from the other end of the phone.

"What kind of complicated?"

"Well, I went to the doctor yesterday, and it seems that…I'm…pregnant."

"Pregnant…Wow! That's great. I mean…are you…okay with that? How are you?"

"Well, I'm trying to figure that out. The feelings are mixed. I'm excited to have a baby, created from love, being knit inside of me, breath by breath, pulse by pulse, the whole awesome art of it. It's incredible to be a part of the wonder of life. But I can't even begin to imagine what it'd look like to have a baby."

He was quiet for a moment, which made me realize, how much I loved him. The hyenas were in halt mode, but I knew they'd be back soon. I could feel their drops of slobber on my neck as the hairs bristled.

"So, do you want to get married?"

"What??"

"Get married."

"Get married?" My parents got married when they were pregnant with me, and that didn't work out so well. I noticed the walls around me. *Was this room so small before?*

"You know, get married. Walk down the aisle, death do us part kind of thing. I mean, we don't have to if you don't want to. I was just thinking…"

"Uh, I don't know. I'm not ready to think about that right now. I'm still getting used to the idea of having a baby inside of me. It's pretty weird." *He is too good to be true. Did I mess things up again?*

"When are you due?"

"June 5."

"Wow."

"I know."

"Are you feeling okay? Are you having morning sickness?"

"No. Not yet. I have weak knee sickness, which I guess just means I'm in shock. I don't know whether to jump up and down or go hide in a closet. I feel both at the same time."

"Maybe you should jump up and down in the closet so you can cover both ends."

"Ha, ha. You are so funny. How are you?"

"Wow, I'm pretty excited! Hadn't thought of being a father just yet, but it's pretty awesome! I wish I could hold you now."

I wriggle, imagining being in his arms. "I know. It really is incredible! And, we have a while to figure this out. I don't want to rush any decisions. It takes nine months, you know. God knew what he was doing on that one."

"I know. Thank goodness."

Visions of the studio came to me while we talked for nearly an hour about everything. That's when I realized that there are those, like the gaffer, who draw us closer to the fire, and because of their influence and skill, the endless possibilities in each of us come into view. Grandma Gertrude was one of those gaffers. She saw things that others didn't see, and wasn't afraid to confront and correct when needed. Yet, she exuded love. Her hand of love was so mighty that it crossed the borders of poverty, age, and race. With great skill and finesse, these gaffers move us from the shard pile onto the marver, and ask us to be patient, while the flame shapes us into something useful, beautiful or both. Matt, I was beginning to see, was one of the gaffers in my life.

"I love you, for being so wonderful about this," I said.

"I love you for being the mother of my child, and because you are the most marvelous human being I've ever met."

"I can't believe you're not mad. I should've used birth control. But I never thought..."

"I could've too. We just got lost in the garden, the passion, and the miracle of it all."

I laughed as I replied, "We kidded about the garden's creation spilling over into our passion."

"Little did we know how much we created," he said with a chuckle.

"How is the garden?"

"It's fine. I picked some beans today. The okra was so big it was tough."

"Yeah, my grandfather said you really have to watch okra because it goes from an inch to a foot in 24 hours."

"I love watching the changes in the garden each day. It's amazing how quickly the little sprouts turn into plants and the tiny leaves grow flowers," I reported.

"I wish I was there to see it, to watch it grow with you," he said longingly.

"You've left a lot of yourself behind you know. Funny how that works."

He added, "Gardens and children..."

"That's what Grandma Gertrude used to say...'Gardens, children, and marriages reflect the care they have been given.'"

"I know. What an inspiration, that woman. The care she gave to that community is her legacy."

"I've got to do some self-care now and get some rest. It's been a long week," I said, not really wanting to get off the phone, but knowing how much rest I needed lately.

"And I've got to get off of this hard dormitory hall floor. But I don't think I'll be sleeping anytime soon. I'm too excited."

"I know. But I'm too exhausted to talk anymore."

"I'll call you tomorrow, first thing. Goodnight for now. I love you."

"Goodnight. I love you too."

Chapter 46
Turbulence and Order

When gazing into the furnace, one cannot bear to see for long
where the hazy flame melds with the invisible shimmery heat:
this is the boundary between turbulence and order. [39]

At one time I wanted to throw everything about being a woman into the shard pile. But then, a hope emerged like the air in a glass bubble, collecting more as it drew to the surface. My hope gained so much momentum that here I was: pregnant. Elzbieta's words kept coming to me, "There is no error the flame cannot correct, no core too weakened if attended to immediately." But...and this is the biggest of all buts...we have to trust the flame and the master's hands to meld, shape, and snip us where needed, even when it hurts.

Like glass, life is all about the bonds. You think everything is strong, but when you add the wily hues, when you stretch the molecular net to breaking, then things become complicated, fragile, and even turbulent. That's what I was feeling-turbulence. But I was beginning to trust the flame.

I learned from my experiences with glass, with Tamira, and Grandma Gertrude that it is precisely in those thin spaces between reason and doubt, sanity and insanity, inspiration and divination that true creativity and boundless possibilities emerge. If I had not gone to Bible study that rainy night long ago, I would've never heard of Basin Street. If I had not met Grandma Gertrude, I would not have the strength or hope I had today. If I had not said yes on that paddleboat...

Matt was so caring. Because of his care and understanding without judgment, I was changed. I was beginning to hope again. But each day was a turbulent roller coaster ride of emotions. And there was no off button on my brain. I kept trying to put things back in order, back in proper perspective.

Some days were hopeful. Some days were not. The doubts fluttered back in and I had conversations with myself:

You know this could be all over with one simple procedure.

Yeah, that's what people say, but most people who have had one are still dealing with it. It's not over for them: they still wonder about it, or regret it for years to come. I have enough of my past hounding me, haunting me, haranguing me. Do I really need anything else?

One simple procedure.

I know; it's tempting. Then I wouldn't have to expend all this energy. But how can I get rid of something that was created with so much love? It would be a waste. It wouldn't be if Roy was the father, or with just a guy off the street. Maybe then I could get an abortion, but this, this is different.

Chapter 47
Vitrification

Glass transitions from a hard and relatively brittle state into a molten or rubber-like state. Super-cooling a viscous liquid into this state is called vitrification, from the Latin word *vitreum*, meaning, "glass". [40]

Matt called and woke me up. "I can't get much sleep. I keep thinking about our baby."

"I know, me too."

"Did you think about marriage?"

"Uh, sort of."

"So, what do you think?"

"Marriage was a disaster for my parents when they were in the same situation."

"I know, but things would be different with us."

"Yeah, that's what everyone thinks."

"I know, I know."

The walls seemed to press right up to my arms, sucking the breath out of me. I heard the hyenas licking their lips; their snorts were like razor blades on the inside of my head.

"I'll call you back. I have to go to the bathroom."

As I sprinted to the overused toilet, I went through my routine. *Think of what is true, what is lovely, what is excellent.*

The truth, plain and simple was that I was pregnant. So I had a heart to heart talk with the baby. "Hello in there. I'm your mother. I know it's not saying much, but I'm all you have right now. I'm really excited about you. I never thought I'd get to have a baby. And your father is wonderful! Your mother is a pretty mixed up puppy, but your father is incredible! I promise you, though; that I will do the best I can for you. So just hold on in there. I don't know what life's gonna look like now. But it'll be all right. Just give me time to figure it out."

The phone was ringing before I had a chance to call him back. The baby and I were snacking on leftover apple walnut cobbler as I picked up the phone.

"You know I'll support you in whatever decision you make, right?"

"I know."

"Are you thinking of an abortion?"

"No."

"Are you sure?"

"I'm sure."

"You are so brave. I love you for that."

"So our other options are..."

"Marriage, or adoption."

"Adoption?" he said with an edge in his voice.

"Yeah, adoption."

"Well...I guess that would work too. But why not marriage?"

I took a few long breaths. This might be the hardest thing I would ever have to say and I wanted to get it right. "You know, marriage is a big deal. I need more time to even consider that as one of the options. Marriage with a baby at the same time could mess everything up. I'm still trying the keep the hope that we can work out as a couple. I don't want to strangle that. Sometimes, when I think of more than one thing at a time, the walls start closing in. That whole Roy incident still messes with my head, and all that happened at college, I'm still trying to believe that you can accept it all, that I can accept who I am and be okay with it."

"You know I'm okay with everything. I think you're amazing with all you've been through. You're faithful, and honest, and..."

"Listen. It is very important that you listen to me, now. I never even imagined I would have sex, much less be pregnant, and then married. I can't even begin to get my head around it. I have to tackle one thing at a time. Right now, I'm still pinching myself that I found you and we are so good together. I'm struggling with what that means. I guess I'm bisexual now? I have a hard time believing that you can possibly accept that. I'm still trying to get my head around that and not let it mess things up. I don't want to mess this up. And I did in a way by having sex. So now we have to rush forward and figure this out before we've even figured ourselves out.

"Marriage kinda sounds like putting me in a corner, and you know I don't do well in corners. Having a baby before we even get married, sounds like a cage for both of us, trapped. I'm not emotionally ready for that yet.

I'm still trying to convince myself I'm emotionally ready for a relationship with you."

"But we are so good together," he replied with conviction.

"But how can I be physically ready for a baby? I barely feed my dog on time and rarely clean the cat's litter box. How am I going to take care of a baby?"

"I can help, even if we don't get married."

"You are in school, and I'm in school. I just got accepted to Princeton. I want to be there with you, to see if we can make this thing work. But I'm not sure I can handle a baby. It's pretty rocky just handling myself, and a move to another part of the country. New Orleans is all I've ever really known."

"You're a whole lot stronger than you think you are. Look at all the things you've been through. You're a fighter and a survivor-strong as steel. You can do anything you set your mind to do."

"Perhaps, but I'm just now getting to where I don't have blackouts. I'm making good grades. I'm starting to be hopeful that things can be different from the shattered life I've envisioned for myself. Do you think I'm being selfish to not want to mess it up with marriage right now?"

"Uh...on...not, when you put it like that." His wobbly voice made it clear he was hurt.

But I was hurt too, from the lacerations of a lifetime and if I didn't watch myself, they would fester again and ooze out on to others. *More time, more time, is what I need.*

"I'm not saying yes, and I'm not saying no. I'm just saying I need more time." I hung up the phone.

But I had an alarm clock ticking inside of me. Before long it was causing a raging battle each morning in my stomach. Before I got out of bed I had to ingest a package of saltines and a can of 7-Up, otherwise I would throw up on the way to the bathroom. *Why, if the child is the size of a lima bean, does it wreak so much havoc on my organs?* It was hard not to think about the baby when he/she was affecting every part of my life: sleeping as much as I could, eating like a horse, and bathrooms drawing me in with the pull of electromagnets.

And the more I thought about it, the more I wanted to do the right thing. *Please God don't let me mess up this baby's life. I've done enough damage to my own. Protect this one please. Thank goodness we don't have to decide anything now, but soon, we'll really have to face some things.*

Chapter 48
Glass Children

You have developed a sense of judgment about temperature based on working with clear glass. As you begin to work with colors, you will have to adjust that sense to react faster to heating and cooling cycles. [41]

My times with Elzbieta in the hot shop were illuminating. Even though I was digressing with glass blowing, she was patient. When I was strung out with yet another broken piece, she would just smile. "How can it be that I work on a piece for half an hour and then when I set it down to admire my handiwork, it crumbles to pieces? I'll never get this; it's too frustrating. How I thought I could just pick it up by watching you I don't know."

"You know I've been doing this since I was twelve, and helping my Dziadzia since I was six, right?" she would console.

"I know. But it is frustrating. I was doing better before. Now, when I think a piece is done, it crumbles under heat stress."

She'd shrug her shoulders and say, "You are working with darker colors now, which makes everything more challenging, and you're using more complicated techniques."

"I know, but still. I shouldn't be digressing."

"You're not digressing; you're just involved in the art now, not just the passing fancy. The more you know about anything, the more you realize you don't know. And you're trying new things, stretching yourself. You're in the middle of the learning curve now, and that's when things get complicated. This is when most people give up. But hang in there-it will all come together in the end."

My art lesson wasn't helping my feelings about life either. I was coming to the studio to cheer myself up after Matt left, to clear my head about my pregnancy, but I had little to show for my efforts. "I know it's hard to see it, Jenna, but you are improving. Remember when you first started on your own, how it would break after two minutes?"

"I know. But a finished piece, a really lovely piece, on my own, without your direction would be nice sometime soon," I sighed.

"You sure are helping my shard supply though," she chuckled.

"Well at least I'm good for something!"

I walked into her back office and saw hundreds of glasses, vases and figurines, some with elegant Reticello latticework and others with twirled jimmies inside. "Your storage room is getting crowded. When will you get these pieces out to market?"

"Well," she coughed, "these pieces are not for sale. There is a gallery in town that wants to show some of my work. So I need to figure out which ones to send." I picked up a beautiful paperweight with what looked like thousands of flowers inside it.

"This millefiori is incredible."

"It's the first real piece I ever made with my Dziadzia. That's why it's not for sale. When he finally bought his furnace, we worked for a long time perfecting the canes. It took days to pull them."

"How old were you?"

"About ten."

"Wow!" is all I could say to describe the tiny repeated pieces of varying color throughout the piece. There was a world inside the glass that was drawing me in, deep, multi-dimensional, and alive.

There was an uncomfortable silence in the room. "I still have a problem selling anything that we made together."

"This one is breathtaking," I said, picking out a purple, red, and orange one. "The colors are so intense."

"I know. I could probably get a good price for some of these, but they're too much like my children to sell. They have too much of my grandfather and me in them, too much of our relationship in them to let any part of it go."

My heart sunk and I found it hard to swallow. "I know exactly what you mean!"

Chapter 49
Formulas

In 1884 chemists Schott and Zeiss produced a glass, which has much lower coefficients of expansion and better optical and heat resistant properties. Their formulas gave way to the modern invention of the borosilicate glass known as Pyrex. [42]

Dear Jenna,

Wow! I always wondered where my interest in taking things apart/building/construction came from! I do the same thing when I'm around construction people and electricians.

The divorce really didn't get to me all that much. The endless years that led up to the divorce were the problem. My dad was quite a bad influence-cynical, critical, narcissistic kind of way. I love him, but it's still taking time to forgive him.

My mother is great, however. It's hard to imagine how so much love can fit inside one person. She is absolutely selfless, and I adore her. She has been such a great influence in my life. Have a great weekend! I can't even put into words how excited I am by this whole interaction with you. Thanks for sharing with me; it means a lot.

-Jeffrey

Chapter 50
Cracking Off

Friendship is like a glass ornament: once it is broken, it can
rarely be put back together exactly the same way. [43]

Since I was pregnant, food didn't have its same allure. Ordering it sounded great, but by the time the kitchen finished preparing it, thinking about it made me gag. So, instead of wasting it, I decided to bring my head waitress meal to the studio. Perhaps Elzbieta and I could share it. Elzbeita was grateful, and threw a sheet over her desk, which was covered with the paperwork of unfilled orders. We ate in her office on the rickety chairs with her glass children surrounding us. She wolfed down the club sandwich with mustard honey sauce and I averted my eyes so I wouldn't get sick.

Her cotton sundress was tight around her breasts. As she ate, the yellow sauce dripped from her lips and her tongue wiped it clean like a windshield wiper. I was picking at the stuffed baked potato, the only thing that had a chance of making it down. I had tried to tell her about the baby several times before, but I couldn't quite muster up the energy. I decided to just blurt it out.

"I'm pregnant."

"What...?" her eyes widened with suspicion and dismay as she reached for a napkin.

"I'm pregnant and due in June."

"How'd that happen?"

"Surely, your mother told you how it happens." I chided.

"I didn't even know you had a boyfriend. " Her voice had an edge in it I hadn't heard before.

"Well, I've been trying to figure that out for a while now. It kinda took me by surprise."

"Is it that same guy? How long have you been dating him?"

"Well, that's just it. We are really good friends. I just kept it in my mind that we were friends so it didn't get too crazy."

"And you never brought him by the studio? I thought you were...I thought we were...closer than that."

"I didn't think...the relationship...just when things were starting to get serious, he moved to Princeton to go to school."

She shook her head a few times like she was trying to force the information down into her brain. "So what does this mean?"

"What do you mean what does this mean? I'm pregnant. How many meanings does that have?"

"Are you happy? Are you keeping it? Are you leaving with him? Giving up school, the studio, everything?"

"That's what I'm trying to figure out now. It's pretty complicated. I've been down a few rocky roads in my life, so I'm not sure how stable this ground is that we are on. But right now, I'm hopeful."

"Hopeful, humph...I guess you're just full of surprises, aren't you?" With that she wiped her face, pulled away from the desk, and walked briskly toward the studio. I followed her, relieved that I didn't have to watch her eat any more.

She began cutting the multi-colored canes we had made the week before into tiny pieces of murrini and scattered them on the marver. But her movements were not as smooth as usual. Taking a pipe from the furnace, she gathered and centered with an urgency that I had not seen before.

I came close as I studied the murrini and its tiny repeating patterns. As they stuck to the clear glass they gave an intriguing depth and perspective to the piece. After adding her jack line, she did her dance from marver to the glory many times before cracking off.

She dipped the tips of the jacks into water and applied it to the line. The three drops sizzled. This created a thermal shock as it hit the hot glass releasing it from the punty on demand. She smiled as she put it in the annealer.

"I've never seen you add water before the crack off," I said.

She grimaced with her response, "I still have a few tricks in my belt you haven't seen. Come here. I found something you may be interested in." Walking back to the furnace, she put her pipe back on the shelf and wiped her hands on her dress as if they were sticky. They must've been, because she went back in her office, to the sink in the closet, and washed them. I followed her and noticed near my chair, the magazine I had brought for her to read.

"I have a something for you too. You won't believe what is in the latest

Science Journal." I took out the new issue and began reading it to her. When I saw her eyes squint and the lines burrow on one side of her face, I began summarizing it. "It pretty much puts our old theory about antique window proving that glass is a liquid to rest. And it clarifies how glass is an amorphous solid." She didn't look interested in the journal at all. I tried to show it to her, but she moved away. Inching toward the desk, she began to clean up the remainders of dinner.

"So you're trying to tell me that everything I've ever learned about glass from my grandfather is false?"

"Well, the latest research has pretty much proven that the thick window bottoms were just how they chose to construct the panes. It was true that while restoring ancient windows, the workers noticed the glass on the bottom of the panes was always thick. But their conclusion that over time the glass had flowed down was wrong. In fact, the thickness difference can be explained by the how the ancient panes of glass were cut from rondels, which were thicker towards the center. Craftsmen installed the panes thick side down for stability. The windows are not proof of anything."

"How can it be that everything we ever learned is false just because some scientist conducted a test or came up with a new theory?"

"That is science. Its business is not truth but process. We use hypotheses and controlled experiments to test everything. No "truth" is excluded. We don't just make these things up you know. We set up rigorous tests and trials for our hypotheses. It's the scientific method."

"You're a scientist now?" she pulled away from the desk throwing the sandwich wrapper and the hefty remains of my potato into the garbage.

"Well, maybe. One of my options is going back for my Masters after the baby. I love how everything can be observed, ordered, and explained."

"What is it with you and science? Don't you see that when you explain everything away you ruin it? All your studies and analyses rob its mystery, its art, its beauty!" She picked up her beautiful millefiori paperweight off the shelf. "Instead of the intrigue of the tiny world inside this piece, all you have is a well dissected and categorized cadaver. What good is that? The manganese, copper and gold in this piece are not the art. They are a miniscule piece. It's the balance and delicacy of how it's put together that makes the art, and that can't be explained away."

"Science is how problems are solved. Without scientists dissecting and analyzing there would be no medicine, or technology without observing, without investigating and classifying. You're not saying you could live without those are you? You wouldn't know what temperature to melt or anneal. You wouldn't have the perfectly heated furnace without science!"

"I'm sure I'd figure something out. Coal and wood would work, just like in the olden days."

"You'd never get colors this vibrant, this perfect," I pointed to the clear paperweight, created by her grandfather, with its colored cane clippings inside. She was rubbing and moving the brilliant piece from hand to hand like a worry stone. "I've seen the ancient glass without the precision of the modern studio. You and I both know the colors are cloudy and distorted."

"I don't know any such thing. It could be the gaffer was not as good an artisan as my Dziadzia."

"You're just being cantankerous, now. Without the processed cane, your art would lack its vibrancy. You couldn't live without the potent colors in the processed frit."

"I *could* live without your ridiculous definitions. Amorphous solid. What kind of a definition is that? It's infuriating, really. Like scientists have to put themselves up higher and mightier than anyone else in the world, more than the people who love glass, who work with glass, in and out, every day."

"It behaves like a solid, so it's a solid," I asserted.

"You said it doesn't behave like a solid at all. Internally it doesn't crystallize; it doesn't really freeze, ever. So how can it be a solid? It's a liquid."

"Well you can be wrong if you like and say it is a liquid. I'm going to go with the facts, myself," I said as I waved the magazine in the air.

"You and your scientific rules, and facts. They are like dogma when you use them."

For all the money in the world, I couldn't figure out what we were really fighting about, but I knew from the intensity in the air it was no longer about the art and science connection we held dear. So terse and constricted was the tone that it seemed each of us was trying to hold together our own fragile internal creed, foundational to our existence. Our conversation had elevated to a whole new level, teetering between the sensual and the spiritual. I wasn't sure I understood, or even wanted to understand, because opening it would be a Pandora's box.

Her breathing was rapid. Her chest heaved up and down. "Well you can take your little textbooks and articles and shove them. I prefer to see life *and* glass as art, constantly changing, challenging, and creeping us into new areas. You waste your time trying to analyze everything, trying to follow all the procedures so much you can't even produce an intricate piece of art on your own if your life depended on it. It's tiring really, your obsession with perfection. Your intensity stresses everyone out. You'll never be able to love glass like I do because you are so busy studying, judging, and working the glass. Why can't you just feel, breathe, love, and create?" She took a long breath and continued.

"If you think you'll be happy going back to school as a scientist, then go for it. I'm tired of the whole thing. Take your over-analyzed life and see where it gets you!"

With her last words she raised her arms like she was dismissing me. In her disgust, she lost grasp of her grandfather's enchanting paperweight. It went flying through the air. I dodged its impact, but its forceful trajectory ended at my toes, crashing it with a throng of pop-clicks. The tiny world of a thousand flowers was decimated. My heart plummeted to the colorful shards at my feet.

A heavy silence filled the room. In that instant an eternity passed through. Neither of us could take our eyes off the destruction between us.

Moving toward me, she fell to her knees. With tears streaming down her face, she picked up the cherished millefiori pieces crying, "Oh my God. Oh my God."

She grabbed the shattered shards in her hands as if they held her life, and her significance. From her fingers dripped crimson blood. As she raised them to her chest, I noticed her eyes, wild and piercing amidst the desecration around me. I was afraid she would bleed to death collecting the fragments, but even more afraid that in her frenzy she was going to cut me with the jagged edges. She began to come near me shouting and gasping, "You, you, you..." I ran out of the studio as quickly as I could.

It was a recurring nightmare that never changed, and never ended, because it was reality. It was the last I ever saw of Elzbieta.

How could it all end with Elzbieta so abruptly? What had I done? What could I have done differently? The fact that I didn't see it coming left me dejected. What if this same thing happened with Matt? I hauled myself to pastor Joe's office before the nightmares, doubts, and decisions turned into self-loathing. The gray-bearded ex-missionary usually had some good advice from the pulpit:

I'm having a hard time figuring out what to do with this baby I'm carrying.

You're pregnant. A baby is a blessing from God. So, what's the issue?

My boyfriend is open to getting married and keeping it but I don't think I can go through with it.

Why not?

It's a long story.

That's what I'm here for.

(I told him the whole thing: about Roy, about my college adventures, and about Tamira and my vow to never let men mess me up again. I also let him know how Matt might just be the right man, but I couldn't trust any feeling that ran through my veins.

What has Matt done to lead you to believe he is not truthful or honorable? That he will leave or hurt you?

Nothing, nothing at all.

How much time have you spent entertaining the idea of getting married and keeping the baby?

Some, but then I see my parent's marriage in full view, screaming about money, with plates crashing, and mom and me sitting on the couch all night waiting for Dad to come home. The walls start to close in and it starts to feel like a nightmare.

What makes you think your marriage would be like your parents'?

No one thinks a marriage is going to detonate before he or she gets into it. It just explodes somewhere along the way. We are really good together, though. I'm always happy when I'm with him, unless I start thinking about budget fights, dirty diapers, sinks full of dishes, and screaming babies. Then it turns pretty quickly into a horror movie. I hate horror movies!

Yes, those are the hard parts of marriage.

And it doesn't help that the voices in my head keep telling me that it would all be over with one simple procedure.

Are you thinking of an abortion?

If I was alone right now, without Matt to love me, and guide me through it, I probably would be. I cannot imagine facing this decision alone. When you have a ticking clock inside, so you have to make a decision-even if it is killing you inside to think about it. But

I've heard of too many people who are still wrestling with the abortion they had four and five years ago. It doesn't seem to be over for them. I have enough of my past locked away in a closet. My options are pretty limited. Do you have any suggestions?

You could give the baby up for adoption or keep the baby without getting married?

Oh, keeping the baby would last about a week. Either I'd kill myself, or I'd kill the baby with so much emotional stress. I can barely take care of myself right now. There's no way I could take care of a baby.

But what if Matt helped and took the baby some times?

I can't do it.

What about parents or relatives to help you?

My mother is on her second marriage, and in the process of ending that one. She has her own issues. And I'm the kind of person that if I feel boxed in a corner; I come out clawing and biting.

That's understandable with your past.

It would be like putting me in a cage. I feel the walls closing in every time I think about it. And I know it's not fair. That I should've thought about this before I had sex, but I didn't. I was caught off guard. I never expected Matt to be so amazing, for me to feel the things most people feel. But is it right to set this baby up for failure just because I was stupid, and didn't see it coming?

Only you can answer that Jenna.

I know. That's the problem. I feel like I'm the real bad guy in all this. Matt is fine with whatever I choose, and is probably leaning toward doing the "right thing" because he is such a good guy. But, I'm not really leaning that way. My past and my genetic makeup cause me to see fractures and shatters everywhere I look. If I'm scratching his eyes out everyday, how could he still love me? And I know I would, I just couldn't help but feeling trapped.

But you wouldn't be trapped. It would be your decision.

No, because if it was my decision, I think I would give up the baby for adoption. Then he or she at least has a fighting chance.

Why do you say that?

With two parents that are ready for a baby, who can pay for it, love it, and not be arrested by their own emotional scars.

We are all arrested by our emotional scars.

Well, my scars just seem a little bloodier than other people's.

Point taken.

When I think about keeping the baby, I have these great visions for a while, rocking her, playing with him, singing to her, but then the dreams take over.

What dreams?

I actually have a recurring dream about people trying to take the baby away from me. I try as hard as I can to keep him but they get him and I stand there crying. Sometimes the baby ends up bloody from the fight, sometimes he just disappears. But each time I'm left standing there with a few pieces of a beautiful but shattered paperweight in my hand. That's what I feel will happen if I keep the baby. Somehow I'll lose her anyway. At least with adopted parents someone will get to keep her. And he or she will be safe. I don't think she'd be safe with me.

Mmmm…. I see. But adoption can have its bad sides too.

I know. They could be rotten parents. I could regret it all later. I could lose Matt in the process of giving up his kid to total strangers. I know, I know, I know. But at least with adoption, the odds are in the baby's favor, and maybe in ours a little too.

How so?

Well, the odds are definitely in the baby's favor. He has a better chance with people who are ready for him. I have no idea about our odds after it is over. I could regret it and crumble with the decision. Matt and I may never recover, but at least the baby will have a fighting chance. The baby should be the one that suffers the least.

Whatever you do for the least of these, you do for me.

Yeah, I'd like to think that's what I'm doing. All out of love.

Then think about it in that way.

Chapter 51
Dimensions

Reticello is an Italian decorative technique, which involves merging two bubbles. Once combined, the opposingly twisted canes cross each other creating a criss-cross or net like pattern. Small air bubbles, trapped in a grid pattern between the crossing canes, add another dimension to the pattern. [44]

My talk with Pastor Joe gave comfort for a while. But then the realization that I couldn't go to the studio anymore out of fear for my life, started to make things close in on me. I didn't have the energy to reach out and try to make it better with Elzbieta because I didn't even know where it went wrong. Was she angry at my endless waste of glass? Did she have expectations of me that I didn't know about? Why did I have to go and attack the very thing that connected her to her art, her faith, her Dziadzia? Why did I have to put truth over art and grace? What is more important, to be right, or to be in relationship?

The ticking clock in my belly was getting me more frantic too. Luckily, Matt had an uncanny knack of calling just as things were getting desperate.

"Time is running out you know," he said.

"Oh, I know. But, I still can't figure it all out."

"When the world seems like it is melting all around you, what do you do?"

"Normally, I go to the glass studio. But things went really wrong with Elzbieta, so I can't seem to find a place to clear my head and think." I told him the bloody details. "What if the same thing happens to us and the baby is the paperweight that gets destroyed in the process? I can't live with that thought."

"You know us, we talk about everything. With you and Elzbieta, it was ethereal. It was about art and balance. I love you even when you are not creative and not balanced."

I chuckled at his honesty. "But, I didn't see any of it coming. I still don't know what went wrong. How can I be so blind? How could I put so much hope and effort into something and it shatters right before my eyes?"

"No matter what shatters, together we will figure it out. Hope and God will get us through."

"You sound like Grandma Gertrude. We must accept finite disappointment, but never lose infinite hope.'"

"That's a Martin Luther King quote, I think," he responded.

"She quoted him all the time. She had definitely seen her share of disappointments and somehow she never lost hope."

Matt came to visit me on his Thanksgiving break. I saw sides of him that I had never seen before. "So this is how I see it," Matt said. He got out his chart with three options. We filled in the blanks together.

Married with baby	Keep baby-unmarried	Adoption
Matt happy	Matt somewhat happy	Matt not really happy
Baby happy	Baby somewhat happy being dragged around	Baby happy
Jenna closed in	Jenna crazy and closed in	Jenna happy
Disillusionment	Both stressed out	Adoptive Parents happy
No finishing school	School? Maybe Matt	School: yes, both

"The next step I usually do is put numbers/weights and write how much each thing is worth." Matt was such a strategist.

"Do we need to do that?" I asked with full heart.

"It's pretty clear if you put it in the chart," Matt replied encouragingly.

"I think it's pretty clear just by what we've filled in so far. Don't you?"

His eyes scrunched up. "It looks...like adoption doesn't it?"

"Yes."

"It's not going to be easy you know," he said wiping his eyes.

"I know. And you may never forgive me."

He paused for a moment, thinking, "That's not what I'm worried about. You may never forgive yourself."

"Yeah, but I really think it's the right thing to do. We've prayed about it so much, we've talked to people, and each other."

"I know." His eyes were anguished.

"But it's out of love."

"Out of love," he said, as if trying to convince himself. "Hopefully that will carry us through."

"I hate this," I added. "I wish we would have done this differently. We would be married first, and then this wouldn't be a problem. But I am <u>so</u> not marriage material."

"Yet." The sparkle returned to his eyes as he corrected me.

I chuckled. *He is always so positive.*

"Yet." I smiled back.

"But in time, we may just get there," he whispered as he kissed me.

"Yes, in time. We may." I was bringing out an imaginary score card of my own as we spoke.

Things that would make Matt a good husband:

Always looks on the bright side
A good analyzer and thinker
A fantastic kisser
Loves me beyond belief
How did that happen

———— ◦◉◦ ————

There were gasps and tears when my obstetrician informed me that he knew someone interested in adopting our baby. After having a daughter ten years ago, his sister had so many miscarriages she had given up hope of ever having another child, so he knew she and her husband would surely want ours if we were serious about adoption. It sounded like a perfect fit.

On Christmas break, we set up appointments with the lawyer and started the paperwork for the adoption. It was counter cultural to think about giving up a baby while the world was preparing for Jesus' birth.

I started thinking more about moving to Princeton with Matt, and giving seminary another try, at least for a year. Without the studio, Elzbieta, or

Gertrude in the picture, staying in New Orleans didn't have the same allure it used to. If Princeton was the same as Conservative Seminary then I could transfer to another school for Materials Science or Physics.

Things started to line up well except that I couldn't bring myself to tell our families about the baby. Matt wanted to, but I knew if I told my mom she would pressure us to keep the baby. I didn't feel strong enough for the battle that would ensue with her, so it was easier to not say a word.

It took all my strength to hash it out with Matt, work full-time, and complete the semester before leaving for Princeton. Matt felt that if we didn't tell my family, then we shouldn't tell his. So we harbored a beautiful secret. The fact that I was moving to Princeton right as I began to show, made it as tidy as the bows on the presents under the Christmas tree.

Making plans for my departure from New Orleans was simultaneously making plans for our baby's exit from our lives. How could I prepare for either? New Orleans had shaped me: its music, its color, its food, and its living life to the fullest with reckless abandon. How would I fit in anywhere else?

And the baby had shaped me too. He/she gave me a purpose to examine my every action and determine its equal and opposite reaction. Her kicks reminded me that my body was but a vessel. Matt's care and concern for me and the baby forged us into a depth of connection that I couldn't even begin to fathom. How could one prepare to cut cords of that significance?

I tried to see it in a different light. Instead of cutting cords, we were leaving behind a piece of art that, though separated from us, would always be a part of our design, our make-up. The adoptive parents would be layering their imprint on the beautiful form we had cast, and together we all would be creating a masterpiece. This image was the only one that could help me endure the pain.

The documents, which said that the doctor's relatives would pay all medical and legal expenses, were drawn. They would pick up the baby in New Jersey after we were released from the hospital. We were to keep them informed of the pregnancy at all the significant turns. We were committed to our decision. They were a good family excited about their new arrival.

Chapter 52
Unnecessary Marks

Pieces of glass are like children; early scars become part
of the final form. Many glassblowers overwork the glass,
leaving unnecessary marks on their creations. [45]

"You don't have to kick so hard. I know you're angry with me for not planning to keep you, but you don't have to take it out on my organs. We both need them to survive, you know. A gentle nudge as a reminder that you are there would be great.

"I know you hear my voice since I talk to you all the time. Are you going to remember me? Will you remember all the songs I sing or the poems I recite to you? One day when you're grown, will you hear my voice above the crowd and think, 'I know that voice. I remember that song, and that prayer.' When you hear the song, 'Bless the Beasts and the Children', will you remember?

"I've been eating healthy lately because of you, and it's not too bad. Giving up alcohol was not so hard either. You're a good influence on me.

"When I think about you growing inside me, I am overjoyed. When I think about giving you up, I am devastated. But we both know I'm not emotionally ready for a baby. It would be too painful, a disaster really, for both of us: too much confusion, too many tortured memories and doubts. They would eat away at any chance we had for survival.

"I want you to have a clean start, a fresh break, a chance with loving parents who can give you all the things that I can't, security, emotional stability, trips to the beach, excitement and joy over your birth.

"Too tired and twisted to be any support for you, I'm still trying to convince myself that my life can be put back together, that the shattered pieces can be sorted through, cleaned off, and arranged into some kind of order. Hopefully there will be enough left intact to create a picture of beauty."

My Child

I need you to know of my love for you
I loved you from the start
And will continue to the end of my life,
But I have to share you
With a mom and dad who will love you
As much as I do
It is breaking my heart
I hope that you never feel
This kind of pain
But I have to put you first
Your parents have so much to offer you
I have too little of what you need
And too much of what you don't
And while my arms will be empty on that day
I leave you with the whispers of my heart:
May my songs, my voice, my prayers,
My force bursting of passion and love
Be retained in your spirit
And nurtured in your soul.

Chapter 53
The Blessed Event

*You use a glass mirror to see your face; you
use works of art to see your soul.* [46]

I still don't understand how something so tragic could be blessed, but there was no other way to describe it. The plan was to spend my entire labor at our favorite pizza parlor in Princeton called Conte's. We were going to get a pizza with everything on it (including anchovies) and spend the evening eating our favorite foods in between contractions. Since I had a very high tolerance of pain, I knew I wasn't going to be one of those belligerent women on TV writhing with the rigors of labor. My plans were dashed in Lamaze class.

"Once you start labor," the instructor warned, "you can't have anything to eat or drink. The most you can have is ice chips."

"What?" I screamed.

Everyone looked at me suspiciously.

"Just in case you need anesthesia, your stomach needs to be clean and clear," said the Lamaze nurse. I didn't remember anything they taught us for the rest of the evening. I growled to Matt, "After nine months of carrying this baby, I should at least get a last supper!"

Matt and I ate our favorite take-out dinner of souvlaki (greek shish kabob sandwiches) near the Princeton graduate tower. We loved being outside on the beautiful lawn lined with colorful rhododendrons. After we ate, we would walk, actually I would waddle and he would walk. The cool New Jersey evenings made you linger for hours after the warm day.

"If I ever have a house, I'd love lots of flowering trees like these, so I can always have cut flowers," I said.

"That means we'd have to live up north. Rhododendrons need the cold weather," he replied pulling a flower off the tree and putting it behind my ear.

"I'm fine with that. I've had enough New Orleans summers for a lifetime."

That's when the sharp pain started. It felt like the middle of my body was strangling the contents within.

"What's wrong?" Matt asked as he caught me from a stumble.

"That must be a contraction. I've never felt anything like that before."

We tried to stay calm but we were too excited. He quickly drove me back my room and helped me pack for the hospital. I had everything arranged; the items just needed to go in a suitcase. Each contraction was a wave of fire through my belly muscles. How a baby could survive the incredible crushing pressure remained to be seen.

So instead of Conte's pizza, we feasted on John Coltrane's soulful saxophone riffs. We danced in my room to numb the pain while Matt measured the time in between contractions. Each moment brought the excruciating reality closer into view. It was a divine mixture of pain and pleasure knowing that we were about to experience the miracle of birth but have nothing to show for it in the end. Eight hours later, at 1:00 AM, we rolled into the emergency room, and hence into the birthing room.

Matt couldn't stand seeing me in such pain, so he crawled in and cuddled up next to me on the hospital bed. Whenever a contraction came he held me for comfort. That was until a nurse came in and gasped.

"What are you doing? You can't be in the bed. Beds are for patients only."

He apologized and sunk into the chair. After about four more hours of gut-wrenching pain, they gave me an epidural. I breathed the biggest sigh of relief in my life. After only a few pushes, they laid a beautiful nine pound thirteen ounce baby boy on my stomach. His pebble eyes seemed to say, "There you are. I've been waiting to see you."

Matt and I just cried and cried in disbelief that it was all over and he was so perfect. His golden strands glued to his head, outlined his intricately small ears. His little hands were clenched tightly. After a few whimpers, he snuggled safely into the crook of my arm.

We agreed that we would spend as much time as we could with him before signing the papers. Matt slept slumped in the chair next to my bed for the next three days. The baby was cuddled, held, fed, and loved with every ounce of energy we could muster.

It was a dangerous game we were playing, but we didn't want his first days of life to be filled with anxiety or the hurried arms of nurses. We wanted him to feel the wonder and awe of parents enamored with their son.

We spent our days as new parents do: counting every finger and toe, examining the resemblances in eyes and nose, unwrapping and rewrapping his blanket, wondering why he stayed so bunched up when finally he had room to stretch and straighten. Keeping an exhaustive list of questions, we bombarded the nurses each time they came in the room.

"How long do we have to keep his skull cap on? When will his umbilical cord pop off? Can we be there for the circumcision?"

But the silence from the nurses was deafening. Whereas the other rooms were filled with well-wishers, flowers, visitors, and rejoicing, our little room was a quiet sanctuary. Knowing that we were not keeping our baby, the nurses tended to stay out of our room, and cut to the chase in conversation. Who could blame them really? What was there to say?

The hardest part was the birth certificate application forms. The nurse handed them to me and said, "Fill out these papers. His name goes at the top and yours at the bottom."

"But you don't understand, we aren't keeping him, so we aren't naming him."

"You *will* name him if you want him to leave the hospital."

I felt the breath being sucked right out of my body. I couldn't name him. It was too personal. If I named him, I'd never be able to let him go. At that instant, I fully understood Kandinsky and his *Without Title* painting. You *could* labor over something for a very long time and not have a name for it. Perhaps it was so close to his heart, held so much of his soul, and had so much of a hold on him, he'd never be able to let it go if he named it. Matt stepped up with suggestions.

"We can name him Robert Anderson Malon, that way his initials will be RAM." I agreed, in fear that any discussion would push me over the edge. His name jolted us back to the fact that we had only one more day together. It was spent in the crystal clear knowledge that, although we longed for him, we had so little to offer him. The short time we had with him, we saw how much care, how many accouterments, how much time it took for a baby. The more time we spent with him, the more apparent we came up lacking.

We gazed into his gray eyes and told him once again that we loved him, and we wanted so much more for him than we could offer. He looked back with intensity, like he really understood. After helping me into the getaway wheelchair and placing that soft little bundle in my arms, the maternity nurse said tenderly, "You know, what you are doing is really a blessing. I know it's hard right now. But we adopted my daughter five years ago, and I cannot begin to tell you what it's like on the other side. There are people waiting for him right now, who are about to jump out of their skin with excitement. Thank you for giving them a chance at a child. God bless you for what you are doing!"

With tears streaming down our faces, we thanked her profusely for her encouragement. The heavy silence of the last four days had been transformed into words that lifted us to a place beyond ourselves. We rolled out with a new sense of purpose and assurance. As long as I live, I will never forget that woman. She was the angel that helped us step into the impossible transition, giving a face to the waiting arms that God had planned for our child.

Chapter 54
Thermal Shock

The effect on a material of rapid temperature change is called thermal shock. In glass it usually involves stress, which is formed as the surface expands or contracts more rapidly than the interior, often resulting in cracking or complete breakage.[47]

The lawyer was waiting to pick us up at the hospital. Did he hire a limousine to ensure we didn't change our minds? Was he protecting his investment, or providing us a safe haven to say goodbye? Whatever the case, we were very relieved not to have to drive with such a precious package, under the emotionally charged circumstances.

Our only desire was to gaze in our baby's beaming eyes and unravel his long, piano fingers. He stayed awake the entire drive from the hospital to the hotel room like he knew he'd better study our faces one last time. Going inside to get the preliminaries settled, the lawyer instructed us to take our time, and come in when we were ready. The motel room door was open. Was it so they could keep a good eye on us?

They were all smiles as we walked in with the living treasure. The man leapt and greeted us with energetic handshakes. The woman hovered around the baby and oohed and aahed. *Was that a tear in her eye?* Matt stayed pretty close and sat on the bed. The woman began with small talk. "He's beautiful...so long and perfect. I see where he gets his hair."

"See his long piano fingers." I stretched them out for all to see. "He's such a good baby, doesn't cry much at all. He's so peaceful." I tried to concentrate, but all I could see was the little girl. She was about twelve years old, sitting on the bed. I held him so close I could feel his little breath on my neck. *He has no idea what is about to take place.*

She couldn't take her eyes off of him. My lawyer spoke incessantly with the wah wah of Charlie Brown adults. There was no need for it; I understood every step of the process. I'd done my part: produced a completely healthy, beautiful baby boy. They'd done theirs: paid for all medical costs and legal fees.

The only part left was signing the papers to make it legal and binding. "You need to put the baby down, Jenna. We have a lot of papers to sign," the lawyer said with authority. But I couldn't, put him down that is. The papers, I knew we had to sign. We couldn't provide for him. I was still too much of a mess.

Things became tense, and the room hushed as I hesitated. Finally, I took a deep breath, smelled his sweet baby smell, gave him a good long kiss and laid him on a blanket in the middle of the bed. I was glad I didn't have to give him to anyone because I hadn't worked up to that yet. As I patted his back to comfort him, my hand could not pull itself away, as if an invisible magnetic bond had connected us forever. He squirmed to find a new position, and settled into a nap.

The girl moved close to him, eyes gleaming with the excitement of choosing a new puppy. Every inch of her screamed with desire to touch him. He jostled with a whine and a wiggle, so she sat with him on the bed, patting and humming to him. I couldn't peel my eyes away. Someone grabbed my arm and moved me toward the table. The pen was like a knife in my hand. I couldn't get my fingers around it.

"Do you have a name for him?" I asked, but I couldn't look at her.

"We're not sure," the mother replied. "Probably Gerard, since he is the saint of motherhood and those who are trying to conceive. It looks like God answered our prayers through you."

What a horrible name!

My lawyer directed me again to the papers that I needed to sign. Matt was watching my every move. I looked from pen to the bed a few times, knowing full well the anguish it would bring, but no blood. I was used to that by now-disguising desolation and distress with a well-layered veneer. We signed. They signed.

The papers meant our rights were terminated. We couldn't check on him, ask about him, or have any contact with him. He was theirs. We had 30 days to change our minds, but I couldn't do it. What did I have to offer?

Studying the people who were going to raise our child, I noticed how beautiful and vivacious she was. Their daughter had flowing long brown hair like Jackie Onassis. He had strong muscular hands and spoke with kindness.

"Is there anything else we can do for you? Or get for you?"

A new heart. "No I'm fine," I said, but I knew I didn't look like it.

"You have given us such a great gift," the mother said as she picked him up. When I was finally able to look up, I saw her eyes brimming with tears that matched mine, drop for drop. I wondered if the same celestial faucet that controlled the flow of desolation pumped jubilation as well, just different ends of the same line.

I sobbed as I watched how easily he relaxed and nestled in his new mother's arms. Their nexus was my nemesis, and another laceration gouged the little left of my soul. There were lots of tears and tissues, but at the end it was silent. It had the feeling of a funeral.

"He will always know he is adopted," his mother said as they walked out of the room.

When it was over, we got into the limo. I immediately noticed the baby powder, and his subtle sweet cuddly baby smell. Funny, I hadn't noticed it when the real thing was in my arms. It wafted to the heart of my despair. Matt wrapped his arms around me more tightly than he ever had before. *Did he smell it too? Did he feel the barrenness in his arms, and want to fill them up as well?*

We cried quietly in the back seat on the way back to the hospital. "Gardens, children and marriages reflect the care that has been tended them," I said with all the courage I could muster.

"They will take good care of him, Jenna," Matt said clearing his throat.

"*We*...are taking...good care of him...by letting him go," I sniffled.

"Yes, we are. He's in God's hands."

When we got out of the car the lawyer reminded us, "You have given a great gift today." He handed us the paperwork, and his card, gave us both good long handshakes while saying, "God bless you."

As I crawled out of the car, I was very thankful. *We really are blessed that it all worked out this well. Thank you, Lord. Take care of him and please help me to keep myself together.* As I watched the limo drive away, I dried my eyes with my last soggy Kleenex. *Yes, that was just like a funeral.*

Chapter 55
He Will Always Know

Every studio has a shard pile whose remnants represent the creative process. When all hope is gone, the pipe is knocked against a solid object, and the glass piece clinks into the discarded pile of shards.

"He will always know he's adopted," she said with full arms on that misty grey day. With a huge chunk of my soul left behind, I walked out empty, except for scads of unanswered questions. It left me with a bump in the road I could never get around, a rupture in my well-ordered plan.

Would it be better if he didn't know? Then he would never have to live with the gut-wrenching question, "Why didn't they want me?"

Once one question formed, the others collected in a hurricane that wreaked havoc on my peace of mind. *Will he look like me, with my wavy hair? Will he want to know about me? Can he be happy? Have we inflicted insurmountable pain and agony on him? Will they be good parents?*

Will he be an inquisitive child like I was, taking things apart and putting them back together again, to see how they worked? Did he get my musical genes? Does he bounce unconsciously with every beat of a song? How long can he stay focused on one thing? Does he bore easily and run from one thing to another like I do?

These questions were always on the forefront of my mind. I tried to block them as soon as they came; otherwise it was a downward spiral with no escape.

Please give him strength to endure the doubts, fears, and rejection. Please help him to fit in like I never did. Please protect him, and help him remember the feeling of love and not the feeling of loss. Please give him courage to fight for what he needs. Please...

He will always know that someone rejected him. No matter how good of a reason she had, no matter how much she endured or had to give up for him, his own flesh-and-blood-mother rejected him. *Will he ever be able to get over that?*

Some days I wish he never knew. It might save him some pain. But that would be unfair on so many fronts.

He will always know that his birth mother was a failure as a mother. But, he will always know that there is a family that wanted him so much they prayed for him, and planned for him. They provided for his every need.

He will always know. What does that mean? Does that mean I can contact him later? Does that mean he'll grow up thinking he's a second-class citizen, illegitimate, unwanted?

Does that mean that everywhere he goes, every room he enters, he will scan every person to see if anyone looks like him? Is there anyone in the room that could be related to him? His brother, aunt, mother?

He will always know that no matter how much his adoptive family loves him, there are real flesh-and-blood people out there that he is blood-related to that he might never meet. He will always know. Tell me, please, is that a good thing, or a bad thing?

Chapter 56
Refractory

A refractory is a material with the ability to retain its strength, physical shape, and chemical identity at high temperatures. Hence, it is used in linings for furnaces, kilns, incinerators, crucibles and reactors.

Princeton Seminary was a totally different type of school than Conservative Seminary. Research papers, panel discussions, projects, and heavy academics were interspersed with all night religious discussions. But somehow amid the heavy academia, there was loads of fun as well: hiding the clapper from the seminary bell, and dancing on the Rat (a painted mascot on the basement floor of one of the ancient dorms). I could barely keep up with the rigor, but I loved it. When we were not researching and writing, we were in discourse with students from Ethiopia, Israel, Korea, India, and Japan. Our world was so vast, seeing the perspectives of so many people.

When Michael Montana, a retired missionary, unexpectedly walked into the dining hall, the entire Korean population hushed, and stood up, in his honor for the lives he helped God transform in Korea. Our Ethiopian friend taught us the "cost of discipleship" watching how he, a bishop in the Coptic Church, endured a ten year exile from his country. Our eyes surely widened when South African friends reported that the major issue in their church was convincing African men they could have only one wife.

But more pertinent than any expansive theological issue I learned in class (or around the dinner table) were the lessons we learned on the intricacy of relationships. The seminary community was a tightly knit group that embraced us solicitously after the adoption. The married friends who knew of our struggles consoled and entertained us. Like a night at the movies, we used them as models of what it looked like to be wedded.

Princeton housed married students in small apartments on the other side of town, near a golf course. There, we enjoyed late night picnics on the green complete with candles, boom boxes and dancing. If only the greens keeper knew. Sometimes Matt or I would dog sit for our friends. We'd light all the candles in the house and dance. Once we committed a grave social faux pas of homemaking-lighting new decorative candles. Questioned by our friend as to why we lit her new candles, we quickly realized there were key differences in how people lived. Some believed every candle should be burned brightly, and others believed in protecting their turf. "Trying to navigate between gender roles and the mine fields of territory is what marriage is all about," our friends warned.

Matt and I both agreed that couples should not get married until they had been through the calendar year twice. So at our two year anniversary, still going strong, I was walking on clouds.

"Get dressed up tonight; I have a surprise," he said, as I called him to confirm what time I needed to pick him up. Dressed in my new pink dress, I drove to his dorm. He asked, "Can I drive your car so our location can be a secret until we get there?"

"Uh...sure." *Could this be the night?*

He drove us to Laheire's, the most exquisite restaurant in town. The first thing I noticed when the brought us into the dining room was how quiet it was. The room was filled with people, but everyone was speaking in whispers at their tables. We adjusted our volume and began our evening of delightful conversation and exquisite food. We had the best dinner ever: stuffed venison, quail, and grilled haricots verts.

"Why do they give such fancy names when they are only green beans?" Matt pondered.

"I guess, if you are going to charge lots of money for them, you need to ramp things up a bit," I replied.

"It is fun to get all dressed up and get out of the cafeteria. Isn't it?" he said taking a sip of wine.

"It's like we are really adults now," I chimed.

"You look amazing. Especially since you just had a baby 4 months ago."

"Thanks, I can't believe it's already been that long. It's still so surreal," I replied with shaky voice.

"Do you think about him much?" he asked cautiously.

"Many times a day."

"Me too," he replied with sad eyes.

"They say a child reinvents the world for you. I think he did that for me. Even though it breaks my heart that we couldn't keep him, just knowing he is alive makes me more aware of the future. I used to see the future as neb-ulous and cloudy. Now, after experiencing childbirth, it's like I'm somehow connected to the future. I don't know how, but that brings me more hope."

"That's good to hear as you have been a bit short on hope," he replied with smiling eyes.

"I know."

"I can't think about him for too long, though, or visualize where he is.

"Me either...I try not let it go too far," I could hear his voice wobble.

"But that doesn't always work, does it?" I asked fully knowing the answer.

"I was hoping it would get easier by now," he said, fidgeting.

"I know. I try to just bring it around to praying for him as soon as I..."

We were both relieved when the waiter broke up the conversation ask-ing if we wanted dessert.

We went back to small talk after that. *Would the baby be the elephant in the room for the rest of our lives?*

After a while, the waiter brought our blackberry cobbler, and coffee with chocolate shavings. My stomach was aflutter with anticipation of the little box.

"Happy anniversary you gorgeous human bean."

"Happy anniversary you haricots vert," I chuckled.

"You know you will be up all night if you drink that coffee."

"I know," I said, "I'm hoping to be awake for a walk around the town after dinner."

"I've never seen you drink coffee before."

"I'm trying to be an adult here, you know."

By the time we finished our meal, our conversation and tone had re-turned to normal. While he paid the bill, I felt the disappointment creep in. As we walked around town, our bellies so full we waddled, I was hopeful his proposal kit was in the car. But he just drove me home. When he kissed me goodnight, my curiosity get the best of me so I asked, "What was the surprise you had for me?"

"Me paying for a really fancy restaurant," he beamed proudly. I sat dumbfounded, biting my tongue not to say what was on its tip. *But I fully expected **that** for our 2 year anniversary!*

Chapter 57
Core Heat

One of the most important facets of glassblowing is retaining the core heat. You should never allow the piece to become so cold that it stops moving. From the moment you gather, the piece should be so hot that it continually moves, even while you are reheating it. [48]

My Dear Child,

You are one year old today. Happy birthday! Please know that June 16 will always be a very special date for me. I had to write you to let you know that you are always in our hearts, no matter how far apart we live.

Your father and I made the most difficult decision we have ever made in our lives when we decided to give you up for adoption. We pondered and cried for so very long. There are so many things to say that I don't know where to begin. I will begin with love because that is where you began. Your father and I were and still are, very much in love. It was out of this love that you were created. I know this may be difficult for you to understand but it is because we love you so very much that we gave you up.

You see, we were both in school, still years away from our degrees and with thousands of dollars' worth of loans to pay off. When we found out about you we were joyous, and remain so even to this day. But we were not ready or able for the tremendous responsibility of caring for a child. We were not physically, emotionally, or financially prepared for such a responsibility, although to this day we wish that we could have been.

We are sorry if our decision   has caused you pain. We really feel that we did the right thing. At the time of your birth, that is all we had to go on. I am hoping that somehow this letter helps you understand our separation and make it easier for all of us to bear.

I must tell you that when you are old enough to understand all this, your father and I would be open to meeting you, but that is your decision. And please don't come to us under the auspices of finding your real parents because your real parents are right there with you. Real parents are the ones who are there when you need them, giving love and kisses when the world seems like it is falling apart. Real parents take care of you when you are scared and alone. Your real parents are Jo Ellen and Bob. I gave birth to you. Believe me there is a very big difference. Almost anyone can give birth, not as many can be real parents.

You are a gift to the world. <u>Let your light shine brightly.</u> You are imbued with a special spirit and a special love. Share it with others.

My wish for you is that you develop to your best mentally, physically, emotionally and spiritually as you continue to grow. We have met your parents and your sister. And we know that they love and care for you. I hope the feeling is always mutual, for they will assist greatly during your journey through life. We are not ashamed of you, nor of having you. We think of you often with fondness and love. May God be with you always!

From the bottom of my heart,

Your birth mother,
Jenna

Chapter 58
The Art of Catastrophe

Glassblowing is an art with the prospect of catastrophe.
Some of the masterpieces are created with thin connections
at the point that can barely hold everything together.

Dear Matt and Jenna,

It's so nice to hear from you. I'm so glad to find out you and Matt are still together. Relationships are a bit difficult for me. I am trying to forgive my father, and I'm almost there, just not entirely. One immensely valuable thing I learned from dealing with him though is the power of words. I learned that even a little rearrangement of your wording or a small change of tone can really affect others, how you come across, and the impression you leave. I know now how effective communication and mutual respect are very important. As well as the importance of venting, and not keeping things pent up within you until you explode.

After my failed college experience, my cousin came to the rescue. He owned a few restaurants around town, and he believed I had the potential to run them for him. He knew I was a businessman at heart, and liked organizing/planning/ etc. So one month before Katrina, I started working for him.

This proved to be interesting. I was working shifts with three of my cousins (we have a gigantic family on my mother's side, and about eight of my cousins are around my age), which I thought was going to be absolutely horrible. I was always the black sheep of the family, never really got along much with any of them. We did our separate things always- me, out of fear of judgment by them. We were very different;

however, working with them, I realized that these people weren't as bad as I had always made them out to be...and they realized the same. Perceptions are a funny thing!

We got along great, and for the first time I felt like I was comfortable with the rest of my family. We started to get to know each other. I was the happiest I had been in so very long. Felt like I belonged-a rare feeling for me. My personality was shining.

Then, there was Katrina. I'll get to that in the next email, though.

I had mentioned there being something that was the probably the main source of my depression, self destructive tendencies, and bad decisions in a previous email. I'm wrestling right now over whether to tell you. However, if I'm going into my background, might as well not leave out an important issue...and well, I would like to think that ya'll are understanding people.

Ever since 7th-8th grade, I've struggled with the issue of <u>homosexuality</u>. It's a very devastating thing, being raised in an uber-conservative Christian home. It's probably single-handedly the hardest thing I've ever had to deal with. I wouldn't wish it on my worst of enemies. Imagine being brought up in that situation...it's incredibly tough. And due to all the faith-related issues regarding that...I'm sure it didn't exactly help in my fallout with Christianity. I'm still incredibly insecure about it, and slowly coming around to accepting the inevitable. I always find it interesting looking at how people subconsciously punish and persecute themselves for absurd reasons. It's sad really.

-Jeffrey

Dear Jeffrey,

It was great to hear from you again. It is important to us that you are sharing too. It is like a lost part our life has been found-or found us. I thank God for that!

I believe I left off with college. But in light of your last letter, I might want to back up a bit. I too would usually not go into such a revealing part of my life on the first few conversations with someone, but in this case it may be warranted-I don't know.

In high school I was in the drama group for the Jefferson Parish High Schools. We had great liberties growing up in New Orleans in the 70s. I had a car at 14, and a mother who knew better than to tell me not to do something because I would run straight to it. I waited tables and bartended all through high school and college so I had lots of ready cash. Hence, I celebrated in the French Quarter every weekend most of my life. I had a wide range of friends from all walks of life that exposed me to things very early on. Some of my best friends were gay. I usually ended up at the Bourbon Pub and the Parade (who knows what they are called to-day?) by 2 or 3 AM most weekends because that is where the best dancing was. Matt even went there with me one night when we were back in town not too long ago, so if you think you are scaring us off, you are not.

But to continue...I gave you one reason why I left LSU, but it was the superficial one. The real reason was that I was getting in really deep in the gay scene. I believe there were a lot of things that led up to that part of my life: hor-rible men, fear, and loathing...there are many details that I have not even told Matt, but he knows enough of how I ran to women, agonized, and still didn't find what I was looking for in love, understanding, or connection.

So, I went to Loyola. The priests fascinated me: men who were not interested in having sex with me. What a concept! It was truly the most healing time of my life. LSU had left me terribly empty and disgusted with life. Neither men nor women satisfied, nor did drinking, or drugs. I had all the money I wanted and it meant nothing. So, a friend and I (one whose fiancée had just died) became roommates. I attended Loyola and she the University of New Orleans.

Who knows what winds blew or spirit fluttered in, but

it moved us toward church. We gravitated to a Presbyterian one around the corner from our shotgun apartment in mid-city. During that time, I came face to face with mortality. One of the people whom I worked with was murdered in a very horrific way, and she was my age. I don't know how to explain it, but at 22 years old, I never thought I was going to die. But there I was faced with death: ugly, bloody, raw, horrible, death. And I had to take a good hard look at my life and how I was living it. The hatred inside was defining me. The reflection of my inner-self was not what I wanted to see, but it moved me toward a change.

One thing led to another and I ended up at Conservative Theological Seminary swearing off both men and women for life. I was going to be a missionary to Africa. Nothing was going to stop me! I write this to let you know that what you think is inevitable may not be. Either way, I guarantee, it does not matter to us.

You are loved, and lovable.

-Jenna

Dear Jenna,

Wow, interesting. I'm glad that you were willing to share that with me! I was unsure how ya'll were going to take in what I had to say. Yeah, that was always the hard part, knowing if that really was my innate inclination, or if it was brought on by traumatic events, stress, or fear of women. You can never rule anything out, so I tended to always stay on the fence, and really do nothing about it. I think I have a good idea now...but am still plagued by doubt. It's an iffy, troublesome thing. My tendency to overanalyze something to death from every imaginable perspective never helped the situation. If you don't mind me asking: What was so different with Matt that made you think you might have a chance of happiness with a man?

Also, I forgot to mention. One of the things I really look

forward to hearing from ya'll in times to come are how intelligent people such as yourselves, very familiar with philosophy, as well as the parallels between Christianity and mythology...could not only believe in a god, but a personal God, and even more strikingly-the whole Christianity thing. For the longest time, this has had me baffled! I must be missing something. If you don't mind sharing, I would LOVE to learn...because despite my very strong opposing beliefs, I am a seeker of truth. And maybe I don't have the truth(?)

-Jeffrey

Chapter 59
Strong as Steel

Glass has a myriad of interesting and useful properties. It is as brilliant as a diamond, as fiery as an opal, as colorful as the rainbow, as light and delicate as a spider's web, as fragile as an eggshell or as strong as steel. [49]

Matt and I shared the craziest idiosyncrasies. Both of us loved everything-but-the-kitchen-sink-and-anchovies pizza; even cold for breakfast. One morning, when Matt came to my room to share our pizza treasure from the night before, he seemed unusually energetic for the morning. "I've been thinking," he said with a gleam in his eyes.

"Watch out, world," I kidded.

"We've been through a lot together. The pregnancy, the adoption, moving to Princeton, and we've come out better. Strong as steel."

"I like to think of us as music," I replied.

"That is a much more beautiful image."

"It's like most of my life I've only heard the melody in music. But then I met people like Grandma Gertrude, the Basin St. kids, and Elzbieta in the glass studio, and I learned to hear the bass line."

"Like the bass guitar?" his eyes squinted with the question.

"Sort of. Any rhythm instrument, piano, drum, bass etc. can play the bass line. It supports and defines the harmonic motion. It gives music its pulse. They taught me to see the things much deeper within, like the bass line in a musical piece."

"Like?"

"Like dealing with racism, violence, the complexities of composition and environment, sexual identity...and although these brought much pain, and fear, they are also what gave me character and definition. Without them my life would not have the depth it has."

"You are a very deep soul," he replied.

"But that's just it. You, your patience, support and encouragement while

I processed everything, helped me to have the courage and hope not just to hear the bass line, but to use it as a new pulse for my life. I am able stand up and to sing that bass line with conviction and hope now."

His hand reached out to hold mine. "You've given me courage and hope too. I think it's because we're such a good team. And we really love each other, support each other, and are totally honest with each other in every way."

"You're right. I can tell you things, I've never told anyone," I said with a smile.

"That's just it. I want to keep hearing those things, and learning about you for the rest of my life. I've been thinking about this for a long time now. I love you, Jenna. I mean; I am head over heels, flutter in the heart when I see you, in love with you, and I want to make that permanent. Will you marry me?"

I was totally caught off guard. Instantly, my brain began to swirl with visions: my dad's flying plates and Elzbieta's bloodied hand holding the pieces of the paperweight. And I heard her words loud and clear, "It's tiring really. Your intensity stresses everyone out. You'll never be able to love glass like I do because you are so busy studying, judging, and working the glass. Why can't you just breathe, feel, love, and create?"

I studied the little plastic to go cup of anchovies on my desk; I could smell its pungency from across the room. A prickle started to arise in my head, which moved to my toes. I hesitated for a moment. Was it a spider crawl? Its warmth radiated through, melting the doubts and fears that had held court over my emotions my entire life. I took a deep breath and remembered the exquisite beaming child we had created together.

I smiled and said, "You know, there will never, ever be anyone in this world who knows me like you do, and loves me anyway. Besides, who else but you would eat anchovies with me before 9 AM? Who else can bring out all of my senses, all of the colors of the spectrum for me to enjoy? Of course, I will marry you." With that he swooped me in his arms, twirled me around, and we sank into another mind-blowing fireworks kiss.

As if two pieces of anchovy/kitchen sink pizza were not enough, we strolled arm-in-arm to the PJ's Pancake House to celebrate. Passing the darkened pizza parlor (I guess others don't share our love of pizza for breakfast) Matt said, "You know I proposed to you last night, right here as we walked to Vesuvio's?"

"What? I didn't hear you."

"I was hoping that was the case, and that you weren't just blowing me off. It took a lot of nerve to ask again today."

"It's a good thing I didn't hear you though. I wouldn't want to have to tell our children that you proposed to me as we were walking to a pizza parlor!"

With his revelation, I had the courage to ask, "So, why didn't you propose on our 2 year anniversary a few weeks ago?"

"Because, you were expecting it," he answered, as if it was the silliest question in the world. I added another point to his rapidly filling scorecard. *This man knows how much I need spontaneity. At least I'll never be bored.*

When I told my mother I was getting married, I thought she was going to jump out of her skin with her response, "I had given up hope of you ever getting married. I thought you hated the thought."

"I did," I replied. "But that is before I met Matt. A lot can change when you find a soul mate."

"He is a gem like no other. And you two are perfect for each other. Both of you with enough degrees to start a small college, but neither with enough common sense to come in out of the rain."

I laughed a belly laugh at her apt description before replying, "But we love the rain. Especially playing and splashing in the puddles."

"My point exactly," she nodded her head in disbelief.

⸺⸺•((◦))•⸺⸺

Planning a wedding while I was in New Orleans for the summer and Matt in Princeton finishing his course work was a little troublesome, but my mother's bridal super-powers clicked into overdrive. It was a good thing because I hadn't spent years dreaming about weddings like most girls had, reading bridal magazines and clipping honeymoon ideas.

I wanted the wedding cheap. I didn't see much sense in spending ridiculous amounts of money on one day, but Mom wanted extravagance, and even limousines. I wanted myriads of color and she said, "Weddings are about white, not the rainbow like gypsies."

"What's the point then?" I questioned. "Expensive and white sounds like boring with a capital B."

Because I didn't really care one way or the other as long as it was cheap, mom got her way on most things. She had a friend with a limousine service who would give us a special price. I found a beautiful dress on the ½ price rack at a bridal store. And she was right, every bridal florist said that white was the way to go with weddings. UGH! I guess I'm more of a gypsy at heart.

We came to a glitch one day when my mother presented me with a box, "These are all the things from the nightstand in your room. I thought you might want them." As I took it from her, I noticed the rough drafts of the letter I had written our beautiful child on his first birthday. My eyes did a double blink.

"So you know?" I questioned knowing full well that she would read any letter in her hands.

"Know what?"

"About the baby. These were my letters to him."

"How was I to know if they were real or not? You always wrote the craziest things."

"They were real," I said sheepishly.

"Humph," she replied. Her flip-flops smacked her feet as she closed the door and the conversation behind her.

I remember thinking: that was a close one. I was really not ready to deal with a conversation like that at that particular time without Matt's strength. But I didn't have to. She strolled out, never uttering another word about it. I'm sure there was a reason she didn't want to talk about it any further. There was probably too much stress already going on with planning the wedding that I had thought little of before my engagement. There were probably unresolved feelings of her difficult choice when she found out she was pregnant with me.

So I did what I had always done when faced with conflicting emotional feelings: I let them walk away, relieved that I didn't have to relive any more of the bloody shards in my life.

———— «(◦)» ————

The rehearsal dinner was a barbeque and a shrimp boil held at City Park's Parthenon Pavilion overlooking the paddleboat lagoon. My heart skipped each time I saw a paddleboat glide by remembering our first kiss. Stuffed with shrimp, ribs and chicken, our family and out-of-town guests danced the night away under the stars.

Our wedding was held on Labor Day weekend at 5:30 pm. *Lohengrin's* "Bridal Chorus" began and I took my father's arm to walk up the aisle of the sanctuary. I heard his continuous refrain, "This is a happy time. Think happy." *Is he thinking I'm going to break down and cry?* Sunlight streamed through the stained glass, illuminating the sanctuary filled with people we knew and loved. All I could think about was: *Why can't I cry like a normal bride?*

Matt's eyes were dripping, though. He pulled himself together the closer I got to him. When he took my hand from my father's, I felt a spark down to my toes. Standing together in the front of the sanctuary surrounded by all of our friends and family, on the arms of a man I didn't even have the courage to dream could be mine, I was the happiest I had ever been in my life. We shared our vows, mine promising to fan the flame of his free spirit, and his to cherish and support the "woman who can't see the rain for the rainbow."

Our reception was held at the Magnolia Plantation. My very large extended Syrian family loves to dance and drink, so we partied the night with exuberance dripping from our heels and hi-balls. Of particular delight was seeing Ari the Greek dancing the Dabke (a traditional Mediterranean dance) with my family and hanging near my mother for the evening. The only family Matt had in attendance was his parents and sister uncomfortably looking on from their seats. *Was that expression utter disbelief or consternation?*

Nothing got in the way of our celebration, though. It was the perfect way to start our life together. I kept pinching myself the entire night thinking, *Can this really be happening to me? What did I do to deserve such a remarkable soul mate to spend the rest of my life with?*

Chapter 60
Levees

> Blowing color has several challenges compared to working
> with clear glass. Although they are the most coveted, blacks
> and blues are notoriously the hardest to work with because
> they absorb heat very quickly in the glory hole. [50]

There comes a time in one's life when the past smacks flat-nosed up against the future. You can let your past define you or you define it. That's when courage is required to take a good honest look in the mirror, a deep breath, and a step forward. I was at one of those junctures and all I could think about was levees.

How could one begin to explain the importance of levees? These walls of dirt, concrete, or stone surround the city of New Orleans like a fortress, acting as stop banks to regulate water levels. Water levels define the city of New Orleans. Imagine being surrounded by water on three sides (Mississippi River, Lake Pontchartrain and the Gulf of Mexico) but positioned 7 feet below sea level. Then you'll understand that in NOLA, water is on a level all its own. One was never far from the realization that the same sultry liquid that brought nourishment, industry, and flavor to the soup-bowl city, could swallow it up in one fell swoop when mixed like a martini with wind and tidal surges. Its sway, its nourishment, its indescribable pull, are all kept at bay by the levee.

So while you are playing tag at the local pavilions, waiting for the steaming cauldron to deliver hot fresh crustaceans to news-papered tables, neighbors, co-worker and friends are squishing mosquitos to a samba rhythm. When the sound is called, everyone oohs and ahs as crawfish, corn, and potatoes are dotted with butter and a little piece of heaven sprinkled on top. You look out at the rippling water amazed that that same force that teems with this shell-sucking goodness could just as easily bring a flood of desecration. The only thing standing in between is the levee.

Walking in to our married-student apartment after our amazing honeymoon to Greece, with boxes from the moving truck piled like Legos all around, I began to feel uneasy. Already we were having heated discussions about where certain pieces of furniture or knick-knacks were going. Each of us had family treasures that the other one was not fully appreciating. Tension was filling the air. The walls started to close in on me as I realized I'd be having these same conversations over territory and belongings for the rest of my life. That's what the marriage certificate meant. I saw the plates crashing, and heard the curse words and screams in my head. Remembering the coldness of the couch as Mom, Jordan, and me, wriggled all night waiting for Dad to come home, I began to dart out the door. But then I remembered the levees.

I imagined myself walking along the levee for a while, taking in the view from both sides like I always did when my friends would swim in Lake Pontchartrain. While they frolicked, I kidded them about the pond scum smell of the water, and kept my eyes focused on the exit route. Yes, my new husband had the power to suck up all of my energy, fighting about boundaries and misplaced assumptions. Yes, I could bolt and have everything my way, like I'd always done. Or I could stay there on the levee, safe and secure for a while and take it all in.

But sometimes even the safety and security we so desperately cling to could fail us. The power of water and the frailty of man could collide with a maelstrom of chaos. All that's left would be a deer in headlights shock that shatters your reality.

I hated to admit it, but marriage was like that. I was beginning to feel caged in after only two weeks. Territory issues, tiptoeing around what you said about relatives, and never having enough quiet time to find my inner-peace, were starting to creep into the surface of my uncertainty. Was marriage going to be the deep dark abyss or the hurricane's tidal surge that swallowed me up and spit me out? The spidery feeling started inching its way down my arms, but I was determined not to let that scare me. I tried the new coping skills I learned from counseling. I asked myself: *What is the worst that could happen?* Memories of the worst experience I'd ever endured took over...

One September morning, when I was about 14, I woke up for school and found Mom staring at the TV screen. The jagged boot-like map of New Orleans had lots of red arrows pointing in its direction. *Uh oh, trouble with a capital T.* Still groggy, all I could hear were the words, "Tropical depression, upgraded, Gulf of Mexico." My first thought was, "Yeah, no school." But my Mom's face was sullen.

"Looks like it's going to be a big one," she stammered. "We haven't had a big one in a while." I made myself some cinnamon toast noticing the swirls I made with the sugar somewhat resembled the hurricane swirls pictured on the screen. *Was that intentional? Did I always swirl my cinnamon sugar?* I couldn't remember. The more she watched, the more her face grew grim. "I don't like the looks of this one."

"Let's go to Grandma's then," I replied. "We can leave now." *And miss school*, I thought with a smile.

"I'm never doing that again," she replied. "Remember last time when we left?"

How could I forget? Edith was a big one, and everyone was warned to evacuate. So we did. Along with our neighbors who didn't have any relatives nearby, we piled into 5 cars toting 2 dogs, 1 cat, 6 children, clothing, and important papers. 10 hours later, (the trip usually takes 5) we arrived at my Grandma's house in South Texas. 11 people began unloading cars in the middle of the night. Kids carried sleeping bags they dreamed of curling into. Parents carried noisy animals and stuffed suitcases, and when we finally get all settled in, we turn on the TV to check the status of the storm. Hurricane Edith had made a sharp turn to the East. Now all the arrows were pointing to Lake Charles, LA, only minutes away from my Grandma's. The storm had not only followed us, but had picked up speed, and would hit within 24 hours. After much shouting, cursing and complaining, it was settled: we were heading back to New Orleans. This time with one additional person: my Grandma who filed right into our already packed-like-sardines car.

No, we were not doing that again. We had all vowed never to leave New Orleans again. So we did what most native New Orleanians did when faced with stress and tension, especially in the midst of hurricanes. We called our neighbors and threw a party!

We all knew the drill really well, and had it down to a science. The children collected flashlights and candles and filled bathtubs and every open container with water. The dads helped each other board up all windows, secure all equipment, and put furniture on bricks. The mothers took to their ovens, cooking roasts, turkeys, and hams, while others headed to the stores to buy water, batteries, and bread for everyone. Gathering all their liquor stashes, the adults mixed their favorite New Orleans potion: the hurricane, which is a hodge-podge of all the types of alcohol you have in your combined houses mixed with all the juices you can muster, and poured into a cooler. When the nights got long, the adults retreated to the hurricane cooler. Everyone brought their coolers of food and drinks to share and lots of games (especially cards and poker chips). We would have lots of time on our hands.

The party was usually at Pam's house because it was raised a few feet above the others. All twenty of us gathered there to wait out the storm. Torrential downpours fell on the streets, but that is a daily occurrence on a New Orleans summer day. We opened the front door every hour or so to keep watch on the rising water only three feet away from the house. By 11 PM the winds came, blowing leaves, limbs and trash cans through the streets. At midnight the winds gusted and the big trees started to bend sideways like a giant hand was using them as slingshots. We strained our ears to hear the fuzzy radio report but we could only make out words. "Eye approaching. The worst part of the storm." Without warning, the electricity surged and then went out, but we were prepared. We lit candles and clutched our flashlights.

The constant banging and thunder were the worst parts. You instinctively tried to distinguish the sounds of metal screeching against metal, crashes and booms right above your heads, windows breaking and screams from all parts of the house. Any moment you expected things to come flying through the plywood-covered windows right at your head like they do in the movies. As the winds grew noisier, the crowd grew quieter. We extinguished the candles and tried to sleep. Every time a clatter arose, we paused and imagined the worst scenarios. We tried to concentrate on positive things, but in the darkness, that was impossible.

What power does the darkness employ that fuels fear and rampant hopelessness? Eventually the noise was too much to bear, and many started to cry. We were too scared to even talk: our brains were crammed with devastating images. We had all been there before: cars overturned, houses demolished, lawnmowers in trees, and boats never seen again.

After an entire night of winds doing demolition, we fell asleep. It's hard to believe you can sleep with such fear, but powerlessness sets in after a while. Your prayers become your breaths, and you fall into a fog. You're sure you're going to die, but then you wake up and you're alive.

We rose to find a tree smashed near the front door penning us inside. Luckily the water had made it to the top of the front step, but not inside. But the back of the house was another story. Water was seeping in from the back door, covering the kitchen floor. Of course all I could think about was moving those coolers out of the water so the ham I wanted for breakfast could be saved. But no one was as interested in food as I was: they wanted to see the damage.

We all waded to the street. At some points the water was up to our waists. We heard Pam's dad say, "I need the boat. It's four feet deep in the street." We hopped into his fishing boat and rode through the water filled streets. VW bugs were floating; doors were caved in, and trees were down. Electrical wires were tied up into a maze, and gas containers and garage contents were littering the streets like bobbing apples. It was like a floating flea market-the grab and pick kind. If we noticed anything belonging to our family, we grabbed it and put it in the boat, or tied it up to something nearby.

After a half-day of trashy treasure collection, we dragged our water-logged selves back to our own houses and surveyed the damage there. Peering inside, we saw water had seeped into some of the rooms, ruining furniture and all our favorite belongings. We knew we couldn't go back until the water receded which could take two or three days. Heading back to Pam's house, we consoled ourselves with cards, food, and hurricanes. We asserted that if the people in Venice, Italy, could live 365 days a year in water, we could live for a few days. The difference between Venice and us: we would just throw ourselves a party!

So even though I was sitting amidst the unpacked boxes in Princeton, New Jersey, miles away from the New Orleans church I was wedded in, I took another marriage-related vow, compliments of the levees in my hometown. Whenever the darkness and dangers of every-day life started to eat away at my peace, gnashing their sharp teeth and making me fear the very things that add adventure and allure to my life, I'm going to fire up a big ole piece of meat, fill up the coolers, and invite the neighbors over for a party!

Chapter 61
Flash the Color

Since it is imperative that you gather onto colored glass at the right temperature, you must look into the pipe and see if there is any glow. If there is any glow at all you are safe to gather. If not, you should flash the color in the glory hole before gathering. [51]

Dear Jeffrey,

I cannot help thinking of you and your questions. I always wondered if you were an inquisitive child like me, and it seems you are. I can never get enough of learning. For each thing I learn, I have hundreds more questions. That's why I loved Loyola so much. They were not always about giving answers. They constantly gave us questions to inspire us to pursue truth, much like Jesus did. The Jesuits' gentle questions turned me inward to search for God. I couldn't get enough of their quotes from Augustine such as, "This is the very perfection of a man, to find out his own imperfections," and "People travel to wonder at the height of the mountains, at the huge waves of the seas, at the long course of the rivers, at the vast compass of the ocean, at the circular motion of the stars, and yet they pass by themselves without wondering." I believe wonder is better than any drug. Those who wonder will never be disappointed with life. There are new pathways of discovery every second; we just have to be aware.

Along those lines, I was wondering, would you be interested in talking on the phone or meeting us in person sometime soon?

-Jenna

Chapter 62
Sea Glass

Sea glass: A magical, mystical, turbulent ride,
which creates a gem of the sea.

Dear Jenna,

Wow, thanks for the background. This gets even more exciting each conversation!

I would absolutely love talking on the phone, as well as meeting. I was trying to decide when to actually ask you, but it looks like ya'll solved that dilemma for me! From the start I was trying to figure out how much to put in the first letters, and how much will come with time. I think knowing that you are open to communication beyond just letters makes it more desirous to take my time and learn... despite my eagerness in getting to know you-its easy to want it to happen right away. I might have to take some time to put the last year of my life into words-for as much as it might seem that little has happened, to me it FEELS as though the world was pulled from under me-in a good way. But this is among so many other things.

Oh, btw, I love those Augustine quotes you sent me. I really had little knowledge of him, despite going to a Catholic high school.

"This is the very perfection of a man, to find out his own imperfections." and "People travel to wonder at the height of the mountains, at the huge waves of the seas, at the long course of the rivers, at the vast compass of the ocean, at the circular motion of the stars, and yet they pass by themselves without wondering," are my favorite of those, but especially the first one for some reason.

Have a great weekend!

-Jeffrey

Dear Jeffrey,

I'd better let you know that patience has never been one of my strong suits and coupled with the fact that I am very excited that you want to meet us, I'm going to let my impulsive side show through and ask if you're ready to set a date. I'll slow down if needed, but there are lots of options for us. We could come to Santa Fe, you to Atlanta, or how about New Orleans? Any chance you will be there after Christmas? If that is too soon, I'll pull the brakes. But when I get excited about something Matt says I'm like a shark in a feeding tank. I'd prefer to think I'm like a dog panting, jumping, and whelping by the master's feet when he gets home, but a shark is probably a more accurate description.

I love your well-written letters, your insightful thought process, and your passion for life. I just can't wait to see that all rolled into a living body. You have truly, made my day, week, month...Off to church now to sing a lot of praises!!!!

Peace and Blessings!
-Jenna

Dear Jenna,

I will be in New Orleans for Christmas so I'll extend my trip to adjust to your dates. Just let me know of your plans. I can't believe this is really happening!

-Jeffrey

What one deems as scrap for the shard pile, another will deem as treasure. So it is with sea glass. A remnant discarded by one is shaped and polished by the rhythm of the ocean. No one knows for sure the turbulent storms or gentle tides that have rounded the edges, or how much time it took for those jags to become jewels. We know only the hastened heartbeats and the squeals of delight when it is scooped from the surf as treasure.

When I heard Jeffrey's voice for the first time it was like being wrapped in velvet: deep, rich, and alluring. All these years I'd pictured him as a baby, and now with words he had proved to be a man.

Opening my computer and seeing the picture he sent for the first time, I gasped. Those sparkly eyes and exuberant smile were the ones I fell in love with so long ago, but on another face. My heart raced at a rabbit's pace, just as it did with the first email. He was truly ours!

Before the picture, Matt was toying with asking for a DNA test to prove he was Jeffrey. "What's the point?" I asked. "We met his parents, and it's not like we have millions of dollars he's after. He just wants to find his birth parents."

But to him, the jury was out. After the photograph, though, he had no doubts. It was as if Matt was looking in the mirror through a wrinkle in time. Glued to the computer, I was late to work.

It was tricky for Matt and me to stare at his picture for so long, because our teenage sons, Taylor and Dylan, didn't know about Jeffrey yet. Still in shock that he contacted us, we hadn't given much thought as to how to include the boys in on our 190-pound secret.

There were lots of secrets in my life, some that rotted and festered, and some that fizzled and died. But as I looked at his face with those deep understanding eyes from birth, I knew that somehow, this ragged shard of a secret that had brought so much pain, had in God's care, weathered into a stunning piece of sea glass. I was dazzled so much, I couldn't wait to get my hands on it, and share its luminous story with the world!

Chapter 63
New Lenses

Glass has been formed into lenses to correct poor vision for hundreds of years and highly refined lenses into telescopes have helped humans look millions of miles into the sky at planets, stars and galaxies. Other lenses have helped to reveal the microscopic secrets of our own human cell structure.[52]

Dear Jenna,

Today I ended up re-reading the letters ya'll sent me when I was one, for the first time in about 4 years. My mom still has the original letters in a safe deposit box for safe-keeping, but I had her fax them over this morning, since I was curious.

It was amazing seeing so much love conveyed in those two letters! I am glad you wrote those-if not for those, I might have never contacted ya'll. I don't know if ya'll ever kept copies for yourselves, but if you ever want a chance to see them again, to reflect on the place, mindset, etc. you were in back many years ago, ya'll are welcome to read them. Also, Jenna, you have incredible handwriting! Even on a messy fax printout it looked great. I always find it really interesting to look at others' handwriting.

A few questions: both of you apparently have a fascination with art. Is it more of a liking and appreciation with it, or did either of ya'll get into creating it?

Also, I hope I'm not being intrusive with this question, but does the rest of your family currently know about the adoption? Do your sons? If so, do they know I am currently in touch with ya'll? Meeting on the 26th sounds great! I will look into changing my flight.

Talk to you soon,
-Jeffrey

Dear Jeffrey,

What a treat! Matt and I have been looking at your picture since 4:30 AM!

You have Matt's gorgeous smile and sparkling eyes but with my narrow face. And I love your hair! I always wanted a child with Matt's dark flowing hair, but Taylor and Dylan have my light hair. It's funny-your hair was light when you were a baby.

Your glasses are cute, but I hope you are not as blind as I am. If I take my glasses off, I can't see to find them. Luckily, contacts correct my vision to 20/20. I'm going to bring pictures of Matt when he was young so you can see the similarities. Please send more when you get them. I can't wait to see you in person!!!!

-Jenna

Dear Jenna,

I know exactly what you mean! This whole experience for me has been an interesting, intense mixture of feelings. And I'm glad ya'll are not hesitant to express that as well! I'm quite excited by all this emotion, even if it is scary in a way at times, and surreal. It's definitely something I've never experienced before! It's such an interesting, and amazing mixture of self-revelation, joy, hopes coming true, and unbelievable excitement!

Oh, I just finalized my plans with Continental today...I

now won't be leaving NOLA till the 28th at ~7PM. Now that it's all set, I'm counting the days.

-Jeffrey

Dear Jeffrey,

I'll try not to gross you out with all the gory details of our relationship, but I do want to respond to the very honest question you asked earlier about Matt and me. I was never attracted to men sexually. The male physique kind of scared me and grossed me out at the same time. So imagine my surprise when I actually was attracted to Matt. And I mean I couldn't keep my hands off this man. It probably had to do with the fact that he was so attentive to me.

If we were getting kind of hot and heavy, and I was uncomfortable moving to the next level, Matt would sense it without me even saying anything. He would respond with, "I can see you are getting uneasy, so let's just slow it down." I had never had a guy say anything like that before. Most of the men I knew were dogs (as you can see I do not have a very high opinion of males) but I am trying to change that since I have given birth to three boys who are all truly amazing creatures! God certainly has a sense of humor giving me three boys.

Loving Matt has helped restore my faith in the male gender. Living in Wynona has helped too. Matt says the men have to be good here, or the wives might leave them for other women. Whatever the reason, Wynona is chocked full of men who adore their wives. They are real family men, walking their children to school, cooking, volunteering around town and in the schools.

We even have a group of couples that go out dancing every so often together. So, I'm slowly revamping my belief that all men are dogs, some are good dogs but they're all dogs. I haven't come up with my final analysis yet. Anyway his hairy chest was no match for me then and it still gets me every time.

-Jenna

Dear Jenna,

I can't believe I finally have someone to talk to about all the conflictions on sexuality.

It's so beautiful hearing how ya'll interact on the telephone. I can only hope to meet someone and have as much chemistry with him or her as ya'll seem to have!

Sorry I haven't been writing much. Once again, the fear/self-consciousness I was talking about. Having to reflect on who I am currently, the things I like, and where my life currently is, kind of hit me in a weird way. I always think of myself as a Renaissance man of sorts, interests in anything and everything: critical thinking, music, philosophy, outdoors activities, mechanics, art, physics, politics, electronics, psychology, animals, food, history, etc. I'm now stuck trying to figure out...is all that really me? Do I love those things, or, am I using those things just as labels-giving me a sense of identity?

I already know that I have a problem with identity, <u>the sexual orientation thing being a prime example</u>. But I find myself thinking...who AM I really? Then again...why DO I need labels? I am an entity that acts in a Jeffrey Gerard Brisure-ish kind of way. Isn't that enough?

Which leaves me with the point of this email; I really treasure our new communication. It helps me figure out who I am. <u>I am an incredibly analytical being.</u>. I live to think. Which brings me to another point-all these interests are all relative anyway. Whether it's the result of me running to them to try and find a piece of myself or not, the thing I need to look at is-the little time I do spend on each of my interests, do I find it enjoyable? Does it make me happy?

However, this viewpoint is conflicting. I tried applying it to sexuality, and I am not pleased (once again, it forces me closer to a conclusion...something I'm terrified of. It's easier to float in ambiguity.) I might have mixed beliefs on which percentage of homosexuality is innate, and how much of it is the result of psychological trauma, or various other factors dealing with the psyche.

Knowing that a percentage of homosexuality is caused by psychological forces, it leads one to hope, if it's possible that if it's just what the mind has come to believe, is it something that you can override?

But then again, that's underestimating the power of the mind. Changing some fundamental building block of the mind, upon which so many other things have already built upon, isn't easy, and generally not even possible.

That is, however, assuming that you are one of those people that it is brought upon them by psychological factors. You would never know. But even if it is possibly just a piece of software that could be rewritten (with much agony) if you are one of the lucky ones for whom it wasn't innate, is it beneficial for you to change it?

If you weren't given at birth an amazing musical talent, however, you came to appreciate music, found enjoyment in playing it, and was a piece of your life, is it any less a part of who you really are?

Homosexuality, although it may not always be innate, becomes who you are in a way. And if it did become who you are, is it a big deal? I know if you are religious, it may or may not be, depending on your creed. But outside of that, what's the big deal? Should I really care? Should I burden myself with trying to figure it out, driving myself crazy in the process? Holding on to that one last thread of hope that I might not be. Is it worth it?

And now that I find out you have homosexual tendencies it makes a clearer picture of what I've felt all along-that it is just part of my DNA. If it's in my DNA, then surely I am, which means I should stop hoping that I am not, right? What if it is already predetermined?

Outside of religion, is there any reason for homosexuality being that horrible? In another society, that sees it as a trivial matter...would there be any reason for caring if you were or not? Outside of it currently being this horrible social stigma, with *persecution-a-plenty*, what's the big deal?

It's all about weighing your reasoning. Should you work to try and offset some disability/trait/etc.? Is it helpful? Is it harmful? Hell, and that's assuming it's even possible...which we aren't even sure of. So I guess it all comes back to religion?

That is who I am. Not any of the labels, interests, or otherwise...that I have stated in this email. No, not that, but the man-driven by analysis and curiosity, who has to rationalize/figure things out on his own. I figure giving you a snippet of my thoughts at this current moment might help you better understand me.

And hell, it helps me as well. I found out long ago that you never know what's on your mind until you try to communicate it to someone! Only then can understanding begin. I find something new about myself every time I pick up a pen, or sit in front the keyboard.

-Jeffrey

Chapter 64
Overlay

When you are almost finished with your piece and want to
intensify it even more, encase it in a layer of clear, unadulterated
glass. Like the most precious of offerings, you drop your
piece back into the crucible for a final overlay of glass.

*T*he ultimate sacrifice in glassblowing is when you drop your completed
*piece into the crucible for encasing. After all the work: the mixing, the
gathering, the coloring, the shaping, the flashing and the marvering, it is put to
the ultimate test-encasing it in another layer of glass. If it hasn't been perfectly
crafted, balancing chemical and heat, tone and center, it will fracture and fall
off the pipe destroying not just that piece but the entire meld in the pot. If and
when you gain enough confidence to risk it all, you dip it into the honey of life.
You place your piece on the altar of hope and gather onto it the most brilliant
substance next to humankind. You lick your lips with anticipation. For if you
dare to look and believe, what you will take off the pipe is your ultimate masterpiece, magnified through the intensity and complexity of glass.*

Chapter 65
Damn Straight

Glass is a buoyant medium. Phoenix-like, it emerges from fire, ash, and sand. The process is extremely theatrical; the colors are dazzling, and the final object is highly resistant to decay, yet simultaneously rather fragile. [53]

We had not been to a counselor since before we were married, so getting back into it brought great insight. And telling the story of Jeffrey brought powerful sensualities to the surface again. Matt and I never lost our passion for each other, but it seemed that each time we told our story a spark of that new-love infatuation fanned into a greater flame. Our counselor encouraged us to tell the boys immediately, so we went home and waited for them to get home from mock trial and track. We sat them down at the dining room table.

"There's something we need to tell you."

Taylor knew something was up and swiftly responded, "Uh, oh. I know you aren't getting a divorce. Are you pregnant?" His quick wit would definitely serve him well in mock trial.

"Well," Matt replied, "funny that you should say that. No, 'we' are not pregnant, but you do have a new brother..."

"What?" Dylan raised his pitch, obviously confused.

I continued, "We had a baby boy, 22 years ago and gave him up for adoption. He has contacted us recently and wants to meet us."

"Why didn't you tell us?" Taylor exclaimed.

"You know, it's a very long story, but I can tell you that it was a very emotionally charged time. We didn't even tell your grandparents. It was a secret, a beautiful secret, not because we were ashamed of the fact, but more so I could have the time and energy to sort out the emotional junk of my past. I'm in a much better state to handle this now than I was then. I can assure you that. And having you guys was a big part of that."

"Where does he live? Who does he look like?" The questions were endless. But telling the boys was much easier than we expected. Dylan was hesitant at first and said he didn't really need to meet Jeffrey, but Taylor was all in, saying, "Wow, another full blood brother I never knew I had. I can't wait to meet him. Do you think he'll act like us?"

When Taylor's friends came over late that night for their regular Friday night home-cooked meal, he showed off Jeffrey's picture like a proud big brother. His friends were eager to meet him, too. I had to explain, "We are taking this one step at a time. We don't want to overwhelm Jeffrey. But if he ever does come to Atlanta, you'll be the first friends to meet him."

Later, we asked Taylor how he knew we weren't getting a divorce and he replied, "You two have the best marriage of anyone I know. If there's one thing we are sure of in this family, it is that you and dad are madly in love with each other!"

Matt and I looked at each other and grinned proudly. As Matt pinched my behind, he replied, "You are damn straight about that!"

The hardest part of our experience was telling our extended family. My mother did not take the news very well. She remembered the incident finding the letters I wrote the baby. When we told her he contacted us, she still had a chill in her voice as she spoke.

"So I've had a grandson for 22 years, that I've never been able to know. That means my mother would've been able to see one of her grandchildren before she died, if only..."

"There are a lot of if onlys in this story, Mom. At least we get to meet him now."

"Well, I guess that's true. I just hope I live long enough to see at least one of my great grandchildren. At this rate, who knows..."

My mother's side of the family was very close. We had family reunions every year with over fifty people in attendance from all over the country. They would not take too kindly to being left out of a secret, because there were no secrets in my family. In fact, the fastest way to get a message spread throughout the family was to say, "Don't tell anyone I told you this." Guaranteed, everyone would know by the end of the day.

So after telling my mother, we wrote a letter and sent it out through our family email:

Dear Family,

I cannot wait to tell you of the most wonderful

Christmas gift Matt and I have ever received. It has deep-ened our understanding of the great gift that God gave to us in the form of his son, as we too have received a son-well, a 22-year-old son named Jeffrey. I'll begin at the beginning.

Matt and I met 23 years ago at Conservative Theological Seminary in New Orleans, and it was love at first sight. I had never felt that way about a man in all my life. We were young and in love and although my beliefs about premarital sex ran deep, I was not prepared for the intensity and intimacy that followed. I found out that I was pregnant at about the same time that I was accepted to Princeton for graduate studies. Matt was already there in school, so I moved to Princeton in January (3 months into the pregnancy) and had the baby there before starting classes in September.

I know some of you may not understand our decisions, but I assure you they were made with much prayer and counseling. Abortion was not an option for us. Marriage would probably be an option for most, but we were not emotionally, spiritually, or financially ready for the respon-sibility of marriage or children at the time. Hence, we gave our beautiful baby boy up for adoption to a loving New Orleans family.

The couple came to Princeton with their pre-teen daughter to sign the papers and take him home. We sent him letters on his one-year birthday, letting him know how much we loved him, and it was out of that love that we gave him to his parents. We also told him that he could contact us if he ever wanted to.

A few years ago, as he was having difficulties dealing with his parents' divorce, his mother urged him to contact us. She knew that there was a void in his life that neither of them could fill so out of her great love for him, she urged him to seek us out. And he did. It took a while, but he con-tacted us through email before Thanksgiving.

As you can see, it has been a pretty big Christmas for us. We have received a very special gift in the form of Jeffrey Gerard Brisures, a gorgeous, insightful, and amazing young man! Raised by adoring parents, he had a large Italian family that lived nearby (his mother's side) so he grew up with grandparents, aunts, uncles, and cousins, who were a very important part of his life just as we all did.

Which brings me to why I am writing you this letter, you are all very important to us! Although we would love to, it would be very difficult to contact each of you individually so we are sending everyone this email at the same time so you can share in our joy. It was the most difficult decision we ever made, but we knew God was with us every step of the way. Now, he has given us a great blessing! I don't think we will ever view Christmas in the same way again!

Much Love,
-Jenna and Matt

Chapter 66
Glass Fusion and Form

The annealing oven is used to cool the glass after it has been formed. The oven decreases the temperature slowly in order to dissipate the internal stresses arising from the natural contraction of glass as it cools.

I chose my clothes and put on make-up that morning as if going on a date. Jeans and my new hip sweater with a colorful scarf would give the youthful look I desired. Matt chose his clothes more carefully too. I'll bet he was in the same quandary. We were to meet Jeffrey at Port of Call, one of my favorite restaurants in New Orleans. Aged beef burgers were paired with huge baked potatoes spilling over with sour cream, cheese, bacon, and chives. Because it didn't close until 5 AM, it was a regular hangout for the wait staff at Malcomb's who didn't get off until 2 or 3 AM on weekends. The boys were spending the day with my mom while we met Jeffrey, and then we'd all get together after that.

On the car ride to the restaurant, my hands were fidgety fixing the bow on his Christmas present. We didn't want to overdo it on our first meeting, so we just gave him our family's favorite book, *The Count of Monte Christo*. Passing by the restaurant looking for a parking place, we saw a giant young man with large dark hair standing in front. Immediately, I felt a tightening in my belly, much like the contractions I endured 22 years before.

"Oh my goodness, that's him," I cried. "He's tall. How'd he get so tall?"

Matt had difficulty parking because he was looking back for glance after glance. I was usually very attentive in the French Quarter, savoring all the sights and smells. But I saw nothing that day except the young man in the stylish striped shirt and jeans standing on the corner of Decatur and Esplanade. Hand in hand, Matt and I walked briskly toward him, "Jeffrey?"

He smiled, moved toward us, and the three of us fell into a deep bear hug embrace. He was the center of our world again, and we soaked in every moment before releasing him.

Matt cleared his throat and said, "Are you hungry?"

"Very," Jeffrey replied.

"Well then, you're in for a treat. These are the best burgers in town," I said as we slipped inside.

Taking a table in the back, we just stared at him until he fidgeted with discomfort.

"I'm sorry, I just can't stop looking at you. I have to keep pinching myself to believe this is all really happening," I explained.

"It's fine, I feel the same way," he said with full eyes.

"How are you so tall? We're all short in our families. Everybody."

"Maybe it's my mom's great Sicilian cooking."

"Could be," Matt interjected, "but my grandfather Judson was tall."

"Oh, that's right; I never met him. The rest of you are shrimps like us," I added.

We all laughed and looked at the menu, hungry but completely full at the same time. We picked up where we left off in our letters, talking with ease and laughing much. He gave us an envelope from his mother with a letter thanking us for allowing him into our lives. Enclosed was his senior picture. "I guess she wants you to see what I look like when I am clean cut, and well groomed."

"But then I wouldn't get to play in all this rich beautiful hair," I said as I ran my fingers through his long curly black hair. "I have a thing for hair. Ask Taylor, I play in his most every night."

"I guess I get this hair color from you, Matt."

"Pretty much," Matt beamed.

"Mine is wavy and curly like yours, but not that color."

Coincidentally, the waitress brought three orders of the same food. I guess I didn't notice when we ordered: prime aged-beef mushroom burgers and potatoes with the works. We talked without interruption for two hours straight. Before we left the restaurant we made sure that he could spend the day with us. We had a few things to show him.

When we left the restaurant, we drove around New Orleans. Jeffrey wanted to show us his childhood home and we wanted to show him all the places that were important to us. We took him to my old shotgun house, showed him the seminary and even where our first kiss happened on the paddleboats. When he started to look bored, we took solace under an oak tree in City Park. Matt pulled out our family photo album and showed him some photos of grandparents, aunts and uncles hoping to spark an interest into one day meeting them.

Matt bravely inquired, "Do you think we'll be able to see more of you, or is this just a one stop meeting your birth parents thing?" I was so glad he had the courage to ask the question that filled my heart.

"Oh, I'd really like to meet Dylan and Tyler, if that's okay," he implored.

"We were hoping you'd say that. How about tomorrow lunch? They're dying to meet you too," I said, excitedly.

"That'd be great. Where?" Jeffrey said.

"What's your favorite food?" Matt inquired.

"Sushi," he answered boldly.

"Man, you're going to fit into this family well. It's our entire family's favorite, but Matt won't usually spring for the bill unless it's a very special occasion. So, we make it at home with sushi grade fish instead."

"I'm thinking *this* is a very special occasion!" Matt said proudly.

"I agree," Jeffrey said, beaming from ear to ear.

The afternoon was filled with grins, laughter and joyful memories. And when we left Jeffrey's childhood neighborhood, we got surprisingly close to a place I knew too well.

Matt got excited and said, "Isn't this near your glassblowing studio, Jenna?"

Jeffrey replied, "You blow glass, Jenna?"

"I did at one time, but I haven't been to a studio in ages."

"Wow, that's awesome," Jeffrey exclaimed. "I've always been fascinated with glassblowing."

"Everyone is. It's even more mesmerizing when you are doing it. I learned a lot about life in the...studio," I hesitated as the garage door came into view. But instead of a glassblowing studio, the building was now an open-air café with a hand written board menu of croissants, baked goods, teas, and sandwiches. I exhaled a sigh of relief.

Matt's phone began to ring and he had to take the call, so he pulled over and parked on the street. Jeffrey hopped out of the car and said, "I'm getting something to drink. Would you like anything, Jenna? My treat."

"I'll come too," I said, wondering what had happened to the studio. "Matt looks like he needs privacy with this call." After 20 years of marriage I could still read his pastoral expressions.

"That's great, because I have some questions I'd like to ask you alone, Jenna." My heart sunk.

Oh no. Here it comes.

"I can't believe I finally have someone to talk to about all these things," he said as he offered me a bottle of water and sat down close to me on the café chair. "Now that I find out you are on the homosexuality spectrum, it makes sense that I would be too. It's part of my DNA. Which means I should stop hoping that I am not gay, right? Do you think it's already predetermined?"

The enormity of his questions literally blew my head back. Here I was sitting where the studio used to be, next to the son I thought I'd never have, facing the same questions I did when I was exactly his age. I knew this was one of those thin spaces of life where the mystic meets the malleable and I needed to be fully aware of the moment. More than anything, I needed to breathe, feel, love, and create, so I took a deep breath and replied.

"I can't believe I have someone to talk with about these things either. Part of my DNA and family conditioning is to brush things under the rug, especially highly charged emotional issues. But before I answer, I want you to know that these are just my thoughts and my experiences. I'm not trying to make universal statements for anyone else. One thing I have learned from life is that we are all very complex beings composed of various experiences and bonds that have shaped us. The chemistry of it all is both fascinating and fragile. The fusion and form of it all is what makes it beautiful. I try to just tell my story the best I can, and let God work out all the details of how others respond to it."

"I need your honesty, Jenna."

"Okay, here goes: When I read about your sexual ambiguities, my first thought was, 'Did he get a homosexuality gene from me too? Did it get passed down as genetic code in DNA?' So, yes, it would seem likely that I could pass that on to you. When I saw the picture you sent, your beautiful eyes and smile, I knew they were from your father. Your wavy hair and thin face are mine. If your sexual orientation is genetic, then it's what God created us to be, out of God's breath, God's ruach."

"What's that word again? Ru...?"

"Ruach. In Hebrew, it means breath, wind or spirit."

"That's powerful. Ruach," he said, over and over.

"Funny thing, though. I'm starting to get proud of it like the fact that you have my analytical and scientific mind."

"That *is* a funny thought," he said with a grin.

"The way I see it is, if homosexuality is passed on genetically, or chemically, then why can't it be seen as a gift from God just like your beautiful Matt-like smile or gleaming eyes? I can't imagine what my life would be like now if it were seen as a gift."

"Me either. All these years questioning...and worrying," he replied with faraway eyes.

"I've spent so much of my life begging for my same sex attractions to be taken away like it was a disability of the worst sort. But then, if I didn't, I wouldn't be where I am today, with a husband and family, and a beautiful connection to you. That's one of the paradoxes of life I live with."

"I can see how much you two love each other. It's inspirational," he added.

"Then again, maybe if I was allowed to live freely without such judgment, I would've found earlier that my hatred was my sin, not my sexual orientation," I added.

"It's mind boggling, all the paradoxes," he quipped.

"And that's life. Paradoxes are everywhere. What helped me a lot with my sexual ambiguity were the lessons I learned right here in this spot, in this 'used to be' glass-blowing studio."

I looked around. The kitchen was where the furnace used to be and the cash register was where the marvering table had once stood. I remembered how after Tamira's murder, my brokenness was placed on the table and with Elzbieta's care and careful addition of color and questions, I was tended and formed into something substantial, though not completely finished.

I continued, "Like the glass on a rod, we are being molded and shaped each day by our environment and the chemicals and people in it. It may not seem like it, but God knows what God is doing. Noticed I said 'God' and not 'the church'. Sometimes faith communities get off track. I believe that is why Jesus came into the world, to get everything back on track with a living, breathing model of how people of faith are supposed to live."

"I'm glad you said that," Jeffrey said as his posture eased. "I've been cautious to say much about my feelings about the church with you and Matt so tied to it."

"I've been there," I replied. "Especially when I was questioning my sexuality. Luckily for me, I had people around whom I could talk to, who loved me through it all, and challenged me to be who God created me to be."

"I wish..." he replied but then hesitated, and took another sip of his drink.

I continued, "I believe the most important questions are not whether we are gay or straight, but how we are treated and cared for on our journey to find our true identity."

"Hmmm."

"I need you hear to hear this loud and clear: God loves you just the way you are. You are loved and lovable no matter whether you are gay, straight, or anything in between."

"That helps, it really does, but it's deeper than that. The feelings and questions are endless. They hound you and never turn off. Sometimes you just need an answer."

"I know. But it is all a process. And good sturdy art pieces take time, and attention."

He shook his head and slumped, "But how did you get through it all? Does it ever end? Do you still have feelings for women?"

"For me, the process was complex. The feelings I have toward women did not just go away when I met Matt. There were still women that I was attracted to. There *are* still women I am attracted to. But I don't have to go down every path where there is an attraction, especially when I am still unsure of my stability or composition. That's why I think most people get so mixed up. We jump into sexual relationships far before we even have time to be formed ourselves. There are many colors and molds in the world of glass-blowing. Every color, which is really a mineral, has its own coefficient of expansion, its own timetable. If they are mixed up too fast, or at too high of heat, or under the wrong circumstances, the entire piece is unstable. It's not only fragile, but can even be dangerous. It can crack or shatter at any time."

"I've had some fragile moments in my life..." Jeffrey said sheepishly.

"I have too, which is why I think the best thing to do is to take your time growing into who you are created to be. Explore the world, yourself, expand your thoughts, your creativity, and your emotions. And if you find someone who ignites your soul, take your time. Study, learn, enjoy. Breathe, love, and create memories together. Learn to love another, no matter who they are, instead of rushing into anything physical. And when you have a soul connection to another, a relationship that helps to create a new world order for you, keep your eyes and attention on that. Fanning the flame of that love becomes more important than the labels or barriers we put on ourselves or others. This goes for a relationship with God as well."

He scooted his chair up and asked, "So can you please tell me what is so wrong about two same sex people committing to marriage? I don't understand how it hurts anyone else's marriage."

"I of all people know how hard it is to find a soul mate. For me, finding authentic love was excruciating, because it's not about looks or the exterior of a person. What attracts me to another person is the depth of their soul. I can only find the depth of another's soul by having deep and inspiring conversations. That is the spark that ignites my chemicals to form bonds, but that takes time and way too much energy."

"I know what you mean," Jeffrey said.

I continued, "I don't seek it. It just happens. It happens rarely, but when it does, it touches a place deep in my soul and I want more. And it doesn't matter to me whether that person is a male or female. When I feel that connection, I lean into it like some infants lean into cuddling when they are held. An infant is too young to choose cuddling. Some just have the natural urge or capacity to nestle in more than others. There's nothing wrong with the infants who nuzzle in to cuddling, nor the ones who don't. It is just the way they are."

"I've never heard it described that way before," he replied, smiling.

"Every time I walked away from a conversation with Matt, I felt that I had been changed. I was a better person. I was more hopeful and more curious: two traits that I regard highly in this world.

"That's funny," he chuckled. "Those are things I look for too."

"What fused our souls was that the world looked much more interesting and hopeful when we were together. We never tire of exploring things together on a very deep level, analyzing feelings, fears, and paradoxes. I was always afraid of my feelings before Matt. But he was safe, gentle, patient and kind."

"He does seem to be. Not the image I had for a preacher."

"I know. And that's what hooked me. I'm sure if I would've found this in a woman, I would've nestled into it, but I never got that close, never trusted anyone enough."

"I can't ever seem to get that close to anyone either, male or female. When it gets too familiar, too intimate, I bail," he added with a painful look I knew all to well.

"This world has so much judgment, hatred and division. It's hard to feel safe enough to be your true self. That's why I can't imagine keeping others from making a commitment when they finally find someone their soul connects with, someone they can let down the walls, and show who they truly are. What kind of hell are we subjecting others to when we keep them from committing to that? A lifetime of isolation, despair, and hopelessness?" I questioned.

"Exactly," he replied.

"To answer your question, there was a woman I was drawn to at the same time as Matt. She was the beautiful soul I was talking about. She was the glassblower who taught me all about glass and life...I was very much attracted to her soul, but I never really could lean into her, no matter how much I put myself there. In the past, I would've gone there, but I was magnetized to Matt. And the love that he radiated was greater than the love she radiated. The voice in my head that had always said I was lost, or worthless seemed to diminish when I was with him."

I leaned in closer and continued, "I have found that the voice I hear in my head that says I am a worthless, sick, and hopeless human being who can never have real relationships has done far more damage than anything anyone else has ever done to me, because the voice never stops. It becomes a wormhole, a trap, and an endless tape that keeps running and running until I am too exhausted to do anything else except feed its self-fulfilling prophecy."

"Are you reading my mind, Jenna?"

"So what did I do when faced with the reality of my attraction for both a male and a female at the same time? I walked away from the thought that my sexuality or sexual orientation was going to define me. I stepped into my identity as being God's child, wholly and acceptable to God exactly as I am. I stepped into being the best instrument of love that I can be. I am a complex being and my sexuality is only a small part of that complex being. When we allow sex, our sexual attractiveness, sexual acuity, or sexual needs to define our lives, then we are diminishing who we are as a complex piece of art. It is a part of us, not all. And like our physical beauty, that small part, should not define the entirety of our lives. That gives it way too much power over us. My sexual orientation or my physical beauty is not my choice. Believing that it defines all of me, is a choice. And that is not a choice I wanted to choose any longer."

"So are you saying, that if I..."

"Jeffrey, I'm not making any empirical statements that relate to anyone else. I am just telling my story. Unconditional love is what attracts me. It's what I desperately needed and what I found among my gay friends in college. And its what I leaned into with Matt. If I had ever found reciprocation in the form of a woman, I would've probably had a very different life. It isn't a choice of sexual orientation at all. It is a choice of love with no strings, no manipulation, and no judgment.

"Matt gave me hope, and encouragement. He saw things in me I didn't see in myself. Because of my history, sex and love didn't really go too well together. But I was drawn to his loving spirit, his bringing out the best in me, his delighting in me without getting too physical."

"Yea, but that was 20 years ago. Things are faster paced now," he replied sheepishly.

"Well," I took a deep breath, "perhaps that is part of the problem. People rush into the physical before their souls are formed. Matt was patient and didn't rush things. He was (and still is) kind, generous, self-reflective, and curious. It was not a choice to lean toward Matt. It was not a choice at all. It was a natural leaning toward authentic, *patient*, non-manipulative love. That is what our souls crave."

"It may be what we crave, but I don't think I will ever find it," Jeffrey said painfully.

"Luckily, I was at a point in my life where I could discern authentic love. With a lot of trial and error, and with a lot of bloody shards in the pile, I finally learned what to look for in love, and it just happened to be Matt. It could have been anyone, a man or woman, but the person who loved me more than anyone else, including myself, was Matt, your father. He loved me in the unique way that I needed to be loved. That is what counts."

He shook his head and whispered, "I don't even know where to begin with what you are talking about, but it helps to hear it."

I looked back at the car to see my soul mate still engaged in conversation, so I continued, "I began by realizing that love is defined by what it leaves behind. If the trail it leaves behind is judgment, denigration, deceit, anger, fear, violence, resentment, or contempt, then that is not authentic love. Perhaps it was because I knew unconditional love from my family, and a church that stayed with me throughout my fragile young adult life. They loved, supported and included me in all activities no matter what I shared about my sexuality. And they helped me to trust God, others, and myself."

"It's hard to believe there are any churches out there like that."

"There are. You just can't give up after the first try any more than you can give up on love after the first date. Dating teaches you about yourself, what is important to you, what to look for and how delicate relationships are. Once I learned to trust and measure love with new standards of joy, peace, patience, kindness, self-sacrifice, and self-control, it was easier to sort things out because there was no longer an in or an out in God's family. We are all in. And so, I naturally leaned toward that love. I bonded to that love. I am fused and changed by that sacrificial love exhibited on the cross.

"Most of the churches I tried, and not just Catholic ones, talked more about what they were against, than what they were for."

I took a deep breath and looked straight into his eyes, "That's how we get off track. We forget that our main focus is that sacrificial love that Jesus exuded. He broke down barriers, and brought in the outsiders. His words and actions should be our primary focus. His love, and a strong community of support gave me the strength to accept who I am, and to not hide behind walls or labels that others put on me. As I served those in need with my community, I began to break down the labels and hatred I had for others as well. That was when true healing began."

"Hatred does spread like a cancer. Ridding oneself of it is not easy," Jeffrey added. "Especially against those who've brought you great pain."

"I'm sure if I went to a church that told me I needed be 'cured' and kept away from the fold and the sacraments in the church until I was 'cured', then I would be a totally different person today. I hope that I would've had the strength to walk away from that church and be able to separate the love of Jesus from the commodity of love that that 'faith' community was peddling. But I'm not sure what would've happened if that had been the case."

"Yea, I went to Christian school, so I got a heavy diet of judgment and guilt every day."

"I, on the other hand, was invited into a place where all of us offered ourselves up (impurities, riches, colors and all) to the furnace of God's creative spirit, trusting God would create art from the meld. They taught me to quit focusing on the sin or pain in my past but to use it to form a more beautiful future. But one thing missing in our church was JUDGMENT!"

I continued, "I have to wonder, if Jesus would be throwing tables around in our churches today, like he did to the Pharisees in the temple? If we could be brutally honest with ourselves, we would admit that our fake piety is what is separating us from each other. Perhaps if each of us was encouraged to examine his/her own life for impurities, lay these impurities and our gifts on the altar (without judging the worth of all those around us) we could not only be agents of transformation, but transformed ourselves."

"You may have a hard time selling that..."

"But if we *could* turn things around, faith communities could produce art instead of dustbins of guilt and shame. Personally, I've had enough of guilt and shame. I've had enough of trying to analyze everything so much that I miss out on the dance of life. I'm ready to worship where people know God is a good and beautiful God, full of creativity and wonder, who only wants the best for us. I'm ready to worship where each one of us is cherished and our unique compositions are added to the gallery of millefiori master-pieces. Have you ever seen a millefiori?" I asked.

"No, what is that?"

"Here, look at this," I said, as I pulled from my purse the first medallion I had made with Elzbieta.

"Wow. That is incredible."

"It's made of layers and layers of colored canes that are fused together and then cut into pieces. You would never know by the outside of the cane what's on the inside. It's beauty lies in being cut open, and laid side by side with other unique canes. Only God knows what's inside each cane and where each one needs to be placed to bring out the greatest contrast."

"Have you ever made one?" he asked.

"Yes, I made this one. And it's a very amateur piece. It is nothing com-pared to the ones a master glassblower can produce. The process is truly incredible. It takes days, and sometimes even weeks. That's what I believe life is…finding our place in the milliefiori masterpieces God is creating in the world."

"If only I could believe that…"

"You are a beautiful part of it, Jeffrey, to me, to Matt and to God. And that's why I'm drawn to church work because it's important right now for people of faith to do some self-reflecting about the damage we have done in God's name. The biggest question I'm wrestling with now is: Why (and this is the biggest question of all) if God is the God of love and mercy, does the church have such a hard time practicing it? Instead we tend to condemn and hate those who are different in any way. We seem to perpetuate fear and contempt. Perhaps the more we learn to include and embrace, the richer our dance, our practice, our art will be."

"I might even be willing to try a church like that," Jeffrey proclaimed.

"It's not easy having a faith like that though, because daily we have to examine our own souls. For me, I wonder if all my questions get me off track. But then I remember that God made me this way, a million questions a day and all. And as long as my questions are helping me to lean into love instead of hate, to trust instead of fret, to hope instead of dread, then I am moving in the right direction," I explained.

"But what if there really are sociopaths or people out there that get you off track?" he asked.

"I get off track all the time," I answered. "We all get off track. I point my finger so strongly at others, so I don't have to look at the three fingers pointing back at me. I judge others who may just be starting on the journey or who have not had the experiences that I've had. I've judged and hated those who have brought me pain. I've spent way too much time analyzing and commenting on their lives, probably so that I don't have to answer the hard questions God asks of me:

- For what sins/errors do I need forgiveness?
  How well do I extend the unconditional love of God to all?
  Where have I been an instrument of hope and grace today?"
  "Those are pretty tough questions. You tackle those every day?" he implored.

"In a nutshell, these are the main questions I need to ask each day. They are the bass line of my life. I used to be afraid of these questions, but I'm not anymore. I try to spend time alone each day answering them. And I try to remember that I am the *only* one I need to judge. I may not like someone else's actions, but it doesn't change their value or worth to God. I've also leaned to give myself and others grace when we fall, because we all fall on the journey. And there is no piece of glass the master cannot shape into art if given enough time. Even the shard thrown out to sea can be formed into sea glass."

"It's funny,' he replied. "It's like you've been reading my journals. I love to analyze things, and having someone to talk to about all these issues really helps."

"I know. It's like transparency and vulnerability are what make us stronger."

"If we live through it," he added with a sigh.

"But we're all a lot tougher than we think we are," I said, waving at Matt who was off the phone and getting out of the car.

"I wish I could believe that," Jeffrey whispered. "Thanks so much for meeting me, and especially for this conversation."

"You have no idea how much this means to all of us. Real conversations like this with Matt, are what helped me realize how strong I am. I never really saw it in myself. His love was like a mirror for me. Eventually, I started believing in what he saw."

Matt sat down next to us, took a sip of my drink and asked, "Sorry about that. Something fell apart at work that just needed a few minutes to clear up. What did I miss?"

Jeffrey and I had the same expression as we smiled. *How can one even begin to explain?*

Chapter 67
Best Mother in the World

Spraying metal oxide on the glass immediately after it comes out of the furnace creates iridescent glass. A resulting finish permanently adheres to the surface, creating a milky-like rainbow.

The boys and Jeffrey fit together as if they had known each other their whole lives. Comparing likes and dislikes with each other, they giggled at their similarities. They bantered about hockey players, Hip Hop music artists, and the latest computer trends. If that wasn't enough, both Taylor and Jeffrey had dressed the same for Halloween the past year-as Hunter Thompson (the beatnik, gonzo journalist).

But there was still one thing that was required to be a part of our family reunions: playing Texas Hold-em. We went back to our hotel room (Taylor had brought his case of poker chips) to rectify the situation. And there we spent the rest of the afternoon as a family.

After several games, Jeffrey commented, "You know, it's obvious how much chemistry there is between you and Matt. I have never seen anything like it before."

Dylan chimed in, "I know, my friends say the same thing. No one has ever seen people that are as happily married as you two. You fight, but there isn't all that frost in the air like with other parents."

"You know, Jeffrey, I have to give <u>you</u> the credit for that. Having to give you up made us face some pretty tough things together. Matt proved himself through it all, like no one had ever done. Because he was so steadfast, so true, so willing to go deep in the mire in counseling for a very long time, we worked it out, and built a foundation that is rock solid. It was your gift to us. I really don't think that would've happened without you."

Jeffrey pushed his chair back slowly, and folded his arms as he took it all in. Then his face beamed as he said, "Wow, I've never thought of it that way."

"Wow," Dylan said, "me neither."

"Then maybe it was worth it," Jeffrey added.

"I certainly hope so," my heart smiled. "I certainly hope so."

Jeffrey had dinner with his mother that night, but promised to call when they were finished so we could go to the French Quarter together. His mother was standing with him outside her house when we picked him up, just as exquisite and Mediterranean looking as I remembered her. She hugged us both and thanked us profusely.

"Oh no," Matt corrected, "it's we who should be thanking you, for urging him to contact us."

"How did you do it?" I asked. "I never would've been able to let him do that."

"Oh yes, you would've. If your child was hurting, and you had tried everything in your power to help him and still couldn't fill his void, you would do anything to help him."

"I don't know."

"I promise you, you would."

"You are an amazing Mother," I proclaimed. "He is wonderful. We will never be able to thank you enough for this."

She opened her arms wide to hug me. "You already have. You already have."

I watched Jeffrey as he got into the back seat of the car. His joy could not be contained in his body. I might have even seen a tear.

"You have an amazing Mother," I said as I buckled my seat belt for the ride to the quarter.

"Yes, I do. Yes, I do."

Chapter 68
Eternal Image

The vast array of colors in glass enchants artisans and craftsmen alike. So too does its permanency. After all, glass never fades. This awesome feature allows the artist to create an eternal image with glass. [54]

The next day, Jeffrey met my mother and sister, Jordan, at a Greek restaurant. There was an awkwardness that hung in the air, and tension that scooted up at the table with us. My mother was worried about how Taylor and Dylan were taking it all and still furious at me for robbing her of her first grandbaby. The five of us were exhausted from the emotional roller coaster we'd been on for the last few days. Having met so many people at one time probably overwhelmed Jeffrey. There was laughter and lots of great Greek food, but the conversation was contrived. We were all preparing for the fact that this was the last stop of the whirlwind tour of our time together. After lunch, Jeffrey would catch a flight, and we would start our long trek back to Atlanta. We dropped him off at his mother's house so she could take him to the airport.

He started his goodbyes with the boys. "It has been great meeting ya'll. Thanks for being so understanding about all this."

"This is great," Taylor said as he hugged him, "to think we've had a long lost brother all this time."

"I hope we can see you again soon," Dylan added.

"I'm sure you will," he said. The boys got into the car while Jeffrey, Matt and I said our goodbyes outside.

"What an amazing adventure we are on! We are so blessed to have you in our lives again," Matt said with a big bear hug.

Jeffrey turned to me with a huge smile and said, "The love in your letters started all this you know. I can still feel it oozing out."

"That's because it's still there, and growing," I replied. "You know it's because of you that Matt and I are still together, right, and so much in love. You are what fused us so tightly. You are the greatest gift to us."

"That's a thought I'll have to grow into with time."

"I understand. Will we ever get to see you again?"

"Of course."

"When?"

"I don't know. We'll have to figure that out."

"But I don't want to let you go again. I don't think I can handle that." He reached out to embrace me. I held him close and got lost in time. Could it really have been 22 years since I felt his heart beat next to mine? My arms felt again the newness of love, birth, and intimacy. The memories brought gentle sobs. "I lost you once, I can't...lose...you again."

When he ended our long hug, he put his hands on my shoulders, looked me straight in the eyes and said, "You're going to have to trust me on this."

Tears streamed down my face as Matt opened the car door for me. I slunk inside, waving to our beautiful child, trying to etch his face into my memory with every ounce of strength I could muster. All the pain, fear, and incertitude began their pull on me. I could feel myself getting sucked in to the hurricane of emotion. Taylor noticed me crying and said, "Mom, I don't think I've ever seen you cry."

Taking a deep sniffled breath, I realized that I was face to face with emotions so raw and real they had the power to devour me alive. My mind had erased them for years in order to survive. They were pooling down my neck, but were finally released when I whimpered, "You know, honey, I don't think I *have* cried for 22 years."

Later that day, on our long drive home to Atlanta, the sun was fading on our seaside dinner in Biloxi, Mississippi. I walked the beach alone to gather my thoughts. The flurry of the past few days blew like hair in the breeze. I was mesmerized watching the lines of my feet make molds in the quartz. The sand had buoyancy to it, taking my stride and bouncing back instead of sinking deeply.

When I saw the glint of cobalt blue glass shimmering on the sand, my heart skipped and reached out with fingers of its own. Part shiny, part dull, some edges of the fragment were worn away, while another was still sharp. As I knelt down, I couldn't help but envision the fire melting the sand, the cobalt being added, and the intensity of the glory hole shaping it into usefulness. I knew the stubbornness of the cold glass and the love of the gaffer for the glass vessel. I could feel the pain it took to get the right mixture of heat, strength, and bold dark color: the delicate balance between turbulence and order. And here it lay as a discarded shard at my feet.

I was reminded of Jeffrey, our beautiful translucent memento of how God could take the raw ragged shards of our lives and turn them into sea glass. I carefully rubbed its jagged edge while taking a few deep breaths. I stood up and walked out as far as I could into the ocean. I thought about all the heartaches and secrets in my life. Doubts about my strength to endure bringing them out into the open again, or to face the complications they would bring, began to pull like the undertow at my feet. Fear that I would never see Jeffrey again drew tears, like rain, from my eyes.

Breathe in God, and out Jenna. The waves, rolling in rhythm, were the metronome to my deep oxygen filled breaths. I pulled my arm back with all my might, and threw those memories, doubts and fears out to sea with the same hope I had for that tiny newborn so long ago. *Can you take this, God, and make it into something vibrant and beautiful?*

The blue shard I hurled sploosh-splooshed into the water. I watched the waves drag it under, out of my sight. And then I heard the gentle wind whisper back, "You are just going to have to trust me on this."

Endnotes

1   Rosa Mentasti. *Glass Throughout Time: History and Technique of Glassmaking from the Ancient World to the Present.* (New York: Skira Press, 2003) 11

2   http://en.wikipedia.org/wiki/Fused_quartz

3   http://en.wikipedia.org/wiki/Fused_quartz

4   William D. Callister. *Materials Science and Engineering an Introduction.* (Utah: John Wiley and Sons, 2003) 437

5   http://en.wikipedia.org/wiki/Glass

6   Thomas Mann. *Death in Venice.* (New York: Bantam, 1988) 274

7   7 James McKelvey. *The Art of Fire: Beginning Glassblowing.* (St. Louis: Third Degree Press, 2003) 201

8   Elisabeth Kubler-Ross. As quoted in The Leader's Digest: Timeless Principles for Team and Organization (Jim Clemmer, 2003) 84 and http://www.ekrfoundation.org/quotes/

9   James Schaffer. *The Science and Design of Engineering Materials.* 2nd edition. (Boston: McGraw-Hill, 1999) 207

10   Charles Bray. *Dictionary of Glass.* (London: A&C Black, 2001) 7

11   Ed Burke. *Glassblowing: A Technical Manual* (Ramsbury: Crowood Press Ltd., 2005) 113

12   James McKelvey. 202

13   James McKelvey. 111

14   James McKelvey. 39

15   http://www.r-e-s-i-d-e-n-c-e.com/glass.html

16   William Bryson. *Notes from a Small Island.* (New York: Harper-Collins, 1995) 91

17   Charles Bray. 170

18   Charles Bray. 236

19   James McKelvey. 25

20   James McKelvey. 27

21   Charles Bray. 172

22   "Bubbles in Glass" http://www.cookingglass.com.au/advanced- kilnforming/cooking-the- glass/Bubbles-in-glass/?searchterm=why%20bubbles

23   Julie Miller. "Broken Things" Used by permission CMG License 591138

24   24 Charles Bray. 65

25   Barrett Browning, Elizabeth. "Aurora Leigh." Book 7 Nicholson, D. H. S., and Lee, A. H. E., eds. *The Oxford Book of English Mystical Verse.* (Oxford: The Clarendon Press, 1917) 236

26   Jalaluddin Rumi, As quoted in *Traveling Mercies.* Anne Lamott. (New York: Pantheon, 1999) 76

27   Charles Bray. 128

28 Isabel Anders editor. *40 Day Journey with Madeline L'Engle*. (Minneapolis: Augsburg Books, 2009) 131

29 William Warmus. *Fire and Form: The Art of Contemporary Glass*. (West Palm Beach: Norton Museum of Art, 2003) 6

30 James McKelvey. 90

31 William Morris. *Glass Artifact and Art*. (Seattle: University of Washington Press, 1989) 82

32 William Morris. 82

33 James McKelvey. 214

34 Anton Chekhov. The Unknown Chekhov: Stories and Other Writings Hitherto Untranslated. (New York: Noonday Press, 1954) 14 Page 14, Noonday Press, New York.

35 James McKelvey. 246

36 James McKelvey. 161

37 James Schaffer. 186

38 James McKelvey. 57

39 Jeannette Walls. *The Glass Castle* (New York: Scribner) 2005

40 http://en.wikipedia.org/wiki/Vitrification

41 James McKelvey. 201

42 https://www.britannica.com/art/Jena-glass

43 Charles Kingsley as quoted in *How to Break Up With Anyone*. Jamye Waxman. (Berkeley: Seal Press, 2015) 65

44 Charles Bray. 200

45 James McKelvey. 139

46 George Bernard Shaw. (n.d.). BrainyQuote.com. Retrieved July 6, 2017, from BrainyQuote.com Web site: https://www.brainyquote.com/quotes/quotes/g/georgebern384892.html

47 Charles Bray. 230

48 James McKelvey. 133

49 James McKelvey. 211 and https://chemistry.boisestate.edu/richardbanks/glass-blowing/glassblowing_history.htm

50 James McKelvey. 211

51 James McKelvey. 207

52 Ed Burke. 9

53 William Warmus. 10

54 media.public.gr/Books-PDF/9780470591321-0534228.pdf

Acknowledgments

I acknowledge that without these people, *The Sea Glass Gift* would still be a jagged shard on the beach: Rochelle Vaughan, my mom, your effervescent spirit is contagious and flows naturally through our entire family. Nate Nardi and Matt Janke, your patience in the studio taught me volumes. Thank you Gail Vogels, my first reader: your honesty, passion and keen artist's eye prompted me to add the glass layer to my love story.

Chris Rockett, you were invaluable in explaining the science of glass in a way others could not. Thank you Patrice Eastham, Beth Damon, Rebecca Schicker, Joan Gray, Maureen Downey, Juliann Whipple, Suzan Reed, Joan Falconer, Mary Ellen Drushal, and Jared Rogers-Martin. Your comments, insights and corrections have shaped this book into reality. For that, I will always be grateful.

Thanks Becky and Scott Messel-your courage whispered to me, "It's time to publish!"

Bo and Maureen and the entire Emerson clan, you were instrumental as many of the chapters were composed at your Hunker Hill house. Thanks Nancy Hammond, Kim Williams, and Michael and Maria Westbrook. You were with me when most of my street schooling occurred. You helped me navigate a world I never knew existed on the other side of the tracks. Jared and Jacob, you are two of the most fun, strong and courageous human beings I've ever known. Your insights have helped me to rewrite my book many times.

And mostly, I must thank my husband, Tim. I never get enough of your radiant smile and passion for life. Your love, joy, patience and humility challenge me to be a better person each day.

Proceeds

A portion of the author's net proceeds from *The Sea Glass Gift* will go toward at-risk children and youth. I am honored to have had many children in my life (in foster care, in classrooms, on city streets, and in churches) who have courageously shared their stories and insights, giving me a glimpse into the invisible reality we have created in our society. Your defiant durability, courage and transparency are what give me hope each day. May you learn to cultivate the gifts that you were given to bring peace, hope and joy into the world!

Afterword

Dear reader,

Please know that this story is an amalgamation of many stories I have lived or heard. I am not trying to make comparisons or judgments for anyone else's life. I am not trying to make blanket statements about anything other than love casts out fear and belonging heals. I believe our chief mission is to bear hope and compassion to ALL people. I believe that in doing so we have an opportunity to create a masterpiece each day.

I know from my experience, that as we move together toward the flame of love, we will be changed. I believe it is the only chance we have for survival in this turbulent world.

> "I say to you, life is hard, at times as hard as crucible steel...
> And if one will hold on, he will discover that God walks
> with him, and that God is able to lift you from the fatigue
> of despair to the buoyancy of hope." -Martin Luther King
> Jr. *Eulogy for Martyred Children 1963*